Warrior

The Morgantown Songbirds

D.E. Mitchell

Warrior

Copyright © 2014 by D.E. Mitchell

ISBN: 978-1503384101

Dedication

This book is dedicated to the many true pioneer families of the West, my mixed Black and Cherokee ancestors, my daughters: Tanya Waltrick and Tina Hill, grandsons: Mason Hill, Benjamin Gray, and Brandon Grey-Mitchell, and great-granddaughters: Chloe Byrd, and Noriah and Naava Grey-Mitchell.

Special thanks to: Frank Young, Anna Renault, David Wren, Juliette McLendon, Barbara Ham, Clara Osborne, Liz Drumgoole, Marilyn Clayton, Constance Reid, Lorenzo Brown, Myrtle Almony, Jim and Pat Holechek, Elaine Wieland, Aja Dorsey Jackson, Jeanette Coulter and The Essex Senior Center Writer's Guild.

Table of Contents

Preface

Since the earliest days of the coal mining industry in East Tennessee, my diverse family of full-blood Cherokee Indians, black Cherokees, blacks, and whites, has produced many generations of workers for the mines. One of them died in a mining disaster.

Our uncle, a retired Cherokee miner, was a wonderful man who loved to bounce his black nieces (the only children of the family living in our town at that time) on his knee. After a stroke, he wasn't able to speak, but he used sign language, and we were able to understand him. We remember the love in his sparkling black eyes, and his black-cat clock that moved its eyes and tail for us. His memory is a wonderful part of our lives.

There were other black families living in our Tennessee town who were descended from Indian ancestors, but ours was the only one that lived among them in every generation.

I cannot remember a time when the differences in race were ever discussed by my mother's family. Now, after many years of reading about the Cherokees, and listening to the slave narratives in my family, I have decided to emphasize the love between the races.

My father's family is descended from slaves owned by plantations in and around Warrior, Alabama. Those who were not in the fields picking cotton were brick makers. Generations of them made pottery, building blocks and paving bricks in the kilns around the vicinity of Warrior.

I have created two historical romance stories about the Songbird, Coulter, Tulloss, and Rhea families. Although they are fictional, they are based on the actual fact that in the 1800s, during a unique chapter of American history, approximately 5,000 black slaves were forcefully removed from this country. The largest population of them made the journey to the Oklahoma Indian Territory as the property of the Cherokee Nation.

By the 1820s, survival of a black slave, or an American Indian, required a person to possess the dexterity to tread lightly around the turmoil fermenting in this country. But, although they suffered during many terror-filled days when their families were torn apart, love and the strength of the human spirit managed against all odds to discover the indestructible truth. The old cliché is undeniably true: Love conquers all.

The stories I have written could have easily occurred during and after their march. Death stalked both the slaves and their masters as Chief Starr Night pushed them farther into the wilderness during their voyage down the mighty rivers of the west. Those black captives who survived the journey were set ashore as slaves for life.

Usually their fates were sealed, but there were exceptions to the rule. The blended, free, black Coulter-Tulloss family was able to rescue a number of slaves and send them away from the Territory.

The black people who were owned by the tribe were forced to overcome a disability not faced by other slave populations in the United States. A great number of them attempted to escape, but their lack of success could usually be attributed to the fact that most of them could not speak English.

Ten years before they were expelled from the United States, the Cherokee chief of the Morgantown Songbirds of the lower towns of Rhea County, Tennessee had found a way to recover from the destruction of their coal mine in Graysville. He had persuaded his band to migrate to their rich, undeveloped hunting grounds in Warrior, Alabama. Starr Night used their highly trained slaves to develop the new mine into Alabama's highest yielding coal-producing property. There was a ready market for the fuel in the voracious, endlessly hungry, iron furnaces in Birmingham.

The tribe also established a successful cotton plantation, "Warrior," named for the river that ran through it. The wise chief purchased experienced Alabama slaves, and they taught the Tennessee captives how to plant and harvest the cotton crop.

In 1839, thugs, hired by white settlers, sabotaged the new mine and forced the band to migrate to the Oklahoma Indian Territory, west of the Mississippi River.

Tolliver, their plantation overseer, was compelled to choose sides. He had to decide if he would remain in the East among the white settlers, or travel with the Indians as they made their dangerous passage westward. The widower's decision to stay with the Indians almost destroyed him. He had given up the chance to erase the evidence of his past history, and now, he anguished over the wisdom of keeping his pact with the Indians.

6

As the trail deepened farther into the wilderness, he was forced to accept the fact that Chief Starr Night held all of the keys to his future. Tragically, he suffered the loss of several members of his beloved family.

After he had been living in the Territory for a few years, Tolliver discovered the way to reunite the rest of his family. On their way to the Territory, His mother, Eliza, and his granddaughter Melinda, managed to survive several near-death experiences, as they neared Tolliver's home in "New Warrior."

By chance, his granddaughter met and fell in love with Sheriff Clinton Coulter, an old acquaintance of his, but their love story hit a glitch when Melinda was kidnapped by Welch, her arch-enemy. Then, the story shifts to a search for Melinda in the mountains and canyons of the Badlands, where the chief used his power to create an alliance between the Songbirds, Seminole renegades, and the Sheriff of Sallisaw. All of them agreed to work together in a desperate attempt to recover the beautiful young maiden.

In "Tolliver's Revenge," extraordinary pioneering skills were demanded of the tribe, their slaves, and the Freedmen, as they labored to establish the New Warrior, Double C, and Willow Bend ranches. Before the wealth of the land could be exploited, the pioneers were faced to confront hostile plains tribes, renegades, and natural disasters. The new settlers endured infestations of grasshoppers, blizzards, and tornadoes in order to wrench incredible wealth from the rich soil. The Morgantown Songbirds and their slaves became the first permanent settlers of Kiowa country in the Oklahoma Indian Territory.

I have included several examples of the blending of the races in the new homeland. Sometimes, the black Cherokees had the ability to make peace between their people due to their unique position as representatives of both races. At other times, they chose opposing sides and fought amongst themselves.

By 1848, Tolliver had spent most of his life working for the Indians. Several times in the past, he had tried to convince the chief of the wisdom of freeing his slaves, but the day came when Starr Night called him into his office and announced his plans to keep his slaves. Tolliver was enraged, and thoroughly disgusted with the chief's decision. At that point, the overseer took things into his own hands. He pretended to be too old and sick to work for the tribe. Instead, he established a vast network of emancipators. The conductors on the escape route included Indians, Freedmen, and Quaker missionaries. All of them worked together to create a series of dangerous escape passages.

The many tentacles of the route stretched from Kansas to Canada. Eventually, it included the barely existent wilderness roads of the Oklahoma Indian Territory to freedom in California and Mexico. Later generations of his family always referred to their ancestor's successful network as "Tolliver's Revenge."

Book One

Chapter One
The Graysville Coalmine (1829)

The overseer of the Songbird 2 mine slashed the naked back of the slave with his whip.

He knew for a fact that the lazy porter was capable of doubling the amount of coal he loaded into the wagon's bed. *That damned fool tries to work as slow as he can*, he thought. *Buck thinks that I'll let him slack off from his work while he asks me a bunch of nonsensical questions. I'm tired of arguing with him. He's not showing me any respect.*

Hart knew that as soon as his back was turned, Buck would find a way to kill time. *What that lazy rascal needs, is another taste of the whip.* Although the sweat-soaked slave jumped away from the flick of the lash, the tail of the weapon hit the mark and slashed his back again.

"Move along, Buck!" Hart yelled at him.

"Please Massa, I'm moving as fast as I can," he said to the Irishman.

"That's a lie. Hurry up your lazy ass bones. When you drop that load, come over here and stack these on the second wagon. That one's about full. And don't take all day with it."

They stood there, both of them bathed in the warmth of the soft April air, just outside the entrance. But neither of them had time to enjoy the day. Once Hart was satisfied that he had the slave's attention, the long, slinky man headed back inside the mine to spur the other men on. He wanted them to achieve greater production numbers. After all, his bonus was tied to the amount of coal the miners produced.

However, in his haste to get back inside the mine, the overseer failed to notice the change in the sullen man's demeanor or his furrowed brow. Nor did he see the wild, insane look in the slave's eyes. But most importantly, he was not close enough to Buck to stop him from picking up the iron sledge hammer at his feet.

Suddenly, the slave viciously swung the tool around his head and hit the upright support beam. Dust particles flew into the air. His second strike dislodged the brace of the entrance.

As Buck continued to smash the wooden supports, he walked farther down into the shaft. Hart was absolutely sure that it was Buck's intention to completely destroy the mine. And, in a last ditch effort, he ran back towards him and attempted to hit the slave in the head with the butt of his whip. But the demented man was strong enough to use one deft swish of his hand to push the overseer away. Hart was astonished!

An unwritten taboo had been breached. The slave had actually touched him. Buck had challenged his right to punish him. *Well*, thought Hart, *there's no ifs, ands, or buts about it, me and the men are about to hit the dust. There ain't no way in hell to stop this bastard, but I sure in hell wish that the Indians had trusted me to wear a gun.*

Just for the hell of it, seeing that there was nothing else to lose, he tried to settle him down. He flicked the whip towards Buck again, but it was soon apparent that he had done everything he could have possibly done to save himself and the mine. Finally, he was forced to admit to himself that he had failed to disrupt Buck's deadly terrorist act.

Once he'd faced the reality of the situation, he ran as fast as he could into the suffocating darkness of the glistening chute to warn the men of the impending disaster. As he stumbled down the pathway, his headlamp threw a pitiful light against the walls of the black slickness of the mine.

"Ahhh! Run! Run men, run!"

They could hear the panic in his voice, and were acutely aware of the terror buried in his warning shout. Instinctively, they ran into the deepest bowels of the mine. And there they stood; helplessly huddled together as they awaited the outcome of whatever it was that the Fates had sent their way.

When the roof of the mine began to collapse, Buck was enveloped in a thick, swirling cloud of coal dust. He could not see more than a few feet ahead of his outstretched hand. He realized that he would never be able to catch up with the overseer again, but at the same time, he was satisfied to know that he'd finally trapped him, and would soon kill his tormentor.

Tears of joy ran down the cheeks of the abused slave as he continued to destroy the underpinnings of the mine. *Ain't nobody ever going to beat me again. All of us will have a place in hell waiting for us, but I won't be nobody's slave!*

There was a good chance that his assessment of the situation was correct, because a spark flew into the air as a glancing blow from the hammer hit the metal coal car. Within a few seconds, Buck heard a series of very loud, crackling noises. Then he saw a flash of light as small as the light from the tiny tail of a firefly.

Suddenly, the roar of the blast grabbed the mountain by the throat and shook it until the loud sound of the explosion reached twenty miles away. The side of the hill cracked, shifted, and melted. The mine was a total loss, sealed beneath thousands of tons of fast-burning coal.

After the quaking ground settled, wagonloads of stunned Cherokee mine-owners began to ride along the five-mile road to the site. When they arrived, they were shocked at the total destruction of the mine, the entombment of their family members, and the loss of so many of their slaves.

The first thing everyone noticed was the absolute silence. No one said anything. The animals that had managed to survive the blast had already thundered away from the smoldering woods. And now, even the voice of the creek had softened to a whisper.

It seemed to the Indians that the men's souls had been captured in the slight, shifting breeze that caressed their faces. This was now a holy place, and nobody attempted to dig into the soil. A white, sulfurous, narrow column of smoke marked the eternal grave.

The Graysville mine was owned by the Songbirds, a band of East Tennessee Cherokees. And now, after the complete destruction of their business, they agreed to gather during the early morning hours of May 10, 1829, for a council meeting. Their chief, Starr Night, thought that it was time for them to decide if they would continue to live in Rhea County, nestled in the gentle Tennessee Valley, or if it was time for them to establish a new settlement.

After a few hours of discussion, they discovered that they were almost evenly divided on the question of whether to uproot their families from the land of their ancestors and settle on another rich tract of land they owned in Alabama, or remain in Rhea County and nurse their other resources carefully so that they could eventually recover from their losses.

If the Morgantown Cherokees decided to relocate, they knew that besides having the task of moving their goods to the new place, they would

13

also face the difficult task of rounding up and gathering almost three hundred black slaves for the journey. The chief was well aware of the logistics involved in herding them to Alabama, without losing half of them along the way.

Although he was only twenty years old, Starr Night had the reputation of being a fierce warrior. He was married to Isola, a member of one of the most powerful Cherokee families in Tennessee, the Songbirds. Her family had convinced most of the men and women of the band to select him as a minor chief of the lower towns.

His parents, Eleven Rock and Kitty Coffee, along with her brother, Clyde Rhea, arrived at the meeting determined to convince their tribesmen to join their wagon train. They were headed towards resettlement on their fertile claim abutting the banks of the Black Warrior River.

The mine had been their primary source of income in East Tennessee, and all of them had realized enormous profits from its tremendous production. The mine had been an extraordinary discovery on the Graysville side of the mountain.

But now that Songbird 2 had been destroyed, the members of the band were divided in their opinions about their future. Several of their elders believed that if the Songbirds and Rheas left Morgantown and relocated in Alabama, there would still be enough of their resources left for the rest of the band to remain in Rhea County.

Starr Night disagreed with their logic. He wanted all of them to go with him.

"There's always been strength to be gained in greater numbers of us. And I'm of the opinion that the development of the property in Alabama will be more successful if we agree to work together. The mine is completely destroyed, and we've lost eight of our brothers, along with thirty-five slaves. There's little value left in our holdings here. We should all stick together and create what could turn out to be a much better place than we have here. We'll be able to make a decent living for ourselves, our children, and later generations to come. Here in Rhea County, the soil is about played out."

Three of the older women disagreed with the chief. They told him that they wished to live out their days in the land of their ancestors.

"But," he said, "you're forgetting that the land in Alabama also belonged to our ancestors. We'll find their spirits there, waiting for us to return home."

It was Starr Night's task to convince them that relocating to Alabama was wise. However, there was another problem with his desire to move. Although his band was accustomed to travel on the creeks that surrounded Rhea County, some of them were superstitious about the demons and spirits who lived in large bodies of water and did not relish the thought that they would be required to travel by raft to the new claim. There had been those times when they had traveled on the ferry to cross the river, but it had not been a common occurrence.

Starr Night and most of the men had fought in battles all over the country, and a few of them had traveled to large eastern cities for school, but most of the women had attended schools within a day's ride of Rhea County, and therefore had stronger ties to the land. Usually, they stayed in Dayton, Morgantown or Spring City, year-round.

After the council meeting, several of the men told the chief that they were depending on him to convince the women that it was wise to resettle. The men from mixed families with white fathers felt that the move to Alabama would be to their advantage, because it would finally be possible for them to decide who would inherit their property. As things stood, the women of the tribe owned everything, including the children.

But, none of the men would consider the move without the approval of the women, nor would they be willing leave them to fend for themselves. Some of them thought that there was always the possibility that once they left Rhea County, their enemies, the white settlers, would establish homesteads on their vacated land.

Another problem arose when Lone Fox, one of the troublemakers, rose from his seat to defend the rights of the women to resist the move to Alabama, and the changes to the old laws of inheritance.

Several of the men shook their heads in agreement with him as Starr Night's rival stated his case:

"If you manage to change our ways, thousands of years of Cherokee law will be abandoned. The women will lose the power to keep us safe from ourselves," he said. "Your idea will destroy the fabric of the tribe. We've already adopted so many of the white man's way of doing things. And now, it seems to me that you want to change our laws!"

The chief's piercing black eyes shot a look of pure hatred toward his accuser. His words were measured, but he was so angry that his burnt copper skin glowed a redder hue.

"Look," Starr Night said, "you've misunderstood me. Even my Scottish father-in-law is concerned about us losing our identity. If white people and their mixed Indian children choose to live among us, then they'll be required to accept Cherokee law. And according to our laws, his Indian wife and her family will control the children's property."

Starr Night's statement caused Lone Fox to slink back into his place at the back of the crowd. He was dissatisfied with the argument, but helpless against the chief's logic.

"Let me make my position crystal clear," said Starr Night, "I don't want you to think that I'd try to browbeat anyone to move. It's just that the women in my mother's family, the Rhea's, and my wife's family, the Songbirds, comprise the majority of the band, and we've decided to leave here. We'll be taking most of the slaves with us. I have a feeling that some of you are going to regret your decision to stay in Rhea County."

A few of them mounted their horses and rode back to Graysville during a sudden, brief rain shower. They wanted to have one last look at the damaged mine. They silently milled around and re-assessed the disastrous site where forty-three men were buried, and made note of the wisp of smoke that still wafted through the air. After many hours of debate, most of them finally agreed with the chief to move with their kinsmen to their ancestors' Alabama territory.

Rather than chance the possibility that he would make enemies among some members of the band, Starr Night made a pact with several of the other minor chiefs whose people had stubbornly decided to remain in Tennessee.

"Any of you who choose to make a living from the remaining assets here in Rhea County, will also have a stake in the Alabama property. All members of the Cherokee nation own a part of that claim. There will always be plenty of land for all of us."

The chief was aware that their red soil, clay-based holdings in Rhea County were not fine enough to grow tobacco, and that the weather grew too cold to raise the best cotton. But still, a great variety of vegetables and fruits grew abundantly. And they owned vast herds of sheep. There were several of them who owned thousands of healthy domestic cattle, and they were tended to by slaves who were experts in animal husbandry.

But, although he continued to discuss the pros and cons of the move with several of his tribesmen, his dreams had already turned to the rich, black, bottomland in Alabama. The chief knew that the property was capable of growing high-quality cotton. The map of the claim showed that it ran parallel to the Black Warrior River in both Jefferson and Blount counties.

There was a large clay deposit on the southern border of the land where they could build a kiln. Their slaves would produce pottery canning jars, and their production of paving bricks would allow them to conquer the muddy, pock-marked roads of the country.

Although they had lost a few of them in the mine disaster, there were another two hundred and sixty-five souls who would be readied for the trek to their wilderness property. The slaves would be forced to labor for the Cherokees and help them create Starr Night's vision of the future: that of a prosperous new life for the tribe as masters of a vast cotton plantation.

Now, what Starr Night needed most was a competent overseer to replace the one he had lost in the mine disaster. After mulling over the problem in his mind, he decided that after things had a chance to settle down a bit, he'd take a few of his men with him to visit Cousin George at his Spring City plantation. He could always depend on him for good advice.

Starr Night had already decided that once they were established in Alabama, he would make an offer to buy another under-developed property in Jefferson County. There, he hoped they would be able to resume their primary business, coal mining. Without a new mine, they would waste their most valuable asset: excellent miners who had been taught the business by Isola's father, an old Scotsman named Ian Mac Donald.

A generation ago, when he had brought his coal mining skills to Tennessee from the old country, he'd been hired by the Cherokees. After he had lived among them a few years, and had been willing to teach the Songbirds the nuances of the lucrative business, the chief had allowed him to marry his daughter. But after Lula's death ten years ago, the grief-stricken man had not let much of anything, other than the coalmine and his love and devotion to his daughter's family, occupy his time.

Fortunately, on the day of the mine explosion, Ian had been lucky enough to be one of several survivors of the disaster. When the crazed slave had gone into the mine to attack the overseer, Ian had been standing atop a slope, well outside the entrance.

He'd often reminded Starr Night of his miracle. He'd raked his fingers through his gray-mixed, ginger-colored hair and recounted his escape from the jaws of death.

"I'd just gone outside to dicker with the lumberman about a load of wood to shore up the walls of the shaft. I'd walked about fifty feet towards the wagon when the force of the blast hurled me across the road, down into the deepest part of the creek. I damn near drowned. I was out cold, but a black man came over and pulled me out of the muddy water."

He'd been amazed at the wonder of it all. "I was just about deaf for a while, but now I'm gradually getting my hearing back," he had explained. "There were mere seconds between life and death. There are only three of us who lived to tell the story."

Chapter Two
The New Overseer

A month had passed since the disaster, and Starr Night was forced to alleviate the concerns of his band. They had gathered to discuss their final plans and details of organizing a dozen wagons, sheep, cattle, and hundreds of people for the journey.

So far, the chief had not been able to find an overseer who could be trusted to treat the slaves with any sort of compassion. According to some of the slaves, Hart, the overseer, had hit Buck so hard with his whip that the slave's mind had snapped, and in his effort to kill the overseer, he had destroyed the mine.

As a temporary measure, until he could find another man to work for him, he had picked out several of his tribesmen to closely guard the slave quarters. One of their greatest tasks would be to maintain control over their workers. The slaves were aware of their plans to move farther south, and their knowledge had made them more desperate than ever to escape from the Indians.

For several generations, their slaves had heard ugly stories from the escapees who'd managed to flee the plantations of the Deep South. The harsh working conditions, cruel masters, deadly diseases, and the sweltering heat encountered in the swampy areas of the country, were feared by the Tennessee slaves. Starr Night knew that some of them would try to run away before they too were faced with the same fate.

The Cherokees tried to avoid the separation of the members of their slave families, but they soon discovered that some of them had complicated their lives by marrying slaves who lived "abroad." They had jumped the broom, a ceremony that was their only way of marrying their loved ones, and had married slaves who did not belong to the Indians. Now, as a consequence, they would be forced to leave those outside wives and husbands behind.

Starr Night and his tribesmen met again in the middle of June, and decided to leave most of the older slaves with those Cherokees who had decided to remain in Tennessee.

"Some of them are not strong enough to be uprooted. It's a good idea to leave them with those families who'll remain in Rhea County. They have little value, and they'd be somewhat bothersome to us out on the

19

trail," said the chief. "I don't think many of those old folks are foolish enough to try to run away. If they do, they could find themselves in a heap of trouble."

All of them knew exactly what he was talking about, because they were aware of the double jeopardy any slaves would face if they managed to escape from them. First of all, slaves could be claimed by any white person or Indian who captured them. They were seldom returned to their original owners, and some of them were hastily sent out of state with newly manufactured paperwork, then sold at auction to the highest bidder.

But the most tragic thing about Cherokee-owned slaves was their inability to speak English. They could not pass themselves off as Freedmen, or even pretend to be American slaves. Worst of all, they were unable to communicate with those people who wanted to help them escape.

Three weeks before they were scheduled to leave Morgantown, Starr Night went to Spring City to meet with Cousin George. He sought his much needed advice, and told him that he was desperately in need of an overseer. Cousin George invited the chief to share the evening meal with him while they tried to find a solution to his problem.

After they had eaten the hearty meal, the two men settled down with their pipes and the checkerboard. *Cousin George*, thought Starr Night as he leaned towards the game board, *could certainly do with a woman in this house*.

He was not sure that the servants were taking the best care of the threadbare furniture. The room was a little shabby, and he did not understand why Cousin George was content to let the place deteriorate. His wife had died a few years ago, and now, the man seemed content to wallow around in the filthy place.

Tolliver, Cousin George's manservant, entered the room and bought them a sample of the latest blend of tobacco from his master's humidor.

Afterwards, the very white-skinned mulatto servant was dismissed, and given permission to leave the house to spend the night in his own cabin. Once he was out of earshot, Cousin George began to brag about his servant. He spoke of the intelligence, loyalty, and honesty of the handsome slave.

"In recent years," he explained, "I've taught him to read, and how to play chess. Then it occurred to me that he should read me the newspapers and some of my latest books. Once he'd conquered the literature so adroitly," Cousin George said, "I couldn't see why he shouldn't also be taught to keep the plantation books."

Then Cousin George bragged about his ability to ride and shoot with him and his neighbors on the hunt. "Tolliver has been trained to be totally obedient to me; I've never had a problem with my faithful servant. He's never done anything to disappoint me," he said. "You know, I'd bet you that Tolliver could handle the other slaves for you, but then, I just can't see me letting him go. It pleases me to own such a magnificent being."

"I really hadn't considered him," answered the chief. "After all, how in hell would I be able to keep him from running away and blending into the white settler population?"

"Nah," said Cousin George, "you'd never have that problem. When I go away from Rhea County to a place where nobody knows him, I let him pass for white. I send him into the settler's stores to do my shopping, and he always comes back home to me," he bragged. "But don't worry yourself about it, because I'd rather keep him here with me. He's good company. It's not unusual for me to get about a dozen offers for him every year. When I go into town, I make money on him. Someone always wants to try to beat him in a game of chess."

Starr Night became intrigued with the slave. He would certainly like to possess such an exotic creature. He decided that if he was able to talk his relative out of the man, he would be foolish not to find him a fine mate. *Imagine the value of their children!*

"Come on, Cousin George, name your price," he said.

"Understand this; I'm not aiming to sell him. But, if I ever *do* want to get rid of him, the price will be steep. Now that I think about it, there is a small chance that I might be interested in the sale, but you'd have to be willing to consider swapping that Arabian racehorse of yours, and the herd of beeves you've got out there in the pasture over by the Jones place."

"You'd want 'Sky?'"

"Yes, and the herd of Angus cattle too."

"Damn! You drive a *very* hard bargain! I hope he's good as you say he is. Since he speaks English, I can use him as an interpreter for half of the members of my band," said the chief.

"You've got me in a bad place, but then again, you know how desperate I am." Starr Night sighed. "When can I pick him up? I have four of my men with me, and I'll bet you anything that I'll need very one of them to help me get that big mulatto home."

Cousin George chuckled. He was satisfied that he had gotten the best of the deal.

"Seeing that I have to pay such a high price for him, I damned sure don't intend to let him escape. I hope he'll come along without a tussle, but I'll hogtie him down if I have to."

Meanwhile, Tolliver walked along the hedgerow that separated the slave quarters from the mansion. He did not sense the danger that surrounded him. He had become very complacent with his position as his master's valet and favorite slave. Recently, there had been a couple of times when he could have left the plantation, but he had always had an excuse to stay there.

Just three weeks ago, he had agreed to run away to the North with Ben, but then at the last minute, Tolliver had decided that he could not leave his family. Besides that, he had explained to Ben, his life as a house slave was very different, for he enjoyed the perks of being his master's favorite. He was proud to show off his skills when Master George bragged about his exceptionally talented "fancy" to his friends.

Ben was coal black, and suffered from the hardships borne by anyone who had to labor in the fields all day. Tolliver had always worked in the house as a personal servant.

"Ben, I just can't leave my family here," Tolliver had told him. "Give me another week, and I'll come up with a plan that includes all of the women in my life."

"Be reasonable. We're not going to be able to carry four extra people with us. Let's take your sisters. They're young, and strong enough to make the trip. Your mother and daughter wouldn't be able to survive in the swamp," he said. "In a few days, the Cherokees will have another council meeting to decide when they're going to move. Cozzy, that old Voodoo woman who lives down in the hollow, says that they intend to move farther south. And I'm determined that I ain't going to pick no cotton or cut no cane. Right now, they're watching us close-like, but as soon as they decide when to move, we won't be able to get away."

That day Ben had wiped the sweat from his brow as he had actually begged his friend to flee from the Rhea plantation with him. "Let's get the hell out of here, now!"

But Tolliver had been in deep thought as he'd walked away from him, fighting with himself, hands dug deep into his pockets, while still turning over the details of the plan in his mind.

Ben had shook his head as he watched his friend walk into his shack, then turned his back to Tolliver and his problems, and headed for the kitchen of the big old house.

The cook, Big Red, had a soft spot in her heart for the handsome man. He made her giggle every time he pinched her. He was bold enough to think that he would be able to scavenge a few scraps of food from the pretty cook. He felt like he would have a better chance to survive his journey if he could charm her out of a few bits and pieces of the master's leftovers.

Two days later, Ben decided that he was tired of waiting for his indecisive friend, and began to make his final preparations for the run. He used the time to gather a bundle of sassafras roots for tea, a balled up piece of brown sugar, a handful of grits, an old pot, and a few clothes into a grass sack. He was certain that he would be able to supplement his diet with the blackberries, wild cherries, apples, and raspberries that grew abundantly in the summer woods.

He would also be able to subsist on the mussels and crayfish that lay hidden under the rocks in the riverbed of the Black Warrior River. That night, as soon as darkness and quiet had descended on the gritty plantation, Ben had left Tolliver behind.

As he had stepped away from the plantation, tears had flooded his eyes. He had been forced to leave behind everyone and everything he'd ever known. But, like every slave who made the decision to flee bondage, he had always known that the day might come when he would have to face permanent separation from his friends and family. It was the price he had been willing to pay for his freedom. Although Ben had left the place without the company of his best friend, the man had been smart enough to know that he was going to run *somewhere north*, because it was better than being forcefully marched *anywhere south.*

Once he had successfully slipped away, Ben reached out with burning intensity to embrace his future as a free man. *Failure to reach his goal was not an option.*

The most dangerous thing he had been forced to worry about, was the power of the hound dogs to retrieve his scent, run him down, and capture him in their razor sharp teeth. The animals had a reputation for being able to track a man to hell and back for a simple pat on the head and the reassuring words from the master: "Atta' boy."

Ben had waded in the tepid water nearest the shore. Those times when he had to walk through the woods, he had taken the advice of the old men in the slave quarters and had rubbed the bottoms of his feet with skunk oil. They had told him that it would make it harder for the dogs to catch his scent.

"Most of the time," they had told him, "when they get a bit of that oil on their nose, all but the most stubborn hounds will leave the trail."

A week later, Tolliver learned that the slave-catchers had aborted their search for Ben. He was free! His feelings were hurt that Ben had just abandoned him like that. He had refused to understand that a man like him had responsibilities. He had a mother, two sisters, and a child to care for. He had told Eliza, his brown-skinned mother, of Ben's betrayal:

"All I needed was a little time to figure out a few details of how to include all of you in our plan. Eventually, I would've been ready to make a run for it with him. I'm mad as hell over his big-mouthed promises to me. He told me that he'd wait for me. Dad-blamed liar!"

But after a few days, Tolliver had recovered from his angry fit of pique, and had whittled down his hurt feelings and returned to his usual high opinion of himself.

Above all, he felt that he was mentally superior to the average slave, and therefore he could certainly concoct a successful escape plan for his family. If a dumb field hand like Ben could do it, surely he could. Already, Tolliver had tried to steal a map from Master George. He wanted to see if he could decipher an escape route from Tennessee.

One day a few months past, Tolliver had looked over the shoulders of his short master and glimpsed a full map of the United States and her territories. That map had scared him. Until that day, he had been totally unaware of the enormity of the country. But once he had discovered the fact that they would be required to cross the vast wilderness, he had used that knowledge as an excuse for his failure to escape from captivity.

The sparse information he had heard from those who planned to escape, mainly consisted of the statement that freedom from slavery was to be had somewhere "Up North." They had put their faith in their ability to follow the North Star, but he had noticed that for whatever reason, most of them had been recaptured within a few days.

When he had talked to his family about the possibility of escape, he had been filled with many unanswerable questions, and now he seemed to be totally confused. Of course, Tolliver was ignorant of the fact that he had been programmed by his master to doubt his ability to perform the simplest task without his input, or approval. He could not have possibly understood that he had been trained to follow his master's orders without question.

Every day, he'd been rewarded by the master for his compliance and blind obedience. But now that Ben had successfully escaped, he had been forced to ask himself a few questions about what he could do to help the family survive once they left the Rhea plantation.

When we're free, how will I support them? Where in the North is safe? How can I escape with all of them in one trip?

He was scared. Eventually the women of the house had to admit to themselves that the man of the house simply did not have any gumption. After all, they were certainly aware of the fact that from the time he had been a young boy, Tolliver had possessed an undeniable route of escape. All he had ever had to do was pass himself off as a white settler.

According to what he'd told them, there had been several times when he had tested the white people in towns where he was not known. And he had not only entered their places of business, but had also been able to buy trinkets for the master in stores that did not cater to Indians.

Then, there were the times he had walked on the wooden walkway down the main street in Rockwood, and nobody had challenged him. If they had known that he was black, he would have been hung for his audacity. But those slaves who'd watched him as he had walked among the whites had not betrayed him. They had cast their eyes away from his direction, amused at his deception. Now, his sisters thought, after all of the wasted time, it had finally dawned on him that he could use the power of his skin color to escape from the Indians.

"Perhaps," he'd said to his mother, "I can pretend that you are my slaves." He knew that his mother's dark skin would not be questioned. One of his sisters, Sue, was brown-skinned, and she too, would easily be accepted as his property. But the other sister was as white as he, and she would have to travel with him as his wife. His daughter, Florrine, looked like her dead black Cherokee mother, but her twenty-five year old father

25

planned to use black walnut husks to darken her skin, cut her silky hair, stick it under a floppy hat, and dress her in boy's clothing.

He had been relieved when the family had finally put their plan into place. They had spent their nights sewing clothes from any scrap of cloth he could barter from the other house slaves. He'd finally awakened and realized that they would have to work quickly, if they were to have a chance to succeed in their escape from the plantation. Before long, according to the information Ben had given him, the Cherokees would soon be ready to take them farther south.

Two days after Starr Night's arrival at the plantation, Tolliver was summoned to the office. It seemed to him that the men were happily enjoying a celebratory drink.

"Well Tolliver," his master said, "you've been a faithful servant to me, and I appreciate the way you've helped me take care of this place. But, I've just about decided to sell the plantation, and either go back to North Carolina, or join the rest of the Rhea family in Alabama," he said as he took another stiff drink. "I've made a decision to sell you to my cousin, Chief Starr Night."

Tolliver was speechless. He actually stumbled back a few steps before he was able to regain his equilibrium. The shock of his master's treachery stung him so hard that it seemed to him that he had been slapped. The tiny bit of color in his face simply disappeared.

Oh my God, he thought, *Ben told me that the Indians planned to move, but he hadn't ever dreamed that any of them would be sold! How could my master sell me away like a common field hand? Why didn't I have enough sense to run away with Ben?*

When he was dismissed from their presence, Tolliver stumbled from the house to the path-way leading to his cabin. The thing he needed most, he felt, was to be embraced in the loving, comforting arms of his family. He was blinded by the tears that kept him from seeing the lane, but eventually, he groped his way home. When he reached the cabin and flung himself through the doorway, the air was sucked from the room. Eliza was shattered by the shocked expression on her son's face. She began to question him, but he was still unable to utter a word.

"What's happened? Did the master hit you?" She was afraid to hear the answer. But, when Tolliver *did* begin to speak, he told them that he had been sold. His words turned their hearts to jelly. It was very difficult for his family to look at him. It seemed to them that the tragedy of his sale had deflated his whole body.

Tolliver's eyes were distant. His soul burned with regret. The women were devastated. What could they do to help their beloved Tolliver?

"Nothing," Eliza told them, "absolutely, nothing."

The women had thought of themselves as superior to the other slaves, and immune to being sold away from the plantation. But now they had to accept the fact that none of them were so special after all because Tolliver had just been swapped for a herd of cattle and a horse.

When he finally gained control of the crying, he had to face the fact that his life, as he had believed it to be, was a lie fabricated by the master. Now he understood that he was not more valuable to him than the cattle he had swapped him for. The shock of the ugly truth cut him like a knife, sliced deep, and twisted itself into his core.

But Tolliver's debasement served to awaken him. It forced him to become a real man, one who finally recognized that unless he managed to change the circumstances of his existence, he would be destined to carry an invisible, but tight, yoke around his neck for the rest of his life.

When Starr Night came to the cabin to collect his new slave, he brought several of his men with him. They were there to help him escort the big man to his new home in Morgantown.

His family stopped crying and looked at their man in astonishment as a new person emerged from the crying, shaking, sniveling, mess that had once been Tolliver. They fearfully waited in breathless anticipation as he looked right into the chief's eyes, and threatened to commit suicide.

"I'll kill myself if you take me away from my family. Without them, I'll have nothing to live for," he said. "But if you'll take *all* of us with you, we'll gladly leave this place," he vowed. "We'll work hard for you. Just as hard as that horse you traded me for."

Starr Night saw the anguish and shock in Tolliver's eyes, and believed him. He had sense enough to realize that any slave who was bold enough to make such a statement to his master was desperate enough to carry out the threat. But the chief had a gut feeling that if he could get him to voluntarily come home with him, it would not take long for them to train the intelligent man to be his overseer.

After thinking about the desperate words the man had uttered, the chief agreed to speak to Cousin George, and ask him to re-arrange the deal.

Later that evening, after talking it over with their master, the chief extracted a promise of loyalty from Tolliver, and agreed to take the whole family with him to Alabama.

The family was so relieved at their reprieve that they all became very docile creatures. But, as recently purchased Starr Night property, the Indians did not trust them, and kept a close watch on them as potential runaways. The tribe had no way of knowing it, but the stuffing had been knocked out of all of them. They had accepted their defeat, and now walked around in a stupor, and followed orders. Their dreams of escape had died.

Eliza castigated herself because of her selfishness. She felt quite guilty that they found themselves in this predicament. She knew that she had encouraged her son to stay on the Rhea plantation with them. They had used his position as a favored slave to ease their lives as privileged house servants.

One day, near or about thirty years ago, when she was a pretty young girl working in the hot, dusty fields, her white master had noticed her fine-boned beauty and ordered the overseer to find a job for her inside his manor. Although her skin was darker than most house servants, he had found her charms irresistible and had insisted that she be trained as his wife's personal maid.

Once Eliza had been given a small room in the cellar, the master had become obsessed with her. He taught her how to pleasure him, and after she had mastered the lessons, he'd seldom found a reason to sleep in his own bed with his wife. She had cried herself to sleep most nights, stayed abed during the day, and learned to rely on a dose of laudanum to ease her heartache.

Eventually, the women had become mortal enemies. The tensions in the house had become especially explosive once Eliza had given birth to the second mulatto baby within three years.

The mistress had been forced to watch Eliza's children play with her own youngsters. She had not been able to avoid the truth of her situation. Her selfish, unfaithful husband had forced her to live under the same roof with his mistress and his bastards. Tolliver and Bea were as white as his other children.

The master's wife seldom left the house. She sent her regrets when her neighbors came to call. She had been too embarrassed to let the white women of nearby plantations pay her a visit, lest they discover the depth of her humiliation, and of the arrogance of her rival.

The master had insisted that Eliza be permitted to remain in the house. And she hadn't been required to do any work, other than to take care of *all* of the master's children. Finally, one drug-fueled day, the mistress grew bold enough to confront her despicable husband. She danced around the room holding a can decorated with cross-bones above her head.

"I can't keep you out of her bed," she said, "but I *will* have the prettiest face in this hell of a house once I've thrown this pot of lye in her face. She'll still be able to serve both of us just the same as she does now, but we'll see how much you want her after I've finished with her. You'll be obliged to look into her scarred, burned face every time you visit her. Either you get her and her bastards out of my house right now, or I'll kill all of them," she threatened. He looked into her crazed eyes and knew for certain that she would carry out her threats. She gave him until the end of the week to get rid of them.

The next morning, Eliza's master loaded her and their children into the wagon, drove them to Spring City, and sold them to George Rhea. He secured the money from their sale in his strongbox, stepped into his wagon, turned the horses for home, and did not look back at Eliza, or his children as he'd rode away.

Although his plantation was located about ten miles away, she never saw him again. But she was always thankful that he had not sold their children away from her.

Five years later, she gave birth to another daughter, fathered by a Rhea slave, but after his death she did not want another man.

Master George seemed pleased with her work. She labored in his house as a skilled seamstress, and worked as a midwife at all of the Cherokee plantations. Up until the time her master sold them to the chief, he seemed to value her and her children for their skills, and their ability to speak both Cherokee and English.

Eliza raised Tolliver to always consider the position of his family. They were the only slaves in the dirt-packed slave quarters to have wooden floors in their small cabin. The other slaves, except for those who slept in the manor, stayed in hovels. They lived like animals. Tolliver was given burlap sacks for his family to stack and use as pallets on the floor.

When Ben first approached Tolliver about the possibility of escape, Eliza prompted him to stay with them, even though he could've easily escaped. She had been well aware that close contact with the master was a perilous position. There had always been the possibility that he would find a new toy, and throw the old favorite away.

Now, Eliza had to face the fact that she had given her son terrible advice. She had been selfish enough to want all of her children to stay with her. So, although they still lived together, she was forced to ask herself some soul-searching questions. *Am I being punished for loving them so much that I could not bear to lose them? Must the price for our remaining together as a family be our imprisonment for the rest of our lives?*

Chapter Three
The Wranglers

Once they were settled in at Starr Night's plantation outside Morgantown, the family gathered around in a circle on the floor to talk about their altered position in the new slave population. During the discussion that night, they made the life-changing decision to aid any slave they could trust with the knowledge of their complicity, to escape from the Morgantown plantation. But before they risked exposing their activities to the Indians, they agreed that they would have to be absolutely convinced that the person had a halfway decent chance to succeed in their attempt to flee the bonds of slavery.

"We'll give them the clothes we've made, and the maps Tolliver has drawn of nearby towns," said Eliza. "But, be sure that this is what we want to do, because if our part in an escape is discovered, the chief will kill all of us."

Otto, and his family of three, slipped away the next week. Tolliver's family was able to console themselves. And although *their* family would probably remain slaves for life, they had made it possible for Otto's family to join the lucky few who had managed to find conductors to lead them to freedom.

Shortly after that initial success, they were able to secretly aid two other families. Tolliver had turned a blind eye to them as they slipped through a fence to the meadow far beyond the borders of the slave quarters.

Meanwhile, Tolliver and his family continued to work on the multitude of details in preparation of their master's journey to Alabama. Once they had packed the Cherokee's belongings and stowed them on the wagons, the tribe was ready to move out.

Most of the tribesmen were prepared to travel on horseback. They met at their gathering and staging place in Graysville for the ride to the boats in Hamilton County. Some of the Cherokee women rode in the bone-jarring wagons, a few rode horseback, but many of them acted as guards, and walked among the slaves behind the wagons.

As the band began to meet other members of their tribe along the trail, they formed the nucleus of the wagon train. Those tribesmen from Meigs

County rode the ferryboat to Hamilton County, and joined those from Sale Creek and Bakewell. Other Songbird family members took a longer trail from the east, and rendezvoused on Lake Richland, near Ross's Landing.

"Hitch that wagon!"

"Watch out for the dog, and line up to the right!" Starr Night shouted. They began to pull out and line up in no particular order. They were just happy to finally get started on their way, early on that slightly windy, overcast day.

Tolliver had recovered enough of his composure to take on his job as the overseer. He was the only slave allowed to ride on a horse. The insight he had gained over the last few weeks had made him a more compassionate man. Now, he did his best to ease the heavy burdens of the other slaves.

He was forced to accept the fact that although his skin was white, he was just as black as any of the other slaves. The only difference there had ever been between his life and theirs had been that George Rhea had raised him to be his special toy.

The Indian had enjoyed his pet, and considered his enchantment with Tolliver the same as he would have any novelty, a favorite horse, gun, or fine book. Tolliver's new understanding of his place in his ex-master's mind forced him to realize that there was no difference between him and any field-hand. It had just been a matter of the skills he had been taught. George Rhea had used him as a diversion from the boredom of living on a lonely, isolated, wilderness plantation.

Now that he was Starr Night's overseer, Tolliver made it a point to reward the other slaves with praise when they worked hard. And it would never have occurred to him that he would ever need to use a whip for discipline. He was determined that he would never misuse his power. Yet, the people seemed to like him, and responded to his orders without question. Even though he was not aware of the fact, there were some of them who had learned of his part in their friend's escape, and now considered him an ally in their bid to flee bondage.

Tolliver had been riding on this particular horse for the past three years. He and the steed were a magnificent pair. The black stallion was marked with a white forelock and stockings. The difficult animal was completely docile with the slave, and refused to accept another rider. The chief had bought him for next to nothing, because the mount was useless to Cousin George. And in spite of the fact that only one person could ride the animal, Starr Night, being an admirer of good horseflesh, enjoyed watching the beautiful horse respond to Tolliver's subtle signals.

The chief had also noticed that his slave could stand to have a haircut. His straight brown hair brushed against his shoulder blades, and his beard grew in the same manner of most white men. All of that hair made him look quite different from any slave they had ever owned.

Maybe it ought to be cut shorter, he thought as he sat in the shade of an oak. *He ought to get rid of that beard too.* Then he saw Tolliver dip down on his horse to pick up a child who had been missing for most of the day, and forgot all about the slave's appearance. The chief watched him return the boy to his grateful, panic-stricken mother. She touched his chap-covered leg and thanked him for his dogged search for the child.

Tolliver had flushed him out of the densest undergrowth of the woods, after almost everyone else had abandoned the search. It marked the first time since he'd bought him that the chief had seen a smile on the big man's face.

Most of his men had stopped looking for the child because they had thought that he was lost to the pack of wild dogs that followed the caravan through the narrow track. He could tell from the slaves' demeanor that today's successful rescue had made him proud that he had not given up the search.

Now that his day was done, Tolliver removed the saddle and tack from his horse and rubbed him down. Once the bit was removed from his mouth, Diamond nuzzled his master, and was set free to graze around the edges of the wagon train, without being tethered or cobbled. The horse never strayed so far away from Tolliver that he could not immediately respond to his master's summons.

Starr Night, and the men of his band, continued to watch their slave overseer closely. The chief sat on his brindled horse and watched Tolliver peer from those hazel-colored eyes. It seemed to him that the man never missed tending to the smallest detail. The Indians thought of him as a confident, laid-back man, but his demeanor was just a show that he put on for them.

Tolliver was always aware of any attention he garnered from Starr Night and his band. He made an effort to discourage their interest in him. He did not want, or trust, their version of friendship. But, he had learned to value a new friend among the house slaves. His new confidant was a black Cherokee.

Tolliver had found that they shared a number of problems. Neither of them belonged to any one race of people, and both of them suffered from their inability to blend in with the other slaves.

"Itty," he said, "the Indians have taught me that there are limits to their relationship with me. Their friendship only goes skin deep. I swear to you that I'll never expose myself to that kind of pain and disappointment again. I really trusted my master to take care of me and my family. But now that I know better, I won't ever be foolish enough to think that one of them is my friend. You always have to watch yourself with them. Eventually, they're likely to find another way to humiliate you."

"Yeah," Itty said, "they know how to tear you apart, work your ass off, and then act as if you're their bosom buddy. Even after they've mistreated you, they don't see any reason why you wouldn't want to go fishing with them the next day. Crazy bastards."

"This is the second time I've been sold," said Tolliver, "and I'm not convinced it'll be the last time. My master played with me like a puppet on a string, then grew tired of me. I don't know who I am anymore. There are times when I just feel dead inside."

Itty shook his head in agreement and acknowledgement of Tolliver's feelings. "You don't know the half of it. I've watched the chief from a distance. I've seen Starr Night pull out his books and study the registrations of the animals he owns. Whether you know it or not, all of us are counted as part of the stock," he said. "You're wise to pay heed to their evil treatment of us. As I work in the house among the chief and his tribesmen, there are times when I get a chance to watch them play a game of chess. I know that they've taught you the game, but when you're not around they play a different game among themselves.
They wager slaves."

Itty pushed his long braids to the back of his neck and wiped the sweat from his brow with his bandana. His emotions were boiling to the surface. After all, Tolliver was the first man who had accepted him for who he was, and he felt the man's pain of being an outsider. Both of them existed in limbo, stranded in a land that had robbed them of an identity.

"There has to be a way to end this nightmare. I just can't fathom a reason why we must be their beasts of burden for eternity. I don't want to wake up every morning of my life without a chance to be free," Itty continued. "Look, I'm part Cherokee, kin to most of them, but as you can see, they treat me just the same as their other slaves. My black blood

34

makes me unable to claim kinship. My blackness makes it easier for them to ignore the fact that I *am* one of them."

After listening to the sorrow buried in his heart, Tolliver began to understand the intricate nuances of the fragile world where he was forced to live. He would have to find the wisdom to guard his heart against the hurtful things that his master had the power to subject him to.

Now that he had discovered this new sense of self, his hidden agenda would dictate who he would allow to enter into the recesses of his soul. He was determined to find a way to deal with the Indians with a smile plastered on his face. Although he was forced to work for them for the rest of his life, he vowed to himself that he would always be sure that he kept a rock tied and pressed solidly around the feelings in his heart.

When Tolliver's black Cherokee wife had died in childbirth, she had left him to raise their tiny, beautiful daughter alone. Mary had not lived long enough to see Florrine's face. Even though the tribe had made it unlawful for blacks and Cherokees to marry, she had been part of a large population of mixed-breeds, and they had married in the slave fashion of jumping the broom.

After her death, his mother and sisters had moved into his cabin to care for the child. They had wanted to live in a place where they could safely raise Florrine, and that had been the main reason the family had accepted their captivity at the Rhea place.

By the time Tolliver and his family were on the road to Alabama, Starr Night was satisfied that the other slaves had completely accepted Tolliver as their leader. The overseer seemed so sure of himself. But, what the chief could not have known was that Tolliver had learned a very valuable lesson from his new masters. He had learned to act as stoic as a Cherokee, and in return, almost everyone thought of him as a deep-thinking man, a man a lot smarter than he actually was. His manner fooled everyone. Most importantly, Starr Night had gradually developed a quiet but unspoken confidence in Tolliver's ability to keep the slaves so busy at their tasks that they did not have the time to formulate escape plans.

As they ambled along the way to Alabama, the southern woods were alive with the noisy sounds of cattle slowly plodding along the trail, sending up clouds of dust and vicious insects. It did not take long for the travelers to discover that the mosquitoes were equally likely to bite either man, or beast.

The hogs aggressively rooted their way past their keepers. Tolliver utilized the energy of several teenage boys to herd them away from the deepest part of the woods, because once they were lost, the beasts were hard to recover, and sometimes managed to mate with the wild boars. The boars, with their long tusks, were dangerous. So when one of them was shot by the hunters, everyone celebrated the event. The slaves quickly butchered the animal, and the meat was cooked and eaten that day.

Many of the slaves carried children on their backs as they walked along the trail. The black women who were more than six months pregnant usually rode in the wagons. They carried the Cherokee's most valuable asset, the next generation of free laborers.

Several of the Indian women and their children walked along the trail with the slave families to help them tend to the large flock of Merino sheep. The women had taught some of their slaves to be highly skilled weavers, and they produced exceptionally fine, wool yard-goods.

When Starr Night's wagon lost its left front wheel, it was quickly repaired by the slave blacksmiths and wheelwrights. The house servants: Itty, his mother, Cook, and his girlfriend, Yellow Girlie; had the responsibility of organizing the repair, seeing that the wagon was repacked, placed back into line, and readied for the next leg of the journey.

They worked under the constant scrutiny of the Cherokees, and felt pressured to perform their tasks as seamlessly perfect as possible. The house slaves always labored under the unspoken threat of banishment from the house to the harsh labor in the fields.

A team of oxen was used to pull the heaviest wagon. It was packed with ammunition and weapons. They carried the small arsenal as protection against the possibility that they would have to defend themselves against bandits, or anyone else who thought they were easy pickings.

A few years ago, the land had been open to travelers, but recently, the settlers had begun to erect fences and toll roads across the landscape. Some of them claimed ownership of the barely improved trail and demanded pay for its use. Sometimes the chief found it better to pay for the shortcut, rather than take the time to search for another way around the barrier.

As they continued to travel through the flat land of the Tennessee Valley, Tolliver noticed that the beautiful hilltops surrounding them were ablaze with the blooms of azaleas, wild black cherry trees, and late blooming dogwoods. When he took off his hat and scanned the sky, not one rain cloud dotted the horizon. Everyone seemed to respond to the glorious day. It seemed to him that the caravan had a festive air about it as they wound through the lightly scented, piney woods of the easy flowing river

The chief pulled up next to Tolliver and told his overseer about a new plan he had been mulling over in his mind for a few days.

"Tolliver, I want you to pick out five of your men to help us manage a new herd of cattle I'm going to buy in Sale Creek. I want to replace those I sold to my Cousin George for you and your family. I've watched how well Cousin George has taught you to handle your horse, and for the first time ever," he said, "I'm beginning to think that it might be possible to show some of the men how to be wranglers. If some of them can learn the basics of riding on a pony while they work, we might be able to train them as drovers, and give them the job of steering the critters all the way to the new land."

"They'll be excited and proud to have lessons from your men. All they want out of this life is a chance to better themselves, and show you that they can put in a good day's work. You have some smart, good-hearted men working for you, Sir."

Tolliver looked around and spotted several men walking behind a wagon. They were lifting buckets of dried cow chips inside so that they could be used as fuel for the nightly campfires.

"I've got an idea," the chief said. "After I buy the cattle, we'll have a contest. That way, the men can compete for the jobs, and we'll have the beeves rounded up and branded before we board the boats."

Later that week, when they came close to another copse of pines, Tolliver told the men the details of the master's plan to build a corral for the herd. And just as he had predicted, they were excited to participate in an adventure and have the chance to change the course of their lives. They would be wranglers. Just the thought of what it would mean to have their women and children see them astride a horse, was a thrilling idea. None of them had dared to dream of the possibility. Now, they hoped that they could somehow improve the circumstances of their existence by becoming cow handlers instead of cotton pickers.

They were determined to work hard and conquer any new tasks their Indian masters required of them. Perhaps, the men hoped, if the Cherokees were pleased with their effort to drive the cattle to the boats, they might be convinced to let them continue their work as wranglers in Alabama.

Tolliver picked out the first three men and gave them a horse. It would be up to the Indians to teach them to ride and perform their tasks from the saddle.

"Tiny, Boneman, and Velvet, step up. You're going to learn how to ride today," said Tolliver. Gradually, after a few bumps and bruises, the three of them learned to stay seated in the simple saddles without falling off, or spooking the horses. The Cherokee masters turned them loose and watched them closely as they honed their skills. After a while, the men were confident and happy to show off their newly learned proficiencies to the Indians.

After several days of steady progress, Tolliver was able to present Starr Night with five slaves that the Cherokees had been able to train as cattlemen. Two of them had not ever sat on horseback before, but had already learned to take care of the cattle and their mounts. *It was amazing*, Tolliver thought, *how fast they'd learned those skills.*

A few days later, Tolliver watched with pride as the men crossed a small, shallow, branch of the river with the cattle. They were all able to hang on to the pommels of their saddles as they swam with one free hand. After the men had landed all of the cattle on the other side of the river, they took turns watching the animals, and guarding them from predators. He gave them a hidden nod and a wink as he rode past. He was proud of what they had accomplished in such a short amount of time, but secretly, he doubted that the Indians would allow so many slaves to have access to a horse once they reached the claim.

With every passing day, Starr Night's confidence in Tolliver's ability to lead the slaves and keep them under his control was magnified. He felt that Tolliver deserved the praise that Cousin George had expressed to everyone about him. The chief was absolutely sure that the slave and his family were worth every cent he'd bartered for them. *And,* he thought, *I almost passed him up, thinking that he'd run away.*

The chief believed that once the overseer had insisted on bringing his family with him to Morgantown, he had trapped himself. *Yep,* he thought, *he's bound to me for the rest of his life. That's the bargain I struck with him.*

Tolliver was well aware that he had fooled the Cherokee into thinking that he was satisfied with the agreement they had made. *And I want him to always think that I'll stay with him. I want his trust until the very day that he discovers that I've flown away.*

The next morning, they arrived at the boat-clogged landing on the deepest part of the river. They boarded paddlewheel riverboats, a keel-boat, several rafts, and a barge down the Tennessee to the Guntersville landing in Alabama. Not every boatman would agree to ferry either Indians or slaves, but finally, the pilgrims amassed enough transportation for everyone. Not every boat owner could afford to deny them service.

Chapter Four
The Alabama Homeland

July

On a hot, humid, dirt-devil kind of day, the drovers pushed the protesting cattle towards the last leg of the journey to the new claim. The dust-clogged trail took them through the sleepy towns of Scottsboro and Albertville, to the stream just outside Royal, in Blount County.

Starr Night allowed the members of his caravan a much needed rest. It was his plan to stay put until the other five wagons from North Carolina caught up with them. Once they arrived, they would form one large wagon train. If the travelers had been lucky enough to have come through the mountains without too much trouble, the chief figured it would be around the week of the Fourth of July before everyone was rested and ready to pull out of Oneonta.

Almost everyone else had a chance to rest, but Tolliver and his master climbed into a buckboard wagon and rode out to Hayden, where they purchased two 100-pound burlap sacks of cotton seeds to plant on the new claim.

"If we stay on schedule, there's still enough time left in this growing season to prepare the ground, plant the seeds, and have a crop ready to harvest. Once the seeds are planted, we'll start to see shoots emerge in about a week," the chief said. "I expect to harvest a bumper crop on that virgin, black bottomland."

When they returned to the caravan near sundown, they could hear the shouts of almost every adult, loudly calling out a name.

"Bea!"

"Where are you, Bea?"

Eliza, tears streaming down her face, ran toward the wagon that was carrying the two men. She told them that Tolliver's sister had simply disappeared into the woods that morning.

"I wasn't worried about her at first, because I thought she'd gone to relieve herself. But later, we went in the woods to look for her. Someone might have taken her, thinking that she was a white woman the Indians had stolen. But surely she'd have screamed if somebody had tried to steal her."

Tolliver jumped from the wagon, and with his master's permission, joined the search. He was scared that he would never find her in those thick woods. *I found that child because I wouldn't give up on him,* he thought. *Now, Bea is gone, and I don't know how long it'll take me to find her, but I'm not about to lose her out here in the wilderness.*

"Bea!" he yelled, as he trampled through the undergrowth.

Although he walked far into the deepest part of the fern covered forest, Tolliver could still hear his mother's cry for her daughter. Sometimes the trail meandered across the landscape in unusual twists and turns, and he found that he was close enough to Eliza to hear her footsteps as she stumbled about the edge of the woods.

The sun was beginning to sink behind the hills when Itty joined his friend on the hunt. He carried torches they would light with a Lucifer, once it grew too dark to navigate the rock-strewn creek bed at the bottom of the hill.

Now that they were running out of daylight, the chief decided to order all of the slaves to join in the search for Bea. The white-skinned slave was too valuable to leave behind.

Earlier that morning, Bea had tired of sitting in the shade of a wagon, and had decided to slip away from the Indians to wade in the water at the base of the hill. Her mother had watched her enter the dense woods. She had not worried about getting lost, because the water ran parallel to the trail, and she intended to stay within shouting distance of her mother.

Bea had not been able to resist a dip into the cool water, but now, she rushed to return to the wagons before the Indians took notice of her absence.

While she was getting back into her cotton shift, she thought she heard the sound of someone walking towards her in the woods. Bea had been frightened enough to hide in the willows near the bank. Maybe *it's a bear,* she'd thought. *It might be a good idea to make a run for it!*

And just as she made up her mind to flee the unseen danger approaching her hiding place, a hand had shot out from behind a tree and knocked her backwards. Her head hit the rocks at the water's edge. Bea blacked out.

When she awakened, the sky was growing dark. She felt sore, disoriented and violated.

Where's my *dress?* She wondered.

"Bea! Where are you, Sis?" Tolliver yelled. He and Itty had climbed down the hill to the water. Both of them had refused to give up hope. Tolliver had to find his sister! They had made it through the hell of being sold, and against all odds, had managed to stay together. Now, he could not bear the thought that he would have to go back to the wagon and tell his mother that they had lost Bea. His throat felt dry as he continued to yell for her.

"Bea!" he shouted again as he neared the large boulders at the edge of the water.

Oh, she thought, *it's Tolliver. My brother will help me stand up.* But when she tried to call out to him, she found that she could not speak.

Tolliver! Help me! Come here! She thought, but not a sound escaped her lips.

Finally, Tolliver spotted her body from the light of his torch, ran to her, took off his shirt, and placed it over her naked body. And just as he moved to pull her dead body from the rocks, she opened her bloodshot, blue eyes.

"Itty," her astonished brother said, "I swear to you that I just saw her open her eyes. Her skin is ashen, and her body is cold to the touch, but, she's alive!"

Tolliver sent Itty to get his mother, a blanket, and the master. Someone had raped his sister and damn near killed her! Most likely, it was a Cherokee, because he knew that Bea had been allowed to walk through the woods without a guard, but it was very unlikely that a black man would have been trusted to stay alone in the woods long enough to accost and rape his sister. And, it was not likely that any white man would care to be around that many Indians either. If someone had seen her, and thought that Bea was a white woman, he would have kidnapped her.

Once he took a good look at the girl in Tolliver's arms, Starr Night ordered his men to let Bea ride in the wagon with the pregnant women, until she got her strength back.

"Then," the chief said, "perhaps she'll be able to tell us who raped her. Eliza, I want you to ride in the wagon and take care of her."

He turned to those who had walked down the hill. "As soon as she's able to tell us what happened," he said, "I promise everyone on this train that the man who committed this crime will be banished from our presence. If a black man did this, he'll be whipped, then sold. And if it's one of my men, all of you know that I don't believe that there's ever any excuse for anyone to rape or kill one of our slaves. So, if he's one of us, my advice would be to pack up and be gone by sundown, or we'll hang you." he announced.

Tolliver was forced to modify his opinion of the chief. He had never heard of *any* master, white or Indian, who punished one of their own when they raped or murdered a slave. Usually, the owner was satisfied if the murderer paid him the value of the slave. But, to his surprise, it seemed as if *this* Cherokee was bound and determined to punish the man who had violated Bea.

I wish she'd wake up and tell me his name, he thought. *Once she does, I'm going to kill him, or die trying. I suspect it's that bastard Lone Fox. All of a sudden, he wants to know how she's doing. I don't ever remember a time when he was ever friendly with any of us.*

After the wagons from North Carolina arrived in Oneonta, Starr Night conferred with his men and the maps, and found that they were within a few days' ride of the claim. And on a glorious July day, after an impatient journey of the last few miles, the Cherokees and their slaves reached their property line. The Indians took one look at the place, were satisfied, and very happy that they had agreed to acquiesce to the wishes of their chief.

The band was convinced that the beautiful lush acres of rich soil would assure a prosperous future for many generations to come. In every Cherokee village, wherever they had settled in the country, their neat towns had always been envied by their neighbors, and they knew that one day, after this place had been fully developed, it would rival any plantation in Alabama.

Their slaves were happy to put down their heavy burdens. They hoped that the masters would allow them to have a few days of rest before their work began, for they all knew that it would be their labor that the Cherokees would use to establish the new, grand plantation.

When Isola laid her eyes on the beautiful land, she cried with joy, and was convinced that her husband had made the right decision for them.

"Starr Night, as soon as we send a few letters back to those who stayed in Rhea County, they will wish that they'd come with us to Alabama. I'll bet you that before long, by the end of the year at the latest, another wagon train will follow our lead," she said. "What a wonderful place! I see just the spot where we should build our house."

The Cherokees named their claim "Warrior," for the gentle Black Warrior River that ran the length of it from Jefferson County, to the middle of Blount County.

Starr Night had sent a construction crew ahead of the main caravan, and they had built dozens of tents and a corral. And now that all of them were there, Tolliver and the rest of the slave men went into the woods to chop down trees for log cabin construction. The builders erected a small sawmill on the banks of the river to cut the lumber into planks.

A few months later, after much pulling and prodding, Bea learned to walk. But now, they began to wonder if she would ever be able to speak to them again. Sometimes it seemed that she had something she wanted to say, and then she would have a hurt look on her face, and would not say or write anything. Tolliver had taught her to read and write when they had belonged to Master Rhea. But, no matter how much Tolliver questioned her, she did not seem to remember who had attacked her.

However, she continued to sew beautiful clothes for the mistress. And though it seemed a shame that a beautiful young woman in her twenties would be maimed for the rest of her life, and forced to drag her left foot a little bit, she seemed satisfied to be ignorant of the details of what had happened to her on the day she had been attacked.

Tolliver had noticed that Lone Fox was apt to ride past the place where she worked just to have a look at her. She smiled when he rode his sorrel past her, and he always lifted his hat to her, but she never seemed to recognize him. After a while, he stopped riding past, but Tolliver was still suspicious of his motives. As a precaution, Tolliver warned his family to never let Bea out of their sight.

"Thankfully," Eliza told him, "she's not pregnant."

Tolliver had plenty of work ahead of him. The Tennessee slaves were not builders. The huts they had occupied in Rhea County had been constructed in their grandparents' generation. Occasionally, they had replaced a rotted log, slathered on missing chinking, or repaired a leaky roof, but they had never been required to build any kind of housing until they had been forced to migrate to Alabama.

Starr Night had hired three Irishmen in Chattanooga to show his servants how to nail together crude dwellings for themselves. Once they had mastered the basics of building their own huts, the master carpenter told the chief that the men were experienced enough to dig the foundation and position the support beams for the mansion's staircase in place.

Tolliver's main duty on the project was to interpret the Irishmen's instructions to the men. They were new to their tasks, and even though he had never built anything himself, he had a good ear for accents and was talented enough to catch on to the essence of other languages. He understood the Irish brogue enough to relay orders to the other slaves. The big boss often set a rapid pace, and insisted that all of them had to work harder and faster, in order to complete the big house for the chief and his family.

Finally, the work on the mansion was finished. And Tolliver would always remember how the Irishman had stood back on his heels and looked at the place as if he had built it all by himself. But, truth be told, the man couldn't have had more pride about his part in creating that place than the slave men. They claimed the beauty of the workmanship on the place for themselves.

It was true that they had learned their construction skills from the Irishmen, but they had been quick to claim credit for their special carving talents. The men enjoyed a sense of accomplishment, because they had used their previously unknown abilities to create the perfectly proportioned mansion. *Their* hands and *their* labor had created the masterpiece. The quality of the built-in bookcases, soaring stairways, plastered ceilings, and tiled fireplaces, was equal to the work done at any plantation house in Alabama.

Within a year, everyone who lived on the property was sufficiently housed. The cabins were the best made slave quarters in Jefferson County. Starr Night had agreed with the Irishman to build wooden floors in all of the cabins, an unheard of luxury for most of the workers.

The gardens had already produced mountains of vegetables, the herd had increased in size, and the cotton bolls of a bumper crop had been successfully harvested.

Neither Tolliver, his family, nor the Morgantown slaves, were accustomed to such hard work. Never before had they been required to work the labor-intensive long hours demanded from them in order to harvest the cotton crop. And now, they were very closely guarded because they were so extremely valuable. Worth twice the price of the ground they tilled.

It was not very long before Tolliver began to see a change in the chief's temperament. Self-interest had begun to overtake his kind heart. Tolliver saw that his compassion had been replaced by his intention to keep them working at optimum speed so that he could increase his profit. His slaves would never again enjoy the freedom of movement they had experienced in Rhea County, Tennessee.

Although the Songbird slaves had always lived with the knowledge that they were enslaved for life, now their servitude had become a much heavier burden to bear. It seemed to them that another chain had been thrown around their necks. At first, the unhappy people increased their efforts to escape, but they were seldom successful. The wilderness land was so isolated that after a time, they felt so defeated that most of them lost the will to change their destinies. And after a desperate few of the runaways were captured and returned to the plantation, Tolliver and his family had subconsciously begun to accept their roles as slaves for life.

By 1839, ten years of deft management and hard labor had turned Warrior into the largest plantation in the area. The tribe had reversed the misfortunes they had suffered in the Tennessee mining disaster, and had grown the value of their resources tenfold. At last, the industrious Cherokee band felt safe and secure in their new home.

One day, the chief held a letter up in the air, showed it to his tribesmen, and shared the contents of the message.

"This letter is from Rhea County," he said, as he waved it around. "It says that there are five more wagonloads of our band coming out here to Warrior next spring!"

The slaves watched them as they celebrated. Whoops of joyful noise burst through the air. The Indians were ecstatic! They yelled and hollered with happiness, but the slaves looked around sorrowfully at each other, and understood that their workload would soon increase by another five wagonloads of demanding masters.

Later that week, Starr Night and his father, Eleven Rock, finally finished their dinner, then headed for the front porch to enjoy the balmy, pleasant air of May. After the men had tamped apple-scented tobacco into their corncob pipes, they ordered Itty to pour the sweet muscadine wine into their glasses.

They had the patience to wait for the servant to go back inside the house, shut the door, and return to the kitchen before they spoke. They pulled their chairs close together, backs to the door, and used hushed voices to discuss tribal business. Both of them were mindful of the prying ears and eyes of the nosy house slaves.

"This is the second time in five years that we've been ordered to attend court in Tuscaloosa," said Eleven Rock. "And every time we go there, we end up losing a couple of hundred acres of our land. We're content to share the land, but it seems to me as if the state of Alabama won't be satisfied until the day comes when they have robbed us of all our land."

"Father, we're so far from the white settlers that we can't possibly be a nuisance to them. This plantation is almost self-sufficient. We've traded with them, sold our slaves and coal to the mills in Birmingham, and shipped our cotton from our own landing. We have quite a few white business partners. Many of them have been permitted to marry into the tribe. Why would their people want to push us out? We contribute quite a bit to the economy of this part of the country," said a furious Starr Night. For a moment, he had forgotten to lower his voice. His father reminded him to be quieter, by putting a finger to his lips.

"And that, my son, is why they want this place. We're too successful, and much too rich. Within a few years, I wouldn't be surprised if they tried to push us completely out of this state. They've already run some of the other tribes out of Georgia."

"But out here, there's no gold to fight about. We've owned this land for centuries. Thankfully, we're protected from their wrath by the agreement with the United States. The state of Alabama does *not* have the power to override a federal decree," he said. "This land is *not* for sale! We'll go to court, fight them, and win."

Now that a few months had passed, the chief thought back to that day, remembered the arrogant words he had spoken to his father, and realized just how ignorant of the white man's ways he had been.

Starr Night had certainly underestimated the power held by their enemies. They had received a notice, and were being forced to return to the courthouse again, to defend their rights to the land.

Chapter Five
The Tuscaloosa Courtroom

"What in hell does that old bastard think he's doing?" asked Starr Night. "He's told more lies today than the law allows. What a nightmare!" His eyes shot a menacing glare towards the lawyer. "Do something else besides just sitting there like a damned log, damn it!"

The fluffy white feather attached to the front of his resplendent, gold-hued turban shook as he raised his fist in indignation. Some people might have called him a handsome man, but others would notice that there was something about his chiseled cheekbones, fierce black eyes, and round, plain face that didn't quite match the long torso on his short-legged body. However, there was one thing agreed on by most of those who met him, and that was that he possessed the aura of a very powerful man.

Starr Night and his wife, Isola Songbird, were stunned at the pronouncement from the judge. Both of them shot ramrod straight up from their seats, shocked at the obscenity that had escaped from the turned-down, sour grape lips of Judge Earl Walker.

It was the first time in his life that the chief had felt powerless. Some of his tribesmen had come with him to the courtroom, and they were devastated by the evil words spoken by their enemy. At first, they were inclined to stomp out of the room, but then they settled down, and were wise enough to understand that they had to control themselves, and remain in the room for the rest of the hearing.

After the fuss died own, the judge continued to read his decision:

"Today, the Appeals Court of the state of Alabama hereby orders you to sell the property in question for the fair market price. This state will never again be held hostage by your tribe. Alabama is willing to guide new owners in the correct way to partition that land into farms and towns. You Indians are no longer going to be allowed to impede the progress of two counties. As of today, July 14, 1839, most of those empty acres of land on 'Warrior,' are declared untenanted. At the end of thirty days, if the land has not been sold to an appropriate party, all property rights will revert to the state of Alabama. It will then be liquidated and sold at auction to the highest bidder."

Their hopes of having his decision overturned were immediately smothered when the tobacco-stained clerk, smiling like the idiot he seemed to be, walked over to the couple and served them with orders to vacate the property.

John Feather, their Cherokee lawyer, was helpless to come to their assistance. By the new rules recently enacted, he was no longer allowed to address the court. However, he was permitted to sit second chair to their white attorney, Zach Howard, who was married to a Cherokee woman of the Rhea band.

Although his face was flushed with anger, Zach managed to speak calmly as he rose to his feet to protest the illegal action of the court. He was a legal resident of Cherokee lands, and he and his family would lose everything if the tribe was forced to cede Warrior to the state. His family owned the general store in a Cherokee town near Sylacauga, and handled a monopoly on the potent whiskey brewed by both the white and Indian bootleggers in Jefferson County. But, according to those unjust words that had just been announced by this judge, all of them were in for the fight of their lives.

Zach motioned to John Feather to try to suppress the Cherokee's unbridled response to their loss. In the meantime, he used a series of hand signs to appeal to Starr Night. He asked him to help him regain order in the courtroom. And after a signal from the chief, every Cherokee in the room followed orders and sat down. Now, it was quiet enough for Zach to respond to the blatant attempt by the judge to steal their land.

It was eight in the morning, and it was already hot enough in that courtroom to make the robed judge wish for a beer. Today was Zach's last chance to persuade the sweat-drenched man to reverse his ruling, because it was the last day for the session.

Their position on the matter stood on solid ground. Zach was shocked that their side had not prevailed in Appeals Court. Now, however, he was nervous about their chance to succeed against Judge Walker's ruling. He asked himself, *is it possible that the judge has been bribed?*

Zach's suspicions were growing because this man had a reputation for being a reasonable, highly respected jurist. A stickler for the rule of law. And yet, he had not called for any expert opinions, asked for further testimony, or used any of his so-called expertise during the hearing. There simply was no legal precedent to support his decision. Surely, the man knew that his opinion would be challenged. *What in hell was going on?*

Zach wiped the sweat from his brow with the white handkerchief from the pocket of his buckskin jacket, and paused to gather his thoughts. The lawyer brushed his long, stringy, gray hair from his mottled face and began to state their defense:

"We signed a treaty with the government of the United States that protects our legal right to possess that land. There are not any *state* laws that have the power to override a *federal* treaty. That agreement permanently set the borders of the Cherokee Indian Territory in this state," said the attorney. "We'll be forced to appeal your decision to the Supreme Court of the United States, as soon as we are granted a hearing."

"As of today," the judge continued, "the federal treaty is declared null and void. It is not recognized by this state to be a binding contract."

With that pronouncement, Judge Walker banged his gavel and rose from the bench. It was his idea to close the court proceedings and leave the room. However, before he could duck out of the back door, the clerk handed him a note.

Meanwhile, pandemonium erupted in the courtroom!

He had expected the Cherokees to have an explosive reaction to his ruling, but he became unnerved as the astonished Indians began to yell at the top of their voices, and walk towards the bench to let him know just how absurd and dishonest they thought he was being.

The townspeople could hear their shouts all the way down Polk Street, far beyond the small shingled courthouse. The hands of the pock-marked judge trembled as he handed the note back to the clerk and asked him to read it aloud.

Once he had their attention, the man began to speak. Judge Walker decided to use the distraction to slide behind the curtain that hid a secret door at the back of the room. It was camouflaged outside of the building by a bush. Once he was in the alley, he looked fugitively over his shoulder to see if he had been followed. The way was clear.

The judge could see that it was safe for him to walk through the dancing heat waves to the path near the stables. He smiled to himself as he tipped the hostler, tightened the cinches on the saddle, and untied his horse from the stall. Now he was free to grab the reins, step up into the saddle, and skedaddle out of town. Yet, he still felt a little uneasy, a little worried that he had forgotten to dot all of the i's, and cross all of the t's, on the document he had left in the hands of the bailiff. *But*, he thought, *right now, the most important thing is* for *me to get the hell out of this town, and put as much distance between me and the enraged Indians as possible.*

The judge would have been a fool not to have noted the condemnation in the cold eyes of the chief. And, he was also very sure that those Moravian missionaries, who had been present at the hearing, would send protest letters to federal officials. He smiled to himself and thought, *lots of good that'll do them*!

Judge Walker spurred his mount to speed things up. That was a fired up hornets' nest he had left in Tuscaloosa. *Whew! I can put this mess behind me.* He was absolutely sure that the Indians would not prevail if they were ever granted a hearing at the Supreme Court. If everything went as planned, the settlers were going to be mighty pleased that he'd had found a way to run the Indians out of Alabama. There wasn't a doubt in his mind that he would be a shoo-in for governor.

Now, he took the time to disguise his trail, settled down to a slow, easy, trot and rode farther away from the melee in Tuscaloosa. He had arranged to spend some time with a friend of his in Moore's Bridge. It was a good idea to get off the road and wait until things cooled off a bit *Best to give those stinking Cherokees time to get back to Warrior.*

It would not do to run into one of them right now. Even though they all lived in the civilized state of Alabama, the Indians' seething anger could easily boil over. After all, they were still savages, and there wasn't a way to stop any of them from putting a price on his scalp.

Back at the courthouse, the Cherokees were still hurling obscenities at the bailiff.

"Thief!" they shouted. "Swindler!"

"Quiet in the courtroom!" commanded the bailiff. "Ladies and gentlemen, court proceedings are closed for the session, but I have an announcement to make." First he cleared his throat, then said, "There's been a disaster at Warrior Plantation," he announced, "and I don't know any details about the matter."

The Cherokees were so shocked at his words that they hardly noticed it when he stepped out of the front door. They began to wander aimlessly around the room, until eventually, most of them were standing near the bench where Chief Starr Night and Isola sat.

"What disaster could he be talking about?" Isola asked her husband.

Before he could think of anything that might be an answer her question, his slave Tolliver created quite a ruckus when he ran into the courtroom. The man was exhausted. He'd just finished a blistering two day ride from Warrior. He was red faced and dirty, because he had not stopped to rid himself of the trail dust embedded in his skin. He spotted the chief and hurriedly walked up to the oak bench where they sat. He pushed past the other men in order to sidle up next to the boss.

In his haste to reach Starr Night, Tolliver almost overturned the smelly spittoon that sat at the end of the bench. He doffed his hat and apologized for the mishap. And then, he began to whisper the details of the tragedy into the chief's ear. The worrisome words he spoke caused the Indian's heart to twist in agony. Now, he was worried that his son, Swift River, and Ian Mac Donald, Isola's father, might be in mortal danger. They had stayed at Warrior while the rest of them made the long trip to court.

Isola wrinkled her nose up to protest the musty odor of the sweaty, dust covered man. The rim of her bonnet acted to deflect some of the scent. *But,* she thought, *he smells as stinky as a polecat. Surely he could've cleaned himself up before he entered the courtroom.* And, although she remained silent about the matter, she began to nervously scratch the end of her nose. Her body prickled with excitement.

She had already been overwhelmed by the ruling from the judge, and now she was forced to wait for the bad news Tolliver had brought with him from home. Isola turned her head farther away from him and sniffed at the contents of her flower-decorated vinaigrette. Somehow, she found the strength to control her emotions. She remained seated a short distance from the men, and could sense her husband's desire to spare her from the details of the happenings at Warrior.

"There has been an explosion at the coal mine." Tolliver whispered to the chief.

"How many did we lose? Was it methane?" he asked.

"Probably, but it also looks as if someone closed all the vent holes to the outside air," he said.

"The mine has been blown to smithereens. It's sealed with so much coal that it'll take months, or maybe never, to get it back in working condition. Most likely, the mistress' father is dead. After the last shift, Mr. MacDonald and two slaves went to inspect the seam of coal set to be mined the next day. That's when I think someone sneaked in behind them, cut off their air supply, set a fire, then hightailed it out of there without anyone seeing them. By the time the rest of us recovered from the shock of the blast, the culprit was long gone."

Starr Night had to blame himself for his lack of insight concerning their enemies. He had left the plantation inadequately protected with a skeleton crew, while they attempted to defend themselves in the crooked courtroom. All of his plans to expand their holdings had just gone down the drain.

They had lost two mines in twenty years, both of them to subversion. Usually, the chief was able to hide his emotions, and his face was an unreadable mask, but now, it was filled with excruciating pain. The most difficult part of this whole matter was that he would eventually have to share the bad news with his precious wife.

Eleven Rock was still sitting in the balcony. He had witnessed all that had passed in the legal wrangling of the proceedings. He had listened to Zach's impassioned explanation of the details of their case, and noted that even though their lawyer had done his best to defend them against the intrusion of the white settlers, the judge had make a ruling that held devastating consequences for their future in Alabama. The tribe had failed to secure their sole ownership of that part of Warrior they called "Frog Level." And all of them knew that if the settlers got their hands on that parcel of land, the tribe would have to defend themselves on three sides of the claim. Then it would just be a matter of time before the settlers were strong enough to run them completely off the last large piece of property owned by the Rhea and Songbird bands.

He rose to his feet when one of the Warrior braves tapped him on his shoulder.

"Eleven Rock," he said, "we've got to get packed up and ready to hit the road for home." He motioned to the other men to follow them out of the courtroom. Eventually, they straggled to the outside of the stiflingly, hot building.

It struck them all that unless they could get someone to reverse the judge's decision, they had just witnessed the end of their ownership of Warrior. They were at the mercy of the Supreme Court to intervene and prevent the settlers from bringing their way of life to a screeching halt.

Isola, still seated in the courtroom, slid closer to her husband. She tried to hear the details of the conversation between the two men, but they continued to whisper. But the bits and pieces that she *did* manage to hear caused her to fear for her father's safety. He had stayed at the mine, determined to keep it in operation, despite the efforts of the settlers to

54

close it down. Now, she wished that she had insisted on his presence in the courtroom. It would not have hurt to have another friendly white face sitting among them.

Isola was filled with a sense of foreboding. When she tried to stand, she actually trembled, and had to take her husband's arm for support. She felt exhausted, tired as a worn out dishrag.

After John Feather stepped up to support her other arm, the other tribesmen fell in line behind their chief. Tolliver walked behind all of them. When they emerged into the blistering sunlight, Starr Night stood at the end of the wooden walkway and raised his hand above his head. It was the signal for Itty, his coachman and personal slave, to bring the carriage around. The green-liveried man pulled over the luxurious, four-seated carriage, and hopped down to the ground to open the door for his owners.

Several white townspeople lined the street, while others peeped from their windows. Most of them had come to investigate the uproar caused by the shouts of the angry Indians as they left the building. They were thrilled to witness the spectacle of the finely dressed chief and his wife as they stepped into their resplendent coach, pulled by four golden palominos.

But once the couple was sheltered from the prying eyes of the public, Starr Night told Isola that he was concerned that his father-in-law might be in trouble.

"Oh, my poor father!" she cried. "I sensed that something had happened to him. I've been shivering since Tolliver first walked in the door. You know how close the two of us are. Is Swift River safe?"

"Before he left Warrior, Tolliver told Eliza to stay at the house until we're back home. We can depend on her to take care of him. I'm sure that Tolliver's mother would lay down her life for him," said the chief.

However, both of them knew how much Swift River loved his adoring grandfather, and they were absolutely sure that he would be devastated if his "Gramps" had been murdered. It was rare for both of his parents to be absent from the plantation at the same time, but they knew that they could depend on those relatives and friends who lived on Warrior to help the slave take care of their child.

"Let's not expect the very worst scenario," said the chief soothingly. "There's always a chance that we'll be able to find him alive. If you'll remember the last time we had a disaster, he was lucky enough to survive the explosion. I wouldn't put it past him to have another tall, miraculous story to tell us at the dinner table," the worried man said. "I want you to return to the hotel and get a few days rest before you start back home. I'm going to ride home on horseback. John Feather and Yellow Girlie will ride with you in the coach, and you'll be escorted by an armed guard. The chuck wagon is at your disposal."

He watched her face to gauge her reaction to his words, and thought that she might object to his plans, but Isola bowed her head in compliance with his wishes.

"I'll join Tolliver and the men for the ride back home, as soon as we're organized. Before we leave Tuscaloosa, we'll need to buy more ammunition. Maybe we won't need it, but the way things are going, it doesn't look as if it's going to be peaceful around the plantation any longer. I've tried to use the court system to protect our property rights, but it seems to me that it's up to us to save ourselves. We might be forced to use lethal power."

Within an hour, Starr Night had changed his clothing and gone outside to find that his men were already mounted, and ready to go home. He asked Tolliver to ride beside him.

"Somewhere, between here and Warrior, I'm going to send several of the men to check on the status of the trading posts, ferries, and storehouses along the upper reaches of the Black Warrior. There's a fortune tied up in our property, but it's scattered all along the river. I think it'd be a good idea to close some of the stores and bring everything within a few miles of the plantation. We might be able to use those men we trained as wranglers. They could help us ferry all the goods by mule train. Most of them haven't been on a horse since they came to Alabama, but I might just see if I can trust any of them not to try to escape."

After thinking about the pros and cons of using the black men as draymen, he decided to employ those slaves who were now idle from their work in the mine, to ferry the goods closer to the plantation.

"There are so many shallow places in the river, that it would be easier to packhorse whatever can't be moved by wagon. There are a few areas where we can use a boat," said Starr Knight. "If my plan works, maybe I'll give some of them permanent jobs as teamsters."

Tolliver knew from experience that the chief had already decided his course of action, but he didn't have much time to think about the details for they faced a hard ride to the plantation.

They were heavily armed, and Starr Night had made it his mission to reach Warrior in time to deal with their cruel enemies. He was determined that he and his men would defend their holdings and fight against the machinations of the saboteurs who sought to destroy them.

For at least fifty years, the Rhea and Songbird families had sought to assimilate themselves into American society. They had copied the dress of their neighbors and sent their children to school to be educated by white teachers. Most of them were at least bilingual, and many of them could also speak a smattering of other Indian languages.

Several members of his band had left Warrior to live in town, but after they'd married white settlers, many of them had been treated shabbily by the townspeople. They had been barely tolerated, and had returned to the village rather than be treated as an inferior race of people on par with the blacks.

In the end, the changes they made to themselves had done nothing to strengthen the treaties they had made between the United States Government and the tribe. They weren't accepted as citizens of the state of Alabama, nor did they have any standing as citizens of the United States of America.

Starr Night had always been wary of the settlers. He had not been fooled by their behavior, and understood the band's position perfectly. He knew that if the Cherokees did not agree to move away and sell the land they had owned for hundreds of years, eventually, it would be stolen from them. The settlers were poised to use a series of questionable maneuvers like the ones they had just witnessed in Tuscaloosa, to loosen their grasp on the land. What the settlers had not counted on was the ingrained sophistication of the Cherokee Indian tribe.

When they stopped to water the horses, the chief squatted near the bank; then the men formed a circle around him as they plotted their next move. He was in a reflective mood as he spoke to them. Tolliver sat in the rear of the Indians with his back propped against an oak tree and listened to Starr Night's side of the story. But no matter how hard he tried to understand it, he still couldn't see why the Indians would want to be slave-owners. *Can't they see that if white men ever get their way, the Indians will be picking cotton too?*

"I've always known how most of them really feel about us. You can see the outrage in their eyes when they become aware of our lifestyle. As far as some of them are concerned, we are 'savages,' and we live far better than any Indian should be able to afford. If our band had been less self-reliant, we would've been powerless to fight the many attempts to run us off our land and out of the state of Alabama," the chief said.

The morning air was still cool when the men reached the village of Abernant. Starr Night gave the signal to them to ride at a slower pace. He knew that they would have to preserve the stamina of their mounts until they reached the next station. After they had gone another five miles, they dismounted, sat in the shade, lit pipes, rolled cigarillos, and smoked.

The chief walked over to Tolliver and said, "Last month, the state passed a flurry of Indian laws. Now, we are forbidden to harvest our cotton bolls that are rotting in the fields, sell the coal to the mills in Birmingham, or produce any more paving bricks. They thought they could starve us out, but as you know, we don't depend on one crop for our living. We're still making money. They haven't been able to break our backs until now. There's a possibility that they've finally found a way to run us off Warrior. It seems as if they've gained control over the crooked court, but they'll still have a fight on their hands," he said. "We're sure as hell are *not* going to give them our land. We'll fight them in the highest court." And, as stubborn as Starr Night was, Tolliver did not doubt his words.

On the scorching hot afternoon of the following day, they arrived at the station. By that time, the chief was irritable. It was ninety degrees, and he was bone tired. The stagnant air was suffocating, and it was the worst possible time for him to be forced to confront blasphemous, face-to-face, wide-open hostility against him and his men.

He could feel the muscles in his broad shoulders grow tense when the way-station attendant refused to let them swap their exhausted mounts for fresh animals. Usually he was expected to pay in advance, then they would get fresh horses. The arrangement had been simple. After they had reached home and rested, some of the men had always returned the station's horses to the corral, then leisurely lead their own animals back home.

They had dealt with this man every time they had come to court, and had never had a disagreement. Now, however, he told them that they would no longer have the privilege of using the facilities. When Starr Night looked into his eyes, the man actually had the decency to be ashamed of himself.

"Look," he said, "last night the White Citizens Council set out new guidelines for the station. I'm bound by the decision of the townspeople.

They could get mad at me and burn this place down. I can't cater to your kind. I'm not going to lose my place because of the lot of you."

Then he spat a wad of tobacco near the chief's shoe, and wiped a dribble of tobacco juice from his mouth with his shirttail.

"There's only one of you who's allowed to enter the station, eat, and swap for a fresh horse." He turned to Tolliver, the only white man present, other than himself.

"Are you serious? You're going to let my overseer eat at your table, but I can't?"

It was hard for the chief to deal with the fickle nature of the insult. "This man doesn't have any money. I pay for his meals."

The stationmaster crooked his finger in Tolliver's direction and said, "Come on into the dining room and get some vittles. These Indians ain't going nowhere, anytime soon."

It smelled like the pinto beans had been seasoned with ham hocks, and the aroma of the food was mighty tempting to Tolliver, but he valued his life, and he was not about to insult his master by eating the food that the Indians were not allowed to purchase. He had opened his mouth to refuse the offer, when Starr Night spoke to him:

"Go on in, Tolliver; let him feed the *white* man. There's no reason for *you* to go hungry, or suffer out here in this heat. It's probably just as hot inside the station, but I want you to enjoy that meal. I certainly hope you're satisfied with the service."

At least the furious chief had a measure of vengeance. He permitted the slave to enjoy the hospitality of the bigot.

"We'll rest the horses and walk them to the spring at the bottom of the road. It's usually cooler down in the glade. Although the horses won't get oats, there's plenty of grass and cool water," he said to his men.

The chief was still angry. He had turned splotchy around the mouth. Over the years, the men had witnessed the strength of his fury more times than they wished to remember. They remained quiet, and let him gradually recapture his usually calm, cool, calculating demeanor. After a while, Starr Night began to retrieve his sense of humor.

"I wonder if our *white* man, *Mr. Tolliver*, is enjoying his pinto beans?" he asked. The chief could not erase the smirk on his face when Lone Fox, who usually opposed most of his decisions, laughed so hard at

59

their reverse situation with the slave, that all of the men began to relax and enjoy the irony of their predicament.

"After the horses are tended to, we'll rest. Be ready to ride later this afternoon, once it's had a chance to cool off," he said. "Our trip will take a little longer because we have to let our mounts recover from the long mileage. The only way these horses will make it to Warrior, is that we let them get plenty of rest. There are people in this world who would give their eye teeth to live as good as our mounts," he said. Then he loosened the cinches so that his horse could take his fill of the pure water from the bubbling spring.

Later in the evening, when Tolliver rejoined the Indians in the glade, he was trailed by nine fresh horses he had managed to talk the old codger into swapping with the Indians. They were not the best of the horses in the corral, but they were healthy and well-rested. The grateful men were relieved and happy to be able to slap their saddles on the station's horses. But Tolliver had a bit of bad news for the boss.

"I had to agree to sweeten the pot," Tolliver told Starr Night. "He wants fifty dollars cash to close the deal."

The chief knew that he was being extorted by the stationmaster, but he also realized the reality of their situation, and understood that their priority was their swift return to Warrior. He gave his slave the money, along with their horses, to hand over to the thieving man. Now at last they were ready to confront their enemies.

They galloped away from the station at a good pace until the near darkness of a late sunset slowed them down. In spite of the fact that they faced an emergency situation, the men dared not travel in the pitch-black night on the wilderness roads of Alabama. The mile or two they might have been able to cover did not warrant the risk of the possibility that either of them, man or beast, could possibly step into one of the many potholes that dotted the landscape.

Tolliver picked out the spot where they would spend the night. The large fire he built protected them from the possibility of falling prey to one of the wild predators in the area. They heard the night sounds of bears, wolves, and bobcats as they prowled along the outskirts of the camp in search of their evening meal.

Part of the trail was situated in the flats, an area easily defended from most things, but it didn't protect the men from the swarm of butterfly sized mosquitoes that buzzed around their heads to attack any uncovered patch of skin. They were able to gain some small measure of relief when one of them thought to place a woolen blanket over the fire to smoke and scatter some of the angry, vicious, insects away from the camp.

Once they were comfortable, the chief and his men were able to work out some of the details of their strategy. Two pots of coffee were consumed while they ate the three wild turkeys they had shot earlier in the day. Later, after they'd filled their bellies, they were ready to settle down for the night. The chief picked that time to give his instructions to Lone Fox:

"I want you to gather some of the men as a back-up force," he said. "We have to be prepared to defend our holdings against the strength of any intruder or enemy force on our land. We're not going to tolerate any further destruction of our property."

Once they had agreed on their counteroffensive strategy against their foes, the chief lay his head down on his blanket-shrouded saddle and went to sleep.

Tolliver took the first watch. He was the calmest man in the group. The Indians trusted him with their lives. And as far as he was concerned, they were right to trust him enough to feel safe and secure under his care. He damned sure did not want them to lose the plantation. He had spent so many years of his life helping them to run the place that he'd come to think of the plantation as his home. He was willing to stand up and fight for Warrior with them. He intended to help the Cherokees save the place from those greedy white settlers.

About noon the next day, the men rode into Horton. It was a sleepy little town about eight miles from the plantation. They could smell the fumes of the coal as it was being consumed by the fire in the mine at Warrior. Starr Night pointed his finger towards the smoke-darkened eastern sky. The putrid air had a gritty, textured feel to it. Minerals sifted down from the wind-blown sky onto their sweat-soaked, irritated skin. The atmosphere created a surer sense of doom. It made the chief agree with his men; their homecoming was not going to be pretty.

A few hours later, the exhausted men rode onto their land and immediately understood the enormous loss they had suffered. Starr Night remained seated on his horse, shocked at the depth of the destruction of their property.

Tolliver could not remember a time when the Indians seemed so profoundly defeated. But now that he had a better chance to examine the damage, he figured that the mine had definitely been rendered useless. It would take months, maybe years of digging to re-develop the mine. He supposed that the decision of whether or not they would try to open it again would be dictated by the ruling on the tribe's appeal to the Supreme Court. He could see that Starr Night's hands were completely tied. *Checkmate.*

What the big overseer could see in the chief's face was sorrow. Tolliver was surprised to discover the amount of residual damage the blast had caused. He'd left Warrior in a hurry, determined to ride hell's bells out of there to Tuscaloosa. But now he could see that not only had the explosion demolished the grounds of Warrior, it had also, for the moment, shattered the chief's confidence.

What Tolliver could not have known, was that the mine disaster had also weakened Starr Night's resolve. He was not so sure that he had the right to insist that his people had to continue the fight against what might be the inevitable outcome of their struggle. The Cherokees had always envisioned Warrior as their version of paradise, but now, the chief did not feel that it was safe for them to remain in this ruined, desecrated place.

Finally, the men began to dismount. They were stiff and sore after the hard ride, but they felt that they could not rest until they had some answers to their queries about the terrorist. Surely, someone had witnessed a stranger on the property. But after the slaves were questioned, the men were forced to admit that they were stymied. Nobody would disclose any information that hinted at the identity of the murderer, nor claim to know anything about the slaves who had escaped during the confusion.

They were able to confirm the deaths of Ian Mac Donald and two of their slaves. The beloved man had been instrumental in their mining operation. Now, the chief would have to tell his wife that her father had been murdered.

"Isola will be devastated," the chief said to the men.

The Cherokees were all saddened at the thought of his death. Ian had been an important figure among them. The widower had lived many years among the tribe, and during that time, he had taught them how to successfully market their coal. While they lived in Tennessee, Ian had passed his mining skills to the slaves in Dayton, Graysville, Morgantown, and Lake City.

As long as they had lived in Tennessee, the slave miners had been hopeful that one day their skills and hard work would lead them to freedom. They had worked among the Irishmen and Freedmen, the paid laborers in the mines. But once they had been marched across the state line

62

to Alabama, the Indians made it very clear to them that they had no intentions of freeing any of them. And the miners grew bitter. The men told Tolliver that even though they were slaves to the Cherokees, it was cruel of the Indians to stand so hard on their backs. It was evil of them to select, and then mate the men with the women, just to increase the value of the resulting offspring. So far, Starr Night had not employed that practice at Warrior, but they had already mated them on the plantation run by Lone Fox and some of the others.

And from the date of their birth, the value of their children could be mortgaged and borrowed against for the next season's crop. The explosive growth of the slave population, and the increased production from their free labor, had earned them the status of "black gold." They were being bred to work in the cultivated, rich bottomlands of cotton country.

One of the men told Tolliver the truth of the matter.

"After treating us like just another farm animal, it amazes me that the Indians really thought that we'd be foolish enough to help them find whoever it was that destroyed their mine. Any of us would be willing to kill the first person who dared to open his mouth with the truth."

Now that they had returned to the plantation, the Cherokee men tried to meet in secret, but the slaves were aware of their every move. They were anxious to find out what the Indians would do in order to keep their plantation. Everyone on the place walked on eggshells.

The slaves were determined to avoid upsetting the already angry tribesmen, and most of them made sure to work hard at their usual jobs. They waited to see what would happen when their mistress came home and found out that her father was dead.

A couple of days later, Tolliver's family sat quietly around the table cracking and eating hickory nuts while he read them the news from the Jefferson County newspaper:

"The settlers have ratified a new law that will harshly penalize any master who attempts to liberate any of his slaves," he read. "Well, that puts another nail in the coffin. They're trying to fix it so that none of us will ever be freed. The chief claims that he doesn't understand why the slaves won't tell him who destroyed the mine, but when I tried to make the boss understand that now that the miners don't have any hope of ever being freed, any of them might have been angry enough to blow it up. He told me that I didn't know what the hell I was talking about. But all of us know how hard those men are worked, and it's a fact that a coal miner usually doesn't live half as long as a cotton picker. They have a right to

63

feel bitter about how things are around here. When those men saw that somebody was able to get the best of the Indians, I guess it made up for some of the misery they've had to deal with every day."

"Starr Night and his men don't seem all that concerned with how many of us they kill. I guess it's because we're so easily replaced. The Indians are rich enough to buy us at auction, but sometimes, I think they get more pleasure out of it if they manage to capture some of us in a raid, then herd us here after they've defeated an enemy," Eliza said. "One of the worst things about us being slaves for life, is that we never know when one of us might be sold away to pay for the master's new furniture, a vacation, jewelry, or even a book. The hell of slavery is that we're forced to live or die at the whim of the master," Eliza answered.

Bea, who would occasionally join in the conversation, busied herself with the work of crocheting a doily. It was a relief to them that she had finally started to speak.

"I feel responsible for your decision to stay at Warrior plantation," she said. "I'm sorry, but the thought of hiding in deep woods makes me sick. And it frustrates me that I still can't remember exactly what happened, or who it was that was so cruel, that he left me there to die."

Eliza was almost sure that her daughter knew the name of the rapist, but she was also sure that Bea would never utter his name. She would protect her brother. He wanted revenge, and she knew that the price Tolliver would have to pay for it would be his own life. Eliza was sure that Bea would take the man's identity with her to her grave.

"We have you back with us, and you're able to talk. That's the best thing that could have happened. None of us are ever going to be willing to leave here without you. Freedom would be worthless if after all these years, we decided to lead separate lives. We've come to terms with our decision. You should never feel that it's your fault. The welfare of our family is much more important to us than where we live," said Tolliver.

"And look at the mess the Freedmen who live here in Alabama face every day. They've been ordered to leave the state without their slave families. If by some miracle they have the money to buy a family member, I doubt their master would accept the money," said Eliza.

Coincidentally, it could not have been more than a week later when Starr Night sent one of the kitchen slaves to the cabin to summon Tolliver to his office.

"I've bought me a tanner," he said. "He's been sold away from his family. At first, he might try to give us a run for the money. His master says that he's a nasty cuss. But, if that turns out to be true, I'll sell him to the Creeks. They'll know how to handle him. Let's go outside and take the chains off him. Put him in the cabin with some of the other single men. I know he's sorry looking, but he has the knowledge to train the other men to help him cure the hides. See what you can do with him, and get back to me."

Tolliver's heart went out to the man who sat in the back of a farm wagon, hands and feet chained to the floor. When they unchained him, he swayed from exhaustion. Tolliver held him up, and escorted him to the empty cabin. Now that the mine was closed, the men were at work in the fields. Tolliver welcomed the new slave to his own, private, little piece of hell.

"M' name's Nut Brown," the man volunteered.

"The chief said that you had a bit of trouble with your old master. Did he beat you?" asked Tolliver.

"Yeah, but after the beating, it took him five more years to decide he couldn't stand to look at me any longer," he said. "Deep down in his gut, my master always felt that I was a problem to him. Although I never threatened him, he still felt that I was dangerous. He told one of the other men that I was a plotting hoodoo man, and that he couldn't shake the feeling that one day, if I ever had the chance, I'd poison him. He was crazy. I didn't work in the house, or have a way to get near his food. He was a foolish man, but, he was right about one thing, I did despise him, and he knew it. I had a good reason to hate him for the damage he'd done to me and my family."

By then, the men noticed that Nut Brown's body was trembling with anger. "The truth be told, he got rid of me because he was determined to have my woman to himself."

Tolliver and one of his friends hunkered down on the floor to listen to the rest of Nut Brown's sorrowful tale.

"He didn't get rid of me immediately, because he needed my knowledge of tanning the hides. But eventually, he was able to work out a deal with your master. I'll live here, but I'll have to cure hides for both plantations," he said.

"Five years ago, the master entered my hut and told me to leave. My woman and me lived in one of his shacks. In the middle of the night, he decided to leave his own bedroom and, as he put it, 'sample the sway in Sally's high-yellow hips.'"

"Dirty bastard," said the blacksmith.

"She was pregnant with my child, and he was very pleased when she told him about her condition. He sent me outside, pulled down his pants, and told Sadie that he wanted to 'sweeten the pie.'"

"Oh hell, I'm sure you felt bad, but you knew better, you shouldn't have tried to stop him," said Tolliver.

"Well, I didn't say that I did, but before he could completely accomplish his dirty deed, he just happened to notice that the roof and the rear of the shack were afire. Someone rang the plantation bell.

"'Fire! Fire!'" they screamed. The lamps were lit in the mansion, and the mistress called out his name over and over again. Eventually, she tired of looking for him, slipped on her housecoat, and ran with the house servants towards the slave quarters. Immediately, she organized a bucket brigade to fight the fire. If the flames had reached the bales of cotton stored in the barn, they would have lost the profits for an entire growing season.

Once her slaves had the fire under control, the mistress continued her search for her husband. When she had given up any hope of finding him, she happened to turn around in time to see the master flee from the smoke-filled, water-soaked hut without his pants. He was trailed by my naked woman."

"I'll bet you a nickel that he kept his ass out of the slave quarters for a while. The mistress probably watched him like a hawk from then on," said Tolliver.

Nut Brown grinned when he said: "The master always suspected me of setting that fire, but several of the other slaves swore that I'd spent the night with them, jigging for frogs. He beat the hell out of me anyhow. He believed that somebody had to pay for the abuse he had suffered from his wife's tongue."

"So why, after five years had passed, did he send you away?"

"I don't know, except that this matter has been sticking in his craw all these years."

"Now," said the blacksmith, he's found a way to get his revenge. I doubt that you'll ever get to see your child or your woman again."

That night, when Nut Brown joined the other men around the fire, he told them his story. It seemed to them that the songs of the Warrior slaves were especially mournful that night.

Although he didn't have all of the words figured out, Tolliver was aware that most of their songs carried secret messages. They knew the code words, and they had put them in a tune. He had been told that if a person memorized a song, it made it easier to find your way out of Alabama and onto one of the escape routes to freedom.

Most Saturday nights, knots of slaves would gather wood for a bonfire and use their precious idle time to visit with their friends and kin. Since they did not work on Sundays, they were able to sit around the fire and repeat the stories that had been passed down from the elders.

Some of the songs the women crooned told of the pain and sorrow to be borne by the slaves until the sweet wings of angels came down from the sky to save them from evil. "Far across the river we fly, sweet Jesus," they trilled. They created lyrics to fit the mood. Nut Brown was comforted by their words. *Perhaps*, he thought, *the day will come when I'll fly away from here and find my family again.*

Starr Night had been apprised of the revision in Isola's schedule by a message sent from his lawyer, John Feather. His wife had needed more time to gather her wits before she returned to the troubles at Warrior. And now, he sat on the porch waiting to see if her carriage might show up sometimes during the day. He hoped that she had not changed her plans again.

He had been married to Isola twenty–two years, and he was still mesmerized by her beauty. She was the only woman he had ever wanted. The first time he'd noticed her, she had been about ten years old. Starr Night had been an awkward teenager, but it had not mattered, because Isola had been too young to notice that he was interested in her. He had been charmed by her brilliant blue eyes and smooth white skin. She had been an exquisite, flawless child. And when he had told his parents of his interest in her, Eleven Rock and Kitty Coffee were pleased.

But, his father reminded him of the sacrifice he would be forced to make in order to claim her. First, her family would have to accept him as a suitor, then, because he had selected such a young girl to be his wife, he would have to be willing to wait several years until she was ready for marriage. He had agreed to the commitment, and was very pleased when he learned that her parents were overjoyed at the match. His love and passion for her were eternal, and he still acted like a young boy around her. He loved her as much now, as he had when he had first looked into the depth of her eyes.

Most people who had known him throughout the years agreed on another important fact about him, and that was the fact that once he had made a decision about a matter, he stuck to his guns, and rarely reversed his original opinion.

Sitting up in the box of the carriage, Itty guided the coach on the road from Tuscaloosa. Once he had finally brought his passengers and the coach within the last few miles of the plantation's boundary line, he had made the conscious decision to slow the pace of the horses. He was not in a hurry to return to Warrior. He needed some time to plan his next move.

Sometimes he wished that he could not read. The thought came to his mind that perhaps the other slaves were better off being ignorant of what was happening to them. The majority of them would never be tortured by the knowledge that new laws, recently passed by the settlers, would tighten the noose of bondage even tighter around their necks. Now, a slave was prohibited from earning or possessing money. And a loophole had been plugged: they would no longer be able to barter their services in exchange for self-emancipation. That's why he had to come up with a plan for him, his mother, and his woman, to escape from Alabama. But then, before he could escape, Starr Night had called them into his office and told them to prepare for the trip to the Appeals Court in Tuscaloosa.

Now that he was almost back on the plantation, he was aware that that he was running out of time, and that he would have to think of a new strategy for their escape.

Before the trip to Tuscaloosa, there had been several times when Itty had slipped away from the house and stood hidden in the shadows, far from the gathering of the other slaves around the fire. Usually, before long, he would see his mother and Yellow Girlie talking to their friends. And even though the other slaves had known him all of his life, they probably would not have accepted his presence among them.

There had been times when their words had smothered him in pain and sorrow. He had wiped away the tears when they had said, "He's too much Indian to suit me." Itty was stranded between both races, and neither of them trusted him.

Now, he planned to use that "other" blood to aid him in his escape. He would steal the women away from the immediate area where he was known. Itty was convinced that once he left the county, it would be hard for anyone to discover that he was not fully of the blood. There was only one thing he wanted to discover before he left Warrior. He'd asked Cook to tell him his father's name, but she had always said, "What you don't know won't kill you." But now that they were leaving the place, perhaps she would tell him her secret.

Chapter Six
The Deal

Itty eased his touch on the leads to the palominos so that he could safely pull the coach off the main road onto the willow-covered, brick–paved lane to Warrior Plantation. He put his bandana on his face in order to avoid the sulfuric odor of burning coal. The air was putrid.

As Isola's carriage entered the ruined grounds of the plantation, she grew excited to see her family, but she was still some distance away, about three miles from the house, when she leaned her head out of the window. It was uncomfortable when her skin began to burn in the noon-day sun. The strong acidic air stung her nose. The mistress was shocked by the eerie sensation of having to wipe at the grit that matted her face, and hurriedly drew her head back inside the coach.

It seemed that the ride home would never end, but it was not very long before the coach pulled into the round-about in front of the man-sion. Her husband stood there and patiently waited for the wagon come to a standstill. Then he opened the door, and assisted his wife from the coach. Isola took one look into his worry-clouded eyes and knew that her father was dead. Starr Night put his arm about her waist, and turned his grieving wife towards the front door. They had to pass the rose garden her father had created for her. He had selected several rare varieties of roses, and had told his daughter that their colors had been selected to complimented her beauty.

Swift River ran from the house and solemnly greeted his mother with a hug. Isola appreciated the love she saw in his blue eyes that mirrored her own. His embrace gave her the strength to face the scrutiny of her people, Indians and slaves, who gathered to greet Warrior's mistress.

She smiled at them, but for the very first time in her life, she felt the loss of the sense of well-being that she usually experienced when she was surrounded by her family. Now, she had to face the fact that her fa-ther was dead. Murdered!

It was time for her to grow up. She could not afford to act like a spoiled child. Isola was stubbornly determined to help her husband lead their people. They would have to face the horrid consequences of their upturned lives. She vowed that she would be strong and fearless enough to be a helpmate to her harried husband.

71

Isola intended to show him that she had the grit to lead the other women. If the band was forced to abandon Warrior, it would be the women's duty to show the slaves how to prepare for the move. It was imperative that they all learned to work together as a unit, to preserve the strength of the band. Their children's future depended on their success.

"I suppose that there are probably some of us who are ready to fight the settlers with guns. Others will want to spend years suing them in the courts, but in the end, they'll just find a way to play another dirty chip, and then we'll still lose Warrior to them," she said. "As far as I'm concerned, the settlers have won. My father's blood has drenched the soil of Warrior, and his bones will lay in that hot, black, nothingness of the mine forever. He lies just over that hill, and I don't think I want to look outside of my window every day and see his burial place."

Starr Night shared her anguish, and he listened carefully to the words that seemed to twist her heart in grief. To his surprise, quite a few members of his band had spoken to him in the same manner. Even Lone Fox wanted him to sell the plantation.

"I'm ready to leave the sorrowful memories of this place. I don't want to fight them any longer. What I *do* need, is peace. Imagine how it would be to finally find a place where our son would be free to live a decent life without having to cope with the fear and hatred that we've been subjected to the last twenty years," she said.

"I'll call a council meeting, and we shall see how many of our people share your point of view," her husband replied. "When some of the men first saw the damage to the mine, they began to wonder if we would ever be able to successfully combat the hatred we've experienced from the settlers. Even if the court rules in our favor, it would mean that we'd be completely isolated, prisoners in our own land."

"As things stand now," said Isola, "we've already been stripped of our rights. Once we leave the grounds of this plantation, we're not citizens of Alabama, or the United States. If they take Warrior and dissolve the rest of the Cherokee Nation of Alabama, we'll be aliens in our own country," Isola said, with tears in her voice.

They walked along the pathway towards the house with heavy hearts, each of them holding back some of the hurtful words that neither of them wanted to say aloud.

Yellow Girlie stepped down from the coach a few steps behind John Feather. She stepped swiftly past the sad couple and their child, then entered the kitchen door at the back of the house and greeted Cook with a hug. Tears streaked her cheeks as she sought to control her confused thoughts. She needed sympathy from Cook, but the woman pushed her away and told Yellow Girlie to remember her place. She was shocked at Cook's reaction to her problems, but before long, she managed to control her emotions. The pretty woman sniffed her cute little button nose, wiped her lemon-colored face, and dried her cornflower blue eyes with the rag she had pulled from Cook's apron pocket. Her tightly curled hair was covered with a bright red scarf, tied neatly around her head.

For the past year, Cook, Itty, and Yellow Girlie had been making plans to escape their captors. The three of them were house servants who slept in the basement of the house.

They looked out for each other. She was absolutely sure that any advice from Cook always had her best interest at heart. She could look at her and tell that the butter-nut colored woman had been good-looking in her day. Both Itty, and Featherman, her other son, were part Indian. *Cook*, she thought, *must be hiding lots of secrets about her past.*

After being away from the demands of their household duties for a while, she figured that it was not going to be easy for her and Itty to slip back into their daily routine. It was going to be hard for them to forget the hours of freedom they had experienced in Tuscaloosa. They had been able to live in a make-believe world while the Cherokees were in court. Every morning, once Itty had driven them to the courtroom, the two of them had explored the town from the driver's seat atop the coach.

They had encountered a few Freedmen on the road who were being expelled from Alabama, and it had been their fantasy to pretend that they were also free. They had imagined how wonderful it would be to exist in a world where their lives did not depend on their ability to anticipate every wish of the master, and they had decided that it would have been heavenly!

Immediately after the explosion at the mine, they had been ordered to prepare for the trip back to the plantation. At once, their dreams had come to an abrupt end. They had been required to resume their real lives as house slaves.

On their way back to Warrior, Yellow Girlie had tried to console her mistress by holding compresses to her forehead. She had lovingly and tenderly held her as close to her as a mother would have held her child, although she was twelve years younger than her mistress.

Yellow Girlie was exhausted. She had been stuffed into the carriage with the Indians for the duration of the trip, and had not slept more than eight hours in the last few days. And, she would not be able to rest until the mistress was in her bed, and asleep. Then, she was required to sit outside Isola's door until someone thought to dismiss her for the night.

Now, back at the house, she was surprised to find that tears flowed from her eyes every time she thought about the Scotsman, his death, or anything that had to do with their secret past.

"Hush up that noise you silly girl! Dry your eyes right now," Cook said. "There's no reason for you to be carrying on and crying like that. She don't have a clue that he's your daddy. Everything will stay just as it's always been. Your life ain't going to change one bit. It don't matter if'n he's dead or alive."

"You're right Cook, I *am* being silly. After all, he never had the nerve to look me in the eye. One night, he just came to the cabin and ordered my mother to get me dressed. He told me to come along with him to the big house. Mother begged him to let me stay with her, but he insisted on me coming here so that I could be trained to serve Isola. My mother cried for me, but she grew quiet when he reminded her that she had the new baby to care for. Now that I'm old enough to understand what was going on, it seems to me that the words he said to her, were a veiled threat. If she'd put up too much of a fuss, he could have decided to sell her, or the baby away from the plantation."

"But then, I remember that his conscience must have gotten the best of him, because his voice softened, and he made an effort to console her. He patted the top of her head and told her that she should be happy that I'd be living in the house with him."

"Did it work, did she quiet'n down?"

"Mother tried to smile, because she didn't want me to be scared. I guess the more she thought about it, the happier she was that I wasn't being sold away from Warrior.

"Hush now, baby," Cook said. "All that stuff is over with. You've got to put it out of your mind." Then she turned around to the stove, and returned to her work. Before long, the food was done, and she began to ladle soup out into Isola's favorite Blue Willow tureen.

She hurried to finish the meal before the Indians entered the dining room. Cook was careful to put Yellow Girlie's problems in the back of her mind so that she could concentrate her duties. It was time to welcome her mistress back to Warrior.

According to Yellow Girlie, the trip back home had been delayed because the day after they had left Tuscaloosa, they'd been forced to ride through a wickedly violent thunderstorm, and had been pelted with hail the size of a pullet's egg. She said that she had helped Itty and the guards remove a fallen tree from the Post road, but they had still been captured in the throes of the raging storm overnight.

The next morning, the men had inspected the roads and realized that they would have to delay the trip long enough to give the waters of the flashflood time to recede.

"If we're lucky," Itty had told the men, "Tomorrow, I figure that we might be able to cross the bridge across Kill Devil Creek."

And finally, after they had camped at the waters side another day, they had crossed the torrentially swollen stream to the other side.

Now that her mistress was back home, Cook intended to fatten her up and put a little color back into her cheeks. The servant peeped around the side of the house as Isola was entering the front door. She could see that her mistress would need lots of care for a while. It would take a little time for her to get herself back together again.

Poor thing, thought Cook, *she just lost her daddy to those awful men who want us to leave our home. What'll happen to us,* she wondered, *if the master loses the place?*

"Yellow Girlie, I can remember the time when there was a horrible sale at the Morrison place. Their master had been killed in a hunting accident, and his wife decided to sell her slaves and go back to her family in the North. I've often wondered about all those folks. A dealer bought most of them and sold 'em down the river."

Since Yellow Girlie seemed to be in the mood to speak of her past, Cook decided to ask her a few questions about the man who had fathered her.

"How did Mr. Ian get you to leave your mother? When I first laid eyes on you, he had set you in a chair near the kitchen fireplace. You had a rag doll in your hand," Cook remembered.

"He held my hand until we were clear of the cabin door. But once we were outside, out of her sight, he dropped my hand, and never touched me again as long as he lived. But I obeyed his orders, just as my mother had told me to, and followed him here to serve my sister. That first night he gave me to you to scrub, clothe, and train. I really can't say that he ever abused me, but I've got to face the fact that he never loved me either. His devotion was reserved for Isola and her family," she said, as she wiped away the last of her tears. "Give me a little time to put these clothes away, and I'll be back downstairs in time to help you serve dinner."

Then she picked up Isola's valise, walked up the winding stairway to her lady's walnut bedroom suite, and unpacked her clothes. She hung some of her sister's finest gowns inside the double-door, mirrored chiffonnier that sat in the corner near the window. It faced the front of the house, where the sun set in its reflection.

It was then that Yellow Girlie looked at herself in the mirror and decided that she would not let herself grieve over the fact that her father had not ever wanted any kind of relationship with her.

Starr Night's arms were still wrapped protectively around Isola's shoulder when they walked into the parlor. They quietly began to make plans to leave their dead, and find a new home for their band in a less hostile area. The court had ordered them to sell their land. Now, they decided to cut their losses. Three people had already been killed in the deadly blast of the mine. Deep down inside, the chief knew that there would be other attacks on the tribe, and that they would probably be just as deadly. He had already made the wise decision to post additional guards around the plantation.

Earlier, when the carriage had arrived at the house, and he had unloaded his passengers at the front portico, Itty had driven the buggy to the rear entrance of the mansion, down past the blacksmith's shack next to the stables. The stablemen had hurried out to clean and refit the carriage.

When the blacksmith checked the wheels, he'd asked Itty about any repairs he'd have to make to the vehicle. One of the other men unhooked the horses and led them to the barn.

Itty had slouched down on a bale of hay and listened to the excited slaves talk about the latest goings on at Warrior. They were full of stories about a daring daytime escape of three slaves amid the turmoil and confusion after the blast at the mine.

"Damn!" Itty said to the blacksmith. I wish I'd been here. I could've run too!"

Smithy laughed at him. "Don't know why you hang around this place anyway. You'd be accepted anywhere outside this part of Alabama, as a full-blood Cherokee Indian."

"But I don't want to leave my women folk here, if I can help it. I wish the other slaves trusted me enough to tell me who to go to for help. I'm as much a slave as any of you, but when all of you look at me, all that you see is an Indian, just another one of your enemies."

Smithy looked him over again. He had to admit that he liked the man, and enjoyed shooting the breeze with him. He liked his off-beat sense of humor. But Smithy also found that he had to agree with the man's assessment of the situation. It *was* going to be almost impossible for Itty to get any kind of information from a black slave.

"You know Itty, until now, I'd never really thought much about your situation. You live in the basement of their house as a servant. They can call on you any time of the day or night. I'll bet that they ask you to do some crazy things. Maybe something so simple as to shoo the flies away from their plate, comb their hair, empty the chamber pot, or tend to the child. I don't envy your job one bit," he said. "If I happen to make a mistake out here at the forge, nobody cares anything about it but me. They watch everything you do. I think I'd rather be sent to the fields to pick cotton all day than to have to live so close to the all-seeing, evil eyes of Starr Night," he said. "The hell of it is that you are probably as much Indian as the majority of the men in his band. But, the others are mixed with the white man's blood, and your mother's a mixed- black woman. Starr Night will always consider you a piece of his property."

"And yet," said Itty, "when I leave the house and enter the slave quarters, the people all think of me as one of *them*. Neither race wants to claims me."

"It's too bad that you're caught up in this mess," Smithy said. He shook his head in frustrated sympathy of his friend's situation, and made a very important decision. *This ain't the time to get his hopes up, but,* Smithy decided, *if Itty ever comes to me with a good plan, I'm going to try to help him escape from this place.*

The blacksmith certainly did not intend to say any encouraging words within earshot of the two stablemen. They were the biggest gossips on the place. What they did not know, of course, was that it was he, and he alone who knew how the other slaves had escaped. Smithy had helped them by sending the patrollers in the wrong direction. He had fed their dogs rancid horsemeat as they sniffed around the barn. The odor of the meat had confused them, and they had misread the scent of the men who were hidden in the loft, awaiting darkness.

77

By the end of the week, the Cherokees had gathered for a meeting in the council house. During their deliberations, none of their slaves were required to serve them. Starr Night had reminded them of the importance of keeping their decision secret.

"If the slaves become aware of the details of our plans, we'll have to face the possibility of a revolt. They should never discover the results of our deliberations."

Despite his words to Tolliver about retaining the plantation, Starr Night, along with the rest of the Songbirds and the Rheas, sadly agreed to sell their land to a syndicate. Their offer for the land had been the only decent one they had received. The chief explained that although their land was worth twice as much as the offer, they would have to absorb the loss and try to accept the fact that they had no choice in the matter.

At least, he thought, *we'll have enough money to get a fresh start somewhere else.* Hopefully, it would be as his wife wished, far away from the hatred that surrounded them in Alabama.

By late August, the paperwork had been signed, and the deal finalized. The band had worked out tentative details with the brokers to locate and purchase new land far away from the state.

But, once they had agreed to move, the federal government announced that all Indians were to be immediately removed from all of the states, and sent to the sparsely settled lands of the Oklahoma Indian Territory, west of the Mississippi River.

About a week after the sale, John Feather came to the plantation to deliver the bad news to Starr Night. He was invited to sit in a velvet covered seat in the richly appointed office, bathed in gold and various shades of brown. The lawyer figured that their meeting would probably be their last time sitting together in that room.

"Chief, the way they've crafted the new law, the land in the Territory will be the only land that we're permitted to settle on. The United States government has given permission to the Alabama Militia to enforce the expulsion. All of the tribes will be sent as far away as possible from where the majority of white settlers want to live," he explained.

"Well, that finishes the dirty work started by Judge Walker. Once we're gone, they'll have finally succeeded in their effort to grab the last great Cherokee hunting ground."

John Feather explained that the Cherokees were expected to swallow a bitter pill and accept that they had to emigrate to the only land that would ever be offered to them.

A few days later, Starr Night, along with some of his tribesmen, gathered as much material as they could lay hands on, and began to read about the plentiful, rich, undeveloped land of the Oklahoma Indian Territory. From what they read in the pamphlets, the virgin land had the potential to be farmland one day, but, when they examined the maps closely, they also found that much of the land included a seemingly endless prairie wasteland, and that there were several deep canyons surrounded by scrub lands, some of them situated in desert-like conditions. It had not taken them long to recognize that they would certainly need every slave they owned in order to convert the land to usefulness.

They were warriors, not farmers. But Starr Night felt confident that as long as their laborers remained firmly under their control, their dreams of a new beginning would be fulfilled. He understood that once they were relocated, none of them would ever be permitted to return to the United States. Their acceptance of the deal meant total separation from the rest of tribe in the East, unless the day came when they too, were forced to emigrate.

There were already several hundred Songbird family members living on an enormous tract of land in Arkansas. Ten years earlier, they had agreed with their chief to exchange their holdings in Tennessee for their new claim, and a sizeable annual allotment from the government.

The letter the Arkansas band had sent in response to Starr Night's query encouraged their kinsmen to join them in the wilderness. They assured the Alabama Songbirds that although things might be a little rough at first, they would be very wise if they decided to establish a new homeland in the Territory.

They encouraged Starr Night to join them in the West, and agreed to supply the band with a herd of Longhorn cattle, once they reached Arkansas. The animals were much more suitable than the eastern strains for survival in the harsh conditions of the Territory, but they could be crossbred with Warrior's cattle.

"You'll need to take a couple of wagons to Birmingham to pick up the parting gifts that the government has given us for our new life in the Territory," the chief told his men. "There are rifles, blankets, kettles, and tobacco sitting at the trading post. Each family has an allotment," he told them. "They've been accustomed to dealing with tribes in Georgia and

Mississippi, but they're less organized than we are. The government has never before had to deal with a tribe that is literate, and has its own postal system. What they don't understand about us is that no matter what new laws they invent, we'll learn to adapt to the situation."

Most of the band agreed with his assessment. They had faith in the chief's ability to sort out any deals with the settlers or the government.

"We'll be doing some of the work ourselves, and that will make the slaves suspicious of us. But everything must be stored upriver until we're about ready to pull out. It's going to be almost impossible to hide our movements from Tolliver, but we'll have to keep him in the dark until all of the details are worked out. I'll send him on an errand far away from our dealings in Birmingham. Our decision to leave Alabama must not be discovered by any of them. They'd be out of here faster than lightning! There'd be no way for us to stop all of them. We'll need to keep this quiet for about two weeks, then I'll make the announcement to them that we're leaving."

"Do you really think they haven't picked up on what's going on?" asked Lone Fox. "I don't trust some of our men. Those with mixed families might be tempted to tell them about our plans."

"So far, they haven't been told. And I'm sure of it, because none of them have tried to run."

"This is a good time to start killing hogs and gathering in the vegetables for canning. Those are the chores they'd soon be doing anyway. They won't be alarmed if we speed things up and gather the rest of the harvest of this cycle of the growing season," reasoned Lone Fox.

"I'll need two men to ride with me to the land office tomorrow. I'm going to follow the advice given by the Arkansas Songbirds. They said that we should renegotiate our deal to include this large tract of land in Kiowa Country." Starr Night stood to point at the place on the map.

"Then, if we're successful, we'd be able to annex thousands of acres of land adjoining our claim. I think that it's only fair that we should be rewarded for our cooperation. After all, as far as they're concerned, we've 'volunteered' to move haven't we? If we get them to agree to those new terms, they'll be able to use us as example to the other tribes, when they try to bribe them to relocate."

Now that the plantation had been sold, the tribe's most valuable asset was their ownership of three hundred black slaves. Most of them would be uprooted from the homeland and forced to be part of a dangerous journey to the wilderness. Starr Night would have preferred to take all of them to the new land, but the deal with the settlers hinged on their ability to exercise the option to buy one hundred of the Cherokee's slaves. The new owners insisted that their two hundred slaves would not be able to provide enough labor to run the place.

Regretfully, the chief agreed to leave some of them at Warrior plantation. When the band had brought them to Alabama, they had tried to keep most of the families together. But this time, he selected those slaves who possessed the skills he needed for the band's conquest of the new land.

Of the one hundred slaves he sold to the settler, he included sixty women, twenty children who were old enough to pick cotton and twenty men who were able to work at a variety of tasks useful to the new owners.

"It's going to be one hell of a problem when they find out that we're leaving some of them here, and I don't want to be anywhere near them when they discover that the new owners are white settlers!" said Lone Fox. "Most of our slaves have never had a white owner, and they don't speak English. They'll be scared of them, sight unseen."

"That's because they've been listening to the old horror stories of how their ancestors were treated in the hands of their cruel masters. I think we're the only slave-owners around here who don't beat their slaves. They have good reason to be scared of them," said the chief.

When the men left the council meeting, several of them were required to make life-changing decisions. Either they would decide to keep their promise and remain quiet about their plans to move, or they could secretly expose the plan to their black friends and family members, and give them a chance to escape. Several days later, Tolliver discovered that two black Cherokee families were missing

Nobody seemed to know when they had escaped, or in which direction they had gone, but in the past, Warrior slaves had seen coffles of black people march past the plantation. Those long lines of the poor wretches were usually led towards the south. And now, even the most ignorant slave would instinctively run in the opposite direction. Although the fact that they always ran towards the north made the job of the slave hunters easier, there had been several families who had managed to escape.

Tolliver had been away from the plantation for several days. His feelings were hurt. Although he'd been working for the Cherokees many

81

years, the master still seemed to feel that he had to test his loyalty. This time, he had sent him to Horton to conduct business for the plantation.

He had carried a large sum of money when he'd ridden into town to settle a bill for cotton seed. It seemed odd to him that his honesty was being questioned. There was no good reason why that bill could not have been paid by mail.

Later in the day, once he was back on the ranch and had a chance to relax a bit, the overseer decided to take a walk around the place and see how things were going. When Tolliver greeted a man he had met at a plantation near Jasper, the slave told him that he had come to Warrior to shoe horses.

That's strange, Tolliver thought. *There are already two black-smiths on the property.* It was not like Starr Night to hire a slave from another plantation without mentioning something to him about it.

What in hell was going on?

"Why are so many horses being shoed at one time?"

"The word I heard from old Paul over at Reston Plantation is that Warrior has been sold to a white man. He told me it was all that they wanted to talk about at dinner. They saluted a man they called 'Judge,' and said that they'd finally found a way to get those damned Indians out of Alabama. It's supposed to be a big secret, but I figure if anybody knows what's going on around here at Warrior, it's you."

At first, it seemed that his mind refused to digest the horrid information. Then, it came to him in a flash, and Tolliver knew why he'd been sent to Horton to pay the bill. The chief had found a way to keep him from discovering that they had sold Warrior. *Damn! How could this be happening to us again?"*

Starr Night had convinced him that they would go to the Supreme Court and fight for the land. But, if what this man said was true, it meant that the Cherokees had given in to the settlers without a fight and had made a deal to sell the plantation to them.

"Is there anything else I ought to know?"

"Paul told me that the Indians have already sold some of you to the settlers, and that the rest of you will stay with them. He sounded like he knew what he was talking about, too."

It had taken him ten years, but Starr Night had finally been able to fool Tolliver into believing that he could trust him. Now he understood why they had increased their patrols around the property. But lately, there had been a few successful escapes by black Cherokees. It didn't take much for Tolliver to figure out that someone had told them about the sale!

He was stunned. He could not think of anything he could do to change his situation. He just sat there, dazed, and not wanting to accept the inevitable. One thing he was certain of, and that was that he was angry enough to kill Starr Night.

Tolliver and his family were trapped again. And this time, according to what this man had said, there was a possibility that some of them had been sold to the settlers. He knew that he had to find a way to rebound from the shock, because he intended to save as many of them as he could.

Slowly, he gathered his thoughts, and walked towards the house to give the bad news to the women in his life. They cried.

"Will he continue to keep us together?" Bea asked.

"He made me a promise ten years ago, but I'm not crazy enough to think he'll keep his word. If he was going to do right by us, why did he hide the sale of the place from me?"

"I don't think we should do anything that might make him want to sell us. I doubt that he'd divide us. And since he depends on you to manage the other slaves, he's not likely to let us go," said Eliza. "Perhaps he's not as fickle as his Cousin George."

Tolliver told a few trusted friends of the sale, and made a decision to free as many of the young men as he could, before they were shipped away. He knew very well that he would have to put his life on the line again, but it was the only way to rescue any of them.

He picked several of the younger men because they had grown up on the Black Warrior River and fished its waters for miles, all along the borders of the plantation. Tolliver advised them to follow the stream to the Tennessee River. He worked hard on a detailed set of maps. If any of them were captured and told the Indians of his involvement, they would kill him.

By the time Starr Night called the slaves together to make his announcement, some of them had already known about his plans for several weeks. What they could not have known, was how much terror they would experience when the chief called off the names of those he had sold to the settlers. Not one single family had been spared.

Every member of Tolliver's family had been sold, except him.

Moans, screams, and cries of disbelief, rumbled through the slave population. Their response to his announcement reminded Starr Night of his tribesmen's reaction to the judges' decision in the Tuscaloosa court-room. They too, had suffered a heart-breaking loss.

Starr Night continued to stand on the porch. He steeled himself to absorb the shock and hate he saw embedded in Tolliver's eyes. *Well*, he said to himself, *that's about the best that can be made of this mess.* He left the porch, went to his office, poured himself a stiff drink of whiskey, and sat there with his head buried in his hands. He wondered if his deeply wounded slave would be tempted to try to kill him.

The chief waited until the next day to send for Tolliver. He would never have admitted to anyone that he was a little nervous to have a one-on-one meeting with the surly man. He had never seen this side of the usually affable slave. As a precaution, he had stationed two of his men in the next room. The chief wanted Tolliver to pull himself together, remember that he was his master, and that he was not obligated to explain his actions to him.

But Starr Night realized that he had sometimes permitted the slave to think that his opinions mattered, and now it was going to be difficult for him to realize that his only job was to carry out the wishes of his master. Otherwise, he was of no use to the tribe. And although they needed his expertise, no slave was too valuable to replace.

The chief lit his pipe and reared back in his chair as Tolliver entered the office. The first thing the chief noticed about him was that he had that same look on his face he had worn the day he'd bought him. But this time, Tolliver did not look him in the eye.

Whether his decision not to hold up his head was through fear, or hate, was something Starr Night would never know. The chief decided to try to strike some sort of reconciliation with him. It was a long way to the Territory, and he had to find a way to regain control of Tolliver. He was confident that this last bit of information would do the trick.

"Well Tolliver, I've got a bit of news for you. Looks like you won't have to leave all of your family at Warrior after all." Tolliver's head lifted. "The new masters of Warrior are sending your daughter, her husband, and the baby to the Territory with us," he said. "They've still got that fever, and I haven't been able to convince them to let us leave them here, so that your other family members can care for them. They want them gone. They're afraid they'll make all of the other slaves sick."

"Master, they'll die if they're sent out on the trail. They can't be cared for in a wagon. If I'm going to be the trail boss, who'll care for them? The baby's only three weeks old!"

"I'll let some of the women take care of them. If they make it to the Territory, at least you'll have some of your family out there with you," he said. "I know how upset you are that your family is being separated, but even though I've kept them together all these years, you'll have to admit that your mother is too old to be of any use to us, and your sister has never recovered from the last time we moved. I decided to leave your granddaughter here too. She's old enough to pick cotton, but she's still young enough that they're willing let her live with the rest of the family.

None of *us* want to leave Warrior either, but this is the best deal I could get. We'll all suck it up and learn how to live with it."

Tolliver was silent. There wasn't anything left to say to the chief that would not get him killed. His family had already been sold away with the land. Now he dared not say, or do anything that might further endanger them.

Their effort to stay together had been shredded into bits and pieces of human confetti, and now they would be scattered from one end of the country to the other. He would do his best to get his daughter and her family comfortably packed into a wagon, then ask his mother to pack a poke of her healing herbs.

Tolliver heard the shuffle of feet in the other room. Until that moment, he had not known if he'd be able to control his temper long enough to let Starr Night draw another breath. The only reason he had failed to kill him that day, was that the Cherokees would have gone into a blind, murderous rage and slaughtered every black person in sight.

Starr Night was pleased. The man had sense enough to know when to shut up. Now, the slaves could start packing the wagons for the journey, while he concentrated on the welfare of his band. He wouldn't have to be distracted by the problem of moving a large population of slaves clear across the country. He gave Tolliver a list of his duties, and dismissed him.

In preparation of their move, Isola organized the women to supervise the slaves as they completed their chores. A dozen hogs had been slaughtered and smoked, new shoes cobbled, glassware and crockery packed, root vegetables dug, stockpiles of peanuts, pecans, and black walnuts were placed in storage baskets in a wagon. Another vehicle was packed with cages of chickens, geese, and rabbits, alongside tubs of salted fish, beef, and eggs. There were sacks of feed for the animals, loaves of bread, hardtack, flour, beef jerky, and pemmican.

Lone Fox urged the men to pack as much ammunition as they could safely carry in the wagon. Although they weren't permitted to arm themselves in Alabama, the militia would provide protection for them until federal forces relieved them of duty, and took charge of the wagon train. When they were settled on the new claim, they would be on their own. The property would have to be protected from all sorts of renegades and bandits. Starr Night had learned from the Chickasaw Map that the nearest fort was several days ride from the claim. Therefore, it would always be necessary for them to maintain a powerful army to defend themselves against their enemies.

They would travel with a large shipment of gold and silver. It was their plan to use the money to pay the United States government for the public lands they wanted to annex to their land grant.

Now that a month had passed since the sale of the plantation, the white settlers wanted the Cherokees to finish their packing and leave Alabama. The new owners had divided the property into three divisions: the coal mine, the Rickwoods Clayworks Brick factory, and the 9,000-acre cotton plantation that wound around the edge of the Black Warrior River. Their engineers had made plans for a new entrance to the mine on the southwestern side of the mountain. The brick factory had backorders to fill, and cotton was just sitting there, rotting in the fields.

Under pressure from the settlers to get off the land, the Indians pushed their slaves to double their efforts to pack the eight wagons. Other Cherokees from the surrounding plantations planned to meet up with Starr Night and his band out on the trail.

Even though they wanted to put this experience behind them, they were still reluctant to give up so easily and leave their successful plantation to the settlers. Worst of all, they had to leave the remains of their dead to the mercy of the white devils.

Later, on that breezy, warm September evening, Starr Night asked Tolliver to ride with him to a hill with a magnificent view of Warrior and the surrounding river bottom-land. They sat quietly on the grazing horses, but Tolliver could feel the stare of the double-crossing Cherokee. *Wonder what's on his mind now? Cold-hearted bastard. He hasn't shown one sign of remorse.*

The thick, short man wore the air of superiority very well. He was soft spoken, but there was always that solid sense of power that emanated from him. Tolliver remained silent.

Finally, his owner turned to face him. Tolliver knew him well enough to know that he was having a rough time. He could see that the Indian was struggling with his decision to accept his banishment from Alabama, and the loss of his beloved plantation.

"Is everything ready for us to pull out of here by tomorrow morning?"

"Yes Sir. The only thing we're waiting for is your signal."

"Your daughter and her family doing any better?"

"No, Sir, but they're packed in the wagon and ready to go. I've found the baby a wet nurse. She still insists on holding him to her breast, but Florrine's milk has dried up."

Tolliver was frightened for them. They were still burning with fever, and neither of them had responded very well to the potions, herbs, and roots from the medicine man. His daughter was a praying woman, and perhaps by morning, her prayers would be answered. Nothing else had come close to helping them out of their deadly predicament.

As the first rays of light of the new day appeared, Tolliver, following Starr Night's orders, led the expatriates, free and slave, down the plantation road. By the time they were at the border of the willow-covered lane, the sun brightened, and they rode beneath the clouds of a buttermilk sky. The coolness of the morning air touched Tolliver's face as he called out the signal to move.

"Ho!" he shouted, and all of them began to rumble down the road.

Most of the slaves walked behind the wagons. They cried as hard as the Indians did, because all of them were leaving the place they had called home. Those poor devils they had left behind did not have a clue to what would happen to them now they belonged to a new owner. But at that moment, they lined the road and mourned for themselves and their loved ones.

The slaves strained their eyes to see their kin as they were led away. Slowly, the tightly shrouded wagons disappeared from sight.

"Lord, have mercy," Cook cried. "They took both of my boys away with them!"

Melinda, Tolliver's granddaughter, blessed with his deep hazel eyes, stood hand in hand with Cook. Her parents, brother, and grandfather were part of the exodus from the plantation. She was stunned at how fast all of this had happened to them. Melinda was too short to see much of anything, but when she stood on tiptoe, she was able to discern the outline of the last wagon, and it seemed to her that the white canvass top was flying away from the rest of the wagon.

Her aunts had already retreated to the cabin to console Eliza. All of them were overwhelmed. They had been forced to face the undeniable fact that their old existence had disintegrated into chaos. Eliza's worst nightmare had become her new reality.

Once Starr Night had cleared the edge of the property, he pulled up his horse, sat on the high, grass-covered knoll, and looked back at Warrior for the last time. His father's wagon, driven by Featherman, was third in line. And once it cleared the gate, the chief turned his horse towards the future, and left the heartbreak of the past behind him.

The Warrior slaves continued to line the road long after the wagons were gone. They were so numb and grief-stricken that they had forgotten to report to their jobs in the fields. When the bell began to ring, they seemed to awaken from a trance, and stumbled along the lane towards the mosquito-laden bottom-land to labor until the evening bell.

Most of the free black Cherokees decided to follow their kinsmen to the Territory. They were accepted by some of the tribe as members of the band. The vast majority of them had remained in Tennessee with the main body of the tribe. Even though Starr Night discouraged them, they continued to form relationships with both races and as a result, their mixed children existed in a confusing limbo. The chief constantly reminded the members of his band that he expected them to maintain a distinct slave and master relationship with the mixed-breeds, and the majority of them agreed with the chief's decision.

By the end of the month, they were able to follow a trail that wound through the woods on a route plotted by the Cherokee scouts. There were several times when they had been forced to cut trees at the edge of swampy areas, lay them side by side, and bumpily roll onto solid ground. Sometimes the soldiers, slaves, and Indians were all required to assist in building long sections of road. Other times they were lucky enough to find a usable section of the Post road, but most of it was in ill repair and deeply rutted. Therefore, Starr Night was happy to pay tolls whenever they were fortunate enough to find roads that were graded well enough to ease their travel.

It seemed to Tolliver that most of his days and nights were filled with requests to solve emergency problems. He gathered the blacksmiths to deal with wagon breakdowns, sought help from the shaman or one of the black root doctors to heal an ailing slave, or organized the men to fight a brush fire. Besides those duties, he was forced to deal with every Cherokee man who commanded him to perform yet another chore.

He had to be diplomatic when he ran his problems past the chief, for he always demanded Tolliver's immediate attention. The men knew that he worked under Starr Night's directions, but that did not stop them from thinking that he had far too much power over their daily lives.

Yet, none of the men stepped in to provide any relief to the overseer. He was well aware of the fact that they grumbled about his decisions. Several of them, including Lone Fox, had questioned the wisdom of letting the man carry out his tasks without adequate supervision. Those words were never spoken in Starr Night's presence, because none of the men wanted to work that hard. But, they owned Tolliver, and he had no choice in the matter. He was required to labor all day and half of the night, while they criticized the quality of his work.

Chapter Seven
September Caravan

Multi-colored leaves spiraled to the ground in September's crisp golden sunlight. The big, lumbering wagons creaked their way through the heavily wooded track. The wagon train was headed north towards the boats at Gunther's landing. Several desperate slaves decided that it was their last chance to escape, and attempted to lose themselves in the dense undergrowth of the forest.

In an effort to show the slaves the futility of their efforts to escape, the Cherokee horsemen decided to make an example of the latest fugitive. They stationed themselves on both sides of a small branch of the river while they watched the panic-stricken man wade knee-deep in the water. The slave was trapped. Starr Night, irritated by this latest troublemaker, promised one of his best mounts to the man who managed to shoot the slave with a stone from his slingshot without permanently maiming him.

The braves were anxious to get started with the game. The chief knew just how bored they were with the monotonous duties of their daily lives on the trail. The slave would supply them with the diversion they craved. He held up his hand to signal that they could start shooting.

"Bam!" Lone Fox hit him with a stone. "Bam!" The rock came closer to the man's ear. The terrified slave dodged, weaved, and begged for mercy. He splashed towards the left to escape the next three stones. The Cherokees began to yelp excitedly. In between shots, they began to count coups. Lone Fox was fascinated with the stupid move made by the captive, and suddenly spurred his horse, wheeled around him as fast as a rogue cyclone, then tapped the slave on his back before he rode away.

The stones came closer and closer to his head, until gradually, the contest took on a more sinister air. When they grew tired of the game, their playfulness disappeared. It was a matter of bad timing when the slave decided that he had nothing to lose by wading to the western shore to appeal to the master. A mixture of sweat, tears, and mud made it difficult for him to see, but he could just make out the place under the oak tree where the chief sat on his pony.

Starr Night rode atop another of his sturdy pintos, and was dressed in a beaded buckskin outfit made of the finest leather. He had remained a good distance away from the goings on while the men terrorized the run-away. But just as the slave reached that side of the riverbank, he screamed. Another stone had hit him. His ear exploded!

Some of the other slaves ran towards the loud commotion in the woods and were shocked when they saw that the Indians were flinging rocks at one of them. None of them could ever remember seeing Starr Night, or any of his men, mistreat a slave. One thing was certain; they intended to tell the other slaves what they had witnessed today. They would have to be made aware that the Cherokees had "baddened," and were rotten to the core.

Of course, they were helpless to aid their friend, and grew afraid to watch the game as the Indians insisted on the complete degradation of the man.

They yelled for someone to go find Tolliver, maybe he could talk some sense into the master. But the overseer had just arrived back at the camp. He had been scouting for a wider trail for the wagons, and had found a path down the southern slope of a hill a few miles away.

"What's the matter, Itty?"

"They caught a man who tried to get away. Now, they've got him cornered, and they're using their slingshots to shoot stones at him. It doesn't seem that master is going to stop them from killing him."

Tolliver spurred his horse towards the river. He reached the clearing just in time to hear the man beg for his life.

"Mercy, Sir, please have mercy. I'll never run again. Please forgive me."

Blood poured from the wound and copiously ran down his body into the water. When the second rock found his shoulder, Starr Night signaled for the men to stop shooting at him.

Tolliver dismounted and stood with the other slaves. They were shocked at the cruelty they had witnessed. Then, they watched the chief leave the woods, ride closer to the riverbank, and march his horse towards the shivering slave.

"Come on out of there, Deadman," he said. The slave crawled onto the riverbank, removed his burlap rag of a shirt, and attempted to stem the flow of blood, but it continued to run down his arm and his back to mingle with that from his shoulder. Whatever his name had been before

that day was forgotten. They called him "Deadman" for the rest
of his life.

Lone Fox dropped a noose around his neck and half pulled him back
to the caravan. Tolliver asked several of the women to bathe and dress
Deadman's wounds. Their salty tears dropped on his injured back as they
worked to stop the bleeding.

All of them understood that something out of the ordinary had happened to them that day. It marked the first time they had ever been able
to say that Starr Night, or any of the men in his band, were mean. They
came to an understanding that the next chapter of their lives would be
even more cruel and regimented.

Although they were easily caught by the Cherokees, there were constant attempts by some of them to flee their captors. It was a mystery to
the chief that the crazy bastards could not get it into their thick, nappy
heads that their attempts were futile. *Eventually,* he thought, *even the
most addle-brained slave has got to catch on to the truth.*

"I don't understand it," he told Tolliver, "Can't they see that we can
find them and bring them back here in less than a day? Why do they keep
trying to do the same old dumb-assed runaway thing? Don't any of them
have an ounce of sense?"

Lone Fox had captured the last one, and Tolliver had watched him
bring Black Boy back to camp with the rope still tied around his neck.
When he'd led him to a place in front of Starr Night, the chief had asked
the slave the same question. Black Boy was scared of the chief, but the
runaway took a deep breath and decided that he might as well try to answer the question.

"I don't have any idea where I was running to, but I know that *this* is
not where I want to be. I'd like to breathe my own air, wherever I'm able
to find it. Everybody here can see this here rope around my neck, but
what you can't see, is the thorn that's thrust into my heart every day that
I wake up and find that I don't belong to me, Black Boy. You say that
I'm yours until I die. Well, I think maybe it's time for me to go
on to glory."

"Now you listen to me. I don't want to beat my property, but you'll be
punished. No matter if it rains, sleets, or snows, you'll walk all the way
to the Territory. And, if you refuse to walk, we'll drag you until you see
fit to stand. But you don't get to decide when you'll die. *I'll decide how
long I'll let you live.*"

When Tolliver led Black Boy over to a wagon, the Indians trussed him up like a pig. Later in the cool of the evening, the overseer brought a blanket to the shivering slave. There was little he could do to help him without drawing attention to himself. He would have liked to loosen the ropes. He did not dare, but he took the time to sit down and listen to the man's crazy explanation of his decision to get away from the Indians. Black Boy was glad to have Tolliver's company. When the overseer held a wad of tobacco out to him, he took a chew, and began to explain the strange day he had experienced.

"When I woke up this morning, I just couldn't stop thinking about it. Something in my head kept saying: Run! Run! Over and over again. It wouldn't stop. I thought I'd gone crazy! I tried to clear my head, chase away the thoughts, but the words got even louder. Finally, I ran away just to silence the sounds running around in my head," he said. "I fought the desire to run all day, but then, the urge just got to me. All of us must be a little touched in the head, or we would've perished long ago. It's damned hard to accept the real truth of our lives. Starr Night and his band own us, our children, and every generation that will be born to us, for eternity."

Both men sat quietly. They knew that their hollow words would never be enough to express the hurt in their hearts, but Tolliver agreed with what Black Boy had said to the chief about his desire to be free of slavery. After a while, the battered man drifted off to sleep, and Tolliver eased back to his place around the fire.

Early the next morning, Tolliver saddled his horse and rode off to inspect the readiness of the wagon train to cover another ten or twelve miles before the evening meal.

He was still the only slave allowed to ride on a horse. He was almost certain that Starr Night would not let the wranglers touch another horse until they were far into the vast unknown wilderness. By then, he might think that they would be too frightened to attempt an escape.

In compliance with the wishes of the chief, the captured runaways were attached to the wagons by rope, and bound together. Their feet were not shackled, but they were now part of a coffle to the west.

It sickened Eleven Rock to see how cruelly the slaves were being treated. Over the years, he had gone fishing with several of those men, and to bed with many of the women. They had always known their place in life, and had shown him the respect he was due. He had always enjoyed their companionship. Most of them were usually good natured

94

about their lives as servants, and as long as nobody agitated them, they wouldn't try to run away.

Lately, Eleven Rock had begun to change the way he thought about slavery. For one thing, he harbored a secret desire to liberate both of his sons by Cook. Before he had left Warrior with them, he had promised their mother that he'd try to find a way to free them, without upsetting Starr Night. The one thing he was sure of was that he would not ever acknowledge parentage to the slave men. His son was the chief, and he would not do anything to undermine his position, or embarrass him and his mother with the truth of his long relationship with Cook.

Tolliver understood the desperation of the other slaves. None of them wanted to live the rest of their lives in captivity. But he remained silent, and always tried to give Starr Night the appearance of being obedient to the tribe. He had figured out that it was the only way he would be able to survive this nightmare. It was absolutely necessary for him to maintain a veneer of supplication as he reined in his total disdain for the Indians.

He kept a watchful eye on the wagons while he bumped along the dust-ridden trail, and used the time to problem-solve. Gradually, small bits of a plan began to gel in the cowboy's mind.

After Tolliver inspected the work the blacksmith had done on the wagon tongue, he rode to the front of the caravan and trotted alongside the one Itty was driving. The horseman reached over to the still rolling wagon and grabbed the gourd dipper from the top of the barrel. After taking a long, satisfying drink of the cool water, he offered the refilled dipper to Itty. Both of them rode peacefully along the monotonous trail under the pink-tinged, cloud-filled sky.

"I'll be glad when we leave this infernal forest and reach that part of the river with water deep enough for the big boats. These long days of dodging hanging tree limbs while I'm working on horseback have worn me out," said Tolliver. "I'll bet your shoulders are tired too. After all, you've had a hell of a time bringing this big wagon through these thick woods. The trail is very narrow through here, and the horses don't care to be confined to close quarters. Just be glad that your wagon is fifth in line. The wagons up front are forced to widen the road."

Tolliver looked up the path and saw that the wagons had ground to a complete stop. He was curious to see why the chief had halted the caravan. When he reached the men, he remained astride his horse and watched the Indian and slave women fish in the shallow water. They had dammed the water at the fork of the stream and trapped the fish in a trough. Before long, they had caught mounds of fish and loaded them into their baskets. Once the women selected the best fish, the waterway was reopened and the surplus fish were allowed to swim away. Later, they were cleaned, dipped in a cornmeal dredge, fried in lard, and eaten as a welcome change from the monotony of their daily ration of ordinary trail food.

Chapter Eight
The Awakening

Diamond-back rattlesnakes sunned themselves on the sandy rocks as the noisy procession traveled on the flat land below, but none of them showed the faintest interest in the horde of intruders, nor did they cause harm to any of the children who played ball and ran unhampered through the brush.

However, sooner or later everyone on the wagon train was attacked by the hungry, blood-thirsty mosquitoes. Luckily, they found quick relief. The itch disappeared when the bites were dabbed with the juice from the snuff-packed mouths of some of the children and adults.

The brilliant sky lifted Tolliver's spirits. He found it hard to feel defeated when he looked around at the endless space of the wilderness. They were still in Alabama, headed for the boats, and it was hard for him to understand why they had to leave the state. There were so many empty acres of land. *Why in hell did the settlers want the Cherokee lands?*

Tolliver guessed he would never understand the greedy ways of the Indians or the settlers. Once he got to thinking along those lines, he lost hope that it would ever be possible to change the most important things about his life. There was no getting around the fact that Starr Night had tricked him again. Once he faced the truth of the situation, a dark shadow fell across his heart. The tightness in his belly returned, and he realized that he would always have to pay attention to that gut feeling if he intended to survive in this hell.

He had become a first-rate actor, aware that he would always have to deceive the Indians and make them think that he would remain docile and willing to accept their decisions. As he went about his daily chores, he was always aware of the master's power. The chief could kill him with the same speed he would squash a bug. The Indian knew that he could not run away, for he possessed a wagonload of hostages, the overseer's daughter, and her sick family.

Tolliver rode along the ridge of the hill and watched closely as the caravan crossed another valley towards a landing on the deepest part of the Tennessee River. They were escorted by the Alabama State Militia, and would be handed over to federal forces when they boarded the boats.

It was later in the evening, almost sunset, when Tolliver led his horse gently down the steep riverbank to fresh water. He pretended that he didn't notice the strange black woman who was hiding beneath the branches of a tree. When he checked out the position of the Cherokee guard, he saw that the man nearest him was at least three hundred yards away.

Once he was sure that he would not betray her position, he locked eyes with the fugitive. The overseer rode closer to her to let her get a good look at him. He wanted her to know that he was not a threat to her. Tolliver hoped that she would be able to figure out for herself that he was not a white man.

Finally, after peering at him in the fading light, she understood who and what he was, then scooted down into the embankment. But she was careful not to come too close to the huge horse, because the animal made a scary, nickering noise once she was within a few feet of him.

Tolliver peppered her with questions. "Are you lost?"

"No."

"Are you trying to escape from your master, or do you want to be rescued?"

"I've been living on this creek a couple of days. I escaped a week ago. Between eating the crayfish and the water cress, I've had plenty food. As soon as all of you pass through here, I'll push on farther north. From the time you rode into this valley, I've been looking at you on that big horse. But I thought you were a white man. None of the other black people ride on a horse. Are you a Freedman?" she asked.

"No. My name's Tolliver, and I'm just as much a slave as any of you. The Indians have made me their foreman. I doubt that they could get a white man to work for them. But since they own me, they can pretend to the settlers that one of their own enjoys their company."

She seemed to think that it was a funny trick for the Indians to play on the settlers, and began to giggle about their joke.

"It's ridiculous. The settlers let me enter their stores and buy goods, but most of them won't let an Indian come into their place. It's a dangerous game. One day I'm going to be recognized, and the settlers are going to be mad enough to string me up. But, so far, the trick has worked. It must irk the hell out the settlers to see me, one of their "white" men, riding with, and working for, the enemy. I get my share of dirty looks."

"But I don't get it, why do you stay with them? Most folks wouldn't ever know that you're black. Why don't you just pretend that you're a white man?"

"It looks as if I can come and go as I wish, but there's a catch to it. The chief is holding my sick daughter and her family hostage. He'd be so mad about me leaving him, that I think he'd kill them for revenge. Believe me, he knows exactly what he's doing. He sold everyone in my family but them. He claims that he had no choice in the matter, that he was forced to bring them along with us to the wilderness. Even though I don't believe his story, I'm trapped.

She felt sorry for him, and wished that she could do something to ease his pain.

"I've not had a chance to tell you my name. I'm Pansy. And even though you can't run away with me, we could have a bit of fun if you could sneak away from them tonight. At least, you could leave them long enough to keep a lonely girl company," she teased. "Why don't we meet over there in that hollow tonight? I've not had anyone to talk to since I ran away," she told him, with a twinkle in her eye. *Dang*, she thought. *I sure like the way this handsome man looks at me with those wonderful, lust-filled eyes*!

Tolliver was very interested in Pansy, and did his best to persuade her to join the wagon train.

"Seeing that I'm not free to leave my family, why not come with me?" he asked. "It's very dangerous for a woman to travel alone in this rough country. You're taking a chance that someone will grab you and do whatever to you."

"It's my dream to find my way to a place called Ohio. Heard about it from my mistress. That's where she's from, and she said that it's a place where black people can live free. She hated the fact that she owned a slave. I'll have to admit that going away with you is a downright interesting idea, but I'm determined to get away from this madness in Alabama. I want to go to a place where I can live free. The mistress was good enough to help me get away from the farm. I can't let her down. She even made me a dress, and I intend to wear it once I get to Ohio."

"Here, take these coins. Every once in a while I manage to steal one of them from the master. I couldn't spend the money in Alabama, but I've heard that it might be a little different in other parts of the country. Once you reach your new home, they might do you some good," he said.

"It'll make me feel as if you're taking a little piece of me with you to Ohio."

Tolliver sadly turned his horse towards the wagons. Pansy slid back under the branches to the safety of the willows, and added almost twenty dollars in coins to her poke.

I wish that hazel-eyed devil would've kissed me, she thought. Then she hunkered down, fell asleep, and dreamed that she and the beautiful man had gone off to Ohio together.

A week before they reached the boat landing, the wagons pulled into a circle while two of the Songbird women gave birth to the last of the Warrior Cherokees born in Alabama.

That night, Starr Night gathered the band around the campfire to welcome the latest members of the tribe. After the shaman had said prayers for their survival, the chief addressed his followers:

"I believe that the healthy babies are an omen of prosperity for our band. As long as we continue to treasure our children and nourish their curiosity, it won't matter where we live, they'll learn the things that are part of their heritage, and we will survive. One day, we might depend on one of these boys to be our leader in the new land."

The new mothers basked in the light of the blessed babies. They were assured that their beloved sons would grow up among the other cherished children of the tribe. For they were their future, and it would be their task to master the new land and assure the continuation of the powerful band. Now that most of them had accepted the forced move from their home, Starr Night could feel the rhythm of their steadily growing excitement fill the air. Finally, they had begun to embrace the grand possibilities awaiting them in the new land. But, there were those who had not yet come to terms with the fact that they would have to live their lives in a land that had not been blessed by their ancestors. Sometimes they danced around the fire and called out to the spirits they had left buried in the east, then begged them to follow them across the mighty waters, through the stark prairies, and across the mountains to their new home. The shaman assured the band of the presence of the spirits, but most of them doubted him.

At last, the pilgrims made their way to the landing on the Tennessee River. The flatboats were loaded with the cattle firmly lashed to the rail. Occasionally, they lost a head of cattle overboard, but most of them survived the transfer from land to boat.

As they ventured farther upriver, there were times when the cattle were allowed to feed on riverside grasses. On those occasions, Starr Night managed to bypass the greedy feed merchants. He was determined to get the breeding stock to the Territory, where they would be crossbred with the wild longhorns. They would be worth their weight in gold, because the band would be able to produce a heavier, healthier, new breed of cattle, envied by their competitors. The Rheas had taught their husbandry skills to their slaves, and an example of their success was evident in the strong, beautifully built animals they rode and trained.

Most days, they were waterborne, carried across the great river by rough sailors called voyageurs. Tolliver watched closely as they expertly poled the watercraft down the river while trying to avoid the angry, worrisome snags that skimmed the water in unexpected places. From his viewpoint, Tolliver saw few roads leading into the dense woods along the water, just the occasional Indian trail that weaved past the cattails along the shore. Tragically, there had been times when he had seen the floating remains of someone who had jumped into the water, or had been flung into the river when they hit a snag. The momentum of the rafts sometimes made it impossible to rescue a person or an animal. Sometimes, as they neared a settlement, they were propelled through miles of filthy, smelly, polluted water until at last, they reached the edge of the unspoiled wilderness.

Starr Night found it difficult to deal with a boatload of irritable children and sick slaves. Most of the time, the chief and Isola preferred to stay in their cabin and let the others take care of the everyday problems of the voyage.

By noon, the high-spirited horses were usually restless. When they reared up to protest their confinement, the sailors would look for a spot where it was safe for them to land the rafts and let the slaves walk them along the riverbank. The men welcomed the task, appreciated the exercise, and relished the time spent on solid ground.

Any of the children who were not ill played on the riverbank. Some of them used the weeping willows to swing into the shallow water, while others were happy to skip flat rocks across the waves, squish mud between their toes, or catch minnows for the fishermen.

After several days of rest, they returned to the rafts for a one-week voyage to the large town of Paducah, Kentucky, where they intended to double their food supply and let the cattle fatten up on the long grass that grew along the waterside.

Starr Night decided that they would pitch their tents outside the city limits. He had become incensed when the town's settlers demanded an entrance fee from the Indians. They did not have a toll road, and as far as Starr Night was concerned, it was just a fraudulent attempt by the white man to steal his money.

Instead of meeting their demands, he sent Tolliver and his men to scout out a way around the town. Once they returned to camp with details of a new route that bypassed Paducah, Starr Night generously gave Tolliver the rest of the day off, time to visit with his daughter.

Tolliver sat by her side and tried to bathe the heat from her brow. The fever was relentless. For a while, it had seemed to him that she was going to fight and conquer the disease. She had been strong enough to cool her husband's brow with compresses. And now, although she held her son to her breast, it became apparent to her that they were dying. That is when Tolliver saw in her eyes that she had given up hope and lost her will to live. Within an hour, both the boy and her husband were dead.

"Well, Pa," she'd said weakly, "they've gone and died on me. If Starr Night had left us at Warrior with Mama Eliza to nurse us, we might have had a chance to make it past this fever. She always had a healing hand, but none of the others knew the secrets of her herbs and potions. The Indians have destroyed my family, but I'm praying that one day, you'll find a way to bring Melinda and the rest of the family out here with you."

"Please don't give up, stay with me. I know it's hard to think about it now, and it's probably cruel for me to talk about it, but I want you to remember that you're still young enough to start another family. I know that it seems that everything is going against you, but all is not lost."

Tolliver continued to caress her hand, but he could feel her life begin to slip away. Tears fell from his eyes as he held her in his arms for the last time. He felt in his heart that he had failed all of them. But now, he wanted her to go peacefully, and therefore, he whispered those words that she needed to hear before she died. The broken man spoke of his vision of the future.

"I promise you that I'll ask Starr Night to buy Melinda and bring her to the Territory. If the time ever comes when he'll agree to let me buy my freedom from him, I'll do whatever it takes to reunite as many of us as I can. I won't abandon any of them."

She looked through the gauze of fever into the truth embedded in his eyes, and agreed with his plan. Tolliver heard the tiniest whisper of a sigh from her parched lips, and she was gone.

102

Now, he had to face the fact that not only had he failed to escape from the clutches of the Indians, he'd also gambled on the lives of his family, and lost. He had been afraid to run off to Ohio with Pansy. He hadn't had the courage to leave them in the hands of a bunch of angry Indians. He had given up all chances of escape because he had supposed his daughter would live, and need his protection.

Now that Florrine and her family were dead, Starr Night had finally managed to get him away from his entire family. And the irony of the situation was that Tolliver had been the only one of them that the chief had ever wanted to own.

Tolliver closed her stilled eyes with his trembling hand. He continued to hold her in his arms until she felt cool to his touch. As he mourned for them, he fastened their faces in his memory forever. Then the truth finally hit him, he was alone, completely, and totally alone for the first time in his life. He had never let himself think that he could lose all of them at once.

Itty, and some of his other friends, had maintained a vigil outside the wagon. And now, they heard the terrible anguish in his sorrowful cry. They could hear the rage in his voice as he tried to come to terms with his loss. They knew their friend well enough to know that he would eventually find a way to stifle his sorrow so that he could go on with his life. Finally, the sobs subsided. When Tolliver stepped down from the wagon to the ground, they could hardly stand to look at him. His spirit was broken.

"Itty," he said to his young friend, "I've never been so alone in my life. I don't know how I'm going to be able to carry on without my family. All of the things I did to keep us together have failed. They're gone. And now, the Indians are taking us so far from Warrior that I'm beginning to wonder if we'll ever see any of our folks again."

"We're captives in this godforsaken land out here in the middle of nowhere," Itty said.

Several of them surrounded Tolliver in an effort to console the grief-stricken man.

"Just try to remember that your daughter and her family are better off than we are. They're finally free of the pain that racked their bodies all the way from Warrior."

Tolliver made arrangements with the men to bury his family. Three of the women washed and dressed them while the men dug the grave. Tolliver left their bodies in the wagon until a few minutes past sunset.

"I'm waiting for the settlers to make their last reconnaissance trip for the night," he told Itty. "Once it's near dark, they won't be foolish enough to bother us, or harass the Indians."

The evening cooled, and the softly whispering breeze wafted through the fragrant trees and gave him solace. Tolliver and his friends did their best to sing a few songs for them.

Earlier, he had carved their names on a wooden marker. And now, he drove it deep down under the soft soil. The men smoothed out the rock-covered grave and used tree limbs to disguise the location of the burial. Hopefully, the grave would not be disturbed by the settlers, or the animals. Tolliver hoped that one day he would be able to travel this way again. He wanted to have a sure way of finding the marker. After the men had finished spreading the leaves and tree branches, he carved his initials into the crotch of a young oak tree.

"One day," he said to the men, "if things are ever different for us in this country, I'll come back here and give them a decent headstone."

The big man knelt down once more to lay a final layer of pine needles on the grave. That was the moment when he began to understand the fact that he had passed another milestone in his life. And, it made him more determined than ever that the Indians would not defeat him. It was clear to him that the main impediment to his own success had been his fear of failure. He had created most of the obstacles that had blocked his bid for freedom. But, his insecurity vanished the moment he realized that there was nothing left to lose.

Now that his family was dead, Starr Night had lost his advantage. A new game had commenced. Tolliver rose to his feet, stretched, and sucked the crisp air into his lungs.

"Right now, we're not in a position to try an escape. We'd just be captured by the settlers. They don't have many slaves, and one man would be worked to death. At least, as long as we're together, we can divide the labor among us."

He had spent a sleepless night, but by the next morning, Tolliver was able to turn his back to the graves. He ordered the men to take his daughter's wagon to the creek for a good old-fashioned lye-soap scrubbing. They burned the bedcovers, removed the sailcloth top of the wagon, washed it, and hung it in the trees to dry. After the wood was dry enough, supplies were stacked in front of the wagon. The rear third of it was left empty. Slaves who were too sick to navigate the trail were allowed to hitch a ride, until they were able to walk.

Tolliver was more in tune with the suffering borne by his people. The blinders he had worn had been stripped from his eyes. Now that his family was gone, he had a new purpose in life. He knew that he would have to expose himself to the constant danger of being discovered, but he was determined to free as many of his people as he could, until the chief discovered his part in their escape and killed him. However, he intended to be very careful, because a dead man was of no value to those who needed his help.

During those days immediately following his daughter's death, his mind expanded to embrace his destiny. His friends began to notice the change in him. He had gained an aura of serenity about his person. He thought that he was probably the only one of his family to survive the holocaust, but one day, if he was ever free, he would spend the rest of his life searching for any of them who might have managed to escape.

But now, he had to pull himself together enough to continue the tasks involved in getting the slaves organized in their work on the caravan. Starr Night's main objective was to reach Indian Territory before the first snows of winter. The Alabamans had yet to experience prolonged icy-cold weather, but now, they began to prepare for a frigid winter.

Once they had skirted around the town of Paducah, the chief and his band found that the merchants in the smaller towns were eager to do business with an Indian who had plenty of cash. There were even those merchants who brought their wares to the wagon train, in an effort to outwit their competitors.

The Indians began to buy heavier coats, shoes, and furs for their families. The chief trusted Tolliver with a small amount of money to purchase additional clothing for the slaves. His overseer managed to hide a few dollars away for himself every time the Cherokee left him to conclude a deal. Tolliver figured that once they were settled on the new place, he would try to give each escapee ten dollars towards their new life as a Freedman.

When he thought about the money he had given Pansy, he wondered if she had ever reached that place called *Ohio.* It sounded like as good a place as any to dream about.

It was not going to be an easy task for him, but he was determined that one day, he would make the chief pay dearly for his bonded service. Although there would probably never come a time when he could openly defy him, Tolliver would try to undermine and wreak havoc on his plans. Then, he planned to just sit back and enjoy his secret vengeance on the cruel, unsuspecting chief and his followers.

The caravan bypassed the shysters who crowded the piers at Paducah, and boarded the boats on the Illinois River at Ragland. When they reached the levee on the Missouri River at New Madrid, the Indians were able to buy coffee beans, tubs of rice, and additional cured beef.

They met trappers, merchants, con-men, preachers, horse thieves, and "soiled doves" amid the churning mass of misfits who traveled down the Mississippi River. All of them were intent on reinventing themselves as pioneers of the new land. And most of them dreamed of possessing those things that were, for one reason or the other, unavailable to them in the East.

The trip down the Mississippi was well organized by the Federal forces. The double-decked boats were capable of carrying enormous loads. Rafts were used to carry newly purchased cattle downstream. The Army guard set up tents on the deck for the off-duty soldiers, while two of the men patrolled both decks each shift.

Starr Night, his tribesmen, their slaves, and their eight wagons, required three riverboats with cabins. Several of the slaves suffered minor injuries while living on the slippery, splintery decks. One of his men, Raincloud, accidently lost a toe when he tried to prevent his slave from jumping overboard. He failed to reach him in time, and the drudge had been sucked down by the deep current to a certain death.

Raincloud had a harrowing tale to repeat to anyone who was willing to listen. Admittedly, he was expected to fully recover from his injury, but the loss of a toe would always serve to remind him of his unreasonable slave.

"I'll never forget the smile on Booty's face as he jumped in the river, rather than begin his new life with me out in the Territory," he told Lone Fox. "He did that just to spite me. I told him I'd get him another woman. I sold Flossie to a man from New Orleans. She brought in enough cash to help me with the expense of building a new ranch," he explained. "That fool refused to accept the fact that she was far too valuable for me to let him keep her as his wife. I told him I'd find him another woman once we were settled down."

106

"I know which one of them you're talking about," said Lone Fox. "Sometimes I think they forget their place in life. We pet them too much. There wasn't any reason why he couldn't start a new family out here. He still had all of his children. Now, you'll have to let that older girl of his take care of the younger ones."

Those slaves who had tried to escape, or commit suicide, were confined to a room on the lower deck, and locked in chains. Starr Night now considered them his enemies. They were always kept separate from the other slaves. Tolliver was not permitted to enter the room located in the bowels of the boat. They were guarded by their Cherokee masters and suffered from heat exhaustion in the poorly ventilated space. The only time they were permitted to leave the boat and go ashore was when they reached a town large enough to have a guarded slave pen for rent. Most of the time, they were better off aboard the boats, because when they were penned up on land, their jailor was likely to feed them cheap, maggot-filled gruel.

One of the boats was caught up on a rock at Montgomery's Point, until the crew managed to pry it from the huge stone. But once it had been freed, they floated down the river past the cataracts to where the Arkansas River gradually mingled into a calm, scenic waterway. The boats pulled in and moored at the pier for the day. The next morning, they rode a few miles to another branch of the Arkansas, and tied up at the dock in tiny Rosedale, Mississippi.

The captain of the boat explained to the chief that there were several sections of the river that were very shallow. The rafts had to be poled out into deeper areas whenever they came too close to a sandbar. A hole had to be mended on one of the boats when it hit a snag. Most of the day was spent making the needed repair. As they neared Pine Bluff, another boat left the channel and had to be towed.

After a week's passage on the Arkansas, the exhausted travelers reached a town a few days away from Little Rock. And, after a short rest, they finally boarded the boats and headed for the fort. Three weeks later, when they reached Fort Smith, Tolliver was the first one to step on land.

"I didn't think we'd ever get here, Itty," said Tolliver. "When I asked the master how long it would be before we got to his new place, he didn't seem to know. He just told me to be patient. He had a map I'd never seen before. They're always poring over it, and studying it, as if all of the answers lie in that piece of paper."

After they had spent a few days at the fort, the Songbird men saddled their horses and readied themselves for a visit to a band of their Arkansas tribesmen who lived in a village not so far away from the garrison. Ten years earlier, they had been persuaded to leave the state of Tennessee and move to Arkansas. Now, they were awaiting their annuity so that they could move to the Oklahoma Indian Territory. They planned to join Starr Night and his band, in Kiowa country. The combined bands would control most of the land allotted to the Cherokee Nation.

In order for Starr Night to get permission to leave the fort without an escort, he had to agree to leave most of the members of his band and the slaves at the garrison. Then, the commander agreed to let him visit their Arkansas tribesmen, buy longhorn cattle, then wrangle the herd to the boats.

"Tolliver, saddle up and come with us. We'll need you to help us bring the critters back here. From what I've read about the longhorns, they've got nasty tempers, but that's what makes them tough enough to survive out here in the drastic weather of the Territory," he said. "I've heard that there are thousands of them running wild. They're unbranded, and free to anyone who has the resources to capture them. Once we're settled on the claim, we'll build a series of corrals to hold them, and then we'll have the biggest damned round-up you've ever seen!"

Later that week, after the Songbirds had spent a few days with their Arkansas relatives, they struck a deal for the cattle. Once they rounded up their purchase, they spent another day branding the cattle. When they had the beeves sorted out, they headed back to the fort through a barely cleared trail. According to the map, it was the shortest route back to the garrison, but eventually, they stumbled into an area where a landslide had blocked the trail with fallen rock.

"Looks like we can cut a new path west of this trail," Starr Night suggested. "There's a small settlement halfway to Fort Smith. We'll stop there and wet our whistles."

Right up to that time, their trip had been a routine excursion and would have remained so, except for the chief's decision to include his slave as a wrangler on the round-up. His next mistake was to stop at Jessup Township to rest, buy supplies, and water the cattle, without realizing that the town was owned by free black men.

Soon after they entered the town, the citizens surrounded Tolliver and his horse. They realized that the powerfully built man on the pinto was probably the boss, or possibly the chief. One of the black men walked up to him and offered to buy the big mulatto.

"What'll it take to free him?" he asked.

"He's not for sale, he's my overseer."

Clinton Coulter, the twenty-year-old sheriff, was a man who had come to Arkansas with a slave yoke around his neck, but he had escaped, and found refuge in this town. And now, when he looked at Tolliver, all he could think of was that the man was a precious commodity that the Freedmen were going to rescue from the Indians, no matter what.

"Look," he said, "we could've ambushed your party outside of town and buried the cattle carcasses. All of you would have simply disappeared. Be reasonable."

"I'm not going to sell Tolliver. He's mine! I meant every word I've said to you. Damn all of you, Tolliver's not for sale!" shouted the chief.

"You have enough men with you to handle the cattle. This man's healthy, but he's not some prime young buck. Why have you decided that he's so valuable that you can't possibly sell him? Is it because we're black men? Our money is the same color as yours. It'll spend just as well as yours, or the white man's. Every man has his price. What's yours?"

Tolliver saw a Freedman's hand touch his gun. Startled, he held up his hand in denial to his would-be saviors. He was not about to allow this argument to spiral into a bloodbath.

"Stop!" Tolliver said.

"Please stop. You can't possibly win this fight. There are another fifty Cherokees at the fort, plus the soldiers who are charged with escorting them safely to the Territory. Usually they'd be fighting the Indians, but in this instance, they have orders to fight you, and defend them. You're greatly outnumbered. You might be able to overpower these men, but make no mistake about it, there's no way for you to beat all of them who are waiting for us to return to the fort."

Reluctantly, Clinton signaled to the men to withdraw. He knew that the man spoke the truth. There was not a slave alive who would have turned down a chance to be free, unless he knew for certain that the attempt would fail.

The men began to slowly melt into the shadows of the surrounding buildings, while angrily uttering obscenities in the direction of the tribesmen. Most of them were forced to relive their own histories, and the helplessness they had felt when they had attempted to flee slavery. They were bitter and frustrated that they could not realize the dream of most Freedmen to assist one of their own to obtain the fragile status they enjoyed.

But, Tolliver refused to let them endanger their lives in order to rescue him from the Indians.

"Thank you for trying to free me from this evil bondage, but as I've explained, the Army will come here hunting for them, if they don't return to the fort in a few days. But I'll remember all of you and what you tried to do for me, for the rest of my life. Perhaps, if the gods are willing, we'll meet again under different circumstances."

The Freedmen waved farewell to the man they had wanted to save, and they understood that they had encountered a genuine hero that day, a man of respect. The sheriff doubted that they would ever see him again, but all of them were sure to remember that day for the rest of their lives. Tolliver's name would always be spoken of with reverence by the people who lived in Jessup Township, Arkansas.

The men would tell stories of the way he had wheeled around on that huge horse towards his Cherokee masters, as he had tried to protect the Freedmen. They remembered the way his chap-covered legs had squeezed the body of his mount, and how the sweat had poured down his face beneath the wide-brimmed hat jammed on his head. His body had jerked around in response to the movement of his horse as he had saluted the men, and galloped away from the town.

Occasionally, Sheriff Coulter would remind the men that all of them could have been killed that day if they had not listened to Tolliver.

"This town might have been burned to the ground like the one down in the valley. A bunch of hooded nightriders fired it up last month."

Chapter Nine
The Faithful Servant

When Tolliver and the Cherokees returned to the fort a few days after the incident at Jessup Township, Starr Night had time to reflect on their experience and wonder how many lives Tolliver had saved that day. *Thank God,* he thought, *the slave made the right decision. He chose the only way possible for the men on both sides to back down from that gunfight.* The chief had to congratulate himself that he had been wise enough to buy Tolliver from Cousin George.

At the same time that Starr Night was patting himself on the back, Tolliver was experiencing quite a different reaction to his decision to remain with the Indians. He walked away from the boats, and used his time to reflect on the reaction of the other slaves to the chief's contentment with his compliant overseer. Tolliver had seen the shock and disbelief in their eyes when the chief had bragged to everyone that their trusted bondsman had probably saved their lives.

That night, he sat on the side of the boat dock and dangled his feet over the edge, wracked with self-doubt concerning his decision to reject the attempt by the Freedmen to rescue him from Starr Night. Now, the Indians trusted him, but the slaves were repulsed by the stories the master told them about Tolliver's complete devotion to him.

Tolliver had seen the wordless scorn in their eyes. They knew that the Freedmen had put their lives on the line for him, and he had turned them down. The disheartened man stood, walked to the end of the pier, and looked down into the dark, brackish water.

His mind was filled with many questions about himself as he raised his eyes to the night sky. *I'm a damned fool! When will I ever have any sense?* He silently asked the stars.

Tolliver felt a gentle hand touch his shoulder. Startled, he turned to see Perry, one of the riverboat men.

"I heard all about that commotion in Jessup Township. It's all that anyone's talking about tonight. While the Cherokees are bragging about your loyalty to them, the slaves are calling you a damned fool. Now, I'm going to tell you how I see things. The way things went, you didn't have much of a choice. But, any doubts you have about the decision you made don't call for you to jump off this pier. Neither of us can swim worth a lick, so if you *do* jump, you're on your own. Don't look for me to come in after you," said Perry, with a teasing banter.

As bad as Tolliver felt, he still had to smile. The men had become friends a few weeks ago, shortly after Tolliver had boarded the boat on the Mississippi River. A week later, the boat with two keelboats attached to it had hit a submerged tree that Perry had called a sawyer. Before long, their boat had been surrounded by a pile of drifting, half-submerged wood.

That day, Perry had taught Tolliver how to walk atop the logjam. A few days later, after the captain had failed to blast his way through the waterway, Starr Night had ordered his slaves, and his tribesmen, to portage their belongings downstream. They had followed the trail near the waterside until they had reached a sawyer–free, open waterway, where the stream was deep enough for them to board another riverboat and follow the westward flowing Arkansas River.

Tolliver and Perry had become best friends as they worked together to get the travelers to Fort Smith. Tolliver had noticed that women seemed to think that Perry was a good-looking man. He looked to him to be about forty, but you could not really tell his age, for he had that smooth, black, wrinkle-free skin, and was in excellent physical condition.

Tolliver had learned to trust his opinion, and was confident that the man would give him the best advice that he could. He had been the first Freedman Tolliver had ever been able to talk to.

"Let's have a sit down over here on this bale of cotton. We'll have to see if you've learned any new lessons this week. First of all, if you really wanted to die, you would've taken your chances in a battle for your freedom. There were men who were willing to lay down their lives for you. Evidently, the price you would've had to pay for your escape would have been the deaths of a number of men on both sides," he said as he wiped the sweat from his brow. "You decided that their lives were more valuable to you than your freedom. This is what I want you to always remember. If you'd decided to fight, a number of the Freedmen would've been killed. Then, how many of the townspeople would've wanted you to stay there as a constant reminder of those who had died for you? They would've always had to think about the sacrifice they'd made for your freedom."

That question got Tolliver's attention.

"Not many," he answered. "Not many."

While the men tried to figure out Tolliver's next move, Perry told him his own story of his struggle to be free. He spoke just loud enough to be heard over the croaking sounds of the over-sized bullfrogs hidden among the grass at the river's edge.

"I was able to escape from the hard work in the rice fields of a plantation near Pine Grove, Louisiana. It took me a week of hiding out in a swamp, but I finally made it to the dock on the river," he explained. "I hid under bales of cotton that were waiting to be loaded onto a barge. Next morning, when the men came to load the cotton, I stood up and joined the work crew. Some of the men gave me suspicious glances, but said nothing. The sailor who was in charge of the cargo noticed my presence too, but he let me continue to work. And I worked that barge until it reached Memphis, then helped them load the cargo onto a seafaring boat. I hadn't asked for wages. It seemed to me that we had an understanding. I'd work for him, and he'd leave me to make a living on my own. Well, that little arrangement worked just fine until one of the men told me that the sailor had purchased forged papers for me in Mississippi, and intended to sell me to a slave trader as soon as we returned to Louisiana."

"Why was he taking you all the way back to Louisiana?" asked Tolliver.

"He wanted to use my labor to help load the barge with tobacco," Perry explained. "He knew that he could get more money for me in the Deep South. Greedy bastard."

"That Freedman probably saved your life. There's no telling what would've happened to you if you'd gone back to Louisiana with him."

"The Freedman gave me a dollar and directions to a house on Woodyear Street, in Memphis. The Presbyterian church sheltered me until a member was able to buy forged Emancipation papers for me." Perry stopped talking long enough to spit snuff into the water. "Since then, I've worked to free as many of our people as I can. I'm telling you about my life because I think I'm a good judge of men. So far, I've not made a mistake, but of course it only takes one snitch, and then I'd be a dead man," he said.

"And what was it that made you think that you could trust me with your secret?" he asked. "None of the others seem to trust me."

"I've watched how you treat the other slaves. They still love you, but right now, they're disappointed with your decision. Give them time to think about it, and they'll see that in was in their best interest that you elected to stay." Perry walked back to the waterside, but continued to

113

speak softly. "One day, I hope that you'll be in the position to help me shepherd some of them away from this hell. You're valuable to the people who're in a position to help us. You can read and write."

"But, what can I do to help them? So far, I've failed to free anyone in my *own* family."

"My value to them is that I have the freedom to travel up and down the rivers and act as a messenger. I also try to draw maps of the places where the boats moor. I leave food and clothes in secret places along the way." Perry reached into his pocket and handed him a note.

"Memorize that name and address. Hopefully, they'll come in handy one day. Maybe you can use it yourself, or give it to someone else who might have a better chance to fly away. I'm sure that it'll seem to you that nothing will ever come to pass that points towards your own freedom, but I have a lot of faith in you. One day, you'll find your own path away from the Indians," he said. "Now, tear up that note."

Tolliver followed his instructions and sprinkled the tiny pieces of paper into the water. Once they had said their goodbyes, Tolliver turned and walked back towards the fort with a swagger in his step, his pride recovered, and spirits uplifted.

The following morning, Perry waved goodbye to his friend as the boats sailed away. The boat had left the Indians, their wagons, and their slaves at the landing near a small settlement at the mouth of the Arkansas River. The wagon train was now within a few days of Fort Gibson, in the Oklahoma Indian Territory.

It was there that they encountered their first blast of very cold, wintry weather. The snow arrived on November 16, and although it was not a big storm, the wagon drivers and the people on foot, were relieved when they were able to stumble into the stockade for the duration of the storm.

They left the animals outside the gate, guarded by slave drovers and a few of the tribesmen who were fortunate enough to have canvas tents for shelter.

Inside the fort, the officers of the United States Army and some of their men were unwilling to hide the fact that they were resentful of the wealth displayed by the Indians. Several among them voiced their opposition to slavery, and threatened to free the slaves.

Usually, unless the Seventh Cavalry soldiers were out quelling a disturbance, or hunting outlaws, they lived in semi-isolation in the wilderness. Now, the lonely soldiers suddenly found themselves in the presence of a large female population, and began to make suggestive moves towards both the Cherokee women, and their black servants. Starr Night and his men did their best to carefully isolate the women.

Thankfully, within a week, the chief and a few men in his band were able to leave the fort to scout the terrain. They found that the muddy ground was stable enough to support the weight of the wagons.

Once they were sure that they would not get mired down in the mud, the rested travelers managed to escape the turmoil that the men were bent on fermenting inside the fort.

Before the Cherokees left the garrison, they visited the sutler's store, where Starr Night increased their supply of weapons and ammunition. Now that they were traveling without the assistance of the United States Army, the new citizens were responsible for their own safety.

Once the goods were packed, the Songbirds, Rheas, and their bondsmen rode out of the gates of the fort just in time to thwart the ambitions of those soldiers who had plans to disrupt their journey.

Two weeks later, when they reached the edge of one of the canyons, three black men leaped head-first from the cliff into the winds of the wide-rimmed abyss. The hysterical cries of the other members of the caravan echoed grotesquely across the canyon walls. Several of the slaves threw themselves prostrate against the rocky soil, unwilling to take another step.

Tolliver shook his head in disbelief. He was shocked at the sudden violence of the suicides. Since that incident at Jessup Township, the men seemed to have lost their faith in his ability to help them solve their problems, but it was still hard for him to understand why they would just give up so easily. After all, they had conquered the harsh trials of their journey, and managed to slog through knee-deep muddy fields in the wilderness to reach this place. Now, for some inane reason, they had been utterly defeated by this devil's den of a hole in the Earth. He, along with the other slaves, had covered his eyes to escape the sight of the tragedy. Even though it was fruitless, they had tried to shut out the screams from their ears. But in the end, they failed to escape the reality of the sudden violence.

Tolliver felt guilty. He had let them down. None of them had said a word to him about their fears, they had just jumped. One of them had remained absolutely silent as he'd held his arms tight to his chest, soared into space, and plummeted to his death at the foot of a sharp, craggy cliff.

When Tolliver had dared to look over the rim of the canyon, he saw that Jack Rabbit remained suspended horizontally, pierced in the middle of his body by a needle of stone, half-way down the cliff. His mouth was agape in a soundless scream, and a surprised expression was etched on his bony face.

While Tolliver stood there at the rim looking at the man, Starr Night walked to his side and tried to see where the other men had landed.

Had they sensed my despair? Tolliver wondered. *Known the depth of my own unhappiness? Was it possible that they had seen the fear and insecurity in my eyes?*

There just hadn't been time for him to hide his shock from them when they had arrived at the open split. He had been afraid, and very careful to ride far away from the edge of the canyon. The Cherokees had calmly peered into the hollowed out place. Evidently, they had already known about the existence of the crack, but Tolliver and the others had never dreamed of the existence of such a monstrous place.

Later that November night, Tolliver walked alone into the cooled air of the penetrating darkness. The bizarrely shadowed night had draped the land in a pattern of lace-covered stars that seemed to dance among the wagons. He turned just in time to see the flicker of the campfire flutter on the canvass covers.

Tolliver imagined that he could see the silhouette of an unearthly being suspended from the bowels of that unending chasm between heaven and hell. The very existence of that enormous hole in the ground was a mystery to him. The few things that he had managed to teach himself with stolen books had not included any information about this part of the country. It seemed to him that they had entered hell. *Surely*, he thought, *the Indians will not settle in this alien place.*

In the light of day, the people of the caravan watched the goats wind their way around the cliff walls to the water at the bottom of the canyon. Eagles filled the air with screeches as they floated through the currents of air in search of prey.

As Tolliver rode through the haziness of the morning sun, he was aware of the skittishness of the slaves as they wandered near the edge, and was afraid that more of them would jump into the canyon. But Starr Night was well aware of the danger. He and his men made an effort to calm them by shifting the route as far away from the cliff-side as possible. By the end of the day, they had managed to skirt around the deepest part of the canyon. Tolliver noticed that the slaves had settled down quite a bit, and were now lethargically subdued. The Cherokees watched them closely. The prisoners tried to stifle their natural instincts to hunt for any other place to be other than where they found themselves.

"Lone Fox, I'm going to depend on you and some of the other men to keep them away from the deep woods. If they manage to escape from us, most likely they'll be picked up by one of the plains tribes. They don't have any use for slave labor, but they'd make us swap something of value with them before they'd agree give one of them back to us."

"Yeah, we'll have to watch them ourselves. Tolliver ain't worth a plugged nickel since those men jumped from the cliff. Seemed to take the stuffing out of him. I still can't figure out why he's so upset. They were just cotton pickers. None of them were friends of his," said Lone Fox. "But, for some reason, he seems downright depressed. I guess that's the no-guts white man side of him," he said, as he rode off to a guard position.

Starr Night thought that it was a good time for him to get away from the myriad of problems he faced daily. He signaled Tolliver to join him on his trek away from the wagons. The chief led the despondent man to a hillock just high enough so that they could keep an eye on the encircled wagons. When Tolliver rode up close to him, they dismounted and strolled along a wooded trail.

His master took this time to astound him. He pulled a deeply folded piece of paper from a place in his leather bag, and showed it to Tolliver. From where he stood, a few steps from Starr Night's hand, Tolliver could just decipher the name "Tolliver Rhea," on the second line of the precious document.

"This Emancipation paper is a reward to you for being loyal to the tribe. I appreciate the fact that against all odds, your effort to ease the way to the Territory has acted as the lynchpin of our effort to reach Kiowa country," he said. "Since our removal from Alabama, we've depended on you to help us with the slaves. The caravan has conquered the wilderness with a minimum loss of life. I wish that I could lighten your sadness over the destruction of your family, but I want you to realize how many unpleasant decisions I was forced to make for the sake of the tribe. We'll all have to be willing to make sacrifices, and work hard to adjust to our new lives."

"Master, I'll make sure that you'll never have cause to regret your mercy. You'll always have my loyalty," promised Tolliver.

"Before the law was changed, I had the idea to free you in Alabama, but then, you couldn't have stayed on at Warrior. You would've had to leave the state. I couldn't afford to lose you. I needed you to help me get the slaves to this new land. Generally, they obey your orders. That fact makes you a very valuable asset to me and the tribe."

"I've not seen a town in the last fifty miles. I'm thankful for your decision, but what good is it for me to be free out here?"

"Well, there are a few things you need to know about your emancipation. You're a free man as long as you remain in Indian Territory. However, if you choose to live in the southern United States, or even in some of the northern ones, your papers from the Cherokee Nation might not be recognized. There's the possibility that you could be returned to slavery. Remember this, I can't return to *any* part of the United States," he reminded Tolliver. "If you decide to stay with me, I promise to do everything I can to reunite you with your family. I'll pay you a salary, and sell you a few acres of land for a homestead. But, if you decide to leave us and start your new life elsewhere, the first thing you'll have to decide, is whether or not you are going to continue to live your life as a black man. It's going to be interesting to see what choice you make. You can walk away from us and spend the rest of your life as a white settler, or you can stay with us, and have the possibility of recovering your family, and living with them under your own roof."

Starr Night chuckled, then shook his head. He was definitely amused by the paradox he had created in Tolliver's life.

The chief signed the paperwork and handed it to the ex-slave. Tolliver reached out to take the paper, then shook the hand that was offered to him. Unshed tears danced in the eyes of both men. Slowly, they led the horses through the rough dried sagebrush towards the wagon train.

Tolliver was stupefied. His voice was full of wonder when he told the people of the master's decision to set him free. He could hardly believe it, but he had proof of his freedom written on the paper he carried in his hand. Amazingly, Starr Night had done a complete turn-around and had set him free. Today marked the first time in all the years the overseer had known the chief, that he had ever seen him change his mind about anything.

He walked to the wagon where Itty was cleaning the mud from the wheels, and asked him to follow him to a place far away from the vicinity of the other slaves. Tolliver knew that he could trust Itty to help him try to understand the chief's latest unfathomable act.

Tolliver had thought that he was *the* expert on the man's behavior, but today, he had actually seen tears swimming in the chief's eyes. Perhaps, he thought, between the two of them, they might be able to figure out the real reason the cunning chief had freed him without requiring him to work as a sharecropper.

His sense of euphoria began to wane as he carefully examined Starr Night's act of generosity. There had to be some underhanded catch connected to that piece of paper, some important fact that he had overlooked. The one thing Tolliver was very certain of was the fact that Starr Night was not a generous man.

"After he stabbed me in the back, ignored my loyalty to him, and sold my family, the unpredictable man has seen fit to set me free," he said to Itty. "What good is it to have my liberty now? I'll just be all alone out here in the wilderness. Everybody in my family is either dead or traded away." Tolliver wrung his hat into a knot as he continued to vent his anger and frustration over the capricious nature of the chief's decision.

"I know that I keep telling you the same old story over and over, but even if it takes me the rest of my life, there *will* come the day when I'll find a way to punish Starr Night."

"Maybe it's going to be better for us to live in the Territory. At least he's made a good start," said Itty. "Yellow Girlie will be excited about that paper, she's been praying for a miracle."

"Yeah, but I can't let myself trust him. You can bet that he'll find a way to use my freedom to his advantage, if it's no more than giving the rest of you a false sense of hope."

"Thank God almighty," was the phrase most often repeated by the slaves when they were made aware of Tolliver's new status. He was the first Freedman they had ever known.

From that moment on, just as Tolliver had predicted, the slaves began to believe that their hard work and loyalty to the chief would be the key to their freedom. However, Tolliver was wise enough to doubt that the Indians would ever free anyone else. Still, he decided that he would not discourage any of them, because there was always the remote possibility that once the Cherokees were settled on their new claim, far away from the influence of the white settlers, they might be persuaded that it was less practical to own slaves this far out in the wilderness.

119

A few weeks later, Tolliver was slouched on his horse, eyes shaded against the sun, as he observed the long, serpentine column of slaves walking in the tall grass of the undulating prairie. He was thankful that the weather was milder in this part of the country. Both he, and the tribesmen, had to be especially vigilant as people wove their way through the grass. The plants grew very high. If a child strayed too far away from the group, they might not ever be found.

"Keep your children with you at all times," Tolliver shouted to the slaves. As he rode atop his mighty horse, he and the other men would usually sit atop any hill within view, so that they were the highest objects on the horizon in order to act as a guide to the walking people. The wagons ground through the grass at a snail's pace, following a path cleared by sweat-drenched men wielding sharp, grass-cutting scythes.

Finally, Starr Night and his people came to the new land listed on the Chickasaw Map. After a few days of joyful celebration, they decided to call the place "New Warrior." The unusual, breathtakingly beautiful place stood between the Wichita hunting grounds and Lone Wolf.

The chief was fascinated by the drastically diverse landscape. In Alabama, they had thrived in the verdant forests. But now, as improbable as it might seem, Starr Night and his tribesmen embraced the harsh, stark beauty of the soaring granite mountains of the Wichita Range. The landscape was so different from the dense, tree-covered, misty, Appalachians, the Smoky Mountains in the states of Tennessee and North Carolina, or the soft hills of the Talladega Mountains of Alabama. Here, the trees were stunted, and the knobby pines grew close to the ground, but the Indians were fascinated by the contrasting landscape.

Until the day that the Cherokees claimed their land, the place had been absolutely absent of permanent settlers. Hunters, trappers, and mountain men had only used the land to hunt their fur-bearing prey during the season. Therefore, the place was pristine, and still populated by hordes of animals.

As the band of Indians and their slaves traveled through the claim, Tolliver and a few of the warriors nailed "No Trespassing" signs on the trees in each section. Occasionally, the men encountered a hunter, but many of the cabins were empty during most of the year, and were only occupied intermittently during the hunting season. When the hunters were confronted by Starr Night, they were astounded.

Usually, they did not see another person all winter, unless they happened to wander into a fort for supplies, traps, or ammunition. The old men met once or twice a year at the rendezvous to sell their pelts to the dealers.

But once Starr Night and his band claimed the land, they made sure to let the hunters know that it was the last year that they would be permitted to hunt on their property. The bewildered men had always trapped in Kiowa Country. The area had been so far from a settlement that they had never bothered to file a claim on the land. Now, they were forced to face the fact that so-called civilization had crept in and closed their open space forever.

With the arrival of the Cherokees, their way of life was completely destroyed. None of them had ever dreamed that anyone would bother to come out that far in the wilderness and set a plow horse to busting up the virgin soil into clods.

But, they had to admit to themselves that they had turned a blind eye to the progress of the easterners. Many of their farms were played out because they had robbed the soil of its value. Now, many of them were headed west to start the process all over again. The new settlers, according to the old-timers, were hell-bent on the total destruction of the rest of the country.

Tolliver felt sorry for those men who were forced to leave Kiowa country. *After all, what would it hurt*, he thought, *if they were allowed to continue to hunt on the claim*? But, he didn't have a say in the matter, so when Starr Night ordered him and the slaves to set fire to every empty cabin on the land, that is exactly what they did.

Any of them would have been happy to have a chance to escape and claim one of the cabins for themselves. But once they set fire to the cabins and barns, they knew that the Indians had destroyed all of the potential shelters for runaways.

As the Cherokees moved farther onto their land, they began to change the very character of the wild country. They made plans to fence great swaths of land to create several enormous cattle ranches. Other sections would be plowed, and planted with cotton and foodstuff.

The Cherokees owned so many thousands of acres of land, that Tolliver figured that it would take a hundred years, and many generations, before that land could possibly be settled. There was enough room for thousands of people. *Why*, Tolliver asked himself, *were the Indians so greedy*?

Starr Night was aware that a band of plains Indians could be expected to occasionally sweep through the claim and assert their right to continue using the hunting ground they had used for hundreds of years. The chief had already made plans to make an agreement with them. He did not intend to start a range war with any of the old tribes.

The chief and Isola began to look for the ideal place to build the chief's residence. Within a week of exploration, they spotted a place high upon a rise, close to the North Fork of the Red River. When they urged their mounts to the top of the hill, they beheld one of the most beautiful valleys they had ever seen. The chief looked into Isola's peace-filled eyes, and both of them knew at once that this was the place where they would spend the rest of their lives.

Starr Night rode closer to his wife, gently touched her hand, took a deep breath, and called to his followers: "We're home. We're finally home."

Tired, and content that they would never be able to find a more suitable place, they decided to dismount and make camp for the night. A fact unknown to them that day, was that if they had traveled another twenty miles to the west, they would have found themselves surrounded by the uncharted, lichen-covered rocks of another deep, wide, pink-hued canyon.

The next day, the exploration party returned to the wagon train. It was already encircled in anticipation of the evening meal. A few hours before nightfall, the other Indians and their slaves pitched tents, made campfires, and corralled the horses for the night.

Small animals scampered around the rocks in search of scraps, while mountain lions scoured the edges of the wagon train and managed to snag two stragglers from the herd. Most of the predators, including wolves, stood hidden just outside the flickering light of the campfire.

There came a time that winter when Tolliver, the slaves, and the tribesmen, all wished for the warmth of the sun at their old home in Alabama. Although this land was beautiful, it was also a brutal place that required back-breaking labor from all of the inhabitants.

When the coldest days of winter arrived in the northernmost part of New Warrior, it seemed to Tolliver that the season would last forever. The ice that hugged the frozen ground was solidly captured until the below-zero temperatures abated.

Buffalo and cattle chips had been gathered by the women to supplement the wood chopped from the timbered areas of the claim. Although most of them trembled in the cold, at least they were able to achieve some small measure of warmth.

But, no matter how hard they worked to keep the fires hot, the hard wind managed to whistle through every hole in the log cabins. Eventually, it became necessary for the chief to put one of his slaves to work patching the holes in the tepees. Then, as the green wood of the cabins began to shrink, that same slave had the job of reapplying chinking between the logs.

Before the bone-numbing cold had set in, Tolliver and Itty had gone into the woods with a gang of men. The chief had made them responsible for felling enough trees for fuel and shelter. Their Cherokee guards were cautious, and were wise enough to stay well beyond striking distance of the ax-wielding wood choppers. The Cherokees thought nothing of their penchant to constantly change their orders about which of the trees they wanted the slaves to cut down and pile into the cart.

"Tolliver," ordered Lone Fox, "these three wagonloads will probably be the last loads we'll be able to cut until next spring. Make sure that you save some of the smaller branches. We can use them for kindling."

He was not satisfied to disrupt and interfere with Tolliver's work; his next instructions were designed to upset and mettle with the mind of that half-breed friend of his.

"You, over there," he said to Itty, "get a couple of men to help you drag those logs to the side. They're the ones we aim to take to the sawmill for the walls of the new cabins. Put your back into it! You'll need to fill the cradle to the top," he said from the saddle of his horse.

Tolliver listened carefully to his instructions, smiled, doffed his hat, then quietly told the men to continue to work in the exact manner as they had before the Indian decided to show him who was boss.

Lone Fox was well aware that technically, Tolliver did not have to follow his orders, but he had just wanted to see if the big man would refuse to obey him in front of the others. He didn't agree with the chief's decision to free his slave, and he definitely didn't think that he should have been allowed stay in the Territory. Several weeks ago, he had told Starr Night exactly the way he felt about the matter.

"One day, you're going to have reason to regret that you let Tolliver stay among the slaves. Now, they'll be asking for their emancipation too," he said. "As soon as one of them can get their hands on a horse, he'll run away. We're the ones who were stupid enough to teach them how to be expert riders, remember?"

"You're a very short-sighted man, Lone Fox. If you'd used your time to understand the changes that have taken root in the slaves' minds, you would've found that they've settled down. Now that we've traveled so far into this country to reach New Warrior, they have had to endure many hardships. They're bone tired. I can guarantee you one thing, and that is that those poor folks just want to have a regular life, and a permanent place to eat and sleep." The chief offered Lone Fox a pipe as he continued to speak: "All of them have been torn away from their families in Alabama, and herded here to the wilderness. They've sailed on the Mississippi River on the big rigs, then waded through the tall grass of the prairie. They'll never want to be uprooted again. Those slaves who jumped off the boats into the water, and those who walked off the cliff into the canyon, were the ones we would've eventually had trouble with," he said. "The wheat has been separated from the chaff. Those who chose life, are here to stay. And, just seeing that Tolliver has been freed will be all the encouragement they need to pick up their spirits and work harder. They'll hope and dream that their loyalty to us will lead to their freedom."

Lone Fox had angrily turned around and slammed out of the chief's house. That day he had vowed to himself that sooner or later, he would prove his point. That had been the reason that he had volunteered to be added to the group of men who supervised the woodchoppers. *Starr Night is our chief now*, he'd thought, *but that does not mean that things have to stay that way forever.*

That day, when he'd ridden away from Tolliver and the slaves, he knew that he would never again be foolish enough to turn his back to one of them, or trust any of them again. They had seemed docile and petted when they were in Tennessee and Alabama, but recently, he had picked up on something new about them.

Never before had they looked him directly in the eye. But that day, they had possessed the temerity to peer into his face and stare at him. There had not been anything he could point to, or put his finger on, but when they held the next council meeting, he intended to make sure that his tribesmen were made aware that their slaves might have become surly enough to plan an insurrection.

After the Indians had ridden away, Tolliver had beaconed to Itty to join him near the tree line. He needed to vent his frustration, and he knew that his friend was usually a good sounding board. The two men agreed on just about anything that had to do with their dealings with the boss. Tolliver wiped his face clean with his bandana, then sat astride a log.

"Lone Fox would have liked nothing better than for me to give him a reason to go to the chief about me. I'm a lot smarter than he gives me credit for. I'll never give him the ammunition he needs to run me out of the Territory. He's one of the men who are pushing Starr Night to send me away. They suspect me of influencing some of the men to run, but they find themselves in a predicament," he told Itty. "They want to control all of this land and glean the profits from it, but they don't want to do the work for it. That's why all of us are here for life. The chief is very wise. He knows how spoiled and lazy they are. He needs me to stay. His men want nothing to do with the actual labor needed to run a ranch."

"Well, don't make him think that you don't need a lot of help. It'll take an army to deal with just that part of their land that we've seen," Itty reminded him. "From what some of the other Indians have said, this is just a small section of their holdings."

"It'll probably be years before the chief will be able to turn me loose to run the place. But, eventually, that'll have to be the way things are here in New Warrior. It'll happen that way, because it's what the chief wants. He'll need all the help he can get if he intends to control this much land."

The other men had decamped, formed a wagon train, and prodded the oxen to pull the cart, piled high with wood, back to the sawmill. Fresh snow had arrived within the hour.

Both the Indians and their slaves had worked to house everyone, but some of them were still forced to live in tents and wagons until permanent housing could be built.

Before the weather had turned bitterly cold, they had packed themselves into rough, hastily built sod and straw houses. They used scattered rugs and hides atop the ground to protect them from frostbite because the soil was solidly frozen until the end of winter.

By the time spring arrived with its long awaited warmth and vibrant greenery, several differences had occurred among the inhabitants. They had gone through hell and high water together, and managed to wretch a cruel existence from their environment. The newest citizens of the Territory were now a tougher breed.

Even though they were forbidden to marry slaves, several of the masters had created new families. Some of those who had been friends were now lovers. Starr Night was not pleased with the new development, especially when the men claimed their children. Nonetheless, he entered their names into his log book. *Those* black Cherokees were his property.

Now that the spring season was in full flower, the builders were ready to construct the main buildings on the southern end of the property. A kiln had been built to make bricks for the big house. Isola wanted the finished residence to mirror the manor house in Alabama.

When the mansion house of New Warrior was complete, the chief's furniture wagon was unpacked of the belongings of previous generations of Songbirds and Rheas, and placed into the rooms in a way that made it seem as if the old place had been moved intact to Indian Territory.

As long as Isola kept the draperies closed, and kept herself busy with chores inside the house, she could pretend that her spinning wheel was set up in the sewing room of the old house. But once she opened the heavy curtains, the illusion was dispelled. Tears sprang to her eyes when she thought of the loss of her father, and the beautiful flower garden he had planted for her. *Those are the things*, she thought, *that I will miss forever.*

One look out of the window, and Isola had to admit to herself that the lush, Spanish moss-covered grounds of the plantation in Alabama could never be duplicated in the wilderness. The juniper trees and butterfly weeds were alien to her, but not as strange as the ever-present tumbleweed. Sometimes it flew down the road on a devil wind and glued itself firmly to the hinges of the massive door to the mansion.

Chapter Ten
Tolliver's Promise

By 1842, three years of hard work by the Indians and their slaves had paid off. They had created an enormous cattle ranch, and the largest cotton plantation in the Territory. Tolliver still functioned as the overseer of the claim that bordered on the western edge of the Wichita Valley to the Texas border.

The chief had seen to it that the slaves were taught new skills. In addition to their usual duties on the plantation and ranch, they had been taught how to produce adobe tiles at a kiln built near the North fork of the Red River. Starr Night's New Warrior Tile Company shipped products to building sites in the Territory, and paving bricks to their old customers in the United States.

Not long after they had arrived in the Territory, the United States had ratcheted up their efforts to finally subdue the Indians who had remained in the eastern states, and expelled them to the Territory. Over the past three years, thousands of them had streamed into New Warrior from their confiscated lands. Although the eastern Cherokees had fought valiantly to remain in their homes, by 1840, most of them, except for small pockets of them in North Carolina, had been forcibly exiled by government soldiers.

Most of the time, they had been whisked away from their goods before they could gather their valuables. Some of them had been ill, and too weak to carry their belongings. They had been forced to abandon all that they had owned, including their hastily buried family members, along the trail.

Once they reached Kiowa country, Starr Night and his band had done everything they could to alleviate their pain. The chief had hired some of them to help him build hospitals, schools, and temporary housing. Most of them were still waiting for their allotment from the United States government. It would be their pay for the land that had been confiscated from them in the East.

Fortunately, there was more than enough land on their claim for all of their tribesmen. The chief was pleased when he began to see the progress made by the new citizens. A new town with several stores, churches, a post office, bank, and a newspaper, was established on the western edge of the plantation.

It seemed to Tolliver that there was no end to the jobs the chief expected him to perform. During the past three years, the Cherokees had used their husbandry skills to breed the cattle they had brought from Alabama, the steers from the Arkansas band, and the wild local stock they gathered from their land, into a vast herd. Now, the chief expected his former slave to run his cattle operation too.

Somehow, Tolliver thought, *I've got to convince him to let me train my replacement, I'm not going to be able to work at this pace forever.*

The chief, however, was occupied with other problems. Once they had begun to develop land that had previously been used as a hunting ground for the nomadic tribes, he agreed to pay their chiefs for their use of the land. But there were occasional run-ins with some of the younger braves who disagreed with the settlement. And now, he was in negotiations for the use of a piece of land owned by the Choctaw nation, so that he could develop a rich seam of coal on their claim.

He hired Cherokee sheriffs to carry out the evictions of squatters, punish outlaws for their crimes, and defuse the almost daily gunfights. Sometimes they were forced to settle the score themselves, then pay the undertaker to clear the bodies from the dust-ridden streets.

As soon as the chief thought that he could relax a bit, the weather could be depended on to upset the equilibrium of Kiowa country. And when they had recovered from the riotous floods following spring thunderstorms, the heat of summer was apt to wither the surviving crops in the fields. Every fall season, tornadoes swept through the land and took everything in its path. In winter, the cold was the adversary that silently killed whole herds of cattle.

Their efforts to survive the hardships of the stubborn country forced them to bond with the land. Now that they had made it through the worst of times, they were now strong enough to thrive and improve their holdings, while several of the other settlements failed to take root.

Starr Night gave Tolliver some of the credit for their success. The ex-slave was beginning to relax in his duties as the manager of New Warrior. He had kept his word, and stuck to their deal to remain on the plantation as field boss. Neither the chief, nor any of his men, wanted the job. They did not want to be involved in the day-to-day operations of the ranch. They still considered themselves warriors and hunters, not plow pushers.

In return for Tolliver's continued servitude, the chief kept his word to him and agreed to aid him in his effort to reunite his family. Starr Night had written a letter to a friend, (one of the last ones who still lived in Alabama), and asked him to see if he could buy any of Tolliver's family from the new master of Warrior.

He had also agreed to give Tolliver a loan. He knew that his savings of three years would not be enough money to buy a slave. Tolliver had certainly tried to earn extra money. He had hired himself out to other ranchers in an attempt to earn every cent he could while doing odd jobs. The chief was sure that Tolliver had not spent any of the money on himself, except for what he had needed to erect the small house on his property.

Both men understood that the deal to rescue his family would further bind the overseer to the tribe. Tolliver was not blind to the invisible, sinewy ropes that held him prisoner, but at least, he had finally developed the dexterity to handle the chief from a distance.

Starr Night held the key to the only possible way for him to find and rescue his family. And Tolliver was willing to pay whatever price the Indian demanded from him for their freedom. Neither man pretended to be a friend to the other, and they both knew that once the chief had helped Tolliver save any of his family, he would never again be in a position to leave New Warrior.

Tolliver contented himself with the 200 acres the chief had sold him, and had built a two-room cabin, a two-seater outhouse, then, a corral and barn for the horses. But, he was a lonely man. He needed someone in his life to share the new-found joy of ownership in his heart. There had been a couple of women to catch his eye, but nothing had come of it. He had not wanted to commit himself to any permanent arrangement with a woman until he had word of his family.

However, in his solitude, he had rediscovered something about himself, a smidgeon of hope had reappeared in his life. Somehow, slowly, without him noticing it, he had recovered a bit of himself in that hostile land. *At least,* he thought, *although I'm without my daughter and her family, I finally understand that Starr Night owns the labor from my body, but no man can own another man's soul.*

In April, after the end a long, hard winter, Itty rode over to Tolliver's place with a message from the boss. Although the plowing at New

Warrior was scheduled to begin next week, he was surprised to be summoned to the plantation so early in the month. After greeting his old friend, he offered him a cup of coffee, and invited him to settle in for a rest while he read the note from the chief. It was written in the Cherokee syllabary. Once he had been taught the letters of the Cherokee alphabet by Starr Night's cousin, it had been easy to learn how to read and write their language. "At first, he taught me to read just so I could read him his bedtime stories!"

Both men laughed at the outlandish claim.

"Before long, he *did* stop doing the books for the plantation. He left that up to me."

The message summoned him to New Warrior Plantation, but the chief had not divulged any details about the reason for the visit. The note just said to come directly to the house once he arrived. There was nothing left for him to do but follow the chief's orders. He gathered his belongings in a trail bag, saddled his new roan, and joined Itty for the eight-mile ride back to the main house. As they cantered along the trail at an easy pace, both of them had many questions about the meaning of the note.

"It'd be great if he's calling me in to give me some news about my family," Tolliver said.

"That would be good news. My brother and I have just about given up hope of ever seeing our mother again. As far as we know, she's still at the plantation in Alabama," said Itty. "If your family still lives there, maybe they'll be able to tell us something about Cook's whereabouts."

"That'd really be a blessing. Let's hope that they've all managed to stay in one place."

The men easily fell back into their role as friends who greatly enjoyed each other's company.

"I've got some unexpected news for you," announced Itty. "Yellow Girlie and me are going to have a child. But, I'll tell you the truth about it. Although I want to be happy about the baby, most of the time, I feel like crying. In the back of my mind I know that we're just providing the master with another poor soul to be bartered, misused, or sold away from us at his discretion."

"Yes, I can see your point. The chief is always very happy when he finds out that one of you is going to provide him with new stock. A

130

child from the two of you'll be valuable, a quadroon," he said. "They get a few dollars richer every time any new slave baby draws a breath, but yours will be 'special.' I know what it is to experience that wonderful, joyful, feeling that you get when you discover that you've have created a new life, but then I also remember the painful memory of having to watch my only child die at the side of a stark wilderness road in Kentucky. When she died, I found out that it hurts to lose anyone, but it's especially hard when you love a person more than you love yourself. There are still those times I think about how bewildered I was when I found out that my family was being sold away from me."

"And I'll never forget the tears and shock plastered on my mother's face when she realized that Starr Night's father wanted my brother to drive his wagon to the Territory. I don't think she had ever dreamed that the Indians would take both of her sons away from her."

The overcast sky brightened in the afternoon, and once the air warmed, the men decided to rest under a large copse of leafy cottonwoods. They sat still long enough to catch a bit of what could pass as a breeze. The hobbled horses tugged at the sparse, spring sprigs of grass while the men sipped water from a ground-fed spring. They loosened the cinches and let the animals drink cool water from the creased crowns of their hats. Then Tolliver decided to see what Itty's reaction would be to a radical idea he had about the child's future.

"We can make it our business to free your child, but I don't know if Yellow Girlie would ever be willing to let it go. Think about it, and maybe the two of you will agree to let Perry hunt for a Canadian family who'd be willing to raise your child as their own."

When his friend seemed to consider his idea without comment, Tolliver did not mention his proposal again. He knew that the harsh sacrifice might be too much for the parents to bear, even if they came to the conclusion that the child would be better off without them.

Before long, the men tightened the cinches, mounted the horses, and resumed the ride to New Warrior. Just before sunset, they rode into the courtyard, dismounted, and tied their horses to the rail. Tolliver walked toward the side door to the office, while Itty headed in the direction of the kitchen.

Before he stepped inside of the house, Tolliver yelled out to his friend, "I'll stop by to see you and Yellow Girlie before I head back to the ranch."

"We'll leave a pot of something on the stove for you!"

131

Tolliver took off his hat as he entered the office and exchanged greetings with the boss. Starr Night reached over the desk to hand over a letter he had received from Long Rogers, a friend of his who still lived in Selma, a small Alabama town near the old Warrior Plantation.

The contents of the note frightened Tolliver. It recounted stories of the near collapse of the plantation due to the misfortunes of the new owner. His inability to turn a profit and pay the mortgage had jeopardized his chances of saving the place from foreclosure. Then, Tolliver came to the part of the letter that was most alarming.

"There has been an auction of Warrior slaves. Tolliver's sisters were sold to a Georgian. The new master of Warrior feels that as long as he has slaves to sell, he'll always be able to raise enough money to plant another crop, and save his plantation," he wrote.

"He's suffered several disasters, and they've forced him to make drastic decisions. Those ripened cotton bolls you weren't allowed to harvest before you were forced to leave, attracted weevils to all of the fields in Jefferson County. It was necessary to burn the entire crop in order to contain the spread of the pests. The next season, they prepared the ground, and sowed the seeds, but as soon as the new shoots appeared, they were infested. The loss of most of his income two years straight, has almost ruined him. He's probably better off than most of the other planters around here, because they just about lost all they had during the panic of '37."

Tolliver looked into Starr Night's eyes. "From what he says in this letter, it's too late to save them. Have all of them been sold?"

"Read on, there's more. It might not be completely hopeless," the chief advised.

Tolliver found these words on the next page of the letter: "The planters who are leaving here, are headed straight for the Territory. They're trying to leave here before their slaves are repossessed by the banks. It'll be possible for them to find land and make a stab at it somewhere else, as long as they can manage to hang on to their laborers."

Tolliver tried to control his emotions, but he was unable to stop the tears from rolling down his face. When he came to another frightening passage, he broke out into a cold sweat.

"Eliza and Melinda are scheduled to be included in the next auction in August. That gives me a little time to finesse a few sticky details, and possibly find a solution to the problem."

Although Eliza was old, Tolliver knew that she would be sold for her abilities as a midwife, and Melinda was valuable as a mixed-race beauty, worth thousands of dollars in New Orleans.

In the last few paragraphs of the letter, Long Rogers said, "If I can find a way, I'll rescue the women. But remember, things have changed around here. Times are tough for any Indian who still lives in the state of Alabama," he informed them. "First of all, it is unwise for any Cherokee to go anywhere near an auction, because it's possible to be arrested as a fugitive. However, I know a desperately poor settler, and I might be able to hire him. Warrior's owner won't deal with me."

"I believe that," said Starr Night. "He bought the land and slaves from the syndicate. He refused to sit in the same room with me."

"My agent might be able to buy the slaves directly from their cash-strapped owner. And if I'm successful in my scheme to purchase the women," Long Rogers wrote, "I'll leave Alabama soon afterwards. It wouldn't pay to stay around here much longer. I sense that the window of opportunity to escape is closing. I'm afraid of being arrested before I can get them."

At least, Tolliver thought, *the Indian has offered a bit of hope.* He wiped his eyes, held the paper in his trembling hands, and continued to read.

"I've heard rumors of round-ups of those of us who have refused to leave the state. The word on the street says that the dirty work is being carried out by the federal government. From what I've heard, all Indians are being interned in resettlement camps."

"If they arrest the Cherokees and put them in jail, what happens to their slaves?" asked Tolliver. "Are they being deported to the Territory with them, or confiscated and sold at auction?"

"In our reply to him, we'll ask him to clarify the details of the situation. But, right now, it's crucial that they all get the hell out of Alabama," declared the chief.

Tolliver agreed with the chief's vision of the situation, and was shocked that his mother and granddaughter were faced with the possibility that they would be sold away from the plantation. He could imagine the heartache his mother had suffered when her daughters had been sold.

"In the last part of the letter, your friend seems to have a good plan to get them out of there. Let's just hope that the owner is desperate enough to take the bait," he said wistfully.

Long Rogers continued: "Hopefully, we'll be out of here before the Army arrives. In the next weeks, I'll transfer most of my money to a bank in the Territory, then we'll be able to travel comfortably, at our own pace."

"There are a lot of things that could go wrong with his plan," said Tolliver, "but at least they have a chance to escape the auction block."

Tolliver was overjoyed that his adversary, Starr Night, had finally done something about the situation, and might possibly have unraveled some of the abominable damage that had been wrecked upon his family. It was beginning to look as if his dream of a happy ending was possible. He was willing to acquiesce to any demand that the chief could think of in order to recover a portion of his family. That day marked the time that Tolliver knowingly sold the rest of his life to the devil, and he was happy about his decision.

Chapter Eleven
Warrior Plantation 1842

It was hot and sticky in Alabama when Melinda was awakened that June day. The overseer, loud and demanding, had flung open the door to the worn-out shack and walked inside to confront the women. He'd ordered Melinda and her great-grandmother Eliza to get dressed, gather their pitiful belongings together, and follow him to the main house.

Eliza looked at the youngster's panic-stricken face and understood that she too, knew that they had probably been sold, just as her daughters had been a few months ago. This time, however, although she was weary, Eliza did not bother to beg the overseer for mercy.

She had tried that tactic when they had dragged her girls from her grasp. But now, after enduring that horrific experience, she docilely accepted her fate. Eliza did not shed a tear as she numbly followed orders. She held Melinda's hand as they walked behind the overseer's horse to the mansion.

Warrior's master did not appear at the sale. Everything was handled by the overseer. He had roughly handed them over to another white man who tied them together and attached them to a rope in the wagon. The men had not exchanged a single word in their presence. The stranger shook the reins on the horse and drove off.

As the wagon ambled down the pike, Eliza and Melinda silently gave a last look around at the slave quarters. They were driven past a few of their friends who were working in a cotton field on the western edge of the plantation. They saw that several of the slaves were crying for them, but they were so frightened that they dared not make a sound, lest they displease their new master.

After a hot, dusty ride of a few miles, the man pulled up in front of a neat little house surrounded by a large garden of sweet-smelling, fully ripened vegetables. The big-boned Cherokee man who stood just outside the door of the house, greeted their new master.

"How much did you end up having to pay for them? Do you owe a balance?"

"I paid twelve hundred dollars for the gal, and five hundred and eighty dollars for the mammy. They are fully paid for. They're yours.

But now, you have to settle up with me, and pay me the two-hundred-dollar fee for making the deal for you."

"But we agreed that your fee would be ten percent of the purchase price. That comes to one-hundred and seventy-eight dollars. Where did you get your figures from?"

"Listen to me, you dumb-assed red bastard, I went against my own people to help you out. The way I figure it, you shouldn't have a problem with paying a little extra for the deal."

Long Rogers heard alarm bells go off in his head when he saw that the settler's face had changed, and red splotches had darkened his face. He was very angry. Long Rogers quickly reversed his position, and agreed to pay him the extra money.

The settler handed him the bill of sale, and snatched the gold from Long Rogers' hand. He cut the rope that bound the women to the wagon and ordered them out of his buggy. Then, he angrily flicked his whip to the rear of the horse, and left the three of them standing in the middle of the road.

Now that the money had been paid, it appeared certain to the two slaves that they had belonged to three different men within a matter of hours.

They quickly obeyed his orders and followed the Indian into the house. He untied their hands and told them to have a seat.

Is this Cherokee crazy? Eliza wondered. Both of them remained standing. Although it meant that they were disobedient, and that they had refused to honor a direct order, the women were so thoroughly conditioned by the rules of slavery that they could not think of any circumstance when it would be proper for either of them to take a seat while in his presence.

Long Rogers had never owned a slave, but he did finally recognize the fear they had of him. He did his best to soothe them by telling them some of the important details of their sale.

"You've been bought by your old master, Starr Night. He lives in Indian Territory. Your son Tolliver is still his overseer," he told Eliza. "It's going to be a long, difficult journey, but if we work together to pack my things, by the end of our journey, both of you will be reunited with your kin. According to his letter, he's hankering to get you away from that plantation, and out there with him. Lately, I've been hearing horror stories about the goings-on out there."

136

The tearful women hugged each other tightly as they danced around the floor. They were so thankful, relieved, and overjoyed to be involved in this unheard of, miraculous plan.

Long Rogers told them that the next critical step of his plan was to get them as far from town as he could, before someone discovered his plans to take them out of state. He had already gathered most of the supplies they would need for the ride to the boat landing. Once the wagon was ready for the trail, any item he had forgotten could be purchased along the way.

"The only reason I was still hanging around this town was for the chance that I'd be able to purchase both of you and take you to the chief. He'll be pleased with my success, and I'm sure that your son will be astounded!"

Melinda and Eliza thought they might be two of the luckiest people in the world. It looked as if they were going to be lifted away from the drudgery of slavery and deposited in a new place with Tolliver. The women worked steadily in an attempt to help the Indian distance them away from the darkness that constituted their lives. As far as they were concerned, the quality of their existence would have to improve, because until today, they had been mired in a deep state of hopelessness.

They had just finished with the last of the packing when suddenly, the front door of the house flew open. A heavily booted foot violently wrenched it from its hinges onto the floor.

"All parties outside!" shouted a soldier. Several men stormed into the house and pushed their captives out to the front porch. Chairs, and several packed wooden crates crashed to the floor. When boiling water spilled into the fire of the cast-iron stove, volumes of steam rose to the ceiling.

Although they moved quickly to comply with his orders, the three of them were stunned. Long Rogers had been within an hour of leaving town with the women. His horses were already strapped to the wagon in back of the house. But now that the barrel of a rifle was pressed to his back, he was persuaded to follow orders from the soldiers without a smidgen of resistance.

Eliza and Melinda were terrified at the thought of being caught up in the Indian round-up. The women cowered together as the soldiers tied them with a rope connected to Long Rogers. They noticed that the other slaves in the wagon were also bound and tied to their masters.

137

Babies and their mothers cried amid the confusion as a general sense of bedlam prevailed in the main street of Selma. Dogs barked excitedly for their master's attention as the white settlers quickly ransacked the Cherokee's houses as soon as the families were removed. They searched for gold and any small treasure that might have been left behind. Houses, cattle, and pets were claimed as spoils of war. Beds were overturned, mattresses ripped apart, opened drawers thrown to the floor, and the chickens scattered, as greed ruled the frenzied minds of the citizens.

When Long Rogers and the women were being removed from the town, they heard someone in the wagon say that they were headed toward a newly built fort, and would be held prisoner there until they were shipped out of Alabama to the Territory.

"The government built that place as a temporary solution to a state-wide problem: Us," said one of the Cherokee men. "Now, Alabama has found a way to solve the question of how to possess our land, and at the same time, the court has gotten rid of a pile of litigation."

"The state always said it would give us fair market price for our land, but most of us have sense enough to know that it's a rotten deal to swap our rich farmland in the east for thousands of acres of wasteland in the west, isolated from civilization."

"In 1839," said Long Rogers, "I wrote a letter to Chief Starr Night about a group of Cherokees who had been given vast tracts of land in 1835, to move west. But, the difference between his band and the others was that the chief had not signed a treaty with the government, or tried to speak for any Cherokees, other than those in his own band."

"Now," said the trussed-up man, "we're in a hell of a mess. Most of us don't recognize that agreement. I refused to sell my land because I felt that the pact opened up all kinds of ways for the settlers to steal our land."

"Well," said Long Rogers, "it's taken them a few years to figure out a way to remove us from our property, but here we are, prisoners in our own land."

As he sat with his back up against the side of the wagon, he thought about his situation. *By a stroke of bad luck and timing, me and these poor devils I bought for Starr Night, are Federal prisoners. And I have to ask myself, why in hell did they pick today to come after me?*

Long Rogers, a sly, cunning, and intelligent man, had survived unmolested in Alabama. The handsome man had made his services invaluable to the white settlers. Usually, he acted as a go-between in deals involving tribe members and the settlers, and was known by all to be a square dealer. The reason he had been able to hire the settler to deal with the owner of Warrior, had been that he knew that the cash-strapped man was almost bankrupt. Long Rogers also knew that he would need to use the services of an agent, because the proud owner refused to deal directly with Indians.

The talk around town had been that the master of Warrior had bought the plantation directly from the syndicate controlled by his brother-in-law, Judge Earl Walker, and had not been required to meet with Starr Night during the sale.

Now, Long Rogers worried that the settler he'd hired to buy the women had double-crossed him in order to claim ownership of the slaves. When he tried to get information from one of the soldiers who had arrested them, his words let him know for certain that his previous life, the one with a favored status, had been obliterated.

"Whatever deal you had going for you that allowed you to remain in Alabama all this time, has come to an end. As far as we're concerned, you're just another dumb-assed Indian we're removing from the borders of Alabama," said the militiaman.

Fortunately, an hour before Long Rogers had been arrested, he had sent a telegram to the chief and told him about his successful purchase of the women. He had set the tentative time of their arrival in the Territory at the last of September, or at the very latest, the first week of October. He was confident that his boyhood friend would send some of his people to look out for them once they entered Indian Territory. Of course, when he'd sent that wire to the chief, he had not counted on entering the Territory as a prisoner. But at least, once they arrived, they would be released by the United States Army, and be free to travel to Kiowa country.

The military wagons and their horses made a thunderous noise as they came to a halt at the solid gates of the stockade. The soldiers dismounted and began to slowly push the prisoners towards the inside of the garrison. Suddenly, the loud wailing of the women became deafening. Once the gates were opened, those people inside the fort tried to escape from the prison, while those who were still outside the walls fought to remain free. But eventually, after a few hours of tussling, the prisoners were intimidated by the show of force, and were slowly contained within the confines of the tall, wooden-barricaded grounds.

Once he entered the fort, the first person Long Rogers recognized was a man who belonged to the Rhea family in Tennessee. Despite the sticky heat, he was swaddled in a blanket. Sweat poured down his face. His name was Clyde, and he was Kitty Coffee's brother, Chief Starr Night's uncle. His body was splotchy with red measles. Long Roger saw that his face was contorted in pain. Spasms and tremors shook his body.

"Don't come near me Long Rogers, I'm dying with the white man's disease."

"You don't have to worry about me. Fortunately, I've already had measles. How long have you been here?" he asked. "Where is your family?"

"Three weeks ago, we watched as the soldiers built this new fort. They were so friendly and helpful around town. They kept the drunks under control. It never occurred to us that this place was being built to be our prison. Then one day, the soldiers just rode into Jasper and rounded us up in the middle of town. They confiscated all of our weapons, then announced that we were now captives of the United States of America," said Clyde. "I'm putting it mildly when I say that we were stunned."

Long Rogers hunched down beside his friend, angered at the sneaky trick they had used to jail his people.

"Most of my family escaped to Rickwood Caverns," Clyde told him. "The soldiers were afraid to follow them into the deep woods. They figured that it would be a good place for an ambush. Those woods are very dense. There's a chance that my family will be safe from capture."

"I wouldn't be so sure about that, there's always the danger that frustrated soldiers will be willing to blow up the caverns if they can't find another way to catch them. I don't put anything past white men since they destroyed the mine at Warrior and killed Ian MacDonald and the slave men."

"Perhaps they did," replied Clyde, "I don't know if they ever figured out what happened. It could have been one of those slaves who ran away. I think that it'll take something that drastic to force our hand, and make us decide to declare a real war. We'd better learn to defend ourselves against our enemies, or before long, the tribe will be annihilated."

"Move on!" shouted a soldier.

"I'll come back to talk with you as soon as I can," Long Rogers said, as the soldier pushed him towards the rear of the fort.

Eliza and Melinda had remained silent and listened closely to the conversation. *Now*, Eliza thought, *Not only are we being held prisoner, but now we have to worry about catching measles. One way or another, these Indians are going to end up killing us.*

The women were still attached by rope to Long Rogers as they walked away from Clyde towards the other Cherokees and their slaves. The soldier settled them in the place he'd selected for them, then cut the rope and freed them from the Indian.

The women were filthy, exhausted, and suffering from a state of shock as they sat among the other inmates.

When Long Roger took a closer look around at their surroundings, he found that most of the Indians were from one of the so-called "civilized" tribes. All of them had been settled on the land for many generations, and now, not only had they lost the land, they had also been stripped of all of their earthly belongings. They found themselves imprisoned in the stockade while they awaited the march to the boat landing. Once there, they would be forced to climb aboard the big boat, and be sent far away from the places they considered their homeland.

Eliza and Melinda stayed close to each other. They were afraid of the strange Indians of some of the other tribes. It was easy to tell by their dress that many of the men, women, and children were from the Creek, Choctaw, and Chickasaw nations.

Most of them had been marched from far-away places, and quite a few of the dirty, ragged, Indians and their slaves were sick. They spoke in a babble of tongues of many dialects. The soldiers were forced to settle many misunderstandings among the inmates.

Even though Eliza and Melinda did not recognize any of the other slaves or Indians, when it was necessary they could communicate with most of them by sign language. They had learned their skills when their master had rented their labor to other plantation owners. Although most of the Cherokees were bilingual, none of the other tribes, or their slaves, spoke English.

Eliza was exhausted, but she was determined to stay alert so that she could protect Melinda from the dangers and tribulations of the journey to the Territory. Once they got there, she was sure that Tolliver would do everything he could to protect them. *My son has done every-*

thing humanly possible to save us, she thought, *it's just that he didn't have any power over the will of the master to keep us all together.*

She watched Long Rogers circulate among his tribesmen and became fearful that he would decide that he no longer wanted to be responsible for their safety. Eliza wondered if it was possible that he would be tempted to sell them, in order to rid himself of a burden. *I hope,* she thought, *the Indian will decide to keep his promise to Starr Night and find a way to deliver us to him in New Warrior.*

So far, Eliza noticed that Long Rogers had not joined in with the Cherokee men as they downed shots of the rot-gut whiskey the bootlegger brought to the fort. It was sold by a sneaky, no-account soldier named Welch. He traded the whiskey for whatever valuables the men had managed to hide from the soldiers when they had been captured. He could have been shot for selling the evil brew, but one of the men had told Long Rogers that Welch's commanding officer had decided to turn his head the other way. His decision to allow the trade to flourish had calmed the Indians down. Now, they were docile, and much easier to manage.

It was an open secret that Welch, who earned thirteen dollars a month as a soldier, was the bootlegger's partner. It was his plan to raise enough money to leave the Army when his current enlistment ended. He dreamed of being a settler of the West.

The soldier was in charge of the worst detail at the fort. Welch and his soldiers were assigned to escort duties. They took families to the burial ground to inter the dead. There had been quite a few inmates who had not survived the trip to Indian Territory. Several dozen Indian children were among those who had not fared so well.

Welch and his men were severely depressed most of the time. The burials had increased as the round-up had intensified. Now, he just wanted to escape the dying Indians and their damned problems. He despised the dirty, conniving drunks. The moaning, screeching, and wailing of the screaming women irritated him as much as the sound of fingernails scratching on a chalkboard.

The only way he'd managed to retain his sanity had been to always keep in mind that if things continued to go his way, one day he was going to be one of the largest owners of virgin soil in the Territory. Welch intended to be a man of means. He was determined to do whatever it took to avoid becoming the failure that his father was. He would never be able to forget the sad look of disappointment and resignation on his poor, tired mother's face when yet another mouth to feed was born every year. *There has to be a way*, he'd thought, *to escape my father's lot in life. I refuse to be just another drunk scrub-farmer like him.*

The soldier's determination to escape his past was the main reason he had joined the Army. After growing up as the son of a sot, Welch was very careful to limit his consumption of the firewater he sold to the Indians. That stuff was poison to the system. *Why in hell do they keep drinking that shit?* He wondered. *They're dumber than hell, and deserve to die with their guts all twisted up in knots, and burnt to a crisp.*

After spending the night asleep on one of the blankets they had been given, Long Rogers walked over to where Clyde slept, praying that his friend had managed to survive another night. The first thing he noticed, was that the man had not moved more than a few feet from where he had lain the day before. *That's not a good sign,* he thought.

When Clyde motioned to Long Rogers to come closer, he immediately noticed that he had developed a far-away look in his eyes. The men spoke of their golden youth; the good old days when they were still great hunters. Neither of them had to exaggerate about the number of animals they had killed for their village. They had belonged to great hunting parties that had provided the towns with all the meat and skins they needed. And then, after every Cherokee family was supplied for the winter, the men had sold their excess deer, beaver skins, fish, and feathers to the white traders in exchange of their guns, ammunition, horses, household goods, and whiskey.

"Our trade is what destroyed our way of life," said Clyde. "It didn't take very long for them to want more and more skins. By the time we recognized our mistake, we'd stripped our best animals from the hunting grounds. But the settlers weren't satisfied to just trade goods with us, they wanted to own some of our land," he declared. "My father says that he can remember when we were strong enough to run them off the claims they cleared. We destroyed their gardens and stole their slaves. There were so many of us, that we had to expand our towns every year."

"But then," said Clyde, "the chiefs permitted a few of the white men to live among us. It wasn't that many years later that the chiefs allowed them to marry our women."

"And now, their deadly diseases are the presents they have given us. This horrible disease is a lousy way to pay us back for our kindness and willingness to make peace with them," Long Rogers said. "Father says that as many as two hundred Cherokees have died from Cholera in his village since their first contact with the mountain men." Tears came to his eyes as he continued to speak. "After a few years, so many of us had died, that there were entire towns and villages left empty. They were completely decimated."

Clyde managed to raise himself on his elbows, but continued to speak softly.

"Yes," he said, "the weaker we became, the bolder our enemies grew. Before long, the white settlers began to build their homesteads in and around our empty villages. There weren't enough healthy braves to push them off our property."

"And that," recounted Long Rogers, "is when the old chiefs began to sell them some of our land. They reasoned that since some of them had already started to build on the land, and we weren't strong enough to push them out, they might as well pay us for the land."

"Those old men never dreamed that so many of the white people would want to live out here in the wilderness. They fooled all of us, huh?"

Long Rogers just shook his head in agreement with Clyde's words. A white curl of smoke drifted above their heads as he sat on his haunches and stared out into space, with his pipe clenched in his teeth.

The next time Clyde spoke, Long Rogers could see that his life was rapidly fading away. The devilish fever had flared up again. Clyde said, "I can feel the weight of death sitting on my chest." Once again, he motioned to his friend to draw closer. His voice had weakened, and as a bone-rattling tremor raced through his body, he managed to whisper these words into Long Rogers' ear: "There's a large hoard of gold in a pouch wrapped around my waist, underneath my shirt. Of course it hasn't been discovered, because nobody has wanted to touch me and take the chance that they would catch the measles," he explained. "Will you keep the treasure safe for me ?" he asked. "If it's my time to die, at least I can go knowing that my wife and children will have the money to develop their claim when they reach the new land." When Long Rogers nodded in agreement with his wishes, he continued to whisper. "Eventually, the soldiers will capture them and bring them to the fort. But now, I'm satisfied to know that I'm going to leave them in your capable hands."

"Clyde," he said, " I promise you that I'll do everything in my power to find them. I'm honored that the Gods have sent me to you. Any house that I ever own, they'll also own, fifty-fifty, right down the middle. The gold will be shared with any and all of your kin," he said to his old hunting buddy.

He continued to sit with him while Clyde dozed. Every once in a while, he stirred himself awake long enough so that they were able to continue to swap old stories of their childhood adventures. It was just after sunset, when the man died in the comforting presence of his friend.

For the time being, he decided to leave Clyde's money belt wrapped around his belly. Long Rogers continued to sit on his haunches, as he recited a prayer for Clyde's soul. He felt very sad when he thought of the loss of his friend, but Clyde's death spurred his determination to find a way to regain his freedom, before something happened to him in the confines of the disease-filled prison.

Finally, he stood and walked in the direction of Welch's office. He had made a decision about what his next step should be. First, it was his task to arrange a decent funeral service for Clyde. Then, he'd pray that Welch was greedy enough for money that he would be open to accepting a bribe.

Long Rogers desperately needed to entice the soldier to abet his effort to escape. When more of the Indians began to die, the fort began to use their blankets as shrouds. Long Rogers intended to prepare Clyde's body for burial himself. He would unwrap the gold-laden money pouch from his body, then find a way to hide it from the soldiers. So far, he had not discovered a secure hiding place in the tight quarters of the courtyard. He figured that eventually, he would have to come up with a way to hide the gold, while it stayed in plain sight.

After reporting Clyde's death to Welch, he passed by a Choctaw woman sitting cross-legged in the grass. He convinced her to accept his knife in trade for the beautiful, big, covered basket that stood at her side. She grinned at him. She knew that the knife was more valuable than the basket she had woven years ago. And after she emptied her belongings from the basket onto her blanket, she handed over the multi-colored, woven container to him.

The following morning, before Long Rogers and the other Cherokee men left the fort with the burial detail, he handed the basket to Eliza.

"Put this basket under your blanket and keep it safe for me," he ordered her. Then, he just turned around without another word, left the women at their sleeping place near the back wall of the fort, and jumped

145

aboard the wagonload of Cherokee men who were headed for the ceremony at the graveyard.

"Melinda," Eliza said, "I wonder what he's hiding in that basket?
And why is it so important that I have to hide it beneath the blanket?"

After a few minutes of discussing the pros and cons of opening
the basket, their curiosity grew to the point where they were powerless to
resist the urge to open the top and peer inside. First, however, they
looked around them to see if they were being watched. And when they
saw that nobody seemed to care what they were doing, Eliza slowly lifted the lid, looked inside, and found a long, leather, beaded pouch tied
with a thong. She untied the bag and looked inside.

The women looked at each other, speechless, stunned and amazed
at the beauty of the gold, as the bright sunlight caught the sparkle of the
treasure.

The snuff bag Eliza wore around her neck was tied to the bodice
of her dress. She quickly opened it and stuffed it with enough gold to fill
the sack. Then, with shaky hands, she retied the precious pouch and returned it to the basket.

When Eliza had made the decision to steal some of the gold,
she'd depended on her inherited, instinctive powers of understanding to
figure out the way the Indian would feel about leaving the gold in her
care. She was one of those rare slaves who had lived long enough, to be
able to gauge the temperament of the people who owned them.

Eliza was reasonably sure that the theft of the gold would go un-
noticed. She figured that the Indian would think that she was too ignorant
to know about the value of gold, and she thought that he would not
dream that she would ever want to steal something that she could not
spend. Even though he had not owned slaves before, he would certainly
be aware that Alabama slaves were not allowed to own, or spend gold.

Of course, he had no way of knowing that the old slave had handled money each time her master had been paid for her services by other
plantation owners. Eliza had worked on the surrounding plantations as a
midwife, or sometimes, a cotton picker, and had always dutifully handed
over every cent of the money to the master.

But now, she thought, *I'm not going to be living in Alabama. One
day my family will be free to use the treasure.* Eliza decided to hide the
money. Whenever they found Tolliver, she would hand it over to him.
He'll know what to do with it, she thought.

Later that evening, when Long Rogers returned to the fort, he did just as she had predicted. The tired, sad, sweaty man grunted a greeting to both of them, took the basket, shoved it under the blanket without opening it, and laid down to sleep. He soon drifted off into a deep slumber, and dreamed of a plan to free them from the fort.

Once she heard him snore, Melinda relaxed. Finally, she felt safe enough to take a grateful, deep breath of fresh air. She leaned over to hug and kiss Eliza. The old woman grinned, pushed the gold-filled bag farther down in her bosom, then fell peacefully to sleep.

Chapter Twelve
The Escape Artists

Welch met the Cherokee men behind the quartermaster's hut with a small vat of whiskey. There wasn't much money to be made in the stockade until a new batch of Indians arrived. But Welch, along with the bootlegger, collected the few pennies the men still owned, in exchange for a sip of the liquor.

Long Rogers pretended to be a drinking man just so he could increase his contact with the soldier. He was trying to fulfill the details of the dream he'd experienced the day he'd helped to bury Clyde. The success of his plan depended on his ability to entice the soldier to help him carry out his unorthodox scheme. He had to arouse the man's greedy instincts to a fevered pitch of excitement in order for his plan to succeed.

A week later, he offered to help the soldier carry out the daily burials. The tall, stringy-haired man was surprised and suspicious of anyone who volunteered to help with the onerous duty.

"Why would you want to be involved with that nasty business at the graveyard?"

"There are ceremonies we wish to carry out for our tribesmen. You saw the way we buried my friend. Well, that's how we want to bury all of our tribesmen, a simple, decent burial. I'm not interested in what happens with the other tribes, it's up to them to make their own arrangements."

Welch was surprised. He had not known that the Indians cared one way or the other about how they buried their dead. When he had been stationed at a fort in the high plains, the Indians lay their corpses on beds of tree limbs, set up high atop stilts. *So, these Cherokees want a funeral, huh? He thought. Well, why not give it a try? Heathens!*

After Long Rogers and a few of the men had accompanied the Army detail to the cemetery a few times, Welch began to relax while he was around some of the Indians. He could see that this Cherokee, Long Rogers, was somewhat different from the other ones, and began to gripe to him about his life in the Army. He shared his plans with him about leaving the service as soon as his enlistment was up.

"Every day, I have to sit here and watch all of your people go to the Territory to get rich, while I'm stuck out here in the backwaters of Alabama. If I wasn't tied down to the Army another year, I'd be on the next wagon train headed west," he told Long Rogers. "I'd like to get away from here right now. A year from now, the best places will be claimed."

Long Rogers always expressed sympathy for Welch's predicament, and pretended to take him into his confidence about his own problems. He told him about his inability to get to the buried treasure that he had been forced to abandon near his home.

"It's a shame we can't get to the gold that I buried. I was arrested before I could get to the nuggets hidden near a stump in the woods," he said mournfully. "One day, some lucky settler will accidentally plow them up, and they'll be rich for the rest of their lives."

Welch's ears had perked up once Long Rogers had used the word "nugget." The Indian had known how to reel the soldier into his scheme. It was a brilliant piece of workmanship, because most of the soldiers believed that the Indians had managed to hide their horde of gold before they had been captured.

In reality, every grain of gold he possessed was from Clyde's treasure. He had sent his own money to a territorial bank a few weeks ago, when things began to get a little "iffy" about his ability to stay in Alabama much longer. But, whoever it was who had been lucky enough to steal the wagon from the back of his house, would have already discovered the money pouch of cash that he had planned to use on his journey.

Now, he had to find a way to secretly use some of the gold in Clyde's pouch. He was down to the few silver dollars he had been carrying in his pockets when he'd been captured. So far, he had been able to use them to buy extra food for him and the women. He figured that the small amount of money he had left deposited in the Selma bank had been confiscated by the state. Long Rogers presented Welch with the last of his coins.

"I promise you that I'll work out one hell of a deal for you, if you can find a way to get me out of this place," he vowed to Welch.

When the soldier didn't shoot him for his proposal, nor seem to be insulted by his suggestion, Long Rogers felt that he had all of the encouragement he needed to expand on his offer. At that point of the negotiations, he had nothing to lose. It was absolutely necessary to find a way to convince Welch that it was possible for him to have a new, wealthy life away from the Army. The soldier would also have to be assured that it was better for him to leave the Army now, than to wait for his discharge from service at the end of the next year.

"You'll have the best of the deal," he reminded him, "the western territories are so vast that a man can easily get lost, escape his past, and never be discovered to be a deserter."

Welch walked away from Long Rogers, deep in thought. He had one hell of a decision to make. Right at that moment, he didn't know what he intended to do about the deal, But Long Rogers was wise, and he knew that he had captured the man's imagination. Eventually, he hoped that Welch would be powerless to turn down his offer. The Indian needed the soldier to help him find a way to escape from the fort. *Of course,* he thought, *the most difficult part of this will be the theft of the slave women.*

Several days later, after discarding several ideas, Long Rogers and Welch finally settled on a plot, but its successful outcome would depend on the soldier's ability to get his bootlegger partner to come in with them on the deal.

On Monday, as part of the arrangement made with the wary man, Welch made a new entry in the log. The names of two women slaves, Melinda and Eliza, were registered on the sick list. By the following Wednesday, their names were included on the list of the deceased.

Slave women owned by other Cherokee masters prepared the bodies and wrapped each of them in their blanket for burial. Welch made sure that word got around to the other soldiers that he suspected that the women had died of cholera. The bodies were to be interred immediately.

"It's best to let the Cherokees handle their own property. I'm not going anywhere near those bodies," he said. "They're beginning to stink, and I'd advise you to stay as far away from them as possible. We can watch them bury them from over there in the shade of the cottonwood."

The day was hot enough for heat waves to dance before their eyes, and the men were glad to join Welch as he sat in the shade. Most of them dismounted and strolled around the tree to hunt for a place to sit and take a smoke, while the Indians conducted the ceremony.

"I don't ever remember seeing them have a service for one of their slaves before, but who in hell knows what the red devils will do next?" asked one of the men.

The Cherokee men easily moved the two bodies from the wagon, laid them in a common grave, secretly slit holes into the blankets, and placed long Indian pipes into their mouths. They were just long enough to peep from the fill dirt. The men were hopeful that the women would be able to breathe underground for a few minutes. None of them could imagine the horror of being buried alive. They knew that any sane person would be scared to lay there and wait for someone to rescue them from a certain death by suffocation.

During the burial ceremony, the Cherokees distracted the soldiers with their loud chants. Long Rogers used that time to melt into the woods. When the soldiers mounted their horses for the return trip to the fort, Welch was the one who counted the Cherokees as they climbed back into the wagon.

Once the detail was out of sight, a sweat-soaked Long Rogers sprang from the woods, ran to the gravesite, and frantically dug at the soft soil to free the women. He brushed the soil from the blankets that covered their faces. Immediately, Melinda took a deep breath, shook her head, and coughed. But, Eliza lay deathly still with the pipe stem barely at the edge of her lips. Long Rogers was so frightened for her life that he began to violently shake her. Thankfully, she began to sputter, cough, and mutter incoherent words.

"Mama Liza," Melinda shouted, "wake up! What will happen to me if you die? I can't do any of this without you!"

The old woman tried to rouse herself, but she hadn't fully regained consciousness. When Eliza did open her old eyes, she was alarmed to find herself lying in the dirt. The other thing she noticed, was that tears were running down Melinda's face. Then she saw that the Indian was sitting cross-legged in the grave with them.

Long Rogers took a deep breath and nosily exhaled. He was relieved that both of them had survived the burial. It had been doubtful that the old woman would be strong enough to deal with such harsh treatment. *But, damned if that old crow hadn't made it out of that hole alive!*

He had to admit to himself that she had been as close to death as he would ever want to be, and gave both of them a sip of water from the leather flask he had bought from a Chickasaw who had used it to hold his whiskey, until he'd run out of money and had to trade it for a drink.

The fugitives continued to hug the dirt. Long Rogers decided that they should stay hidden in the grave. Eliza was still too weak to walk. Melinda enfolded the exhausted woman in her arms and held her close to her breast, until the tremors left her body. Sweat ran from her brow to mix with the sandy soil. After Eliza was a bit calmer, they laid her down on an indented place in the dirt so that she could sit sideways and rest her black, ashy face against the cool soil of the grave.

Melinda watched her closely. She hoped to see more signs that Eliza was recovering from her desperate escape from their underground imprisonment, but she was satisfied that her great-grandmother was able to speak, and could understand what she was saying to her. *That's enough progress for now*, she thought, *just stay alive my sweetie, I need you!*

"I've never been so scared," Melinda told her. "The thud of the dirt that covered our blankets is a sound that I doubt either of us will ever be able to forget. The soil was so heavy that it must have knocked your pipe from your mouth. Our hands were tightly wrapped across our breasts. It was impossible for either of us to get free."

She turned to Long Rogers. "Thank you for getting us out of there when you did. What did you use to open the grave and pull us out? I don't see a shovel."

Long Rogers explained how he had frantically retrieved them from the grave with his bare hands. Then, he fell silent, because he could feel a slight vibration in the soil that surrounded them. A few small stones from the fill dirt began to fall into the grave. They hushed their voices and hunkered down deep in the hole.

From a distance far across a large field, they heard the sound of a wagon as it approached their location. The women were alarmed, and frightened that the soldiers might have returned to the cemetery with another body to bury, before they had managed to escape.

Finally, when Long Rogers lifted his head up past the dirt pile, he heard a two-note whistle. It was the signal from his accomplice. Melinda tried to follow his gaze, and raised her head just high enough to see that the old bootlegger had arrived in his covered wagon.

"Am I glad to see you!" Long Rogers said, "I'll need your help to get the old woman into the wagon. She's just plumb tuckered out."

The bootlegger stepped down from the wagon, walked over to peer into the grave, and shook his head in wonder at the bravery of the slaves who had allowed themselves to be buried alive.

"I believe that it's the nature of every living critter on Earth to struggle to be free. But you women let those Indians hide you in a grave," he said. "Both of you have got to be a little bit touched in the head to agree to something like that." He reached his hand out to Eliza. "I sure as hell would never have done it. If you'd waited a few weeks, they'd have shipped you out of Alabama to the Territory without all this fuss."

"I thought about that, but the old one would have died on the march to the river. It was the only way to save her. She belongs to a chief, and I promised him that I'd do my very best to deliver her to him in the Territory. I aim keep my word."

After a struggle, the three of them managed to half drag Eliza onboard the wagon. The slaves settled on the boards with their blankets from the grave. A few hours later, when Long Rogers looked behind him from his seat in the front of the wagon, he saw that both of the exhausted women were asleep. They had succumbed to the rocking motion of the wagon.

When the sky was at the verge of the slightest tinge of nightfall, Welch joined up with the fugitives on the edge of the woods near the spot he and his partner had mapped out, a few miles from the fort. When he tied his horse to the rear of the wagon, Long Rogers moved inside so that Welch could sit on the seat next to the bootlegger. Originally, the soldier was supposed to have met up with them earlier in the day, but before he had been able to make his own escape from the fort, he and his men had been ordered to perform another burial.

"Well, old partner," Welch said to the bootlegger, "we've made about all the money to be had until the next batch of prisoners arrive. But don't worry about anything. I've already found a way for you to keep up your work. A buddy of mine by the name of Tom Wilks will be working with you. I can vouch for him. He'll be square with you."

"Next trip," the bootlegger told him, "I'll have two barrels of rot-gut with me. I plan to sell it by the cup. I've got a new head-banging recipe."

Later that night, the horses trudged their way back home on the familiar, well-worn track to Buffalo Mills. Finally, when the weary travelers arrived at the bootlegger's shack, they began to transfer their supplies from the inside his house to the wagon.

Once the men had tended to the horses, Welch and his buddy re-entered the stifling hot, stuffy cabin, and opened the doors and windows to air it out. Welch dropped his saddlebags to the floor, and reached into his pocket to pay the bootlegger for the supplies, and his wagon. Then, both of them lay down on the bed, and were asleep soon after their heads touched the straw-stuffed mattress.

The women washed their bodies in the rill behind the shack to rid themselves of the sandy dirt from the grave, but they were relieved to walk out of the deep woods, and climb back into the wagon. Long Rogers lay on his pallet beneath the wagon, looked out at the bright stars, and called them by name. He used the peace of the night to come up with a few ideas that would allow him to put a fine point on, and finesse the final touches of his scheme.

The morning air still held the touch of dewdrops when the wagon pulled away from the house. The bootlegger waved farewell to the travelers, and Welch promised to write to him as soon as he was settled. But, both men knew that they probably would not see each other again.

Later, around noon, Long Rogers steered the wagon toward a shallow path near a town not far from Selma. He took the trail through the woods towards his home so that he could "find" the hidden gold, and fulfill his obligation to Welch.

"I'm a man who keeps his word. Soon, it'll be time to dig for the treasure I've buried," he reminded Welch. "We're coming close to my property. Once I have those nuggets in my hands, we'll be able to leave our troubles behind us, and live the rest of our days out West."

Their wagon, horses, supplies, and new clothing had been bought from the bootlegger with the money Welch had saved from his salary, along with his cut of the whiskey money. He had already decided that he would kill the Indian if he found out that he'd been tricked. Deep down, he had known that he was taking a chance on the word of a dirty redskin, but, he also knew that this might be the once-in-a-lifetime opportunity to satisfy his desire to be a man of means.

I'm never, he vowed to himself, *going to be content to be a dirt farmer for the rest of my life. I refuse to push another plow behind some bony, worn out nag of a horse.*

Welch decided to let the Indian drive the wagon while he sat beside him on the front seat. He had traded the government horse to the bootlegger for the nice sorrel tied to the rear of the wagon. He had confidence that his clever ex-partner would find a way to change the brand, and get rid of the Army tattoo in the animal's mouth. He was right handy that way.

Welch planned to sell the wagon and the horses when they reached the boat landing. He would replace them when they were closer to the Territory.

Daybreak turned out to be the best time to travel. Their goal was to beat the worst of the heat of the late July days. Sultry Alabama was extremely hot by noon. Usually, Welch called a halt to their travel until the cool of the evening.

Within a week of their escape from the fort, Long Rogers told his fellow travelers that he had to be very careful not to be spotted by any of his old neighbors on his trek into the woods, for they would sound an alarm to the soldiers who had expelled him from the area.

When they were about five miles away from Selma, Long Rogers pulled off the road into a turn-a-round, and jumped down from the old wagon. He picked up the shovel attached to the side of the wagon, and advised Welch to be patient, because it would take him a bit of time to find the spot where he had buried the gold.

"All of you should to stay with the wagon and guard our supplies," he said to the others. "Don't wander around. It'd be dangerous for me to have to hunt for you in these woods."

After he melted into the pines, Melinda, Eliza, and Welch sat pensively waiting for his return, and peered into the forest to see if they could discover the place where he had gone.

Long Rogers watched them from his hiding place behind a large, sandstone rock with a flat table top. It was a safe place where he could crouch down, untie, and unroll Clyde's money pouch from around his waist. He found it difficult to separate the nuggets from the gold dust without getting specks of it all over the place. He estimated how much gold it would take to satisfy Welch's greed, and still have enough money to assure their safe passage on a riverboat.

Long Rogers wanted the man to be satisfied that he had received a fair portion of the gold for himself. Enough to begin his new life as a 'person of means.' That is how he'd described his wishes to him, and the Indian decided to reward the man handsomely for saving their lives.

At first, Long Rogers had worried that as soon as the soldier got his hands on the gold, he would desert them, but now he felt more secure of their position. After all, the man was now as much a wanted fugitive as he was. And, it was safer for him to travel with them, than to travel alone. He would be able to use them as a cover, and act as their master as

156

he traveled across the country. No one would suspect him of doing anything illegal.

An hour later, Long Rogers emerged from the woods while shaking dirt from his hands and clothing. He approached the wagon from the rear, and his sudden appearance startled Welch and the slaves. The soldier put his gun back into his holster. He had feared they had been found out by either the nosy neighbors, or the Army. All of them were relieved when the Indian climbed back into his seat in the wagon. There had been no guarantee that he would ever return.

From the looks of him, with so much dirt on his clothing, Welch surmised, *the Indian must have had to dig* a *very deep hole to get to the gold.* Welch held out both hands to Long Rogers, and received more gold than he had ever seen. A smile deepened on his face. *Yes*, he said to himself, *I'll enter the Territory a very rich man.*

Eliza looked at Melinda and winked. They watched the men as they handled the gold. A secret smile lit her face as she touched the gold-stuffed bag in the bodice of her dress.

Welch's plans, however, were slightly different from those he had described to Long Rogers. Now that he had the gold, he planned to kill the Indian as soon as they left the state of Alabama.

I wonder where he put the rest of the gold. All that digging in the woods probably produced a lot more gold than he forked over to me. Why shouldn't I have all of it?

Welch kept his eyes on the black wench. He had plans for her and her silky, caramel-colored skin. He did not intend to be bothered with the old mammy either. After he figured out a way to "accidentally" kill her, the girl would be alone, and he would present himself to her as her savior. *Once the old woman is dead, she'll be grateful for my protection.*

A man needed to bring his own woman to the wilderness. And he would keep her until he could find a suitable white woman to bear his children. But, meantime, she would do very nicely. Welch did not know anything about the value of slaves, but he would learn. *I'd have to be a complete fool not to understand that she's very valuable. Melinda will bring in a pretty penny when I get ready to sell her. Owning a slave,* he thought, *would be like having another gold nugget. I'll be able to sell her any time, any place, for anything I want.*

Neither Eliza, nor Melinda trusted the former soldier to get them safely to the Territory. They were aware of the fact that he had only

157

agreed to help them because he wanted to leave the Army, and he wanted the Indian's gold. And now that he had some of it, they watched him closely.

Their well-being depended on the Cherokee. A few days before their escape from the stockade, Welch had told Long Rogers that they were scheduled to take the ten-mile long walk to the boats. That fact had forced him to devise the elaborate escape plan that had freed them. They had agreed to follow his bizarre scheme, because Long Rogers had told the women that he didn't believe that Eliza would last one day on a forced march along the rough trail to the boat.

Melinda despised the way Welch watched her every move. His lingering gaze made her feel awkward and dirty. She did not want his attention. She was sure that there was something about the smirk on his face that was pure evil.

The beautiful slave girl always tried to keep Eliza close to her, and usually managed to sit as far away from the soldier as possible. The icy looks he sent to Eliza chilled Melinda to the bone. His aggressive behavior reminded them that he was the only one of them with a gun. They were at his mercy. Melinda figured that the Indian was in as much danger as they were.

As the wagon bounced along the trail towards the Tennessee River, near the north branch of the Warrior River, they began to relax, and dream of a future void of most of the problems they were leaving behind.

Long Rogers and Welch were anxious to board any riverboat ready to travel to the Territory. The most important item on their agenda, was to get the hell out of Alabama.

The men were tired of the salt pork and cornpone cooked by Eliza every day. Melinda agreed that she too was sick of the monotonous menu. While they were camped on the banks of a small lake, she decided to try to catch a few fish for dinner.

Melinda was able to dam a small portion of a narrow branch of water with rocks and logs just long enough to confuse the fish into entering her trap. Within an hour, she had caught a large carp. As the fish struggled to free itself from her grasp, she lost her balance and tumbled into the water. She came up sputtering. Once she had regained her stance, she became aware of the uproarious laughter from her trail-mates as they bent over, holding their sides, thoroughly amused at her antics.

The young girl stood there with a sheepish grin on her face, embarrassed that she had failed so miserably in her attempt to catch dinner. Then, she noticed that Welch was not laughing.

His eyes were glued on the way her wet shift hugged her body and caressed her curves. Eliza and Long Rogers could see that Welch had actually begun to tremble with excitement as he noted the heaviness of her perfect breasts, and the way her body was shadowed by the thin cotton material of the dress. His body was poised to spring into the water and grab her.

Although Melinda was aware of the danger of his menacing stance on the riverbank, she stood frozen, prey, unable to save herself. When his body tensed to run into the water, the Indian spat out one word:

"No!"

Long Rogers had not moved an inch, but the word stilled Welch's progress towards the girl. That single exclamation from the Indian was strong enough to let him know that he would have to shoot him, if he was determined to jump into the water and grab the girl.

And, if he had not needed them to continue the charade as his slaves, that is exactly what he would have done. But this time, he managed to regain control of his temper, shook the demon thoughts from his head, and walked back toward the woods.

Eliza walked down to the water's edge and handed her blanket to Melinda. After she had wrapped it around herself, she went inside the wagon to dry off. She handed her dress to Eliza through the canvas flap, to dry on the limbs of a bush.

The spell was broken. Welch walked away from the camp into the dense woods. When he had gone a few yards, he spotted a rabbit in the brush and decided to kill it for dinner.

"I'll be back later. Melinda's right, it's time to eat something besides salt pork and hardtack. Seeing that I'm the only one carrying a gun, I think it's up to me to go hunting for supper."

While the women were still in the wagon, and Welch was out hunting, Long Rogers used his time to weave a rabbit trap together from twigs and vines. He decided to set it every day. There would come the time when they were closer to a town and would not want to draw attention to themselves by the sound of gunfire.

Long Rogers decided to talk to Eliza about the girl. Up until today, they had both done a good job of hiding Melinda's beauty from the soldier, but now that he had seen her almost naked, they would really have to keep an eye on him. They had both seen that flare of raw passion in his eyes.

Later in the day, Welch returned to camp with a wild turkey flung across his shoulder. Before long, the women had cleaned it and had it roasting on the spit that Long Rogers had built. The deserter gathered a handful of the turkey feathers, mixed them in to a bouquet with white ones he had found in the woods, walked over to Melinda, and before Eliza could stop him, stuck the best of his treasure, a black feather with a red spot, into her long, raven-black braid.

In her innocence, Melinda thought that it was a nice thing for him to do, and felt that perhaps it was his way of showing her that he sympathized with her about her mishap earlier in the day. "Thank you," she said. "We really appreciate the turkey. After all, I failed to get us the fish." He smiled, entranced with her dimpled cheek when she said, "At least, you were able to provide a meal that had nothing to do with pig meat!"

Eliza and Long Rogers said nothing, but they both felt pangs of uneasiness in their guts. They knew that it would be necessary to redouble their efforts to keep the girl safe.

Chapter Thirteen
The Voyage to Arkansas

Three weeks after their escape from prison, Welch and his three slaves stepped aboard a riverboat that was tied up to a wharf far from the main landing place. Once he was settled into his quarters, Welch slept in his comfortable bed, while his slaves slept under a tarp he had provided for them on the deck. At last, they were on a boat in the Tennessee River, headed towards the wilderness lands on the other side of the Mississippi River.

Once they had boarded the boat, Welch had assumed his new identity. He was now a man named Charles Locke, a rich settler relocating to the new territory. Although he took precautions against being discovered as a deserter, there was not much chance that anyone would identify him. Almost all of the soldiers from his fort were tied up with relocation plans for the Indians and their slaves. *By the time they recover from their march from the fort to the river, I'll be far from Alabama,* he thought.

The riverboat was packed with a varied assortment of people, their horses and oxen. There were a few wagons from a Tennessee fort, escorted by soldiers on their way to Fort Gibson.

Scattered among the passengers were a few rich Cherokees who had managed to emigrate with their fortunes intact. They seldom left their cabins to mix with those Indians of different tribes, and none of them tried to communicate with Long Rogers.

The slaves were completely dependent on "Locke," their master, to provide them with decent food, ample clothing, and the canvass cover on the deck. They were at the mercy of a man who routinely spent money at every port. Long Rogers, as part of his disguise, could not spend or possess gold.

"I bought me a pair of beautiful Tennessee Walkers," Locke boasted to some of the other men. "I'll ride this one, and the other will pull the buggy when I take my slaves home."

They were nearing their destination in the Territory. The next time he sat down near Long Rogers, he had a decent conversation with him.

161

"By now," he said, "some of your folks should be waiting for you to reach the Territory. It shouldn't take you long to hear from them. Most likely, they'll be at Fort Gibson, or Sallisaw. I'll be leaving you before that happens. I was stationed out here a few years ago, so there's a remote possibility that someone might be able to recognize me. No use tempting fate. There's plenty of wide open country out here, and there's no reason I need to go anywhere near there."

After a month of sailing on the muddy, unforgiving Mississippi river, they entered the waters of the mouth of the Arkansas River, at Ozark. The sweet water was a godsend, especially so for the children. Many of them were ill.

When the soldiers took inventory, they recorded ten deaths among the passengers. One woman had died during childbirth, while another had lost her life when her child was a week old. Two slaves had committed suicide when they had jumped overboard, four men had died of fever, and two children had been defeated by red measles.

On September 5, the boat pulled into a landing a short distance from Fort Smith, Arkansas. By then, so many of the passengers suffered from different illnesses, that the commanding officer was forced to order wagons to transport the majority of them from the boat to the garrison.

After a thorough inspection, the commander decided that the travelers would need at least two weeks of rest before any of them were fit enough to continue their trek.

"That'll give us time to refit the boat and resupply the food," he said. "By that time, they should be in better shape to complete their voyage to the Sallisaw riverboat landing. I'm doing all that I can to help them, but there's a chance that they might lose another child today."

According to Sheriff Clinton Coulter, that sun-filled September day would always be remembered by him as the day that changed the course of the rest of his life. He was at the fort because he had just solved a case of cattle rustling by catching the settler red-handed with a branding iron in the fire. He had committed his crime near Jessup Township, where he was sheriff. Ordinarily, the townspeople would have strung him up in the nearest hanging tree, but by law, the black town could not try, or hang a white man. Therefore, he had brought the scoundrel to the base commander to seek retribution for his crimes. Sheriff Coulter asked Commander Reid to exile the settler from the Territory before he could get into more mischief.

"I can't be responsible for his safety if he comes anywhere near the town again," he said. "If the owner of the cattle discovers that he's still in the area, the man will find a way to make sure that he suffers some kind of punishment, just short of killing him. I can't babysit him. If I hadn't sneaked off with him before dawn, the men would have thought of a way to retaliate. Then, your soldiers would have been ready to turn the town to ashes."

"So far," the commander said, "Jessup Township has been one of the best-run towns in Arkansas, and I agree that banishment is the best remedy for his crime, but, how in hell would we know if he decided to come back?"

"I really can't say, but I know what you mean about him. Usually there's no cure for a rustler. Let's hope that the next time he steals a steer, it belongs to someone who can hang him. Believe me, that critter knew exactly what he was doing. He knew that we were powerless to hang him, unless we were ready to put our own lives on the line."

Once he released the prisoner into the custody of the commander, Clinton stepped outside into the brightness of the noon day, and greeted several of the men he was acquainted with. He walked into the sutler's store to buy a plug of tobacco, then stopped by the blacksmith's.

Clinton hoped to convince the man that it would be well worth his time to come to his town, shoe some horses, and respond to the message he'd brought with him from Salty Sal.

"She told me to tell you that she was looking forward to spending more time with you. She's been a widow for two years now. She's getting lonely. Salty Sal is not a gal you're going to be able to leave by herself very long. She wants company!"

"Tell her to give me a few weeks, and I'll load up the wagon and head her way. I've been thinking that I need to get away from the wilderness, and finally settle down in town, but the money is good here at the fort. More than I could ever make in town."

But after he weighed his options, he said: "Well, money's not everything. And it sure don't keep a man's feet warm during a cold winter's night. The more I think about it, it seems to me that Salty Sal might use her very lovely, fat feet to warm my bed."

The two men laughed uproariously at the blacksmith's joke. Tolliver slapped him on the back as he headed outside. And as soon as he stepped into the yard of the hot, open shack of the forge, the gates of the

163

fort burst open in a gush of dust-laden air, to admit a wagon train of weary looking travelers. It had seemed to him that this one was larger than most of the groups he'd seen traveling through Arkansas that time of the year. Clinton's heart filled with compassion for the slave prisoners. He watched them enter the fort the same way he had twenty years ago, under almost the same circumstances.

"At least," he said to the blacksmith who now stood at his side, "they don't have slave collars around their necks like I did." The ironsmith could not bear another moment of the pain he felt as he watched the poor wretches enter the fort. He walked back inside his shack.

Clinton closed his watering eyes and sorrowfully held his face behind his helpless hands. He was stunned when he raised his bowed head in time to look into the striking, hazel-colored eyes of an unusual-looking, beautiful, caramel-colored slave woman. She was clutching the arms of an old mammy: a woman much too old to be her mother. She was gracefully seated in a small carriage pulled by a Tennessee Walker. It seemed to Clinton that she held herself as if she were seated on a throne.

Behind her, a row of heavy wagons filled with Indians was followed by a line of walking, rope-tied slaves. Unconsciously, Clinton began to run alongside the wagon, eyes fastened to hers. The wheels of the carriage ground to a halt, and he watched as a white man directed his Indian driver. The slaves got out of the carriage, and when they stepped to the ground, they had stiffly stretched their travel-worn bodies.

Clinton practically ran back to Commander Reid's office, and asked to be allowed to enter. He was as excited as he had ever been in his life, and did not realize that he was shouting.

"Sir," he yelled, "I need your help!"

"Hold on there, Sheriff Coulter, what's the matter? Got a bee in your bonnet? "

"Yes Sir, I guess you're mighty right about that. I would definitely say that's the truth," he said.

"Here's every penny I own," he said excitedly, as he pulled a leather bag from beneath his deerskin shirt.

"A wagon train just pulled into the yard, and just possibly, I've found a reason to hope a black man might be able to buy himself a brighter future. There's a woman sitting out there. She just stepped out of a carriage. If you agree to play along with my plan, there's the possibility that I could end up with her as my wife!"

"I want you to know that you're not making one bit of sense. Have you gone daft?"

"Please help me get her out of this mess. It's hard to explain this to anyone who has not lived in slave country, and I realize that you don't know one thing about the rules of the slave trade. So let me see if I can simplify the matter for you," he said.

Clinton took a deep breath, and launched into his explanation, the best he could.

"I need you to act as my agent, and offer to buy a slave woman from her master. I'm almost sure that I have enough money to buy her, but, as a black man, I'm not allowed to approach her master and make an offer for her. If you decide to help me buy her, you'll have to be aware of the fact that he'll ask for an outrageous amount of money for her. He'll expect you to make a counter offer, but don't argue. Give him whatever he wants for her."

Commander Reid hailed from Boston, and could not understand why the sheriff could not make the offer himself. He did not want to become involved in the slave trade. If anyone discovered that he had participated in such a dishonorable practice, he would be ashamed of the fact for the rest of his life. He was sympathetic of the sheriff's problem, but he did not have any desire to get involved.

"Sir, most slave owners don't like the idea of any black person having enough money to seriously bid for the freedom of another one, especially if they are not kin. They think that it sets a bad example for other owners. They are of the opinion that there are too many of us free ones in the West."

Reid scratched his dry beard with his thumb, sat back in his chair, and considered Clinton's plea. The longer he thought about the situation, the more he had to admit to himself that what the sheriff had said was probably true. And, in this wild country, it must have been almost impossible for a black man to find a wife.

"My only hope of ever getting that woman," Clinton reminded him, "is that he believes that you are the buyer."

After mulling over the facts of the matter, and realizing how truly lonely the man seemed to be, the commander felt that the highly respected lawman deserved a break. Now, Commander Reid had to decide how

165

to accept the fact that this man had just handed him an enormous bag of gold. *How in hell had a black man put his hands on so much gold? Surely, he hadn't collected that much bounty money,* he thought. But, in the way of the West, he did not question the man. He trusted him, and accepted the fact that he was an honest man. Reid kept his mouth shut, and decided to intercede and try to help the sheriff purchase the woman. He stood, pulled on the jacket to his uniform and headed for the door, while Clinton continued to school him on the nuances of slave buying.

As the commander walked across the middle of the parade grounds, Locke spotted him, and began to fidget with his collar. The commander came forward, introduced himself, and asked him a few questions about his trip from Alabama.

The clothing he had bought for himself, resembled that worn by a riverboat gambler. He had grown his hair longer, and sported a neat beard. Now, he walked with a swagger, and no longer carried himself with bearings of a military man. In the short span of time that had passed since he'd changed his identity, he had successfully transformed himself into his version of a southern gentleman. His hands shook as he nervously smoked a cigar.

Reid sized the man up, paid notice to the cheap suit and the strong cologne he'd splashed all over his body. *You can smell him a mile away,* Reid thought, *if he doesn't tone down some of that perfume, he's going to have to fight someone in every saloon in the Territory.* The soldier felt like holding his nose, but he managed to continue the conversation.

Locke plumped out his chest when Reid said that it was nice to have a gentleman in their midst. And when he invited him to dinner in his quarters, Locke accepted.

At dinner, Clinton Coulter pretended to be the cook, and served the meal. He watched closely as the men ate, and seemed to enjoy the other's company. When Reid questioned Locke about the possibility of buying his young slave, Locke seemed hesitant to discuss the possibility of a sale. *He must want to keep her to himself,* thought Clinton.

"It's lonely out here in the wilderness without my wife," Reid said. "She prefers to stay in Boston. That wouldn't bother me so much if I could have that lovely girl to warm my blankets. If we can agree on the price, I'd really like to have her. She's young enough to earn her keep. I'll hire her out as a laundress. She'll be a legal resident of the fort, and I'll pocket the profits."

"Forget about her," Locke said. "She won't go anywhere without that old mammy. She's as stubborn as a mule."

Although Locke was greedy enough to sell her, he knew that he would never be able to separate her from the others, and, he still had an itch for her himself. But he knew how to get this man to shut up and stop worrying him about Melinda. He decided to have a little fun with him before he left the table. He would pretend to be interested in the sale, name an outlandish price, and watch Reid's face when he realized he could never hope to buy her.

"She's what the trade calls a fancy," he told the commander, "I couldn't think of letting her go for less than two thousand dollars. She would bring in three thousand in New Orleans, he announced with a sly grin.

When Commander Reid pulled out the money pouch to pay Locke, the deserter almost lost his breath. *Where in hell did a soldier get that kind of money?* Locke wondered.

Immediately, Locke back-tracked, and invented a new story. "I haven't been completely honest with you. I never dreamed you'd have enough money to buy her," he said truthfully, "and I thought I'd impress you with her value. But, the truth is, she has already been sold. I'm on this trip to the Territory to deliver her to her new owner. He'd kill me if I failed to deliver her."

Clinton hung his head in defeat as Commander Reid offered Locke a thousand dollars more, and the man refused the offer, and stuck to his story.

Reid, however, felt that the man was lying about the sale for some reason. There was something oily about the man. He was disappointed that he had failed to help the sheriff buy the woman. He had seen her from a distance, and he could tell that once she'd shed the dirt from the trail, she would be gorgeous, absolutely beautiful. Sheriff Coulter had good taste. Too bad things did not work out for him. *How will the man deal with his disappointment?*

Clinton was forced to absorb the bad news, but at the same time, he made up his mind that even though the man had refused to sell the girl to Reid, it was not the end of the story. In that moment, he made up his mind to follow the slaves and their master until he discovered who her new owner was, and then, he would find a way to make an offer of everything he owned, for her.

After dinner was finished, and Locke left Reid's quarters, Clinton told him what he planned to do. "When they resume their trip to the Territory, I want to find a way to be a passenger on that boat too," he said. "I'm willing to do whatever it takes to win her heart. I just pray that I can persuade her to start thinking the same way about me."

Commander Reid gave Clinton what information he'd managed to glean from the settler.

"Her name is Melinda," he informed him.

"Oh my goodness, even her name sounds sweet. But just looking at her, something tells me that she's a little spitfire. Now that I've seen her, no other woman will do. I've become obsessed with the idea of claiming her for my own."

Clinton knew that he would follow her until the silent promise and wonder in her eyes were his to keep. "I think what touches me most, is the fact that I'd never even thought that such a beautiful creature actually lived and breathed. She's the very thing that dreams are made of."

None of the many white, slave, or Indian women he had ever seen, could approach Melinda's beauty.

The next morning, Clinton sat among some of the soldiers and listened to them describe the rough trip down the Mississippi. Locke, his slaves, and the Cherokees, had encountered many difficulties on their way to Arkansas. The deaths of ten people during the trip had robbed many of the passengers of their will to live.

"They'll need at least two weeks of rest before they re-board the boat for the final leg of the journey," said the sergeant.

That was the best news Clinton could have heard. It gave him time to make some adjustments to his life. The sheriff left the fort on his sorrel, and after attending to a matter in a nearby town, he headed down the road towards his home in Jessup Township. Within a day, the muscular, powerfully built man stepped into his office, greeted his second-in-command, and arranged to have his deputy take over his duties and keep a careful eye on the sometimes difficult inhabitants of the town.

Clinton felt that Anderson was sharp enough to keep everything under control until he returned from his trip. He needed to take off time from duty so that he could follow Melinda, and the man who owned her, to her new master's place somewhere in the Territory.

It was absolutely necessary for him to stay nearby until Locke had consummated the deal with the new owner. Then, Clinton planned to make an offer on both Melinda and her old mammy.

He was taking one hell of a gamble. It was very dangerous for a black man to admit that he owned gold, but he had decided that he would just have to take his chances, for there would never be another time when he might be able to save Melinda. And, there was no limit to what he was willing to go through to have her.

The gold nuggets and gold dust he carried beneath his shirt were from an unregistered claim he had discovered two miles out of town. If word got out that there was gold to be had near Jessup, miners would move in, destroy the town, and the government would find a way to run all the black people off their land. Clinton was not foolish enough to think that he would ever be allowed to claim ownership to a gold mine. So far, he had contented himself with whatever gold he could pan, and had not disturbed the ground surrounding the stream.

The land was as pristine as it had been when he had found the first nugget. *One day,* he thought, *perhaps it'll be safe enough for me to mine it.* He had been lucky enough to sell some of the gold to a riverboat gambler who had traveled through Jessup on his way to Fort Smith, to catch a boat headed to New Orleans. He had not asked Clinton any questions.

When the sheriff had purchased the land, the townspeople were relieved. They had encouraged him to put down permanent roots in the town. Several of them complemented him on his choice of several large lots, and told him that he had made a wise investment. Primarily, because of the icy-cold spring water that ran through the claim.

Most of them had used the waterhole at one time or another. Long ago, the Indians had nailed antlers to a cottonwood tree to mark the location of the spring.

Clinton was watering his horse when he found the first nugget. Later, it had been easy for him to pan for the gold without anyone becoming suspicious of the activity, because he had limited himself to a few hours of exploration at a time.

Clinton had never used any of his gold in Jessup. Now, he hoped that the hoarded treasure would be enough to establish his future with Melinda. His greatest desire was to create a family with her. He wanted to replace some of those that he had been robbed of. He did not want to

169

live the rest of his life as a lawman. And Jessup Township was as good a place as any to raise children.

The sheriff wanted a new life. He was tired of being haunted by the terrors he had suffered in the past. *I deserve to be a real part of this country I've helped to create.*

Clinton had worked most of his life as a free laborer, and had worked to help his master to realize his dreams. But now that he was free, he was determined to have a small part of his life comforted by the love of Melinda. There was a chance that she could heal his damaged heart.

Within two weeks, he had returned to Fort Smith. He was pleasantly surprised when he discovered that Commander Reid had arranged passage for him on the riverboat.

"I've got a job for you," he announced. "You can do me a favor, while you take care of your business. On your way back, I want you to pick up a murdering thief by the name of Almony. The sheriff has him sitting in a jail cell in Bonanza. I want you to bring him here to the fort. I intend to hang him. When you get him be very careful, he's a mad-dog of a man. This is the third bank he's robbed. This time, two men died. Rattlesnakes don't come any meaner."

Once Clinton was aboard the boat with the immigrants, he tried to locate Melinda. He squinted against the glare of the morning sunlight. When he finally found her, she was sitting cross-legged under a tarp with her mammy. She turned, and a smile lit her face when he looked straight into her wonderful eyes. Her heart flip-flopped. Melinda tried to take a deep breath and calm herself down.

Oh my goodness, she thought. *Once he left the fort, I didn't dream that I'd ever see him again!* For the most part of the last two weeks, she had asked Long Rogers to ask the men around the fort if they knew anything about him. She had felt some kind of connection to him, and then one day he had just disappeared. She had felt let-down and deserted, and wondered where he had gone. Melinda had asked herself why Clinton hadn't felt the same way she had--that they shared a common bond? Or, had she just created a fantasy about a man who had not bothered to tell her that he was leaving?

Long Rogers thought about the day he had sat on the steps of the fort commander's Quarters and listened to Locke as he had pretended that he could sell Melinda. He'd heard every word. For a brief moment, he had thought the man was serious. He was certainly greedy enough to try to

170

pull a dirty deal like that. Long Rogers had made up his mind to kill him. But, after a while, he realized that Locke was just twisting the commander's tail. But it had made him decide then and there, that if Locke ever tried to sell either slave, he would expose him as a deserter. He had given his word to Starr Night that he would bring the women to New Warrior, and that was exactly what he was going to do, come hell or high water.

Clinton had been willing to travel hundreds of miles, for the chance to save Melinda. It took his breath away when he dared to think of the consequences if he failed in his attempt to secure her release. The very sight of this woman overwhelmed him, and he wanted to always be close enough to her to admire her beauty, and be dazzled by the sunlight in her beautiful face. The overwhelming feeling in his heart was that nothing would ever happen to him that could possibly surpass the contentment of beholding her serenity. As she sat there, he suddenly knew that his reason for being alive was to be with her forever. He had to make that happen, or both of them would be lost.

Eliza watched as the tall, handsome man continued to follow the movements of her fascinated great-granddaughter. She could almost see the tension in the air. Both of them seemed to be mesmerized at the mere presence of the other. The man looked at Melinda with so much love in his eyes that she decided right then and there to invite the Freedman to sit with them and share the fatback and cornbread she had cooked for the morning meal.

Clinton was delighted to accept her generous invitation, and they were joined by Long Rogers, who immediately began to question the stranger. He was astounded to learn that it was possible anywhere in the country for a black man to be a sheriff, or have the power or nerve to arrest some of the worst criminals in the West.

"It's a hell of a way to make a living," he told Clinton. "And you ride alone, and don't have a deputy to watch your back. You're lucky to be alive. There are bushwhackers on every trail."

Clinton shrugged. "When I was a slave, I learned to have a second sense, and a finely tuned set of survival skills. So far, they've kept me a step ahead of my enemies."

Now that a crewman had told him that the black man was a lawman, Locke made sure to give him a wide berth. He was reasonably sure that he had little power to arrest him outside the state of Arkansas. Evidently, he didn't make much money and would do anything to earn his keep, or he would not have had to moonlight as a servant for the commander of the fort. But, he did not want to take a chance that he would become curious enough about him to ask the soldiers to take a closer look at him.

Locke was disgusted at the way the man looked at Melinda. He did not like it one bit. He had that puppy dog look in his eyes. *That bastard will ruin my plans if I'm not careful,* he thought. *The women and the Indian had better have sense enough to keep their mouths closed about me.*

So far, everything had gone the way he wanted it to. Even the Indian had been easy to get along with. Locke figured he would have to speak to Long Rogers about the black man, and set him straight. They did not need the complications this man could bring into their lives. Better to cut him loose before he could put any kinks in their plans.

When Melinda and Eliza were left alone, the young girl giggled as she told her great-grandmother how much she liked the attractive lawman. Those dimpled good looks, strong built body, and wide shoulders, brought Clinton to the attention of quite a few women sailing on the boat.

"Did you notice the way his hair peeped from under his hat? When he took it off, it reached all the way to his shoulders. I know he looks good, but what I really admire about him, is that he's found a way to make a decent living as a free man. He's already earned the position as a peacemaker among the unlawful, hard men of the wilderness," said Eliza.

"The bad thing about his job is there'll always be someone who feels that they have to challenge his right to man the position. But, I have the sense that Clinton is definitely capable of defending himself," Melinda answered.

As the days of the voyage rolled past, Melinda and Clinton used the time to become better acquainted. One of their favorite things to do was to stroll around the decks of the boat. They took the time to tell each other the stories of their lives. Clinton listened carefully as the orphan described the loss of her parents and brother.

"I wasn't aware of their deaths until Long Rogers told us about a letter he received from Chief Starr Night, a few weeks before we were captured in Selma."

Then, on another day, she told him of the horrible sale of her aunts to a slave-master from Georgia. He held her to him, and when the tears she had suppressed in front of Eliza rolled down her cheeks, Clinton encouraged her to let go of the bottled-up pain.

Later, when she told Clinton of the loss of most of the members of three generations of her family within three years, he looked into her sad face, and saw the strength of the blood from her black, red, and white ancestors. Her beautiful plaited hair was a gift from the Cherokees, and her softly shaded skin spoke both of the white man and the African. Her blended racial features had produced a creature of rare beauty. But her most striking feature was her gentle countenance.

Later, just before the boat pulled into a small landing, they took another walk around the deck while Melinda listened to Clinton's stories about his life as a Freedman. She was enchanted when he told her the stories about the little place on the map called Jessup Township.

"Some of us escaped from the lowland cotton plantations in the delta. But gradually, we've attracted Freedmen and their families to the town, Clinton explained. "Now we're armed, and strong enough to defend ourselves from those who would re-enslave us."

The sheriff went on to tell Melinda about the beauty of the area.

" Jessup is located in the foothills of the most thickly forested land in the area. Slaves aren't needed there, because there are only a few small subsistence farms. When the town was first built, there were raids by patrollers looking for runaways, but now we have finally grown large enough to shoo them away. The Indians who live among us are not slave owners."

"One day, if I live long enough to come back to Arkansas, I'm going to come visit that town. It's hard for me to believe that there's a place where black people are free. Sometimes, it's hard to believe that you don't belong to anyone. You're the first Freedman any of us have ever met."

Of course Clinton wanted all of her dreams to come true. But, he could not make her any promises, nor could he fully express his love for her. At the same time, Melinda didn't think that she was free to tell him that she did not belong to Locke.

The sheriff toyed with the idea of telling her about his plans to buy her from her new owner, but through pitiful necessity, both of their hearts were wrapped in layers of secrets. Instead of talking, Clinton dipped his head, and touched her sweet lips to his. Melinda thought that she would surely faint. *How wonderful!* She thought. She could hardly believe she had shared her first kiss with this wonderful man. Of course Clinton pretended to be calm, and tried to act as if he had not been stunned by the kiss. In reality, his heart threatened to explode with excitement. Weak-kneed, he gently released her from his embrace. She reached for his hand, and they resumed their walk around the deck. But both of them continued to keep their secrets down in the deep recesses of their hearts.

Melinda squeezed his hand, and Clinton's hope soared. *There's always the chance,* he thought, *that we might be able to carve a little place for ourselves out of the chaos in our lives.*

"What if we?" and "how can we?" dominated their thoughts. They wanted to be together forever.

When Locke rounded the corner of the deck and saw that Melinda was wrapped in Clinton's arms, he was shocked. He had not been aware that their relationship had progressed to the point that she would let him kiss her. Now, there would only be one way to get rid of him. He would have to kill him before he messed up his plans. He had to find a way to get Melinda away from the two people who had made it their business to keep him away from her.

He certainly did not have a moral problem with murder. As a soldier, he had been paid by the government to kill the enemies of the state. And, as far as he was concerned, that black sheriff fit the bill. *I'll have to be very careful, but I will eliminate my enemy.*

During the voyage, Locke had made friends among the sailors, and a few of the desperately poor Cherokee men. He plied them with whiskey at every boat landing, and before long, he was able to pick out those men he wanted in his gang. He felt the need to hire the men to do some of the dirty work he had planned. The Cherokee men he picked were in need of some kind of security in their fractured lives, and Locke promised them that he could be depended on for steady employment and a place where they would belong.

After being torn from their families in the East, the men, all of them handy with a gun, would be ideal trail mates, and indispensable once they reached Indian Territory.

When the boat reached Sallisaw on October 2, the air was crisp, and the trees were bathed in scarlet, orange, and yellow. Long Rogers, glad to be off that boat, took a good look around the town, and was pleased to find that it was well-developed, and included a general store, bakery, haberdashery, post office, newspaper, barbershop, and of course,

174

two saloons. Whiskey was illegal in most of the Territory, but there were more bootleggers within a square mile than preachers. Several of the streets boasted painted houses, and there was a school for the many children running around the town.

They were two days away from Fort Gibson, but still clear across the country from Kiowa country. The travelers were careful to get plenty of rest, and prepared themselves for what lay ahead of them. Soon, they would tackle one of the most demanding parts of their journey, the final push along the rough trail to Fort Gibson. But, the reward for their diligence would be that many of them would be able to reunite with their family members who were already residents of the Territory.

Long Rogers sure hoped that Starr Night had received his wire in July, and had made flexible arrangements for someone to be there to greet him and the slaves. He thought, *maybe, I'll give it a day or two to see who shows up, and then, if we seem to be stranded, I'll send him another wire.*

While he waited for someone to contact him, he decided that it was time to get a much needed haircut. After the barber had finished the trim to his hair, he looked into the mirror, and was pleased with the results. He stepped from the chair, gave the barber a generous tip, walked onto the wooden sidewalk with a smile plastered on his face, and deeply inhaled the autumn air. His eyes opened wide with surprise when he sensed the bullet that whizzed by his right cheek.

Long Rogers felt the heat of the lead before the sound of the shot reached his ear. He dived behind the water barrel, and it was pierced by the second round. The water spilled down the dusty street, but since he did not possess a weapon, wisely, he stayed hidden. Then he heard the sound of fast paced horses thundering away from his position.

The Indian raised his head and saw the Sheriff of Sallisaw and his deputy run from the jail. They had drawn their guns, but were too late to challenge the two horsemen who were galloping out of town. The men walked over to Long Rogers. He was dusting himself off, now that the men rode off hell's bells down the road.

"Who wants you dead, Stranger?"

"Damned if I know. I've only been in town a couple of hours."

"If that's so, I'd have to say that you brought the trouble to town with you, mister."

Long Rogers agreed with the sheriff's assessment of the situation, and knew that there could only be one answer to the question, for there was only one person who could possibly want him dead: Locke. But he asked himself, *Why? Is he trying to get the rest of the gold? Does he want to steal the slaves?*

Still standing in the street, the men were startled when they heard the report of another two rounds of gunfire. The sheriff and his deputy ran to the other end of town towards the big barn. That is where most of the poorer Cherokees and their slaves were housed. As they neared the commotion, they could see confused and panic-stricken people pouring out of the large shelter towards a hoped-for safe hiding place in the dense woods.

Long Rogers entered the barn behind the armed lawmen, and saw that Melinda was sobbing. She was sitting on the dirt floor, covered in a spreading cowl of blood, as she held Sheriff Clinton Coulter's head in her lap. He was sprawled motionless on the hay-scattered floor. From a cursory look at him, the men figured there was a good possibility that the wound to his head would prove to be a fatal one. Long Rogers was very sad. He and the black man had united for a common cause during their journey: the safe passage of the women to their new owner. He was aware that Melinda had not told Clinton the name of her master, or that once she was in New Warrior, she would be reunited with her grandfather.

He considered the sheriff to be his new friend and ally. When he turned around to survey the damage to the barn, he noticed that Eliza was sitting quiet. She seemed to be in a state of shock. Both women were stunned.

"Run, go get Doc!" shouted the lawman. He recognized Sheriff Coulter from the time he had backed him up during a showdown with one of the most dangerous men in the country. Now he was afraid that his old friend was mortally wounded. He had seen many gun-shots, and this one was nasty.

"But," he said to Long Rogers, "Old 'Doc' is pretty good at mending and sewing the bumps and scrapes of our town. If he can be saved, I believe Doc might just be the one to pull him through. I damn-near hope so."

Long Rogers watched two of the Cherokee men drift back into the barn. He asked them to go on a very important mission for him.

"Find the medicine man for me. Ask him to come here and do what he can to save my friend."

The men noted his distress, saw the desperation in his eyes, and turned and sped away in two different directions in search of the healer.

When both doctors arrived at the barn, they found it difficult to pry Melinda's arms from around the injured man, but eventually, she had been forced to let the black-frocked doctor and the feather-wearing medicine man administer to their critically injured patient.

They completely undressed him while they searched for more wounds. The men removed his heavy money-belt from his waist, and handed it to Melinda. By the way she was grieving, they assumed that she had to be his woman.

Eliza walked over to her baby, wrapped her in her arms, and convinced her to leave Clinton's fate in the hands of the skilled healers. She watched as they laid him on a board to keep him steady while Doc removed the slug from his head and sewed up the wound. The medicine man applied an herb-tinged salve on the wound, and wrapped a bandage embedded with an eagle's feather around his head. Now that both of them had done their part in the healing, each of them, in their own way, prayed for the survival of the giant.

Chapter Fourteen
Lockewood

Three weeks before Clinton's shooting, Locke had discovered that he had a great deal in common with the riverboat pilot and some of his crewmen. All of them were white men who were quite resentful about the way that their window of time to become settlers was rapidly fading away from them. Every time they brought a boatload of the damned Indians and blacks to the Territory, their chances of claiming a large tract of property for themselves shrank. But, the men were determined that they would find a way to get in on the next land bonanza. They had not given up on the possibility that sooner or later, a good deal would come their way.

And within the week, according to some passengers they had picked up in Arkansas, they picked up on a bit of information about a settler who planned to sell his claim, then head back to his old family place in Virginia.

When the pilot told a few of his men about the possibility of getting their hands on a prime piece of land, they agreed to pool their money together so that they could make a bid on the property. But it had not taken very long for the men to realize that they needed a partner who had a little cash to boost their buying power. Their pitiful savings from their sailor's pay was not nearly enough to tempt any landowner into selling his land to them.

During the last leg in the voyage to Sallisaw, the pilot approached Locke with an offer to get in on a sure-fire deal. And after he listened to what the pilot had to say, the deserter became consumed with the idea that he should become his partner in the scheme. The pilot told Locke about the large, mainly undeveloped claim near Tahlequah.

"And," he said, "from what I've heard about that land, it's ready to be sub-divided into lots. But the problem with it is that it's so far away from the beaten track. The owner wasn't able to attract families to the area. He'd planned on developing that place into a good-sized town, but evidently, he failed to advertise the benefits of settling down in a place with ready access to water."

Immediately after studying the map, Locke could see that the land was located far enough from the fort that he probably would not have to deal with any sort of interference from government representatives from Fort Gibson. He could not foresee any problems surrounding their plan to buy the 150 acres of land.

Locke put Long Rogers in charge of the slave women, while he joined the expedition to inspect the land. And as soon as the boat pulled up to the pier near Akins, he and several members of his gang--the pilot, and some of the crew-- saddled up their horses and rode off into the interior, while the boat resumed its course towards their destination in Sallisaw.

On the short ride to the claim, Locke and the pilot agreed to share equally in the profits of any deal they might manage to grab hold of. Locke was positively jovial as he rode along with the men. Once they had made camp for the night, the rough sailors, Cherokee men, and the pilot, listened to his stories of adventures in the East, and counted themselves lucky to have stumbled into such a fine gentleman.

Of course, Locke thought to himself, *eventually, while the pilot works on the riverboat, I'll be in town selling lots. He'll make a small profit, but he just might end up losing his stake after a time. One thing's for sure, he can't keep an eye on the land, if he intends to carry on with his work on the riverboat with his voyageurs.*

Another thing that the pilot and Locke had in common was their jealousy of the people they had provided services to. They had acted as guides and provided protection for them, but now, both of them wanted their share of the wealth. They had been stuck in low paying jobs, until this golden opportunity had fallen in their laps. If they had spent the rest of their lives in the United States, they would have been doomed to spend their time connected to the dirt-poor, penniless families who had spawned them. But, If they could successfully grab this land, it could prove to be their chance to escape the unyieldingly, hard labor of the lower classes.

Locke felt that it was his right to search for the chance to gain some of the enormous wealth of the unspoiled land of the West. *All a man has to have*, he thought, *is the nerve to go after his dream.* He was prepared to wrestle a good living out of the land. The West was the place where a man had a chance to re-invent himself.

In the early morning light, he sat by himself and watched the riverboat men gamble their money away, and made up his mind that he would find a way to make himself the sole-surviving partner of the deal. He'd left the Indian and the women slaves on the boat, then he had sent two of his men to ride ahead of the riverboat on horseback. Their job was to hang around the streets of Sallisaw for the chance to eliminate his rival for Melinda. *That sheriff might be strong as a bull, but he sure as hell won't be able to dodge a bullet,* he thought, as a smile lit his face.

Locke was determined that the black man would die, just as soon as his men had a chance to ambush him. But he'd told his men to be sure to rob Long Rogers before they shot him. Locke wanted every penny of the Indian's treasure.

When the men arrived in the small, poorly developed town, they agreed to let Locke and the pilot act as their spokesmen. They followed the directions on a rough sign to the land office. At first, neither of the white men said anything to the settler. Then Locke's Cherokee gang stood menacingly around the room, while the boss made his offer to the settler.

His bid for the land was a lot less than the man had asked for the property, and although the owner was dissatisfied with the offer, he looked around at the rough bunch of Indians and sailors, and decided to take the money. At that point, he just wanted to have a chance to escape from the deal with his life.

"Well, fellows, it's not all that I asked for, but it's enough for me to go back home and buy me a small homestead. I want to live in a place where my scalp is mine to keep," he said. "At least, I'll be back in civilization. When I came out here in '28, I almost got scalped. That day I made myself a promise that after a few years, if I still wasn't satisfied with my life, I'd go back home," he said. "You're welcome to it. If you can keep those Indians from stealing every damned, gosh darned thing that ain't nailed down, you're a much better man than I am. It's been an adventure, but now I'm old enough to know better, and I'm sick of it," he said as he walked out the door, and handed the key over to Locke. "I wouldn't bother to lock the door if I was you. They'll just pry it open, or take it completely off the hinges. You can't keep them from walking in here any time they feel like it."

Once the deal was signed, the pilot, a man who trusted that his new partner would always be square with him, happily picked out a lot at the corner of a tree-lined street. He imagined the contours of the house that he would build on it. Those years of hard work on the riverboat had taken its toll on his body, and now, he looked forward to his retirement from his life on the water.

Locke had decided that there was not a good reason for him to go into Sallisaw. The men would be able to handle everything, and bring the girl to him. It should not be necessary for him to go anywhere near that town. He was determined that there would not ever be a way to connect him to the crime.

Next week, he thought, *once my partners have gone back to the boat, I'm going to name the place for myself. 'Lockewood' sounds good to me!*

Now that the sailors left town, he spent his days riding around town plotting out lots, or sitting at his desk waiting for customers. He had plenty of time to daydream about Melinda, and how she would look when he dressed her up like his own, personal, little brown baby doll.

He envisioned her chiseled cheekbones, hazel eyes, and the ebony hair that hung down her back in two thick braids He wanted to see the expression on her face when he slowly unraveled them from the thongs that bound them, and twisted her hair in his hands.

Locke anxiously awaited word from his men that they had robbed Long Rogers, then killed both him and the black sheriff. They had been instructed to bring Melinda to a dog-trot shack buried in the woods outside of town. *If my men have managed to grab her, and have moved her away from town, I'll find a way to get rid of her old mammy later,* he planned.

It had taken a little time to sort things out, but by the middle of September Long Rogers figured that he was pretty damned sure who had tried to kill him and Sheriff Clinton Coulter. There was only one thing the two of them had in common, and that was that they had kept Melinda safely away from Locke's clutches.

There was something that bothered him about the men who had shot at him that made him slightly hesitant to name Locke as the would-be assassin. *Why didn't the men try to rob me?* He wondered. *Locke would have wanted them to rob me of my gold. I might be wrong about him, but I wonder why he hasn't contacted me since he left the boat. He was going to see about buying some land out near Tahlequah. Could it be that he has been attacked too? Could he have been deranged enough that he would murder us in order to possess the girl? If that's true, the man has acted like a rabid dog.*

A week ago, when the sailors had returned to the boat without Locke, Long Rogers noticed that the Cherokee men were often intoxicated. Yet, they had not made him feel that he was in any kind of danger.

182

They had acted friendly towards him. Then, after they had pulled into Sallisaw and left the boat, all hell had turned loose, and Clinton had been shot.

Well, he thought, *this is certainly a mystery. But I don't intend to stick around Sallisaw until someone else decides to take another shot at me.*

Thankfully, the big, black giant of a man was still alive. He was not completely out of the woods, and he wasn't in good traveling shape yet, but Long Rogers decided that it was time for him to take a hike over to the telegraph office and send another wire to Starr Night. He wanted him to know exactly where he was. He also decided to ask the chief to bring enough men along with him to assure their safe passage to Kiowa country. But he knew that it would be damned near impossible to get Melinda and Eliza to leave Clinton until they were assured of his survival.

After he had made it through the second week, Clinton was able to walk short distances, but he still had a long way to go before he would be completely recovered from his wound. The ideal situation, would be that he would heal fast enough for them to safely transport him to Fort Gibson. There, they could safely rest until their saviors arrived to pack them up and take them to New Warrior, before the first snows of winter.

October 30, before the United States Army forces pulled out of Sallisaw on route to the fort, they counted the Indians and their slaves again, and found that most of them had recovered enough to finish their journey. Long Rogers watched them as they pulled out. At the last minute, he had decided that he, the slave women, and the sheriff, would remain in Sallisaw. He had the papers that proved his ownership of the women. And now that they were in the Oklahoma Indian Territory, as far as the soldiers were concerned, Long Rogers was free to come and go as he wished.

Long Rogers had decided to accept the protection of the Sheriff of Sallisaw, rather than expose them to the dangers of being bush-whacked somewhere out on the trail by their enemies. Even though they would have had the Army escort, he felt that they would have been subjected to the possibility of an attack, out there somewhere along the deeply-wooded terrain.

The sheriff had given him a list of the Cherokee-owned ranches in the area, and he had utilized the information, and hired an express rider to take a note around to each of them. The note explained who he was, and why he needed their help to extricate himself from a dangerous situation. He also asked his tribesmen to provide a safe place for his party to stay until Chief Starr Night, of New Warrior Plantation, could rescue them.

Melinda kept herself busy in the backyard of the Sallisaw house by washing their clothes. Now that Clinton's condition had improved, she felt happy as she stirred his pants around in the boiling water of the old black cast-iron wash-pot

She could not keep herself from singing a silly little tune she had heard somewhere along the trail. She, Eliza, and the two men had arranged with the sheriff to live in this deserted little soddy, while they waited for her grandfather and Chief Starr Night to arrive. The house must have been empty for quite a while, because it had been necessary for them to cut tender young shoots of weeds from the dirt ceiling. But, otherwise, the house was sound. They had been homeless for a while, and now, they were extremely happy to have use of the crude, but solidly built hay and soil shelter.

She felt like dancing when she pictured herself as Clinton Coulter's wife. She had been encouraged to fantasize about that possibility ever since the day a letter had been delivered to him by the sheriff. It had been handed along from man to man, all around the Territory, until it had finally caught up with him in Sallisaw a few days ago.

After Clinton had read the letter from his deputy in Jessup Township to himself, he shared the contents of the latest news from home with all of them. "The state of Arkansas has ordered the Cherokees, (who had settled there a hundred years before), to leave the state and resettle in the Territory. The government used the same dishonest laws they utilized in the East to expel them," he explained. "But now, there is a new wrinkle in their bloody method, and they have enacted what they call "Black Laws."

"What does that mean?"

"All of the black towns like Jessup Township, have been destroyed." Clinton held up a couple of ragged, tattered, pages of paper. "These are sale papers for my property that the state has already seized. My deputy writes that I can't enter that state as a free man. Once they issued bills of sale for all of the properties, the houses and businesses were burnt to the ground. He says that once I sign the paperwork, and send it back to Arkansas by courier, or the mail, I'll be paid for my loss."

184

Later, when he and Melinda were alone, he told her of some of the other details included in the letter. "Although I haven't signed the damned papers, the white settlers have already obtained my land in a state-run lottery. It's a 'take it, or leave it' situation. Evidently, none of the new families wanted to live in our houses. The Indians and the black people were expelled and forced to sail away on the same boat. None of them had much of a choice of where they'd build their new lives."

"Now that the Indians and the black Freedmen have been forced to emigrate westward, neither group will be welcome to live in total freedom east of the Mississippi," said Melinda. "I'd dreamed so much about Jessup, and the possibility of going there one day. Now, that's not possible, and I feel the loss too," she had told him that day.

Now, as she continued to scrub the stain on the knee of a pair of Long Rogers' pants, Melinda started to hum her little off key song again, and thought about the details of their conversation. *Perhaps*, she thought, *we'll have to struggle a bit to get this mess straightened out, but in a way, the court in Arkansas has done us a favor. Although Clinton's gold claim was lost to him forever, he doubted that he'd have ever been able to claim it anyhow. The good thing about the situation, was that he had brought every penny of his treasure with him on the trip. Mama Liza and I hid his money for him when they shot him. Both of us knew that he'd have to be extremely careful of how and where he spends any of it. Now, Clinton says that he's going to try to buy me from my master. I wonder if the chief will agree to let me go. Maybe my grandfather can convince him to sell me.*

Melinda was deep in thought as she continued the task of rinsing out and hanging up the clothes. Clinton was wise when he'd told her that if he was able to purchase her, he would claim that he had spent his last penny. He would not ever appear to have as much money as any Indian, or a white settler.

"Someday," he had told her, "it might just happen that our children will be free to live anywhere in the United States. But even then, I don't think there'll ever come a time when a black man will be allowed to possess great wealth. But, I've learned to accept that it's just the way things are, and that's fine with me. The poorer they think we are, the longer we'll be able to live in peace."

Melinda had agreed with Clinton's viewpoint that they should hide anything he had left, after the sale. Otherwise, they would arouse someone's jealousy. The last thing any black man wanted to do, if he intended to live a long life, was to draw attention to himself.

When Melinda was about finished with the rest of the laundry, the medicine man stopped in to check on Clinton's progress. He was astonished. It was hard to believe that the man had healed so quickly. And now, he was acting feisty, wanted to stir up trouble, and go hunting after a man named Locke.

"Although I can't prove his guilt in the shooting, I'd just like to lay eyes on the man, and be convinced of his innocence."

The medicine man advised the big man to take a few more days of rest before he tried to ride horseback, but Clinton and the sheriff were beginning to hear of more crimes being committed by a gang of rabid Cherokee desperadoes. Clinton and Long Rogers had told the lawman about their suspicions. And after he had looked under Clinton's bandage, the medicine man decided that it was no longer needed. Once he was finished with his examination, the men decided to take a walk down to the sheriff's office, to see if there were any new reports of criminal activity.

Eliza sat near the stove picking stones and dirt from the pinto beans. Later, she would wash them, season them with a piece of ham hock, and put them on the stove to cook.

Melinda finally hung up the last piece of clothing across the rope to dry. Eliza still had not grown accustomed to living in a town. The odor from the toilets was pungently strong in the midday sun, and her eyes stung from the smoke from so many cook stoves. At night, the dogs howled at everything that moved. But, the scariest thing about the place, was the presence of so many white people. Once, when she was a young girl, she had belonged to a white man, but she had been sold, and for the rest of her life, she had lived on plantations where she was surrounded by other black slaves and her Cherokee masters. It had not occurred to her that there were so many of them around, until she had been arrested by the soldiers. She had been completely isolated from reality until she had been sold away from Warrior.

Melinda gloried in the warmth of the October sunshine while she finished her work, still singing her nonsense of a tune as a big hand snaked around from behind a sheet and covered her mouth. In a few swift moves, she was grabbed, hog-tied, gagged, and flung across the rump of a horse that calmly trotted across the backyard of the house.

Eliza welcomed the heat from the wood-stove in the cool, sunny, leaf-blown day, but she missed the sweet companionship of her great-granddaughter. She decided to cover up her old bones with a sweater, and go help Melinda with the clothes.

"Melinda!"

"Melinda, Melindaaaa!," she called as she stepped outside.

When she looked around the small yard, she saw that clothes were scattered around on the ground. And when Melinda did not respond to her call, panic grabbed the heart of the old woman. She held her hand across her heart in an effort to contain her panic, but when she turned toward a noise at the edge of the property, she saw that an Indian man was riding past the house holding the reins of a pinto pony. There was a large bundle tied to its back.

Eliza continued to cry out Melinda's name as she walked as fast as she could to the sheriff's office to sound the alert. She wanted Clinton, and the rest of the men, to help her search for the girl.

The sheriff, Clinton, and the deputy, all spilled out of the office with guns drawn, in response to her cries. Clinton ran to her and tried to understand what she was saying. He could not make sense of her babbling. Finally, she settled down enough so that he could unravel some of what she was saying.

"Help! My baby's gone, she hollered. Someone took my baby!"

"Who took her? Which way did they go?"

"I didn't see her leave, but she's gone!" After uttering those words, Eliza remembered to tell the men about the Indian with the two horses. He had been riding on a pinto, and leading the other horse that had a package tied on its back. She managed to point towards Tahlequah before she collapsed into Clinton's muscle-bound arms. He gently scooped her up, walked to the house, and put her in the bed. Then, he determinedly stuck a big hat on his sore head, saddled his horse, and grabbed a sack of grub. Enough, he figured, for what might turn out to be a long ride to find Melinda.

The sheriff, along with Long Rogers and Clinton, and some of the men in town, formed a posse. Against all odds, they would try to catch the kidnapper before he had a chance to take her into the deep wilderness of the Badlands. The town was usually a peaceful place to live, and the sheriff aimed to keep it that way. He handed out a rifle, and plenty of ammunition to any able-bodied man who agreed to help him catch the criminals and bring them to justice.

187

He asked one of his old friends, Maude Tulloss, a free black woman, to care for Eliza until they returned to town. The widow lived in a house behind the jail with her son Esau, the town carpenter.

Chapter Fifteen
The Seminole Trail

The letter that Long Rogers had sent to Starr Night in June had created an electric urgency at New Warrior Plantation. He and Tolliver had immediately begun to plan the trip to rescue the travelers to coincide with the cattle roundup and annual drive to the market in Kansas City. They figured that it would be safer to travel across the wilderness in the company of New Warrior's black wranglers, and their handlers.

Tolliver still worked for the chief as his trail boss, and planned that both of them would be able to lend their expertise to the newcomers, and sharpen up their skills as wranglers. The men planned to stay with the wranglers until they were sure that the men had the ability to drive the cattle the rest of the way to the stockyards.

Once they were confident that the men were capable of handling their tasks, the boss would be ready to leave them with their new Cherokee trail boss. Then, he and Tolliver would leave them to steer the cattle to the stockyards in the north, while they headed towards Straight Arrow Ranch in the east. Starr Night knew that he could depend on Silas, his brother-in-law, to help him get the travelers back to his ranch in Kiowa country.

By September, confident in the abilities of the new leader, the men had split off from the drovers and the herd, and were on the road to Chickasaw. Both men were dressed Indian style with beaded leggings, moccasins, and leather shirts. But they also carried English clothing stashed in their saddlebags, strapped to the back of the mule, just in case they got into a situation where they had to interact with the settlers.

All along the trail on the way to Tahlequah, they stopped at other Cherokee ranches and asked if there had been any news of the whereabouts of Long Rogers and the slave women. But so far, there had not been any sightings.

Tolliver was very anxious to find them and give them the good news about their new lives. He knew that they wouldn't have a way to know that they had been freed from slavery. He figured that it was hard for any man to make the trip across the country, and doubly hard for a woman. Most likely, his mother and Melinda had experienced a rough time on their long journey to the Territory, but now they would be rewarded for their successful journey, with a big payoff: They were Freedwomen for life. As the men rode along the trail towards Straight Arrow, Tolliver's head was filled with visions of what the faces of his mother and granddaughter might look like after a three-year separation.

When they were just a few miles past Henrietta, Tolliver and the chief decided to make camp earlier in the day than usual. The overseer intended to go hunting for a fresh supply of meat, preferably, the chief's favorite, rabbit. He turned around just in time to see that the chief had stopped dead in his tracks, and was looking towards a mile-long plume of dust. He could see that the disturbance was caused by another wagon train, one of the many they had spotted during the week.

Tolliver watched him as he pulled out his spyglass. *It's getting harder and harder for those Cherokees who are being shipped from the East to find open spaces,* he thought. At first, the settlers had told the tribe that all of the land was theirs, and that the Territory would always be their refuge. But now the laws had changed again, and they were losing ground that had been promised to them.

"White settlers are coming to our land in droves," the chief said, "the next thing you know, they'll insist on moving us farther away from them. I'm afraid that we'll never be able to satisfy their thirst for more and more land. Their quest to conquer the West will run out of space again. Eventually, if they continue to migrate westward, my people will have their backs pressed up against the Pacific Ocean."

When they reached Okmulgee on October 12, Tolliver and Starr Night ran into a group of men. Some of them were black, and there were a few Cherokees, but most of them were white settlers. They were sitting around a campfire drinking chicory and gossiping about a white settler who had bought a man's homestead with more than 150 acres, and then divided the claim into one acre plots. Now, he planned to sell the lots to other settlers. Recently, he'd named his new town Lockewood.

Jacob, a free black man, told them the latest details: "Last week, a house was burned to the ground by three masked men. I heard that they threatened to burn down the entire village if the Indians don't agree to leave the area. The damned thing about it, is that the townspeople suspect that the men are members of their own tribe. Renegades, who work for the white settler. Why in hell would they do such a sick thing?" he asked. "Those men are the same ones who we suspect of shooting a black man in the head. Shot him while he was sitting in a barn in Sallisaw, waiting for an Army wagon to take him to Fort Gibson. I heard that he's still alive, but he's hurt bad."

A white settler piped in, "The story I heard, is that it took both the doctor and the medicine man to save him."

"Why would anyone want to kill a slave? If he was new to the Territory, he shouldn't have had any enemies," said the chief. "It doesn't make any sense."

"Maybe he was just in the wrong place that day. Perhaps the bullet was meant for someone else," Tolliver said.

They found out from one of the men that they had gathered themselves into a posse, determined to capture the gang and hang them high. Those same men were also suspected of robbing a wagon train. The men had come from several towns, and they intended to catch the thieves and punish them for terrorizing the poor, hard-working settlers. The posse assured the chief that they were sure that they carried enough rope with them, to seal the deal.

"One thing's for sure," said the chief, "I'll bet you anything that they won't go near the Choctaw nation in the Quachita Mountains. The Lighthorsemen are the strictest, most lethal lawmen in the Territory. They don't bother themselves with taking the time to build a jail."

After they had spent the night among their new friends, Tolliver and Starr Night were well rested and ready to resume their journey to Straight Arrow. Before they saddled their mounts, they took the time to reach into their saddlebags and give a bag of their sugar to the men. It was their way to show their gratitude to them for letting them use the warmth of their fire, and for the information they had been willing to share with them.

"Thanks for the warning about the bandits," Tolliver called to the men. Both of them took the time to check their guns and ammunition.

"When we leave here, we'll he heading for Sallisaw. We've got lots of ground to cover, but when we reach town, I'll call on the sheriff and tell him about the latest trouble. He'll probably request a detail from the fort to help you capture the outlaws," the chief promised.

The next leg of the trip would carry them into dense trees and scrub brush. It would slow them down a bit, but once they reached Straight Arrow, they would be furnished with fresh mounts that were accustomed to the terrain.

Tolliver felt a bit uneasy. He remembered the area as being one of the most difficult places that he and the rest of the slaves had been forced to navigate, when they'd been led from Alabama to the strange environs of Kiowa country. The trek to the Cherokee's new claim had been a living hell for them, and he still had nightmares about the day that three of the men had jumped from the cliff.

Three days later, a hard-riding, sweaty messenger arrived at Straight Arrow Ranch in a flurry of dust. The exhausted man had come to deliver an urgent message from Long Rogers to Silas, an old friend and neighbor of his from Alabama.

His note told Silas of his plans to stay in Sallisaw until someone came in town to rescue him, two of Starr Night's slaves, and a wounded friend, from a dangerous situation.

"I was on my way to New Warrior with your brother-in-law's property when someone tried to kill me. I suspect that he was trying to rob me of my money and steal the slaves," he wrote. "The sheriff has done his best to watch out for us, but I think we'd be better off if I could get us out of here, and onto a Cherokee plantation."

By the first light of the new dawn, Silas and six of his wranglers set out on the road towards Sallisaw to save his tribesman. The horsemen were trailed by a fully equipped wagon that would be used to transport the slave women and the wounded man to the ranch. Starr Night had already warned him to be on the lookout for the travelers, and he had expected all of them to be at the ranch by now. *Something must have held them up,* he thought. *Well, the note from Long Rogers explains a lot of it.*

The next morning, Starr Night and Tolliver arrived at the ranch. Isola's sister greeted the men with the news that they had missed Silas's departure from the ranch by one day.

"He thought it was best to go on ahead of you. A message came in from Long Rogers saying that he was in trouble. Silas high-tailed it out of here to see if he could bring him out here, away from the trouble in Sallisaw."

They were disappointed that they had missed the ride with Silas to pick up the immigrants, but after they had rested a few hours, eaten, packed a fresh supply of trail food, changed clothes, and saddled fresh horses, the men lit out on an extraordinary mission to intercept Silas and his men, out on the trail. They listened carefully to the directions from the ranch-hands, and discovered that they knew about a shortcut to the ferry on the Illinois River.

The foreman advised them to check with the men at the Seminole village perched on a round-about table of a place in the verdant, lush mountains surrounding Webber's Falls.

"The people who live there are on friendly terms with both the Cherokees and their slaves. Usually, we stop there and visit with them when we cut through there on our way to town, a couple of times a year. It's a good place to let off steam once we're headed back home. If you go through there, you might just be able to catch up with Mr. Silas and the men at Cherokee Landing. If you catch up with them there, you'll be able to ride with them through the Bushy Mountain Pass to Sallisaw."

Before they left the ranch, Starr Night took the time to unroll the map from his saddlebag. Immediately, he came to the conclusion that although he would try to use the shortcut, he could see that it would be a dangerous and difficult business to get through those dense woods without getting robbed by bandits, or having one of the horses go lame in the steep terrain.

Several gangs had hideouts in the caves that dotted the mountain sides. But the chief decided that their experience in the wilderness would help them to get through the trail, as long as they remained extra vigilant every inch of the way.

The men were very alert as they rode single-file through the tight trail. When they finally came to a flat clearing, they could tell by the slightly warm ashes of an old fire that someone had camped there overnight. They agreed with the logic of the previous visitor that the back of the site, protected by an overhanging crag, provided the safest place to build a fire.

Starr Night had a sleepless night. He thought he'd heard something rustling through the woods just before dawn, but he'd not found any tracks. As the chief had circled the camp, he had looked for the source of the noise. Tolliver had lain still with his hand resting on the Henry rifle. But when he saw that the chief had returned his gun to the holster, he had shut his eyes and slept, until he heard the horses stir.

After the animals were fed, the men sipped coffee, ate a couple of hardtack biscuits, then resumed their search for Silas and his men. They hunkered down into their coats. A strong wind whistled loudly through the trees as they came to a place called Hanging Rock, a stronghold of the Seminole Indians and their ex-slave friends.

A shot rang out, and Tolliver and the chief ducked their heads and tried to find a place to hide. A bullet came so close to Tolliver that he

193

was forced to dive from his horse, and seek cover behind a boulder. Meanwhile, he couldn't figure out why Starr Night, who still sat astride his horse, seemed to be immune to attack.

"White man, get your ass back on that horse, turn around, and leave this land. If you weren't riding along with this crazy red man, you'd be dead," said an anonymous voice from the safety of the woods. "Injun, why in hell would you bring a white man into our camp?"

"I'm not dumb enough to enter Seminole country with a white man," the chief replied. "This here is Tolliver. He does look mighty white, but he's just a light-skinned black man. Come over here, look at those eyes, then you'll see the truth of my words."

Three black men, and six Seminoles, emerged from the woods and surrounded the strangers. When Tolliver stood up from behind the rock, he walked towards them with his hands in the air, far away from his guns. A short black man with wild, nappy red hair was the first to speak.

"Sorry about that shot, but you look so white. A few months ago, there were a couple of white men who were so desperate for money that they had the nerve to check the woods for runaways. They were foolish to hunt for any of them so far away from the plantations. Believe me, if any slave managed to get this far into the mountains, we'd never allow anyone to catch him. I guess that I'm willing to take your word for it that you're a black man. Because there is not a white man living who'd try to be black."

One of the Seminole Indians who seemed to be the leader of the group, decided to join the conversation. "We're a hunting party. We're about ready to take our kill to the village. You're welcome to eat with us. You'll have to tell us why the two of you have come to our camp."

"We've been watching you since you set foot on the trail to the village. We left our sign, but we didn't think you'd be fool enough to follow us," Hairy told Starr Night. "Last night, when you heard that noise and went to search the woods, you almost stepped on my toe!"

All of the men laughed at the near miss, and it put them all a jovial mood as they followed the faint trail towards the village. They found themselves surrounded by nine men. When they arrived at the campsite, the village men were greeted by their wives, children, and dogs. The village inhabitants were amazed to see that their men had brought a Cherokee stranger and a white man into their midst. The majority of the denizens of the village were Indian, but some were black, and others were half-breeds.

Tolliver thought it wise to leave his Henry in the scabbard strapped to the saddle of his horse. The chief agreed with his logic, and decided to tie his guns down with the leather straps of his holster, in order to gain the trust of their hosts.

Hairy walked with them to point out the place at the stream where they could refresh themselves while they tended to the horses. Once they had removed the saddles, the animals were fed, then tied to a tree. When they returned to the center of the encampment, they were joined by the other men around the fire. They threw their blankets around their tired shoulders against the sting of the brisk, cool, night air.

The New Warrior men talked to the Seminole braves while the women cooked the food. Their way of cooking game was foreign to anything Tolliver or the chief had ever seen. The Seminole women used an elaborate set-up of a series of spits that hung above the fire. The flames flared up every time fat dripped down from the suspended meat. Tolliver was totally mesmerized by the aroma of the spices they used on the meat. He decided to ask Hairy for a sample of the seasoning. Once he was settled in with his family, he intended to experiment with the Seminole method of cooking.

After the men had filled their bellies, Tolliver began to tell them the story of his quest to free his mother and granddaughter. "I want to give them a home far away from that nightmare they lived in at the plantation. The last three years, they have been used to do some back-breaking labor in the cotton fields," he said. "Hairy, when we come back through here on our way to Kiowa country, I'm going to need your help getting them home. I'm a Freedman, and he's a chief. Like you, he's an honorable man, and the chief has promised that he'd try to help me recover my family."

However, Tolliver did not explain the details of the reason his family had been scattered with the wind across the country. If he had told them the truth, he did not doubt that the ex-slaves among the tribe would have been angry enough to kill Starr Night. Then he would have been forced to defend him with his own life.

Tolliver needed the man to stay alive. He was the key to the possibility that he could end the hell he'd been living in. He needed the chief to continue to use his influence, and to act as his protector against those Cherokees, especially Lone Fox, who wanted all Freedmen to be expelled from the Territory. And, there was another matter. Eliza and Melinda would not be free until he actually signed their papers.

195

Other than the day he had been freed, he could think of only two other times when the chief had changed his mind about anything. The first time, he had sold Warrior without waiting for the decision from the Supreme Court, and the other one was his guilt-ridden decision to free his relatives. Tolliver and his family had been the only slaves Starr Night had ever owned. The rest of the Warrior slaves belonged to Isola and the members of the Songbird family.

Of course, the chief would have never admitted to anyone that his Bible-toting wife had influenced his thinking, but Starr Night could remember the day that he had brought Tolliver and his family to the plantation. Isola had been displeased with his purchase, and he could still hear her angry words:

"It's enough that I have to live in the house with Cook, and her half-Indian sons. I agreed to let them be my house servants. But I've never liked the idea of owning mixed-white slaves," she'd said. "From what I've observed about that slave when he was here with Cousin George, he's only useful as a toy. We have no use for him around here. What we need, is someone to help us control the other slaves."

But now, after all of Tolliver's faithful years of service, Isola had changed her mind about him, had become his advocate, and encouraged her husband to reunite the family.

"His skin color sets him apart from the others. And look at him. So far, after all these years, he's not been able to find a woman he fancies enough to marry. His only friends are Featherman and Itty. It's cruel to expect a man to live alone for the rest of his life. He should be surrounded by his family. I feel sorry for him. He's worked very hard on our claim. Now, he deserves some happiness in his own life."

Starr Night had listened to her words and had finally written that letter to Long Rogers. *Now, here I am,* he thought, *riding along with my ex-slave through Seminole country, hell-bent on finding the two women I've agreed to sell to my overseer. Isola will be pleased.*

Hairy and the other men were touched by Tolliver's story. Most of the black men of the tribe had always dreamed of finding their own lost families and bringing them out to the West, but they were wise enough to know that it would never happen. First of all, they wouldn't have any idea where they were. Many of them were probably still being held captive on the same plantations the men had fled. Most of their parents were probably dead by now, but if they were alive, they might not even recognize their long-lost children. In those dark days, there was a

196

vagrant, lost generation of slaves who wandered all over the back roads of America, dodging the patrollers who sought to capture them for the reward money.

The men agreed to provide an escort for the travelers when they returned to their territory. Starr Night and Hairy parted on friendly terms too. He asked him to use his skills to translate his English into the Seminole language whenever he spoke to his chief. The Cherokee chief promised to speak to Silas about trading and selling goods to their isolated tribe. And, most importantly, Silas could supply them with the horses they were going to need if they intended to extend the range of their hunting grounds, and protect their land from the settlers who were determined to settle on their land. Tolliver did all he could to encourage Hairy's tribe of Seminoles to form a coalition with the Cherokees. Then, they might possibly be able to expand the power of both tribes over the mountainous territory.

After the men had spent an evening bragging about the superiority of Seminole tobacco blends, they swapped pipes and sampled a mix from New Warrior. Finally, after an evening spent teasing each other, an agreement was reached between the combined Songbird and Rhea Cherokee band, with the Hanging Rock Seminole band.

The next morning, just as the sun began to peep from the day's stack of fluff-filled clouds, Starr Night and Tolliver bade farewell to the village, and resumed their attempt to join Silas in his pursuit of the immigrants.

Chapter Sixteen
The Wilderness Reunion

On October 20, Starr Night and Tolliver finally were coming down from the high mountain pass when they spotted Silas and his men riding towards Sallisaw with the wagon in tow. To get his attention, the chief fired a couple of rounds into the air. Even from that distance, they could see Silas draw his gun. Tolliver waved his kerchief in the air as they rode towards the men. When they were close enough to the men that Silas could recognize them, he spurred his horse towards them, and yelled a greeting to his brother-in-law. *What a surprise!* He thought. *It's a good thing he sent those shots into the air to warn us that they were there. Me and the men are a little skittish. We've been expecting trouble to find us. Maybe from the same people who attacked Long Rogers, you never know. I didn't expect to see them until later this week.*

"Glad to see that it's the two of you that's come to meet me and the boys. It's getting late, let's make camp. That way, we'll have a chance to fill you in on the mess that's going on in Sallisaw," Silas proposed. As they set up camp, the men spread around and checked the woods for bushwhackers. After what had happened to Long Rogers, they knew what kind of men they were dealing with.

"We heard about a black man being shot in Sallisaw, but we heard that he was a slave. Where did he come from? And, how did he hook up with Tolliver's family?"

"I don't know," answered Silas. "Long Rogers sent me a note asking for help, but he didn't go into details about the man. Just said that he was his friend. I think we're riding into a hornet's nest. That sheriff is tough. He's strong enough to keep them safe until we get there. He wouldn't have offered them a safe haven if he wasn't sure he could protect them."

"Let's get a little shuteye. We're within a day from town, Silas said. "We've got enough ammo with us to start a war, but I'm hoping that we'll just be able to get in there, retrieve your folks, and leave the town without having to fire a shot."

The brother-in-laws hadn't seen each other in over a year, and after Silas secured their position, the men relaxed and began to plan their strategy.

Tolliver slept peacefully. It was the first time in many moons that he could tell himself that he had done everything possible to reunite his family. Tonight, he was happier than he'd been in years. There was a good chance that he would soon be able to see both of his loved ones.

Starr Night looked over to the sleeping man and wondered how he could sleep after he had waited three years to see his mother and granddaughter. He shook his head and thought, *I'll never be able to figure this man out.*

At daybreak, the men gathered around the fire to shag a cup of coffee and a piece of hardtack before they hit the trail. There were nine of them now, and they were confident that they could go into town and take care of business. Five miles into the ride, Silas spotted a plume of dust. Someone was coming their way. The men took cover.

As the horsemen drew nearer, Silas saw that it was the Sheriff of Sallisaw, and what looked to him to be a posse. When he rode out to meet him, the rest of the men stayed back, guns drawn, until he signaled them that all was well.

Now Starr Night and Tolliver followed his lead and rode over to greet the posse. Silas was pleased, but shocked to see that his friend Long Rogers and a black man rode with the posse.

"Well I'll be damned if you didn't find us, instead of it being the other way around! We were on our way to Sallisaw to rescue you."

Starr Night rode up to the men. "Good to see you. I was really worried. After all, I'm the one who asked you to bring those slaves out here with you."

When Tolliver followed the Indian out towards the saddled riders, he locked eyes with the black man. At first glance, both of them were speechless. Then Tolliver and Clinton yelled at the top of their voices at same time. They were speaking so fast, and were so excited, that the other men around them could not make sense of their gibberish. But from what they *did* understand about what was going on, the men of the posse were shocked at the astonishing news of the reunion of the black men.

When Clinton spotted the man he had tried to rescue in Arkansas, he jumped down from his horse and sprinted over to the older man. Almost simultaneously, Tolliver slid down from his roan and met the sheriff halfway. He was immediately engulfed in a big bear hug as they danced around in the vast wilderness of the Territory. Everyone grinned at the sight of the two burley men as they continued to hug, cry, and jump about. Finally, they were so exhausted that they could do nothing else but sit down in the dirt and look at each other.

They peppered the air with questions. The odds of them meeting again were astronomical, yet, there they were. Who would have ever thought they'd find themselves together, riding in the highest mountain pass in the Territory? As they settled down a bit and exchanged a few sentences, they discovered that both of them were searching for the same woman: Melinda. The main difference between their missions was that Tolliver had not known that his granddaughter had been kidnapped, until now.

He looked closely at the shaved section of Clinton's head. "What happened?" he asked.

"The man who took Melinda is probably the same one who's responsible for this wound. It's an old story of greed and jealousy. Long Rogers told me that he paid a soldier to help them escape from a prison fort in Alabama. He posed as their master, and they all came out here to the Territory on the boat together. I met them when the boat came into Fort Smith. I tried to buy them from him, but Locke claimed they belonged to someone out here, and I followed them in hopes of buying them." He took a deep breath. "I'll give him credit. He's a deserter, but he had the gumption to travel in close quarters with a bunch of soldiers and a sheriff."

"Melinda never told you about him?"

"No, I think she came close to telling me, but she still didn't know what I'd do about him. I'm still a Lawman, and she was probably afraid I'd mess up things for them. They depended on him to protect them while they were traveling to the Territory," he said.

Clinton was very pleased to discover that Melinda, the woman he loved, was Tolliver's granddaughter. When he told him that once she was free, he intended to ask her to marry him, Tolliver was happy. So happy, in fact, that he started to yell all over again.

"Clinton, she doesn't know it yet, but she's already free," he said. "So am I. About three years ago, not long after we met in Jessup, Starr Night freed me. And, over the years, I've saved up my money. I was able to make a deal with the chief to buy her and my mother's freedom."

What Tolliver failed to say, was that he had tied himself to Starr Night forever. But he doubted that he would ever tell anyone of his sacrifice. The important thing right now, was to find Melinda. Both men knew that it was going to be a difficult task, because she was just a speck of humanity in an enormous part of the country.

"We're going to find her," Tolliver vowed. "The two of us will search for her for however long it takes. I'm determined that one day you'll be able to use your money to build a new life for the two of you. But, be careful. Don't ever let them know anything about you having gold. They're not your friends. Pinch small bits of it at a time and it won't draw attention to you. There are a few small changes in our place here in the Territory, but it'll never be a place where a black man can feel free to spend his gold."

He reached into his saddlebag and retrieved two precious documents that the Indian had finally signed. Then he told Clinton about the small homestead the chief had sold him.

"If you marry Melinda, he'll want you tied to him too. He seems impressed with you. Long Rogers has told him that you are his friend. It wouldn't surprise me if he offered you a job as a lawman for the tribe. There are many criminals who are raiding Cherokee lands and creating havoc all over the Territory, he told Clinton. "But, I'm warning you now, there'll always be strings attached to any deal you make with the chief."

Tolliver smiled. He was happy that this man who had risked his life for him, wanted to be part of his family. He knew that Melinda would never be able to find a more compassionate young man.

Later, when they had explained their miracle to rest of the men, Starr Night, Silas, Long Rogers, and the sheriff walked away from the celebration. The chief began to tell them of the time when Tolliver had saved him and his men from certain death in a little town in Arkansas.

"Any of us could've died that day, but he convinced them to back down. That's when I decided that I'd free him. So far, I haven't had a reason to regret my decision."

The Sheriff of Sallisaw looked back to the black man he had thought was white. If his life had depended on it, he still could not see it. *How in hell do these southerners tell which one of them is mixed?* It simplified matters for him that he accepted the fact that every man was a man.

By morning, the posse had split up into three sections. The sheriff would keep most of the townspeople with him to block the roads in and around Sallisaw. They would try to keep the bandits away from the caves that they used as hideouts in the Badlands.

Long Rogers and some of the men made camp within a few miles of Fort Gibson. That evening, he told Silas the story about how the three of them had been captured by the Army, and their imprisonment at the fort.

"I was forced to use some mighty gruesome methods to get those slaves out of prison," he explained. And when he told them how he'd buried them, the men were shocked beyond belief. Then he told them about the slave woman who had been kidnapped.

"I've got an idea she's being held prisoner somewhere near Lockewood, unless he had sense enough to hide her away, until the search for her dies down. But, if I ever get a chance to lay eyes on him again, I'm going to let him know that he picked the wrong woman to grab. I don't think the day will come when Clinton and her grandfather will ever give up and stop looking for her. I paid him lots of money to help me escape, and now the greedy bastard has double-crossed me."

"Do you still have your receipt from her sale in Alabama?" Silas asked.

"The sales receipt is still in my name. I have it here. How about letting me borrow one of your men go with me to the fort? I'd like a chance to speak with the commander and ask him for his assistance in the recovery of my property."

Since Long Rogers and Clinton were known to Locke and his gang, it was up to Tolliver and Starr Night to make up the third leg of the rescue effort, and ride into the town alone.

The last leaves of the cottonwood trees were falling to the ground when they spotted the big hand-written sign on the land office. The gaudy sign was hard to miss.

Tolliver was beautifully dressed, and played the part of a rich planter handsomely. He rode up to the office and introduced himself to the man who sat just outside the door, tilted back in a soft-bottomed, cane-backed chair. The over-anxious salesman introduced himself.

"Name's Charles N. Locke, owner of this up and coming metropolis. Welcome to Lockewood!"

"My name is Tolliver Rhea, and this is my friend Jack. I'd like to look at three lots, if you have that many left for sale. I don't want to live on them, I'm looking to turn a profit on any land that I buy."

After a stroll around the poorly developed town, the men haggled over the price and size of the lots. Once they had agreed on the small details of the deal, Tolliver signed the paperwork.

"Of course I don't run around the Territory with cash on hand, but you'll be able to cash my draft at any Territorial bank."

To celebrate the successful deal, Locke insisted on buying Tolliver a drink. The men walked into the saloon, bellied up to the bar, and both of them ordered a shot of whiskey. Locke was in an expansive mood. *I wasn't much of a drinking man until I came out here,* he thought. It had changed him since he'd been out here in the wilderness with nobody to brag to but his Cherokee gang, or the girls who worked in the saloon. Although he was apt to take a drink now and then, he still remembered his father's drunken history, and tried not to make a habit of it.

Once the new townspeople had bought their lots from him, most of them tried to avoid his company. They felt stuck in this place where his gang victimized them. He had done nothing to control his men, and enjoyed the fact that most of those holier-than-thou citizens of Lockewood feared his power.

"Jack" stayed with the Cherokee gang members and swapped stories with them about their removal from their homes in the east, and the destruction of their families. They told him how they had thrown in their lot with the white man. He had offered them shelter, and the protection of living in his town. "Jack" agreed with their decision, and told them he might be interested in living in Lockewood too.

While the white men were in the saloon cementing their deal, the gang allowed him to follow them to the general store at the end of the street and watch while they took food without paying for it. The store owner didn't protest the robbery; his wife and children were in the back room.

The gang leader, Buttram, told them to saddle up so that they could take care of some business for the boss. They all rode out of town on the westward trail towards the mountains. After they had gone about five miles, they arrived at a small dog-trot shack.

"You guys stay out here near the corral, tie up the horses and take a smoke. I won't be long. I've got to check on her, make sure she's all right."

He tried to stay cool while they rolled their cigarillos, but "Jack" felt his heart skip a beat. The chief was certain that Melinda was the woman they were holding captive. He thought that Buttram might decide to bring her outside, and as a precaution, he decided to turn his body to the side, so that his face couldn't be seen from the door of the house. If by chance she still recognized him, the men would shoot him from one side to the other without even thinking about it. He didn't see a horse in the corral for her. Maybe they weren't moving her today.

"Brought you some more vittles to eat. Stop whining, and try to settle down. It shouldn't be too long before we're able to take you to town," Buttram said as he came through the door.

"Please don't leave me out here again, I'm afraid of this place. Why did you kidnap me?"

"Everything will be explained to you soon. Sometimes you're better off not knowing what's going on. Just don't try to go anywhere by yourself," he advised. "You're miles away from the nearest town, and if one of the settlers grabs you, you might be sold to someone a lot worse than your new owner."

"Who is he? Does he know that my *real* owner is a man named Starr Night? If he has papers on me, they're not real. Does he know that my owner has plans to free me?" she asked.

He wiped his brow with his hand, and pushed his braids to the back of his neck. Something about her made him jumpy. He'd never been around a slave who had the nerve to ask so many damned questions.

"If you follow orders, everything will work out. You'll probably live a lot better than you did in Alabama. At least you're not out in a field picking cotton. A pretty girl like you could've been auctioned off to one of the whorehouses in New Orleans."

Melinda was determined she would not cry, but he was really scaring her. At least he didn't keep her tied up any more. The Indian was probably right. It was better to stay put. It was possible she'd get herself into all sorts of trouble if she strayed too far from the house. After all, she didn't know if she was still in Cherokee Territory. *Not that it makes much difference,* she thought, *I'm still a slave anywhere I go. It doesn't matter who's country I'm in, it's not mine.*

205

As Buttram turned to go, he took a long look at the beautiful woman and felt sorry for her. It occurred to him that he could steal her for himself, but he knew that Locke would be relentless in his hunt for them. It he'd been ready to kill the black sheriff and the Cherokee to have her, he certainly would not allow a poor, Indian cow hand like him take her from him.

Before their leader returned to the rest of the men, "Jack" had a chance to listen to their tales about the robberies they had pulled off. And, he had pretended to believe all the lies they told about the women they had bedded. But, their most humorous tales concerned Locke. They laughed at him for being so obsessed with the slave woman that he was willing to gamble everything he owned in order to possess her.

When Buttram returned to the corral, the men took one look at his clouded face and decided that they wouldn't be asking him any questions. All of them just mounted their ponies and slowly headed back to town.

At the saloon, Tolliver and Locke wrapped up the last details of their deal. Locke promised him that he would advertise the lots in the newspapers, and that most likely, the investor would double his money before the end of the year. Tolliver turned around just in time to see that the bartender could hardly hide his disdain for Locke. But the man's hatred for him was so subtle that Locke would never know that there was a chance that the man would poison him one day.

When they heard the clip-clopping of several horses' hooves, they figured their men were coming back in town. Both gentlemen strolled out of the swinging batwing doors of the saloon on very cordial terms. "Jack" rode across the street and joined his boss for the ride home.

Tolliver mounted his horse, they waved goodbye to their new friends, and left the town on the main road towards Tahlequah and Straight Arrow Ranch. And now, finally, the chief could tell Tolliver the good news. He'd found out Melinda's whereabouts.

"I rode with his men out into the deep woods to an old, beaten-down shack about five miles out. They told me that she has not been molested yet, but Locke is itching to get to her. It's my opinion that we need to shake a tail feather and get out there to grab her as soon as we can, if you intend to get to her before Locke comes to collect his treasure. The men told me that he has the idea that once he beds her, she'll never want to leave him."

"Sick bastard," said Tolliver. "What woman loves a man who forces himself on her?"

As they reached the edge of town, a white settler, formally of Selma, was astounded when he spotted someone from back home. When he took a closer look, he realized that he'd come along just in time to see that Indian they'd run out of Warrior, riding out of town with his slave.

He waited until they were out of sight, then walked over to the saloon to see if anyone knew why the men were so far away from the chief's spread in Kiowa country. The first thing he wanted to know, was if that Indian intended to buy land in their town.

Locke had just sat down with another shot of whiskey. "If you feel the need to meddle into my business, I'd be glad to fill you in on a few facts. I'll never sell any of my land to an Indian."

"Well now, I'll rest a little easier. It took everything we had to push him out of Alabama. And now that we've got him, his band, and his slaves hemmed up out there in the wilderness of Kiowa country, we want to be sure that he stays out there in that untamed, old Indian hunting ground."

"You're crazy. That Indian works for a white man, He's like the Cherokees that I have hanging around here. He's nobody's chief of anything."

"You've been snookered. He fooled you too. He's always liked to parade around that half-white slave of his. Don't ever let them sucker you into a hand of poker, he's right smart for a black man."

"You must be drunk, and out of your cotton-picking mind. I just sold Tolliver three lots. I've got his check right here, and I know damned well that he's not a slave!"

The men in the saloon started to laugh when the settler insisted that he was right. They got a big kick out of the knowledge that Locke would have refused to sell to a Cherokee, but instead, he had sold three of his lots to a slave. The settler from Alabama thought that it was hilarious, and laughed so hard at the look on Locke's face, that he spewed whiskey into the room as he almost choked on his drink.

Locke was furious. He finally had to admit that the settler knew what he was talking about. He had been duped into selling land to Tolliver. The other men joined in the merriment as Locke reluctantly accepted the truth of the matter. He'd just spent most of his day drinking with a slave. On his way out of the saloon, he banged against the doors in such a fit of anger that he did not notice that his Cherokee gang had already melted into the night. They had been standing just outside of the doors of the saloon, and had heard every word the white men had spoken. All of them had heard of Starr Night, he was one of the most powerful Cherokee chiefs. The men compared notes, and it did not take very long for them to realize that they had exposed themselves to the wrath of two powerful Cherokee families.

Buttram decided that what they needed was a grubstake, and that meant they had to find somebody to rob. Once they found a way to get the money in their hands, he knew where they could hide out until things cooled down a bit.

As he walked back into his office, Locke recalled a conversation he'd heard between the slave women and Long Rogers when they had been aboard the riverboat. They had talked about how it had been when they had lived at Warrior Plantation before it had been sold. And he now understood enough of what they had said about their master, to understand that lots of trouble was about to come his way.

When he wondered why they had come to Locketown, he came to the conclusion that they were searching for Melinda. After all, she was the chief's stolen property.

Now that he had managed to increase his fortune quite a bit, Locke felt that he couldn't think of a better time to get the hell out of that sinkhole of a town. The newest land boom was in Missouri, near Neosho, and he was inclined to try his luck across the border. However, there was another thing he had to do before he was completely satisfied. Locke was determined that he would have a taste of the sweet Melinda before he left the Territory. She had caused him to too much trouble to just abandon her in the woods. His appetite for her had not been quenched. However, he was sure that once he'd bedded her, he would finally be released from his insane obsession with her. She had bewitched him, and now, he wanted to be free of her vise-like power over his dreams.

Of course she would have to die. He couldn't allow her to identify him as her kidnapper, or as a deserter from the Army. According to what his men had said before they'd left town, Clinton Coulter, her crazy–in–love boyfriend, and Long Rogers, his ex-partner in crime, were still alive. And between them, and those fierce Cherokee Indians she belonged to, any of them would like to catch up with him and administer their own brand of justice.

Locke dragged his carpetbag from beneath the bed and stuffed it with paper money, gold, and a few clothes, then picked up his bedroll. It was a great day to go for a ride. He walked over to the barn, saddled his horse, and rode out of town. Nobody paid much attention to him when his beautiful Tennessee Walker pranced towards the woods.

Melinda blew out the coal-oil lamp when she heard the whinnying of the horse. She was afraid, and wondered why the gang would come to the cabin so late. It was almost too dark to ride a horse in this rough country. She was not brave enough to peep out of the window. Instead, she decided to hide in the corner of the room behind the cord of wood stacked inside the shack.

When Locke saw that she had extinguished the light, he took the flint and a piece of steel from his pocket, and struck them together to light the torch that Buttram had stashed beneath the porch. He walked into the cabin to confront Melinda. She ran into his arms, relieved to see his familiar face. *They had misjudged him*! Melinda hugged herself as she danced around the room.

"I'm so happy you've found me," she cried. "Let's get out of here. Hurry! If you saw them, you'd recognize the Indians who came here on the boat. One of them, a man called Buttram, promised me that if he could find a way for us to leave the other men in town, he'd try to take me to Kiowa country, and sell me back to my master." Melinda told him. "They're probably holding me for ransom. Have you seen Mama Liza? I'll bet she's having a hissy-fit over me being gone. I'd say that by now, Clinton is frantic."

Melinda stopped talking. Now that she had calmed down a bit, she frowned when she noticed that Locke had hardly said a word. *He's acting awfully mysterious,* she thought. *Those men on the boat were his friends.* She asked him another question, just to see his reaction.

"How did you find me?" she inquired, as she stepped back into the shadow of the re-lit lamp. She wanted to look directly into his eyes. It looked to her that he held keys to the solution of this mystery.

Locke was sure that she had no idea he was involved in her kidnapping, and decided to make himself the hero who had come to rescue her from the bandits. He pulled a piece of paper from his pocket.

"A man came into a saloon that's next door to my office. He'd lost most of his money playing poker, but when he finally got a decent hand, he wanted a chance to win some of his money back. He took this paper out of his pocket and put it on the table. Then he laid his cards down. When my full house beat his hand, he handed over the document. Then he drew a map to this place. He said he was giving up on the Territory, and had decided to head out to California."

Of course Locke had no way of knowing that Melinda could read, and she pretended that she was as illiterate as most slaves were, and ignored the writing on the paper.

"This here piece of paper says that I'm your new owner."

"Oh, what a miracle! Well, I'm glad you were able to win me from him. There might be a happy ending to this nightmare after all. You'll be rewarded with more gold when you return me to my master. And now, I'll have a chance to be back with my family, all thanks to you," she said. "I want to try to erase all of this turmoil from my memory. First, I was a prisoner at the fort, then there was that nasty business of being buried at the graveyard, and now, I've been snatched from Sallisaw. Finally, all of it is over with, and I just want to find Clinton, and begin our new lives together. Are we still in the Territory? If we are somewhere near New Warrior, will you take me back to him?"

When Melinda turned to look at her savior, she saw that Locke's face was flushed bright red.

"Why are you still so intoxicated with that man? He's not the one who is here to save you, I am. Why aren't you willing to take a closer look at me? Can't you see how much I care for you?"

Melinda tried to soothe his feelings. She thought flattery might dilute the intensity of his outrage over being ignored. His jealous heart had stifled his ability to be reasonable. She tried to get him to think about the money he would earn.

"Just think of the reward the chief will pay you if you return me to him," she reminded him.

"Right now," Locke said, "I'm just so relieved that you're still innocent of the things that could have happened to you out here. And from now on, you can count on me to protect you from those animals that kidnapped you. I'm willing to put my life on the line for you."

Now Melinda knew that he had not listened to anything she'd said! She became aware of the way his eyes raked over her supple body, and alarm bells went off in her head. Suddenly, she understood that she was trapped in that cabin with a man who was a dangerous predator. She tried to focus on every word he said. An uneasy feeling crawled down her back. Her body tensed as her spine tingled. She was ready to spring away from his touch. The hair on her arms stood stiffly erect as a warning sign of imminent danger.

This man was determined to have her, and he wanted her now. Melinda tried to calm herself down so that she could try to reason with Locke. *How can I convince him that I need more time to accept his right to have me?* Melinda had to think fast. She might be able to buy a little time if she could convince him that eventually, she would be willing to come to him.

"Out here in the wilderness," Locke said, "everybody minds their own business. A man can have any kind of woman he wants. When I take you to town, you'll be treated just as good as the rest of them. Nobody has to know that you're still my slave," he promised. Her refusal to seriously consider the value of his proposal, had left him flummoxed. *Why would she pick Clinton Coulter, a man with no means to care for her, over me, a man of means?*

Melinda stalled for more time. *What can I do to convince him to wait?* She asked herself.

"I've been a prisoner in this filthy place for weeks," she said, "I haven't had a bath since I've been here. Don't you want our time to be special? You promised to buy me a new dress, but I've had to wear these rags for months." Then, she changed tactics. "You'd be better off if you'd just turn me in and take get money. If you take me to town, eventually Clinton will find me there and take me away from you. That's if the Indians don't find me first. Then they won't be willing to pay you a cent."

"Oh hell, I forgot, you don't know about it do you?" His sudden concern made her leery of him.

"You're scaring me, what is it that I don't know?"

"Sit here, Melinda. There have been many changes in your life since you've been away."

Melinda was frightened, and when she saw the sorrowful look on his face, she began to tremble. Locke sat next to her on the edge of the bed and took off his jacket. First, he told her about Clinton's death, then Eliza's demise, a week later.

"The story I heard out of Sallisaw, is that Eliza was so heartbroken that you went missing, that the old soul couldn't cope with your disappearance. She just gave up hope and withered away, after Clinton died.

He didn't have enough time to heal before he went to hunt for you. His wound became infected."

"No!" she shouted. "How could all of our lives fall apart so quickly? We'd finally found our way out of slavery. It's not fair! Aren't any of us destined to be happy?"

"Later, I'll try to find out more about what happened. But all I can tell you now, is that both of them are gone. Just remember that I'm here for you. I can be depended on to take care of you."

In her grief, she didn't notice that he was using one hand to remove more of his clothing, while he held her with his other arm. Suddenly, his hand shot up inside her thin cotton dress to touch her thigh. Melinda screamed. His pants were completely unbuttoned.

His next move forced her to touch him. She snatched her hand from his grasp and jumped up from the bed. The material threatened to rip, as he began to pull at her dress.

Melinda, like most slaves, had never worn underwear, and Locke was excited to find that there were no barriers to his advances. He had complete access to her body when he reached inside the shift to caress the recesses of her body.

"Stop!" she yelled. "What has gotten into you? Are you mad?"

"Be still, damn you!" he said. "Why can't you behave? Can't you see that you're better off with me? If you'll stop fighting, I'll be gentle," he said as he pressed her body closer to his.

It was the first time she had ever seen a completely naked, aroused, man in her life. And now, she was more frightened of him than she was of any animal she might encounter in the dark, unknown woods outside the shack.

Locke managed to secure both of her hands while he forced her back down on the bed and pushed himself between her thighs. Horrified, Melinda used the last of her strength to twist away from the thrust of his body. Once again he rose to his knees, sure that this time, his next lunge would strike home. He celebrated the knowledge that he would be her first, and last lover.

She could see the demonic smile on his face, and pushed her body sideways in a last-ditch effort to escape his grasp. Somehow, her knee hit his nakedness, and suddenly his body stiffened above her. He groaned as his seed spilled onto the bed. His grip on Melinda loosened just enough for her to slide from beneath his spent body. She bolted away from the shack to the edge of the forest, stumbled, and fell into a gully deep enough to hide her when she flattened herself against the ground.

When she saw a flash of lightening in the sky, she prayed that it would not rain, for then she would be in danger of drowning in a flash-flood. And most likely, Locke would be able to catch her if she had to leave her hiding place and run for higher ground. She decided to take a chance that the storm would pass them by, and stayed in the hole.

Now that Locke had recovered from the kick, he walked outside the cabin and lit a torch. He cursed Melinda as he angrily searched for her, but the hole in the wash was undetectable from his uphill position. The tobacco-brown dress she wore acted to camouflage her presence in the hollow recess.

Melinda was scared. She dreaded the punishment Locke would inflict on her for being willful and disobedient to him. He was her new master, and it was his right to use her body as he wished. Horrible things happened to slaves who defied their masters. Nothing would happen to him if he killed her. Most people would be less tolerant of him if he harmed a good horse.

After he had spent an hour scouring the woods for her hiding place, Locke gave up looking for her and headed back inside the house. He stood in the door and angrily hurled insults at her. Then he tried to speak reasonably, hoping that she would leave her hiding place and come back into the cabin.

"I don't know what the hell you think you're doing girl," he shouted, "but sooner or later, you're going to have to come back to me. I've got all the food and water. If you want to stay out there in a forest full of cougars, go ahead. I'll be here when you get some sense back in that thick head of yours."

When she didn't answer him, he shut the door and stretched out on the bed, confident that she would give up once she'd had a chance to think about the consequences of her decision to run away from him. He reached under the bed, took his bottle from the bag, and downed a slug of whiskey. *When I've had my fill of that bitch,* he said to himself, *I'm going to shoot her and bury her behind the house. Once her spell is broken, I'll go on with my life, unencumbered.*

Melinda was left to imagine which of the wild animals would come to attack her. *No matter what happens to me,* she thought, *I'm going to stay right down here in this hole.*

Chapter Seventeen
The Possum

At first daylight, Melinda hoisted herself from the depression. She was stiff from sleeping on the damp soil, but she began to walk rapidly through the woods to distance herself from Locke.

She ate a few berries from a bush that had been overlooked by the bears. Farther into the woods, she found a peck of sweetly-tart persimmons, and folded them into a large leaf to eat along with the other food she had found during the day's hike.

The water in the creek sparkled, and she ate crayfish from beneath the rocks. Then, from about a hundred yards from where she stood behind a cottonwood tree, she watched a woman work to clear a garden spot. Melinda avoided contact with her.

She had lived among the Cherokees all of her life, and was well aware of how to cover her tracks in the woods. She moved so quietly on the sun-dappled forest floor, that she was able to come very close to a whitetail deer before it noticed her nearness and leapt away.

By sunset, Melinda began to miss the warmth from the cabin's stove. The weather had begun to cool. She took stock of her clothing and knew that she was pitifully dressed for someone living in the woods. First though, she had to stop and remove the beggars-lice from her dress. She had picked them up when she'd run through the grass near the cabin. Now, they stuck to her skin as she looked for a place to sleep. The depression under a sassafras tree seemed like a secure place to stay. She began to gather leaves so that she could cover herself. She wished that it would have been possible to build a fire to ward off the four-legged animals, but the smoke would have given her location away to the two-legged beast that followed her. She had enough problems, and the worst one was that she could still be claimed by anyone who captured her. Buttram was right; she could find herself in more trouble than the situation she had left behind. *If I could convince someone to take me to New War-*

rior, I'm sure that the chief would pay them a reward for me. It's my only chance, she thought.

Melinda knew that it was not possible for her to escape slavery in the Territory, and she was not likely to find the chief or her grandfather. Clinton and Eliza were dead, but she was still determined that if she had to, she would accept any master but Locke. There was nothing honorable about his sick determination to subject her to his desires.

Her "master" conducted a thorough search of the woods as far away as Hulbert. Locke also contacted the patrollers, men who were adept at catching runaways. After giving them her description, he promised the men a bonus if they scoured the woods and ran her ragged until she gave up. She was on foot, and he was sure that they would run her down within the week.

"We'll catch her as soon as she steps out of the woods. There's no way for a slave, especially one as beautiful as you say she is, to just disappear," stated the slave-catcher.

As Locke left the men to the task of hunting their prey, he doubted that Rice, their leader, would be able to resist the temptation of having his fun with her, but Locke wanted her back anyway. It was her punishment for running away from him. If the greasy, smelly man attacked her, it would be exactly what she deserved. Cold anger had replaced his burning passion. He took out his whetstone to sharpen his knife, and salivated at the thought of the torture she would suffer in his hands before he killed her.

Melinda kept herself safe by walking in the deep paths of the chaparral. There were several breaks in the brush, but their size made it impossible for a horse to penetrate the dense growth. Sometimes she felt like jumping out of her skin, when one of the small animals that lived in the thicket skittered across her feet. But she was convinced that she could use the skills she had learned at Warrior to help her escape from Locke.

When he was riding on the Post road within a few miles of the fort, Locke met a small group of men who told him they were the third section of the large posse. Most of them were a tobacco-chewing, smelly lot. *Either they've been on the road a long time, or they're allergic to water,* Locke thought.

They invited him to share their campfire. Just for the hell of it, he decided to accept their invitation, and asked them about whomever it was that they were hunting. He set the men at ease when he offered them the makings of a pot of real coffee. They threw out the chicory that was brewing over the fire, and replaced it with the ground beans, so that they could have a true bit of a rare drink for most of them.

One of the black men told him a story about a Cherokee gang that had robbed a stagecoach of a federal payroll.

"Now, they'll be running from the Army and our posse. We think they're also holding a stolen slave girl that they snatched away from Sallisaw."

"Are you sure they're headed for the Badlands near the canyon?"

"Nah, you can never figure exactly what they're up to. But we're going to split up. Some of us are going to take the western route over the trail. There might be two gangs."

After Locke fed his horse and rubbed him down, he spent a pleasant night with the men. He enjoyed listening to their stories of their rough-scrabble existence in the Territory. But, he knew that it was necessary for him to change his plans. He'd heard enough about the posse being on the hunt for his gang, and the details of their search for Melinda, to make him give up the hunt for the elusive bitch. He saw that he needed to get as far away as he could from his old Cherokee gang, and the slave woman.

Early the next morning, he saddled up and said his goodbyes to the men. When he was about a mile down the road, he attempted to disguise his trail. First, he rode east, then made a switch-back at the creek and headed north on the old cattle trail, and followed the Texas Road to Neosho, Missouri.

Locke's plans were well seeded with his gold and good luck. Now, he planned to go into an area that was far away from the manhunt. He reasoned that if the posse had not mentioned anything about hunting for a white man, it meant that they hadn't captured any of his men yet. *But*, he thought, *as soon as one of them is captured, he'll tell them I was in cahoots with him, just so he can try to save his own neck.*

He decided then and there that it was time for him to change his life-style. And as he rode deeper into the forest, thinking about his future, he decided to buy himself a saloon in Missouri, and forget about trying to deal with the Indians again. From now on, Locke figured that he would be better off among his own people. He decided to leave those damned heathens alone.

Locke made camp along the banks of the Neosho River, and though there was little chance that someone was on his trail, he took the precaution of not lighting a fire. A meal of hardtack would do fine as his meal for the night.

One of the first things he intended to do was to find himself a white woman. She didn't have to be as pure as the driven snow, she might even have a checkered past, but she would have to be absolutely, unquestionably, lily white.

Now he realized that Melinda could not have given him the things he wanted most from life, sons. All she could have produced was a bunch of mixed-breed bastards. Locke was thankful that he had not bedded anyone out of his race. Too many half-breeds were already polluting the Territory. During the long ride, he had time to clarify his thoughts about the future, and he came to the conclusion that if the white man wanted to rule the country, then he'd better keep his pants up, or keep to his own kind.

Yet, he had to admit to himself that it still left a bitter taste in his mouth when he thought of how he'd been cheated in the land deal with Tolliver. And, he was still very angry that Melinda had run away from him. She'd had no right to defy him. That is when he decided that if it took him the rest of his life, one day, he would find her. And then, the games would begin.

As Melinda traveled through the woods, she began to see densely populated Indian settlements. Once she entered the forest near Tahlequah, she could see that there were black slaves on most farms, but she was afraid that once she exposed her presence to them, they would betray her.

She could smell venison roasting on a spit behind a cabin. She wasn't able to get close enough to it to steal a piece of the meat, but once darkness fell, she managed to retrieve a few meaty bones that the settler had thrown in the trash.

There had been several times when she had spotted men who might have been patrollers on the lookout for runaways. They usually had a pack of dogs with them, but she had learned one of the old Cherokee tricks, and had evaded the dogs by rubbing wild garlic on the bottom of her feet. So far, the dogs had run past her hiding place.

As the weather grew cooler, it became more difficult to find food. One day, she ripped a pillowcase from a clothesline and gathered fruit from a chokeberry tree. Most of the withered grapes, still clinging to the vine, were at the rear of the shack.

By the end of the next week, she was desperate for food. Melinda crawled on her belly to the edge of a vegetable garden to steal the remnants of a turnip patch. Just as one of them plopped from the ground, a big, black-booted foot stepped on her hand. She screamed. A big-knuckled boy with calloused hands and huge eyes filled with the excitement of catching a thief, was just about ready to shout to someone who was working in a faraway field.

" Shhh!" Melinda whispered, "Don't tell!"

He looked down and saw that she had tears in her eyes. "Why -why you stealing Master's turnips?"

"I ran away from my master, and now I'm hungry. I've been out here in these woods for weeks, and now it's getting hard for me to find food. Your master won't miss that old withered-up turnip."

That's a outlandish lie! He thought. *There ain't no other masters but mine around here.* He cocked his head in disbelief. This beautiful woman was lying, but for the life of him, he certainly couldn't figure out why she would want to eat a bitter-tasting, raw, turnip.

"Where's your master?"

Melinda held up her berry-stained hands. "Look I'll be honest with you. That master was a white man who stole me from the Cherokees and locked me up in a cabin. He almost ripped my dress off, but I got away. I need a place to rest for a while. "Can you hide me? What's your name? Where do you live?"

Her questions were coming at him so fast, that he just needed her to be quiet and let him think. When Melinda took a good look at him, she saw that he wore thick-soled brogans, a tattered shirt, and pants. Even though he worked in the fields, he did not smell dirty. She noticed that he seemed very shy, and afraid of her. Finally, he spoke:

"Name's Lucky. I li-live in a cabin by the cr-creek, with four other men. We take care of the gardens and do odd jobs around the place, like cleaning the stables. I'm the youngest one on this place. None of us have a family, it's just us. And if they see you, they'll tell Master. There ain't many secrets kept on this place."

But Lucky was so enchanted by the beautiful woman from the turnip patch, that he had already decided that he would help her hide from the other men. But first, he would have to find her a hiding place somewhere far away from the shack. *There's that old empty pigsty down on the other side of the garden,* he thought.

219

"Look here," he told her. "See that pigpen down yonder? Go get inside there and hide out, while I try to rustle up some vittles for you."

When she saw that the sod structure had been abandoned, she was grateful for his offer to let her use the shelter. She was so tired. The only difference between the pigsty and the shack she had lived in at Warrior Plantation was the height of the door to the hovel. For the last two weeks, she had slept beneath piles of leaves every night. Now, she enjoyed the luxury of being inside, away from the elements and the dangerous animals of the forest.

Lucky was able to sneak into the cabin without being discovered by any of the men. As usual, they had left a big pot of food boiling on the stove while they worked. He used his bowl to scoop up enough of the beans to feed the girl, found a piece of cold cornbread to add to the meal, and picked up an old rag that she could use to cover herself against the cool, damp ground inside the sty.

Once he had handed her his gifts, he assured her that he would try to come back to the hut the next morning, and bring her more food. He explained that he would have to wait until the other men had left the house for the day's work in the fields.

Now that Melinda's belly was filled with beans, she drifted off to sleep, comfortable, and content to spend the night in the old abandoned pigs house, near the slave quarters of Silas' Straight Arrow Ranch.

On the porch of the main house, Starr Night and Silas sat in cane chairs, while Tolliver relaxed on the steps with his back propped against the upright post. The men discussed their planned raid on the town of Lockewood the next morning. They would meet up with the posse at Two Forks, and try to capture Locke. Then they would ride to the cabin in the woods to rescue Melinda.

When she awakened at dawn, Melinda could smell the salt pork and grits that Lucky had left outside the door of the sty. She had slept so soundly that he had not had the heart to disturb the exhausted woman. But he had stooped down low so that he could have a good look at her. He had just wanted to watch her sleep. It had been several years since he had been sold away from his family, and he had not seen a black woman since he'd been brought to this plantation.

Lucky had backed away from the sty without making any noise that would awaken her, and gone to work in a nearby field with the other men, who were preparing the ground for the next season's crop. But most of the day, he sent secret looks in the direction of the pigpen. He was unaware that his behavior had alerted Hiram, the oldest slave, to suspect that he was up to something. And Hiram was the master's informer. He was rewarded for his loyalty with special treatment, and the freedom to travel about most of the local area.

Earlier that morning, he'd noticed that Lucky had bundled up food into a rag, and left the shack to dig turnips in the lower field before any of them had their clothes on. Usually, Hiram had to kick at his pallet just to get him up for work. *Something's going on. Probably thinking about running away, I'll keep an eye on him. If he tries to run, I'll catch him and tell the master all about it,* he decided, as he stood near the cabin door and looked out into the fields. That is when he noticed that something was stirring around in that old pig house down in the hollow.

"Look, Moses," he said to one of the men, "must be a coon rooting around out there by the sty. Usually, a possum won't come out 'til night. I don't have clear sight of it, but I do swear that it sure acts like a possum."

The three posses converged at Lockewood, and discovered that not only had the Cherokee gang escaped to the Badlands, their boss was missing too. According to the townspeople, the last time they had seen Locke, he was riding out of town with a bedroll and a carpetbag tied to the rear of his horse. He had not said anything, about where he was going, or when he'd be back.

They made it clear to the lawmen that they were glad to see law and order arrive in their town. The place had been overrun by soiled doves, gamblers, and con men. And, the merchants had been at the mercy of the whims of Locke's men.

The Sheriff of Sallisaw requisitioned Locke's office as his headquarters. Then he and a few of his men planned their next foray into the forest around Robber's Cave, in Quachita country. They had a long ride ahead of them. The sheriff was a lean man of forty, and he wanted to clean up the messy situation and go home to his wife and kids. His deputy had an idea of how they could catch the thieves without firing a shot.

"I'm not looking forward to looking in those caves in canyon country. The scrub brush around them is so dense that a man could get himself twisted up in the switch-backs. Then he'd be a sitting duck for the outlaws. The way I see it, if we find them holed up in those caves, we ought to gather up some dry brush and set fire to it. It's the only way to flush them out of there without any of us getting shot. We'll just smoke them out of the canyon," he said.

"It wouldn't take much for something to go wrong with your plan," answered the sheriff. "If the wind changed direction, we could end up trapping ourselves in the same fire we were crazy enough to set. Come to think about it, years ago, somebody told me that there's a way to come into the back of the canyon from the south. Some of the old tribes have used it for ages."

The sheriff lit his pipe. "I've heard from Silas that he has a Comanche guide working at his place. He knows the way, and I intend to hire him. We might be able to set up an ambush."

Tolliver, Clinton, and some of the other men followed Starr Night through the woods to the little shanty. They were determined to recover Melinda. Tolliver cautiously rode up in front of the house with his guns ready to do battle, while Clinton covered the rear. But they returned their guns to the holsters when they saw that the shack was empty. When Tolliver touched the woodstove, it was cold to the touch. He could see straight through the house and see that the bed had been slept in. The coverlet had been pushed back, and the pillow had been thrown to the floor. The room was musty and stale, as if someone could have been caged there for a long period of time. At least, there weren't any signs of a struggle. He didn't see any clothing, and it made him wonder if they had ever brought anything, other than food and water, out here to her.

When the men surrounded the place, they had expected to find the hostage. But now that they saw that the place was deserted, they decided to spread out and search all of the immediate area. Then one of the men spotted a dirty shovel propped against the house, and they silently began to search for a grave. Clinton and Tolliver were relieved when they couldn't find evidence of a burial. But one of the Cherokees did discover that someone had once laid in a hole in the wash, then had stood up and walked off into the nearby woods.

A Straight Arrow ranch hand said, "Hey! Look over here." He pulled several strands of long black hair from the dirt and held them up in the air. "For some reason, she left the house and came out here and slept in this here hole." They followed her trail into the woods, and then it just disappeared.

The chief smiled. He understood that someone who knew their ways had erased the evidence of their presence. Now that the men were convinced that Melinda was still alive, they knew that eventually, the Cherokee scouts would be able pick up her trail again.

At sunset, they gave up the search for the day. Starr Night and his men joined Silas and his cowboys in town for the ride out to Straight Arrow. They wanted to sit down together and coordinate their plans to catch the thieves, but Silas left three of his men at the shack so that they could continue the search for Melinda in the thick, mossy woods

Tolliver was torn between his decision to continue the hunt for his granddaughter, and the temptation to break off from the search and go to his overwhelmed mother. They had been separated for three years, but, instinctively, he knew his mother well enough to know that she would want him to continue the search for Melinda, find her, and bring her back with him. His granddaughter was the foundation of their future.

Once they were back at Straight Arrow, Silas, a scrawny looking, tough man, paced around the room while he issued orders to his men. There was something about the way he carried himself that warned other men not to mess with him. Starr Night and Tolliver listened closely to his instructions. He wanted them to form even smaller groups in order to cover a larger part of the country. He'd ranched in the area seven years, owned thousands of acres of land, and he wanted all of them searched. He decided to send messages to the other Cherokee ranches within a hundred mile radius. He asked them to join the posse in their pursuit of the criminals. Silas intended to expand the circumference of the trap they hoped to spring on the outlaws.

"They've been spotted near the Missouri border, and yet there's another report that someone has robbed a stagecoach in the south. I'm beginning to think that they've added more men to the gang, or we're dealing with a copycat bunch," he guessed. "The fort has sent a detachment to the Texas border. My men know every inch of this area, and will continue to search the woods for the girl, all the way to Fort Gibson. We'll find her."

"Thanks Sir," Tolliver said, "I've been separated from my family three years, and I guess I'll be able to last a few days longer. It's too bad that the man they trusted to get them here to the Territory turned out to be such a rotten stinker."

Silas looked at the two discouraged men and said, "Tolliver, I'll send a wagon to Sallisaw and have them bring your mother out here. Once you're all back together again, we'll help you and Clinton get them on the road to New Warrior."

Back in the slave quarters, Hiram decided that the creature stirring around in the sty had to be a possum, and made plans to kill it for dinner.

He went over the steps that he'd have to take in order to prepare the animal for the meal. It would take him most of the day to clean it, *but nothing*, he thought, *tasted as good as possum!*

He'd have to ask the master for a bit of lime to remove the stubble from the skin. Once it was cleaned, he'd stuff the belly with yams, season it with salt, throw in a bunch of hot peppers from the garden, stick it in a cast-iron covered pot, and cover it with the ashes from the grate. After it had simmered all day while they worked, the men would feast on it that night. Now, he went to hunt for the heaviest club he could find. And once he had the perfect weapon, he walked stealthily up to the sty and hit the back of it as hard as he could.

Whack!

"Help! Help me!" Melinda screamed as she scrambled from the door of the enclosure. Hiram had already raised his arm for the second swing of the club, and could not stop the momentum of the stick as it glanced across the crown of her head. When he saw that he had almost killed a woman, both he and Melinda screamed at the same time. Hiram could scarcely believe his eyes. A woman! A dad-blamed woman!

"What in the hell are you doing in the pigsty?"

"Why are you determined to kill me?" she asked, as blood began to trickle down her face.

Immediately, Lucky sprinted across the field and ran to her side. He had always stuttered, but now he was so nervous that he could hardly get the words out.

"Wha-what happened Melinda?"

"He tried to kill me with that club."

"Why-why'd you try to kill her Hiram?"

"I thought that she was a possum running about the pig pen. I was going to kill it for dinner. Where in hell did a woman come from?"

Melinda continued to cling to Lucky, afraid and hysterical from the near-assault from Hiram. Lucky didn't tell him anything about her. He was desperately trying to think of a way for them to escape. After a few minutes, they were trapped. The other slaves had run to the sty when they had heard the scream.

The men were astonished when they saw the beautiful, black woman. She was crying, hysterically. Lucky continued to hold her to his side.

Hiram signaled to the other men to back away from the couple. And after Melinda had time to grasp the fact that they meant her no harm, she calmed herself down enough that she was able to make an appeal to the men.

A few minutes later, the men sat themselves in a circle around her, and after one of them handed her a cloth to wipe the blood away, she told them the story of her escape from Alabama.

"Now," she told them, "I've got a different problem. I have to find a way to get away from the monster who owns me. He intends to molest me, then punish me for running away from him."

"I barely escaped his grasp. A few days ago, I spotted him sitting on his horse near a clearing. He was looking through a long pipe, still scouring the woods, determined to catch me. I hunkered down beneath a chinquapin tree, until he gave up the chase and rode away."

The men decided that they'd help her escape her owner, but Hiram reminded them that there were probably a few glitches ahead of them.

"I'm worried. If your master finds out that you're here at the ranch, my master will have to give you back to him."

The other men disagreed with his decision to tell the master about Melinda's presence on his ranch, but they were helpless to stop him.

"If I knew a free black person, I would do everything in my power to take Melinda to him, but although there are a few of them living in the Territory, I don't know them, or where they live. No matter what the master decides about the girl, I still have to let him know that she's on his ranch."

But the men decided to stretch the truth. Hiram would take Melinda to the master and tell him that she was a free black woman, and she had been separated from her wagon train. A gang of bandits had attacked them before they could reach the fort. They told her to ask him to send her to the fort so that she would have a chance to reunite with her husband and children.

Maybe, Hiram thought, *she can stay at the fort until her real owner finds her.* They took her to their shack to feed her, and let her clean herself up a bit before Hiram took her to meet their owner. He and Lucky tried to soothe her nerves by telling her that their master had never mistreated his slaves. Hiram explained that the property was a more ranch, than plantation. The master used his slaves to care for the animals, grow and gather fodder for them, and plant and maintain a garden. He did not grow cotton.

After she had done her best to remove some of the smudge from her body, Melinda followed Hiram across the ranch yard towards the back door of the house. They dodged the dust devils that swirled toward a clump of tumbleweed that was poised to run in the wicked wind. They had not managed to get very far down the pathway before one of the ranch hands spotted the couple and ran over to them. When he peered into her face, he was speechless, then astonished. What in hell was Hiram doing with a woman?

"I'll be damned if she ain't a black woman," he said. "When I first laid eyes on her, I thought she was a Cherokee, but the closer I get to her, the more I can see that I'm right about her. Here we are, just searching all over the dad-blamed country for her, and she just moseys right down the lane to the big house. We've looked all over tarnation for her, and under every tree trunk and rock between here and the badlands. We've been trying to find a woman who looks just like her!"

He ran ahead of them, opened the back door to the house, and shouted for everyone to come outside. Silas was angry. What in hell had gotten into the man? He knew better than to yell in his house.

"You all better git out here and see what Hiram's got. You ain't gonna believe your eyes!"

Silas was angry that the dirty cowhand had pushed himself into his house with all that caterwauling and commotion, but he followed him outside to the yard. He intended to give him a piece of his mind about his rudeness, once he was out of earshot. However, he lost his bluster once he stepped outside.

When he reached the walkway, he spotted a black woman walking down the lane with Hiram. *Could she be?* He wondered, but then dismissed the thought. There was no way that she could be the woman they were hunting. But then, he saw that she was a mixed-breed, and quite lovely, despite the fact that she was filthy. If this woman was actually Melinda, then Silas could understand why Locke had kidnapped her. She was exquisite. *How can anyone be so beautiful?*

Finding his voice, he asked, "Where'd you get that woman, Hiram?"

"In the pigsty, Master," he answered truthfully. "She says that she got lost from a wagon train on its way to the fort. Says they were attacked by

226

white men trying to steal slaves. She hid in the wash, but when she came out of hiding, they had gone on without her."

Silas didn't believe one word of that story, whether she was Melinda or not. "Who's your master, girl? Where is he?"

Before she could answer his question, Starr Night, Clinton, and Tolliver all spilled out of the back door. They had waited patiently for Silas to return to the house, but when they saw that he'd been delayed, they had become curious enough to go outside and see what all of the commotion was about. They decided it wouldn't hurt to lend a hand, and help Silas with whatever problem he was dealing with.

Clinton was the first one of them out the door. And when he saw the black raggedy woman, his heart skipped a beat. His mouth opened wide with wonder. That filthy creature looked just like his woman! *Surely,* he said to himself, *this can't be my Melinda!* But, when he looked into her hazel colored eyes, he knew for certain that somehow, his love had found a way to return to him. Damned if it wasn't her!

Melinda stared at him in the bright sunlight, but the glare made her squint as she managed to pick up the red highlights of his mahogany skin. She was looking into the face of a dead man!

But no, he was alive! Locke had lied to her. He had wanted her to turn to him in her grief. He had wanted her to be desperate for his protection.

Those few seconds seemed like an eternity as she reached her hands out to her man. As Melinda walked toward him, she thanked the heavens for keeping him alive. Now, she could return to the comfort of his loving arms.

Clinton ran to her and swung her around in circles as the other men spilled out of the house. Everyone was a witness to Clinton's tender embrace of the wonderful woman who had been lost to him. When Tolliver stepped from the house, he shouted her name. He didn't hesitate for one second to rejoice in Melinda's miraculous recovery. He walked over to them and became a part of their circle of love. Melinda rewarded her grandfather with a kiss. She was so relieved to see him, that she said nothing to him about the fact that his hair had turned completely white. Neither of them thought to wipe the tears away from their eyes. Tolliver's lonely three-year separation from his family had ended.

He held the couple tight against his chest. *Now I can finally take a deep breath. We've got our Melinda back. Starr Night has single-handedly, almost erased my family from the Earth No man should have that much power over another man's life. From this day, I vow to fight him and free as many of my people from slavery as I can, until they catch me and skin me alive.*

Tolliver and Clinton were in awe of Melinda. This strong woman had managed to rescue herself from her adversary, and had found her way to safe haven at Straight Arrow Ranch. Both of the men had known that the odds had been stacked against them. Most likely, they would have never found her in that vast, untamed land. Women were scarce in that part of the country, and that fact alone had only amplified their problems. Most men would not have been willing to give her back to them. Instead, he would have been willing to fight them for her, until he was ready to take his very last breath.

Silas returned to the house and called for his wife and daughter to come outside with him to witness a miracle. Norstella and Litcher came quickly in answer to his summons. They were aware of the urgency in his voice, and walked quickly away from the loom where they had been working. Norstella could sense her husband's excitement.

"This woman is the one we've been looking for. By some great miracle, she's found her way to our ranch. But from the looks of her, she's been through hell. Will you clean her up for me?"

The Songbird women looked at her closely. She was a shade or two darker than they were, but Melinda looked very much like a Cherokee. She was filthy, and she smelled as if she had been rolling around in a patch of wild onions. Her black braids were matted with dirt, but the gorgeous woman seemed to be intelligent, and answered all of their questions in their language. She seemed relieved when Norstella summoned Hiram to fill a tin tub with water. It would be the first time she would bathe inside a house. Later, when she stepped from the tub, she looked around for her shift, but the women had consigned her grimy garment to the trash.

Litcher offered to replace the rags she had worn with a simple cotton slip of a dress. It was the finest piece of clothing Melinda had ever worn.

"I'll never be able to repay you for your kindness, but I'll do any work you have for me. Please understand that I'm overwhelmed. It's hard to believe that you've actually let me come inside your house. Until today, I'd never been inside anything larger than the two-room shack where I was held hostage. I feel like I'm dreaming. Yesterday, I was almost killed when Hiram thought I was a possum. I spent the night in your pigsty!".

There had never been a black woman on the ranch before. But the Cherokee women obeyed Silas, and accepted her in the house. Norstella and her half-sister Isola had grown up in Rhea County among their slaves, but her husband had not owned slaves until she had brought her people to the marriage. Silas had told her about the black Cherokees in his father's family in North Carolina, and she had agreed with him that although they needed slaves to do the hard work of establishing the ranch, eventually they would free themselves of the burden of owning other people. They looked at their possession of their slave men as an unwanted necessity. Now, except for the last five men, all of them had been freed.

They expected their Cherokee hands to teach the remaining slaves how to be wranglers. Norstella agreed with her husband that once they had learned a skill, they would also be liberated.

Her sister Isola and Starr Night thought that they were foolish to release their valuable men, but Straight Arrow was not in Kiowa country. They were free to make their own decisions. The two households could not have been less alike. At New Warrior, the chief's family lived among their tribesmen, out here, Silas was his own man, and cared nothing about his brother-in-laws opinions about slavery. He was not *his* chief.

Later that afternoon, Melinda told the men most of the details concerning her captivity. Afterwards, they stepped outside to the veranda to piece together all the details of the case. She had not been able to shed much light on the situation, because she had spent much of her time in the cabin, blindfolded.

Although she was sure that men were Cherokees from the riverboat, only one of them, a man called Buttram, had shown his face.

"Well, I can connect some of the dots for you," said the chief. "The men told me about their boss, and about the jobs they had pulled after Buttram was able to kidnap Melinda from Sallisaw."

Later that evening, a messenger rode in from town and brought a telegram from the Commander of Fort Gibson. A posse from Okmulgee had captured Buttram, and two other members of the gang. They had already been arrested, tried, and hanged by the citizens, after they had tried to hold up a bank in Granite City. They hadn't been able to get them to talk about the other gang members or their boss before they died.

Buttram had remained loyal to Locke. He'd made a statement before they had strung him up:

"I'm going to die out here today, and there's nothing that's going to change that fact, no matter what I say. So, I'm not going to give you any ammunition against him. That's just the way it's going to be. I'm getting ready to die with my boots on, no use taking him with me. If we hadn't been cheated out of our land in the states, none of us would have been out here in this mess."

The next morning, when Tolliver looked to the horizon from the porch of Straight Arrow, he saw a dust cloud from the horse of a lone rider, as he rode to the ranch. He turned out to be another messenger from the sheriff in Sallisaw. The note said that a wagon would arrive at the ranch the next day, carrying Eliza, the woman who had nursed her to good health, and her son Esau.

Tolliver was so pleased with the news, that he could not wipe the smile from his face. He sent the rider to the bunkhouse to rest, eat some vittles, and visit with the other men before he hit the trail back home.

In all of the years they had been in New Warrior, Tolliver had not been allowed past Starr Night's office in his house. But from what he'd seen since they had arrived at Straight Arrow, Silas and his family were certainly more liberal than any Indian family he had ever met. He had been shocked when they had bathed Melinda in the house, and then, the women had given her a dress! Then, Silas had allowed Melinda, Tolliver, and Clinton to eat in the kitchen, while his family and the chief ate in the dining room. Tolliver knew that the chief didn't like the arrangement. Although he was gracious to his hosts, he could not wait to get back home and tell Isola how her sister and her family lived out here on this ranch.

In the kitchen, all of the black folks looked as if they expected to be struck by lightning. For one thing, none of them had ever used a fork. But Hiram, who was acting as the butler tonight, showed them how to spear the food. Although he had never used one of them himself, he had served the Indians many times before, and had watched them use the silverware.

Starr Night was uncomfortable knowing that they were eating in the kitchen while he was still having his meal. He managed to push down enough food to last him for the night, and excused himself from the table. Once he'd stepped outside, he decided to walk down to the barn and have a look at the palomino mare that Silas had bragged about earlier. Perhaps he could talk him into trading her. Then, he'd have another horse to mate with the studhorse.

230

Tolliver sat at the kitchen table, happy to bask in light of the love between the young couple. He figured that it was the ideal time to give Melinda her Emancipation papers. She saw Eliza's papers when they fell out of the same pouch. Tolliver waited for her happy reaction. Why did she have that mortified expression on her face? It seemed to him that she was heartbroken. Tolliver was at his wits end to discover the reason for her irrational behavior.

Melinda started to sob. "It's so sad that she lived every day of her life as a slave. If Mama Liza had lived just few weeks longer, she would have been free too," she cried.

Tolliver was flabbergasted. "What in hell are you yapping about? What makes you think that she's dead? Tomorrow they're bringing her out here to the ranch. She stayed in Sallisaw to wait for news of your whereabouts."

"Oh, for goodness sake!" she said as she held her hands over her mouth. When she recalled Locke's words to her, she was appalled. Now it all made sense to her, and she grew more angry by the second. He had known that she would be devastated when he told her the bad news about them. How could he have been so callous? When she told the men about his dastardly deed, they were not at all surprised, they had already heard some of the nasty things he'd done to those poor folks who were unlucky enough to have bought land in Lockewood.

They had tried to befriend him, but he had classified them as his inferiors, and had betrayed them. After she recovered from the shock of Locke's double-edged deception, Melinda left the men sitting at the table and went outside in the dry, crisp, much needed air. After a few minutes, Clinton joined her on the porch, and wrapped his arms around her. The stars blazed in the velvet night sky as Melinda began to tell Clinton the details of Locke's ruthless, evil plan to capture her heart for himself.

"It's a miracle that you were able to escape from that cabin before he had a chance to rape you. When I was about ten years old, I happened walk into the house in time to see my master wrestle my sister to the floor. When I tried to save her, he told me to scat, but I refused to let him have his way with her. He kicked me in the head with his boot. Mother pulled me away and hid me in the woods. That didn't make a bit of difference. Within a week, he had rounded up all of his slave boys from about ten, or twelve years old, and sold us to a traveling dealer. The last time I saw my mother and sister, I was being led away in chains to the slave pens in town."

231

Just the thought of what Melinda had been through to get away from Locke, made him so angry that he could feel the muscles in his back twitch with pent-up frustration and anger. He hid his balled up fists from her, and did his best not to alarm her, but he ached to find Locke, beat the tar out of him, and mash him to pulp before the posse could get their hands on him. He'd get no trial, he was a deserter. It would be a matter to be settled by the first posse lucky enough to string him up in the nearest hanging tree.

Clinton had worked as a sheriff in some of the toughest lands of the west, but so far, he'd stopped short of killing a man. Now, he wanted vengeance. The scoundrel deserved to die a thousand deaths.

Melinda noticed that Clinton was rubbing the spot on his head from the bullet wound. She pretended that she didn't see the grimace on his face, a sign of the pain he still suffered. She was so proud of him. This injured man had gotten on his horse and rode clear across the country in an effort to find her. She stood on her tiptoes to kiss him. Neither of them could think of anything to say. The brisk night folded them in a caress of endless devotion, an eternity of indestructible love.

The next evening, just before sundown, a covered wagon from Sallisaw arrived at the ranch carrying Eliza. She was accompanied by her new friends, Maude, and her son Esau. The family reunion was bittersweet. Eliza had lost her granddaughter and most of her family to the fever. Both of her daughters had been sold at auction. Still, she was thankful to have Melinda and Tolliver back in her life again. She knew from past experience, how rare it was for a slave family to be reunited. She gathered them to her breast with such sweet tenderness, that just the sight of the grateful family was enough to touch the hearts of everyone who witnessed their serenity and happiness.

Tolliver thanked Maude, a graceful, ebony-colored woman, for the care she had given his beloved mother. And immediately, she became aware of the way his exotic hazel-colored eyes swept over the contours of her body. *Whew! He's all that his mother described to me, and more,* she thought.

Initially, the sheriff had hired her to nurse Eliza, but the two of them had become such good friends that Maude had agreed to accompany the old woman to New Warrior. She wanted to see for herself, if the town was the place where she and her son could start a new life.

Esau was a master carpenter, and he was excited to migrate to a place that was putting up new buildings as fast as they could be constructed.

He had listened to Eliza's fascinating talk about what she had heard about the new town, and had made up his mind to join her and her family in Kiowa country. His mother knew that it was his way to escape from their tragic past, and, if she had not agreed to leave Sallisaw, she would have lost her only child. He would have gone without her.

It would have been impossible to wait until later and visit him after he was settled in the town. There weren't many white women who dared to make the trip across the Territory alone, and it was next to impossible for a free black woman to go anywhere without the added risk of being captured, imprisoned, and accused of being a runaway slave. The fact that she possessed Emancipation papers would not deter a slave rustler from stealing her. The only public transportation was the stagecoach, and black people in the Territory had never been allowed to ride in one of them.

Now that she'd met everyone at Straight Arrow Ranch, she had become more confident that it was highly probable that her life in New Warrior would be much better than the one she had left behind.

"Well I won't lie to you," Tolliver said. "Nothing like our experience here is ever likely to happen to us again, in this lifetime. Silas and his family are rare people. They've treated us like we're human. But there are Indians in Kiowa country that would burn this place down if they had any idea that this family had fed us in their house. We must be very careful not to say anything about what happened at Straight Arrow. It could cause them a heap of trouble."

Even though Tolliver seemed to appreciate Maude as a nurse for his mother, he had not really shown her much attention, but she secretly harbored the hope that he would seek a romantic relationship with her. At first, she had been surprised to find that she wanted him. She hadn't entertained such thoughts about a man since her husband died. But now, every time Tolliver came near, her heart fluttered, and it made her want to shake him, and make him take a better look at her. She wanted him to see her as someone who could play an important part in his future.

During their search for Melinda, she had read her Bible to Eliza, and the time they had spent together seemed to ease Eliza's pain of losing her great-granddaughter to the kidnappers. She had tried to boost her spirits when she'd taught the old woman how to pray for Melinda's safe return. It had been Eliza's first brush with religion, and she had seemed to find great comfort in the scriptures. The women had become close friends and confidants.

The slave mother had told Maude about her widowed son, a free man who lived in a place called New Warrior. After a while, Eliza had discovered that she really did not want to lose her friendship.

"Why don't you and your son come with me?" she had asked "We can start a new life for ourselves out there. The two of you are alone here in Sallisaw. If you come with me, I'll make you part of my family. Come on, take a chance, share our adventure. You've got to look straight ahead. Forget about the past. I'm an old woman, but I'm going to live long enough to see you happy and settled down. Both of you deserve happiness."

Now that they were at Straight Arrow, Eliza could see that Maude was attracted to her son, but he was so busy getting them ready for the next leg of the trip, that he hadn't noticed how much Maude wanted his attention. She gave Maude some sage advice:

"Be patient, love is sneaky. There's nothing more beautiful in this world than the sight of love in bloom. Most of the time it has to hit a man square between his eyes before he sees it."

Silas had offered Tolliver's family the use of a small cabin near the bunkhouse, and they were glad to accept his generosity. But after a couple of days rest, Starr Night was ready to leave the ranch. It was well past time for the first snowfall of the season, and he didn't want to be stranded out here, so far away from his plantation.

Melinda had begged her grandfather to ask one more favor from the chief. A loan, so that she could offer to buy Lucky and Hiram, and take them with her to her new home. Silas encouraged the deal because he knew that Melinda wanted to reward her saviors. When the chief hesitated, Silas agreed to sell the chief the palomino mare, and a deal was made.

Hiram and Lucky would drive her wagon to their new home. Melinda hoped to make them a permanent part of her life. If they had refused to help her that day, she might have been caught up in another disastrous situation. But instead, they had convinced the other slaves to help them rescue her. She would have never found Tolliver and Clinton at Straight Arrow if Hiram had not been wise enough to take her to Silas. She would have still been out there wandering around in the woods. There was a good chance that eventually, Locke would have captured her.

"Who would have ever thought that we'd get freed because Lucky caught you stealing a turnip, and I almost whacked you across the head in the pigsty!" exclaimed Hiram. "Miss Melinda, I'm so glad I belong to you. Mr. Tolliver says he's going to teach me to me to be a cowhand, and Esau is going to teach Lucky how to help him build houses."

"You're going to be proud you bought us. You'll see how hard we work for you," pledged Lucky.

Melinda did not tell them that they would be freed as soon as she and Clinton had their home place established. She'd have to be a legal resident of the Territory before she could emancipate them.

Silas and his family had been touched by the rare family reunion of the slaves. And now, after reflecting on the pain endured by Tolliver's fractured family, Silas made up his mind that he would recognize the black relatives in his family. From now on, he would look upon those black Cherokees in a different light.

Just before dinner, Long Rogers finally got up the nerve to speak to Silas about a serious matter.

"I appreciate the fact that you put everything on the back burner and came to get me out of that mess in Sallisaw. There aren't many men who would've been willing to treat blacks as well as you and your family have. We'd have been goners without your help. It's been a pleasure being around the graceful women in your house, it's made me want to be part of your family. Can I have your permission to come visit Litcher once I'm settled in New Warrior?"

"Long Rogers, you'll always be welcome in this house. Consider this place your own. When you come here, stay as long as you wish."

"I'll warn you now. Eventually, I intend to ask you for Litcher's hand in marriage."

Silas was amused as he listened to his friend's prepared speech. Did he think that he and Norstella were blind? They had watched the two of them making cow eyes across the table at each other since the very first day they had met.

Litcher had confided in her mother that she was smitten by the man who had been brave enough to risk his life in order to save the slave women from certain death. When Silas and Norstella issued the open invitation to their wealthy, heroic friend, they were confident that a highly respected man of his caliber would be a good match for their daughter.

Chapter Eighteen
Homeward Bound

On November 20,1842, Silas received information from Sallisaw that Locke had been seen by one of the cowhands from around Nevis, riding across the Missouri border near Neosho. And now, they were almost certain that he was probably beyond the reach of their wrath. It was absolutely sickening news to Tolliver and Clinton. Both of them had fantasized about a fit end to their enemy. It was disheartening to discover that they would not have a chance to punish the rogue. But somehow, they knew that the day would come when they would cross paths with the evil man again, and perhaps then they'd be playing on an even playing field. But the stench from that rotten egg would not be easily forgotten.

"As soon as he thinks the trouble has died down, he'll slink back into town to try to collect his rent and sales money," said Starr Night.

"But now that he doesn't have his gang to back him up, he'd do well to stay away from that town. Seems to me that those folks are mad enough at him that they might be willing to string him up themselves," Silas replied.

Now that the hunt for the bandits was over with, the men turned their attention to the problems involved in getting everyone back to the chief's plantation. Silas lent them several of his wagons. They would need them to take the women and their supplies on the deep winter trek.

The Songbirds and their visitors gathered to say goodbye. The women sent presents to Swift River and Isola, Norstella's half-sister, home with Starr Night. A few days earlier, Litcher had presented Melinda with a tough, small, paint pony that she had trained to be gentle with a new rider. The young women had hugged, determined that they would be friends for life. Litcher planned for the pony to be the foundation of Melinda's own string of ponies on the ranch she and Clinton planned to establish.

The slaves and the Freedmen packed the food chests of smoked meats, barrels of flour, six dozen hard-boiled eggs, fifty pounds of beef jerky, red and yellow apples, hardtack, and beans.

Eliza, Maude, and Melinda rode in the same covered wagon. It was exciting to Maude to watch the newly freed women stretch out and spread their wings of discovery. The good news had just barely penetrated their brains. They were free!

And now that they had pulled out and left the borders of Straight Arrow, Tolliver rode ahead of the wagons and took charge of the caravan to New Warrior. As they bumped along the way, the women looked up and out of the wagon to watch him work from high in the saddle. He rode alongside them and told them the details of some of his plans for their new lives. Listening to his soothing words helped Maude to let go of some of her apprehensions.

Melinda and Eliza were glad for her presence, for she could tell them of the days when she had first been emancipated, and how she had felt when she'd first held her papers in her hands.

"In those days, when I had just barely learned to read, my husband had to explain each word to me," Maude explained. "But, before the end of the year, I'd memorized every word of the paper. I hate to think about how things were before I was set free, because it was a soul-breaking existence, working in the rice fields of Louisiana."

One morning, after about a week on the road, Tolliver told Maude about his two-room house.

"I'd always hoped that I'd have a reason to expand it, and now that I can claim all of you as my family, I guess I'll have to get to building," he said playfully.

She climbed to the back of the wagon as he rode away, and Maude thought, *If that man keeps looking at me with such longing and passion in those beautiful eyes, I might just give him another reason to add several rooms onto that house!*

Clinton rode up to the wagon and spoke to Melinda. She had decided to sit on the bench with Hiram, and watch him guide the team down the trail.

"I'm going to teach you to ride that pony Miss Litcher gave you. Then you'll be able to ride along with me. That way, you won't be confined to sitting in the wagon, or walking behind it in the dust. We need the time to talk. I intend for us to know a lot more about each other than we do now by the time we reach Kiowa country," he promised.

His heart had been captured by the willowy swing of her step. He admired the fragile, yet strong young maiden he knew her to be. She had escaped that white-livered scoundrel Locke, by having the nerve to defy him. Melinda was the kind a woman a man needed out here in this rough country. If he was hired as a sheriff, there would be many times when she would be alone, living out here on the edge of the frontier.

Tolliver had already suggested that both Melinda and Maude should be taught to use a gun. *Perhaps*, he thought, *I'll start them out by teaching them to load both a rifle and a revolver.*

Melinda could remember the days when Tolliver had been the headman of the plantation in Alabama, and how proud she had been when she had watched his horse canter across the field. But she had never sat on a horse until the day that Clinton saddled her pony for a lesson in canyon country.

First, he pulled her into his lap atop his roan, and they rode away from camp. Melinda held the rope to the blanket-saddled pinto that trailed behind them. But when the pony came to a dead stop to grab a blade of grass, Melinda was almost pulled from Clinton's grasp. After that, unless Melinda was astride the stubborn critter, they kept the pony tied to the pommel of Clinton's horse.

The rolling motion of his horse would have frightened her if Clinton had not held her so close to his heart. She was aware of his shortness of breath, the slight tremble of his arms, and the heat that seemed to seep through the cloth of his shirt. She enjoyed the warmth of his embrace, and contrived to remain with him onboard his horse, rather than sitting on her own pony. Clinton could see the way she wiped the moisture away from her upper lip, and knew that she was just as affected by their close contact as he was. He smiled to himself, satisfied that both of them felt the same passion flaring hot in their hearts and minds.

"Look," he said, as he pointed to the pastel shadows of the canyon walls. They rode closer to the surrounding abyss. "I saw this canyon a week ago when I scouted the trail with Tolliver for the safest way to New Warrior. There's not a name for it on Starr Night's map, so, I named it 'Melinda Canyon.' Tolliver marked your name on a paper, and he promised to register it with the Territorial Land Office."

"Clinton! Are you sure that you can do that? A slave name for this beautiful place?"

"You're no longer a slave. And if you were, who'd care enough about it to make a fuss?"

Melinda was pleased that he loved her so much that he thought of her when he was inspired at the beauty of such a spectacular place. She wrapped her arms around him as they watched the sunset in hues of color that changed from pink to yellow, then green. Mauve tinted shadows danced across the air and left a warm glow on their faces. They hobbled the horses and walked over even closer to the edge, and peered into the deep, jagged rock.

Standing there arm-in-arm, they pledged their lives together until death. The vast canyon was their cathedral, the flower-covered grass their laced bouquet, and the murmur of the water, the music of their love. Clinton removed his bedroll from the horse and spread it over the crunchy leaves as Melinda flung the bag from her neck to the ground. She unpacked the meat and bread she'd gotten from the cook. As they sat on the blanket to eat, they watched the display of the brilliant explosions of color on the face of the silvery rock.

After they had eaten, Melinda and Clinton stretched out on their bellies, inched closer to the edge, and looked deeper down in the broken hole.

"I've traveled all over Arkansas and Indian Territory searching for outlaws, and I've seen other canyons, but I'd never seen anything like this one until Tolliver showed it to me. He told me a story about how it was when Starr Night brought his slaves through here the first time. That day, the slaves began to realize that they were hopelessly trapped. They were too far away from Alabama to ever go back home, and this hole in the ground seemed to the slaves to be the entry door to hell," explained Clinton. "Several of the men jumped from this cliff to their deaths. Tolliver thought about jumping too; he'd just lost your mother and the rest of your family. It was the only way to get away from the Indians. Back then, there were no roads, just faint animal trails that were known to the tribe. They carried around a map they had bought from the Chickasaw tribe. That day, Starr Night took one look at Tolliver, and was smart enough to see that he had also lost his will to live. He emancipated him the next day."

Melinda trembled, and Clinton pulled her into his arms and held her close to him. She enjoyed the way his body molded itself into the crevices and hollows of her lithe form. Their bodies blended together, a symphony of perfect harmony. Her innocent tongue imitated a tiny hummingbird, and touched his cheek to taste a bead of sweat from his neck. Rivulets of pleasure shot through her body as she discovered sweet pleasure within the circle of his arms. Clinton was bewitched by the expression of wonder on her face, and reveled in the awe of the moment. Melinda unleashed a torrent of electric passion. Both of them were left breathless in the wonder of the aura of simultaneous ecstasy.

Afterwards, they spoke with voices that carried a new tenderness, a caress. Now, Melinda understood the value of what Locke had sought to steal from them. When their minds returned to reality, shadows danced across their faces, casting a warm glow on their skin. While she was still enshrined in his arms, Melinda reached out to capture a honeysuckle bloom from a vine. She opened it from the bottom, and shared the nectar from the flower. Finally, the day was darkening, and they reluctantly walked to the sweetly trilling spring near the hobbled horses. They washed their bodies and prepared themselves for their return to the wagon train.

They did not attempt to hide the change in their relationship from the others. The evidence of their love was present for all to see. Their tender words and loving glances were as smooth as their caresses.

Most days, after Tolliver had finished his chores, he and Maude used the time to stroll away from the others to talk about the things that mattered the most to them. And they found that generally, they agreed on the important things in life. Although they were both still filled with the tales of their pasts, they held their tongues, and were able to concentrate on the beauty of their romantic moments together. Within a week, Tolliver was sure that it was the right time to propose marriage to Maude, and she readily accepted his offer. Eliza was overjoyed!

"Maude," Tolliver told her, "Now that we've pledged ourselves to this new life together, I want you to understand that I'm in a hurry. I intend to look for a preacher man in every town between here and New Warrior. So, don't you get started making plans for anything fancy," he teased. "I wish we would have been hitched up yesterday!"

Maude was pleased with his reaction, and traced his strong jaw-line with her fingertip. He dropped his head to kiss her hand and tried to hide the fire in his eyes. But the beauty of the wonderful day struck his senses, and he forgot all about the people who stood around them, and kissed her soundly. The kiss was unexpected, and Maude forgot about whatever it was that she was going to say and concentrated on the fascinating thrill of his lips on hers. The goose-bumps on her skin might have been from the slight breeze that stirred the trees, but she was very sure that his kiss had a lot to with the way her body flushed with heat. But, although she could see the hunger in his eyes, she decided to make him wait. Despite his eagerness to be wed, she intended to wear one of the doeskin dresses that the Songbird women had given her and Melinda.

Two weeks later, the wagon train pulled into a circle to protect it from a huge herd of buffalo. The heavy, stubborn animals were winding their way through the land to their winter quarters, dropping late season calves along the way. The plodding beasts were not in a hurry to move. They were protected from cold weather by their matted clumps of thick hair. And according to the way they moved, Tolliver figured that they were only interested in one thing, and that was nibbling at the abundant, short, stubby grass of the plains.

The dogs were kept on their leashes, and everyone went about their duties as usual, but they were reminded that the beasts were easily spooked, and the chief warned everyone about their tendency to stampede, once they were frightened.

The wagon train was able to rest beneath the cottonwood trees another day, before the animals were clear of the trail. After the trip resumed, the women walked along the trail behind the wagons and collected a bonus amount of dried buffalo chips. They would be used as fuel for the campfires.

Once they reached the edges of the deep prairie, the grass seemed to touch the sky.

"There's no getting around the fact that we've got to get through the plains before we reach Wichita country," Starr Night told Tolliver. "But, if we follow the trail through Shawnee, we'll shorten the trip by fifty miles."

The chief was getting worried about the weather, and he tried to hurry the travelers toward home. He could feel it in his bones that they were running out of time. His intuition about the weather was usually very accurate. And once they had gone another twenty miles farther, the wind shifted, the sky darkened to a solid gray, and bone-chilling air cut through their clothing and made them shiver.

Even the prairie dogs lay with their bellies flat to the ground, tails a-twitch in the wind. Then, suddenly, without any apparent reason for alarm, they scampered to their vast, underground sanctuary. It was quite a trial for the horsemen to avoid the hundreds of burrows under the seemingly endless acreage of the underground town.

By mid-evening, the chief lifted his head, noticed that the sky was the color of lead, and took a deep breath as the wind spat tiny ice crystals like twisted needles into his face.

He called out to Tolliver. "Tell the men to bring the wagons back into a circle."

The chief had sensed that a heavy snowfall was imminent. But, before they could complete the circle, snowflakes had already covered the ground.

Quickly, canvas tents were constructed using the scrubby, post oak pine trees they had cut down from the ridges of the now distant mountains in the south. Horses and oxen were herded into a hastily built corral, and were protected on the windward side of it by a tarpaulin.

Three inches of snow had already landed by the time the wagons were ready for the storm. The wind slipped down between the Wichita Mountain slopes with a cold fury that blinded the animals and the people who had not reached shelter. The blizzard lasted all night. Everyone hunkered down to escape the effects of the deepening mounds of ice and snow.

Melinda and Eliza survived their first snow storm while snuggled up in the wagon with Maude. They were buried deep beneath the fur throws that Tolliver had used to line the wagons. After the livestock had been secured and fed for the night, the men pushed past the snow to climb inside the haven.

Tolliver and Clinton removed their gun belts and set them down in front of the wagon. Then Tolliver began to tell the women all about the cabin he had prepared for them.

"Now that Clinton has decided to come with us to New Warrior, the chief has offered to put him up in the bunkhouse with the wranglers until you two are married, and have time to build a house," Tolliver explained.

"It's going to be a lot different out here. Before, everything belonged to the master. But now that all of us are free, you'll see that things are really going to be different," Clinton told them. "From now on, anything you plant and harvest is yours. But if you decide to let it rot in the fields, or you're too lazy to prepare for winter, that's your business too. You've got nobody to tell you what to do, but if you don't get up off your behind and work to feed yourself, you'll die out here. There's no master to hand you seeds, food, meat, or a cabin to live in."

"I've been free for a few years now, and I've always had enough work as a seamstress," Maude told Melinda. "Both of our men have unusual jobs, one a lawman, and the other an overseer. So far, we've managed to carve out an existence as free blacks, but it's not easy. If a black man doesn't have a skill, he might as well tear up the papers, because he's at the mercy of the old master, and he'll always be in a position to buy his labor so cheaply, that the man just ends up being another kind of slave, one that the master does not have to feed."

"Since Mother is a midwife, and I think it'd be a good idea for her to teach you to help her, there'll always be a demand for your services," Tolliver advised.

He told them about the large population of free black people who lived in the area.

"Some of them are ex-slaves who were emancipated, but there are others who entered the Territory as free people looking for a town where their children could live without the Black Laws. But now, there's a movement among the Indians, led by a man named Lone Fox, to expel the Freedmen from their land. So far, Starr Night and the rest of his band have fought to keep us here in the Territory. They need us to help them keep control of their huge claim."

Eliza motioned to her son to follow her to the back of the wagon. They made themselves comfortable, and then Eliza began to speak of her lost daughters who had been sold away to a man in Georgia. She picked that time to tell Tolliver about the nuggets she carried in a bag snuggled between her breasts.

"If you ever find your sisters, we'll use the treasure to rescue them from slavery," she said as she turned away from his eyes, opened the bag, and handed it over to him for safe keeping. Tolliver was dumbfounded! It was unbelievable that she possessed any amount of gold, but the horde that she had just handed over to him in that snuff bag was worth a fortune!

Eliza decided that she would not give him an explanation of how she came to own the gold. And since she did not tell him that Melinda knew about the treasure, the secret origin of the gold would remain a mystery to Tolliver for the rest of his life.

He already knew how some of the treasure would be spent.

"As soon as I get back to New Warrior," he whispered to his mother, "I'll contact one of the men working on the escape route to Tennessee. I trust him to take a sum of the money to my friend Perry. He's hides the fugitives in the safe house in Memphis. They need all of the money they can find to buy their families and try to move them farther north into Canada. With these new slave laws on the books, Ohio is too close to the slave catchers in Kentucky for an escapee to be safe. The patrollers simply cross the river at night, kidnap the slaves, and bring them back to their owners. Now that I have these funds to send to Perry, we might be able get more of them out of their reach."

"Do whatever you can to help them without alarming the Indians," Eliza told her son. "Our lives won't be worth a dime if anyone finds out that we have gold."

Eliza felt vindicated that she had somehow made up for some of the past mistakes she had made with her son. Now that she was reacquainted with him, he had told her about his work to free the slaves, and she had the satisfaction of knowing that against all odds, her son had turned out to be a most honorable man.

And now, by handing him the gold, she had given him the tools to achieve greatness. Not one cent of the money would be spent for anything that did not have the possibility of producing a miracle. Freedom would be their unsung legacy to their people.

The wind whipped the canvas cover, but the warmth of the wagon was bolstered a little bit by the almost non-existent heat from the oil lamp. Clinton opened the flap and put his backside to the wind on his way to the chuck wagon. Despite the blizzard, the cook had managed to warm a pot of beans and bacon from the day before. He'd been smart enough to set a tripod over a lantern he had sat in a hole in the ground. The metal-clad bottom of the wagon was surrounded by a leather skirt, and it was tied to the soil with wooden pegs. Cooky pulled back the covering and scooped a mess of beans into Clinton's pail.

When he returned to the wagon with the warm vittles, all of them ate heartily.

It was a good time for Maude and Clinton to listen to Tolliver's family as they tried to catch up on some of the stories of the missing years, those times when they had been separated.

"You don't know about the other time when someone else tried to snatch me," Melinda told an astonished audience. "Sundays at Warrior, Mama Liza and me would walk down the pathway near the river. We'd pick wild greens and baby pokeweed for dinner, and speckled-dick for the medicine she brewed for our winter colds. We always carried our fishing poles and big old fat worms for the fish. The new master had made it clear to all of us that he expected us to catch fish, gather berries, and feed ourselves. After the Cherokees left Warrior, some of the slaves escaped into the bush and lived in the caves. At first, patrollers tried to capture them, but eventually, they gave up the chase. Some of the men were secretly fed by their families who still lived on the plantation. They called the men 'Wild Ones.'"

"Sometimes, they managed to steal a woman," said Eliza. "After a few years, you could see young children running into the caves. None of the women ever returned to the plantation. There are about twenty of them living there now."

"One day, when Mama Liza stooped to pick greens, one of the men grabbed me and tried to pull me into the woods. But she looked up, saw what he was up to, and beat him across the head with her cane pole. He yelped like a whipped dog and ran away," she said proudly. Everyone laughed at the thought, and was impressed with the old woman's spit and grit.

Tolliver watched the glow of the flame in the lantern dance in the light of Maude's eyes. He was anxious to make the wonderful woman his wife. But he was a little worried that he might be too old for a woman in her thirties. She was still young enough to bear children. Now, when he looked at her, he realized that he wanted to know a lot more about how she really felt about him. He wanted to explore the promise in her eyes and see if they truly expressed her feelings about him, or if he was just a convenient solution to her problem of being a single woman living alone in the wilderness. Tolliver wanted a truly romantic relationship.

She has not said a word about how her Jim died, but, he thought, w*ill she be willing to let me replace the love for her dead husband in her heart?*

Maude had never removed the scarf from her hair in his presence, and he wanted to uncoil her plaits to feel their texture between his fingers. He had not realized how much he wanted her, until his hand had accidentally brushed against her shoulder, and the spark he felt between them had set him afire. He'd heard the sigh escape from her lips. And though there had been several women in his life since he'd come to the Territory, he had never felt so such passion. Maude suited him, he had been lonely too long. What a wonder to have these three women in his life! He liked the idea of belonging to all of them.

During the rest of the wind-driven night, Tolliver told the rest of them about the beauty of the harsh land named New Warrior, and the stories of the summer of '40, when the grasshopper infestation had stripped away most of the vegetation in the area.

"Thankfully," he told them, "most people had preserved so much food in the root cellars and smokehouses, that we were able to feed everyone at the plantation. Before the swarm, we had harvested a bumper crop. The cotton-picking had been done, the wheat winnowed, and the children had husked the corn. Of course, Starr Night was able to feed the other Indians and their slaves, nobody went hungry."

"I heard Starr Night tell his brother-in-law about his profit from the sagebrush brooms the children produced," Clinton said. "That plantation sure is independent. Those Indians have a pottery business, coal mine, ranch, salt company, and their own police force. It seems to me that chief has built himself a kingdom out here."

"Now that you can see the whole picture, you can figure out why he holds onto me. I'm his eyes and ears. And now he's accepted all of you. Each of you has a skill that he needs. He wouldn't do anything to bring you out here if it didn't benefit him or the tribe. And even though he's signed our papers saying that we're free, you'll find that most of the time, we'll be obliged to work as much for him as ourselves. Once you're on the place," Tolliver told the women, he'll expect you to learn new skills, one of them being that you'll have to learn to work with the other women to bake bread in the adobe ovens."

As Maude listened to Tolliver's description of the plantation and the town that surrounded it, she felt confident that she and her son, the builder, would fit nicely into their new home.

Starr Night and Long Rogers sat in one of the wagons and played cards with the ranch hands. They tried to forget about the mounting problems presented by the blizzard. Once the storm ceased to be, they would have to order the men to shovel the heavy snow from the tops of the tarps before they collapsed.

In the light of the next morning, Tolliver measured the snowfall. It was over a foot deep in some spots. All of the wagons were stuck in the snowdrifts. But within a week, with help from the melting effects of the sun, the men were able to chain logs to the oxen, and use the guy rope to plot a pathway through the snow.

When they reached the last pass into the valley, the women walked carefully behind the wagon while holding onto a piece of rope. They were frightened as they slid along in the tracks past the edge of the dangerous cliff. Hiram shouted to them.

"If this wagon starts to lose its grip on the road and slides closer to the edge, let go of that rope, jump to the other side of the hill, and hold on. Me and Lucky will come and get you."

But slowly, all of the wagons remained upright on the trail as the caravan plowed through the heavy snowfall. They finally reached Cox's Point. And once they passed the incline, they were able to roll downhill towards the road to the plantation, past the small towns that had sprung up around New Warrior ranch.

On the tenth day of hard labor, they entered the valley down through the steep mountain pass. The wagons had made good time. In this area, the snow-covered earth was not deep enough to slow them down. Later in the afternoon, when the wagon train plowed its way through the gates of the plantation, Starr Night looked towards the front porch of his house and saw that Isola was standing watch. His wife was trying to get sight of him as they lumbered through the lane to the turnabout.

She had wrapped herself up in a fur robe in an attempt to shield herself against the wind. Tears of relief were in her eyes. She had asked her husband to do the right thing about Tolliver's predicament, but it had been difficult waiting for him to return to her. Now, her beloved husband had come back to the embrace of her waiting arms. She looked past him to the wagonload of new arrivals as they rode beneath the wooden archway.

"New Warrior Plantation." Melinda read the emblazoned script aloud. *At last*, she thought, *we're here!* It was almost unbelievable, but they had actually arrived at the place that held the keys to their future. And from what she could see of the place, it was just as Tolliver had described it. A beautiful, self-contained land where they would be allowed to set down roots.

Clinton and Tolliver dismounted, and went to help the women climb down from the wagon. They were shod in the canvass boots Maude had made to cover their shoes. Once they were standing on solid ground, they looked around at their surroundings, astonished that they had actually reached this place, "New Warrior," where they prayed that their dreams might be realized. They tried to absorb the meaning of what it would be like to live free in a place that would let them thrive, encourage them to build a future for themselves, and not suck the breath out of them.

Eliza squiggled her feet through the snow to the naked ground to plant herself. She felt like they were brand new seeds in search of a place to spread their tender tendrils and call this place their own. As she stood with one hand on her hip, she hugged Melinda to her side with the other one.

The weary travelers were suddenly struck with a spectacular once-in-a-lifetime display of the setting sun. The reddish-orange sphere seemed to have rooted itself into the ground. Then, the wondrous ball of fire sank below the horizon to greet the newest citizens of Kiowa country.

Gradually, as they continued to look into the dimming light, hope began to take shape in their minds that it was really possible that there was a chance that they would be able to anchor themselves to this wonderful land forever. Home. December 25, 1842.

The End

Next Read Part II: Tolliver's Revenge
warriorbydemitchell@gmail.com
www.facebook.com/AuthorDEMitchell

If you enjoyed Warrior: The Morgantown Songbirds, please visit the book on Amazon and leave a review.

About the Author

Doris Mitchell is a member of a large, fifth-generation East Tennessee Black-Cherokee family. Many of the men in her mother's family were coal miners.

She graduated from Carver High School in Dayton, Tennessee, attended Knoxville College in Knoxville, Tennessee, and became involved in the Civil Rights Movement as an Organizer in Knoxville, and later, in Oklahoma City, Oklahoma.

After completing an apprenticeship in Dental Technology, she became the first Black woman in the state of Maryland to earn a National Certification in Dental Technology with a specialty in Crown and Bridge. During her career as a technician, she became the co-owner of Ceramalab Dental Laboratory in Knoxville, Tennessee, and later, owner of Permalab Dental Laboratory in Richmond. Va.

After an illness she retired from dental work, and became a salesperson for a Maryland car dealer. Several years later, she was hired by the Social Security Administration as a certified clerk, and worked in offices in Washington, D.C. and Maryland.

She is a former member of Fifth Baptist Church of Richmond, Va., and is presently the church clerk at Northside Baptist Church in Baltimore, Md. She is a member of the Sandalwood Social Club, The Red Hat Foxy Belles, and the Writer's Guild at Essex Senior Center.

After participating in classes at Baltimore County Community College in Owings Mills, The Writer's Guild in Essex, and the Renaissance program at The College of Notre Dame, she has completed two books in the Warrior series.

22001161R00152

Made in the USA
Middletown, DE
16 July 2015